THE BELL TOWER

THE BELL TOWER

ANDRE CHARLES

Published by Konstellation Press, San Diego

konstellationpress.com

Editor: Lisa Wolff

Cover Design: Teresa Espaniola

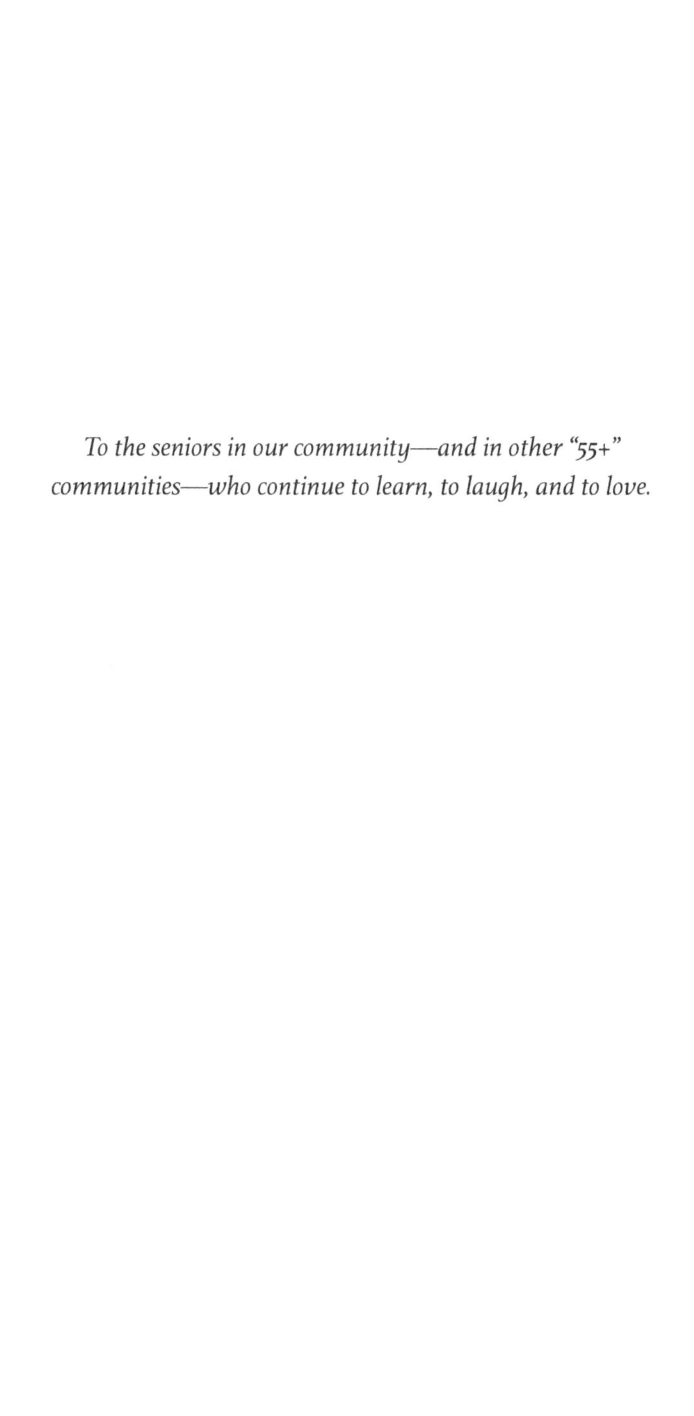

To the seniors in our community—and in other "55+" communities—who continue to learn, to laugh, and to love.

PART I

DOUGLAS HOLDEN

Early March 2019

If Doug Holden had known he was filling his coffee thermos for the last time, he might have added an extra shot of whiskey. Late winter in Northern California was still very cold. But the task he was embarking on required a sober mind, so he hesitated a moment, added the usual tot, and put the whiskey bottle aside.

Although he was nearing his eightieth birthday, Doug rarely thought about his own mortality. Sometimes, his friends warned, he pushed that casual disregard a bit too far and took risks even a younger man might avoid. But today, his mind troubled by what he was already thinking of as "that damned DNA test," he was impatient to get out to cut down the huge leaning pine tree menacing the power lines that ran along the ridge behind his house. Physical labor always helped him with weighty decisions. A tall, once powerfully built man, he was still relatively strong, even if he'd lost a lot of bulk the last few years.

It wasn't really a one-man job, so Doug decided to call his neighbor and good friend Bert O'Shea to help. He briefly considered discussing his personal dilemma with Bert while they worked, but the notion of Bert as counselor was so bizarre that Doug chuckled.

Bert did have considerable expertise as a handyman, and he was in much demand. "Doug, I'm real sorry, but I'm on my way down to Colfax. Donna Wilcox's basement's filling up from a busted hot water tank and she's purty hysterical. How 'bout tomorrow?"

"Nah. It's no big deal. The guy line is already set and anchored, thanks to you, and I just need to make the two cuts. Easy-peasy."

"Maybe not that easy," Bert warned. "You could use a second guy line. And that's not some little Christmas tree. The first wedge is gonna take a lot of effort on your part, even with the big Makita. You sure you can't wait a day?"

"Tell you what. If I find the first cut is taking a lot out of me, I'll hang up the chainsaw and wait for you. I appreciate the concern, but the day hasn't come yet that I can't fell a tree. And in the meantime, I'll give Rod a buzz and see if he's available."

Bert did not sound enthusiastic. "Okay, but...honestly, I wish you'd wait for me."

Doug wondered a bit at Bert's note of caution. Rod Staley was just as competent in the woods as Bert. Was it possible that Bert felt a bit territorial about their friendship? Or was it genuine concern? Doug shrugged it off, called Rod and left a message, went back to the shed, and picked up the chainsaw. He waited a few more minutes.

When he didn't hear back from Rod, he headed up the slope behind his house toward the pine grove. The morning sun sent shards of light slanting through the dense canopy. He was conscious of being short of breath. *Damn indigestion. I'm not exactly climbing Everest. Either the DNA stuff must be making me a little anxious or I'm letting Bert make me feel old. What trouble does he think I could get into, in my own woods, just cutting down a tree, for cryin' out loud?*

Doug took very seriously his stewardship of the old family homestead in the foothills of the Sierras where he had retired. Wildfires that fed voraciously on any dry brush or trees weakened by drought or insects were a constant threat to his heavily timbered acres. Not only was the leaning pine vulnerable to high winds, but he didn't like the look of the upper branches, either. After so many years of assessing California forests for disease, he could tell when foliage looked "off" somehow. He'd heard friends compare his ability to that of older doctors who could sense a patient's impending health crisis from cues invisible to less practiced eyes. One of the few benefits of growing old was the wisdom earned through years of experience.

He checked the guy line that would guide the fall of the tree, found the line taut and well anchored, and estimated again the direction. *Yeah, Bert's right; I could use another line, but it is what it is.* The tree would fall a little closer to him than usual, because he had to avoid both the overhead lines and the nice oak he was planning on harvesting next year to make a cabinet and a couple of small tables. *I'll have plenty of time to get out of the way.* Doug began the first cut. The chainsaw roar hardly registered. *There are some advantages to going deaf,* he thought with grim amusement. But he knew the growl must echo through the woods clear to Rod's house. He checked his phone. *No message. Guess Rod's not coming. Well, no biggy.* He looked around, feeling a swell of pride as he always did among the majestic trees. It wasn't virgin forest; his great-grandfather had cleared a lot of this land in the mid-1800s. But these second-growth trees had been reaching for the sky for decades. Some were a hundred feet tall, five feet across. He actually hated cutting any of them down, but the old ones needed thinning to make room for the saplings underneath. That thought brought an unaccustomed twinge of regret that he could see life's end racing toward him. He had maybe, what, ten more years? And no human saplings in sight to grow up here in these woods when he himself was felled. If only he had grandchildren.

He shook off the familiar pang of useless regret and surveyed the pine with a practiced eye. The first cut would have to be a big one, he agreed with Bert. *Just take your time. No use hurrying when you're out of sorts.* He was almost through the cut when he felt a tightness in his chest. *Time for a break.* Doug took a couple of swigs from the coffee thermos he'd left on a nearby stump, wiped his brow, removed his hat, ran a hand over his unruly white curls, and attacked the second cut—this one on the front-leaning side. The first cut was maybe a bit deeper than he intended. A heavy push could send the tree crashing.

He shut off the saw, grimaced when the pain edged up a notch, and looked for the thermos. *Where did I put the damned thing?* A sharp crack alarmed the primitive part of his brain, registered as danger. Just as he started to move, he caught a glimpse of movement partially obscured by the tree. *Rod?*

2

RENEE HOLDEN

Later that day

When Renee Holden answered her doorbell, she was startled to see two uniformed police officers standing on her bright-colored Mexican doormat. Behind them, the huge saguaro cactus in her front yard seemed with its raised arms to be reacting with alarm at the patrol car parked on the curb. Renee blinked against the sudden flood of bright afternoon sunlight reflecting off the light pink flagstones paving the patio, as the police removed their sunglasses. *Uh-oh,* she thought. *Do I have unpaid parking fines? Or are they raising funds for some police charity?* Neither was smiling. Instead, they seemed...embarrassed? Confused? *What's going on?*

She looked from one officer to the other. The policewoman appeared to be in her late forties. Her companion was a very young man with a meager approximation of a mustache and a soul patch that could easily be mistaken for a dirt smudge. The woman introduced herself as Sergeant Partridge, the young man as Officer Kurtz.

The officers seemed taken aback by her appearance;

they glanced at each other uncertainly. "Uh, are you Douglas Holden's daughter, Renee Holden?" Partridge ventured. Renee smiled to herself. *They were probably expecting a wrinkled old lady in sweats, like most Sunrise Acre residents.* She was accustomed to being told that she didn't seem old enough for this "fifty-five and older" retirement community. Just moments before, in anticipation of her dinner date with Peter, she had pulled her fashionably streaked hair back into a ponytail and dressed in the elegant gold-trimmed pantsuit that set off her slim, athletic build.

At Renee's curt nod, the policewoman stumbled her way through a brief explanation that Renee's father had died early that morning. But before she could utter the standard condolences, Renee interrupted her.

"Wait. Wait. This is a mistake. What are you saying! My father doesn't live here in Arizona. He's in California."

"Ma'am, I'm really sorry. We got the call from the Placer County sheriff. He knew your father. He would have called you himself, but he thought it was better if someone told you in person."

"He's...dead?" She pictured her dad as she had last seen him. Standing in front of the house in his trademark red plaid flannel shirt, he was waving a farewell as she drove away. Old, yes, but still hardy, still vital. How could he be dead? Various scenarios ran quickly through her head: *Gas explosion? Some drunk ran into him on I-80? A bear attack?*

"I'm very sorry for your loss."

"Yeah, yeah," Renee said, waving her hand dismissively at the pro forma and, to her, meaningless statement. "But what happened?"

What Partridge said next was the last thing she expected. "Ma'am, we were told that while he was cutting down some big tree it, uh, fell on him."

It took a few seconds for Renee to process that. Then she exploded.

"Impossible! There is no way that my father could have been killed by a tree he was felling!" Renee said furiously, as if the police were accusing him of a crime.

Startled, Partridge took an involuntary step backwards. She glanced for help at Kurtz, who was nervously rotating his hat in his hands. But he appeared equally cowed by the unexpected anger.

"He's a certified forester," Renee said. "He's felled trees for more years than you've been alive. What the hell do you mean telling me that?"

"But ma'am," Kurtz stammered, "that's what they told us. This morning a neighbor found him under a tree that your father had been cutting down, and—"

"A neighbor!"

"Yes ma'am."

Renee's voice hardened. "Rod Staley?"

"Yes, that's right. So you know him?"

Renee's face was set, grim in anger. "Oh yes, I know him! And if it's Rod Staley who 'found' him, it was no accident!"

"What do you mean?" Sergeant Partridge asked, leaning forward, interested now.

Renee appraised the policewoman through narrowed eyes, taking in the neat hair bun, the dark jacket tight across her shoulders suggesting well-developed muscles, the pressed trousers, and black shoes with thick soles. "I mean that my father would never go out to fell trees without another person along and that Rod has a very good reason to be happy he's dead."

Partridge shifted uneasily. "I'm sure that you could raise those issues with the Placer County sheriff's office."

"Oh, believe me, I will."

"I have contact information for the sheriff and for the coroner," Partridge said. "I can text them to you if you'll give me your cell number."

"I don't give out my private information. Just write it down on something and give it to me."

"I have Mr. Staley's phone number as well," Partridge volunteered, as she wrote down the information on the back of her card.

"I don't need it. Tell the sheriff I'll get there as soon as I can." Renee grabbed the card and shut the door, leaving them still standing for a few awkward moments on the stoop. Through the glass panel at the side of the door, she watched as Partridge shrugged and said something to Kurtz, who was shaking his head. Still talking, they walked to the curb. Kurtz glanced back at the house, said something —"bitch," Renee thought it was—and climbed into the patrol car.

She sat down heavily on the couch, remembering how she had convinced her father to delay selling the land to Rod Staley. *My God. Am I responsible for Dad's murder?*

A MONTH before her father's death, he had phoned Renee late one evening.

"Hi, Renee. Sorry to call at this hour; I know you like to get to bed early."

Renee made a noncommittal grunt, just letting him know she was there and listening.

"I have an interesting situation that I wanted to tell you about. You know Rod Staley; he's just offered me a really good price for our land—all 150 acres, with just one acre carved out around the house, which he doesn't want. I can continue to live there, and the road access would be included in the sale."

Renee said nothing and Doug went on rather uncomfortably. "I mean, *we* can continue to—well, I mean for the couple of weeks a year you're here, the big bedroom would still be yours. But hey, you're basically full time in Arizona now." Doug continued to fill the silence at Renee's end of the line. "I don't think you really appreciate the work I do to keep the house and land up. I'm not so young anymore, and it's getting to be more than I want to be responsible for. It's a good offer, Renee. We'll never get a better one."

Renee gripped the phone hard and finally erupted. "Dad, I'll never agree to sell that land to Rod. Never! You know that. His mother screwed us out of those ten acres of meadow. My favorite piece of land. Where I wanted to build someday. Grandma promised all the land to you; she said it was in her will. And then when she died, who gets those ten acres? Rod's mother, that's who. Why couldn't Grandma have given her the eight acres of swamp?"

"Renee, that was more than twenty years ago, and it wasn't Rod's fault. After all, June Staley did take care of your grandmother during her last, what, six months? A year?"

"Dad, get real. Rod or his mother—or both of them— preyed on an old woman who was dying and not exactly compos mentis. Grandma got a bit squirrely at the end, from what I heard. I'll bet anything June made Grandma feel grateful, then hinted about how much she would appreciate a little something—like those ten acres—then got Grandma to rewrite her will. I didn't trust June Staley, and I certainly don't trust her son. He was still living at home then—probably changing Grandma's will was his idea. He's always wanted our land—especially that piece. Guess we're lucky your mom didn't sign the whole 160 acres over."

"Oh, come on, Renee. That's not fair. You don't know why Grandma changed her will. You were off working in San Francisco then. Besides," Doug said, changing his tactics, "you aren't around here to enjoy the place anyway. Why do you care if I sell it? You basically treat it as a nice resort. And a free one at that, with one guy who maintains it."

"I'll be coming back every summer, Dad—at least during June, when Arizona is frying eyeballs. Maybe winter as well. And if you need help, can't you hire someone? Maybe Bert? I'd split the cost with you. Dammit, that land's been in our family for over 150 years. Rod would probably either sell it for a housing development or clear-cut it for the timber—or both—and you'd hate that. It would take forever for the land to recover..."

"He promised he wouldn't," Doug interjected. "He's a friend, you know. Our families have been neighbors, helping each other out for decades. And," he hesitated a long moment before adding, "I really had no idea you'd be so opposed to selling to Rod. I've...already told him I would do it."

"What! How could you do that without even asking me? Dad, you can't trust him. He doesn't care about the land— not the way you do. He won't.... You've always said that we are stewards of the land, caretakers. Can you honestly tell me he sees himself that way? Why is he trying to buy the land right now, anyway? He's never offered before, right? He's got some harebrained scheme in mind, I guarantee it."

There was another long pause.

"Dad, you still there?"

"Renee, we shook on it," he said finally. "I was just calling to let you know. Dave Elby's drawing up the agreement. How can I go back on my word?"

"You didn't sign anything, did you?"

"No," he said slowly. "But Renee, I've never broken a promise. You know that."

"Dad, sorry to say that the code of the West and making land deals on a handshake went out with six-shooters. If it were anyone else, I might agree. But I tell you, he's got something up his sleeve. He's not being honest with you. Please think it over. Look, do this: Tell him you need to wait a year or two before selling. If he gets mad or pushy about it, you'll know he's got some idiotic scheme in mind."

Doug sounded relieved. "That's a good idea. That way I won't be going back on my word—just asking him to wait. He should be willing to do that. And if he isn't, well, you could be right."

Renee hung up, somewhat reassured. But the question she had posed to her dad kept buzzing in her head: *Why is Rod so eager to purchase land he's never before offered to buy? Maybe he's just come into some money. But maybe he has another reason—one he isn't divulging. I should get Dad to push for an answer.*

3
___

DOUG

Mid-February (a month earlier)

The snow had picked up again, swirling in small tornados. The brisk wind cut through Doug Holden's brown leather jacket as he restacked the firewood more tightly against the wooden siding of the small ranch house. Bert O'Shea was bringing by a fresh load of wood cut from a downed tree and Doug wanted to stack it at the far end of the pile where it could season before he would need it next winter.

He could hear the signature sound of Bert's pickup coughing its way down the driveway. *How he ever got an emissions sticker for that old beast is a mystery.* Bert backed up almost to the porch and pulled the tailgate down. He stood in the truck bed and tossed the logs one by one to Doug, who added them to the pile, then replaced the tarp that kept the firewood dry from the wind-driven snow.

"Come in for a hot toddy?" Doug offered when they were finished, brushing snow off his shoulders with one hand, while wiping sweat from his brow with the other.

"That would go down good," Bert allowed. "Colder'n a witch's tit out here today."

The fire was down to embers, so Doug threw on a few seasoned logs. The pines would catch immediately, while the oaks would burn nice and slow. They pulled up by the fire, Bert in the wooden rocker and Doug in his mother's old blue overstuffed armchair, each with a hot mug of whiskey and sweetened lemon juice.

"Say, you know how I alluz told you I was Irish? Not a big surprise, me bein' an O'Shea. But turns out my family's all Italian on my mother's side."

"How'd you find that out? You find a long-lost relative or something?"

"Well," said Bert, looking a little sheepish. "Not 'xactly. I did one of them gene things? You know, you send them some spit and they send you a report about your Dee En Ay." Bert carefully enunciated each letter.

"How'd you think to do that?"

"My grand-niece got me into it. She's doin' some big college project on family ancestors and she's buggin' everyone—my brother, her sisters. Even cousins. Anyway, turns out somebody lied to somebody way back when, I guess, 'cuz when I got the Dee En Ay report from this MyGenes company, turns out I'm more Italian than Irish! The email they sent me also gave a list of all the people I'm related to, along with how we're related. Like, you know, I have a whole passel of third or fourth cousins over in Illinois. Not that I'm gonna email them; I mean I really don't care. But it's kind of interesting."

"Uh-huh," Doug grunted, putting another oak log on the fire.

"You oughtta do it. Din't you say you might have Indian

blood, what with your great-grandpa maybe marryin' an Indian woman back in Minnesota?"

"I don't know for sure that he did. It's just kind of a family rumor that's been passed down, probably because of that old photo of him with a whole pack of Native Americans back in Minnesota, taken when he was, what, maybe in his twenties?"

"Well, you look like an Indian, kinda. Those high cheekbones. And you look tanned even now in the middle of winter. It's real easy to do this test thing," he said. "I'll bet you..." Bert hesitated, calculating odds, "five bucks that you've got some Indian blood."

"I'm not going to bet against myself," Doug protested. "I'm the one who said I might be part Native American. Kinda hope I am. It'd be nice to think I have a legitimate tie to the land."

"Okay," Bert said amiably. "I'll bet you five bucks you ain't got any Indian blood at all."

"No wonder you're always broke," Doug said. "You'll bet both sides against the middle."

"And even if there ain't no Indians back in your family tree, mebbe you'll find some cousins or somethin' hangin' from the branches."

"Maybe," Doug allowed. "But seems as if the urge to reproduce kinda peaked a couple of generations back. Some of the older generations had five, six, even ten kids. Of course, a lot of them didn't survive, but each next generation had fewer and fewer. My parents were both only children and you know I don't have any brothers or sisters. And just the one daughter." He paused a moment, thinking about the baby son who had lived only a few months and the way that death had doomed his marriage. He took another sip of his toddy. "And since Renee doesn't have any kids," he concluded, "the Holden genes are going to die with her."

But Bert's comments renewed his curiosity about the old photo. It was a little faded and creased in one corner, but still in remarkably good condition, considering it was over a hundred years old. On the back of the photo, someone had written in elegant script, "Harold." A young man in overalls stood stiffly at attention, as the cameras of the day required. He held a long rifle by its barrel, stock resting on the dirt. On either side of him stood a row of Native Americans, probably Ojibwe or Chippewa, given that the photo was taken in northern Minnesota. Some were in native dress, others in trousers and shirts.

Doug had no idea whether the rumors about Harold's marriage to a Native American woman had any basis in fact. There was probably some stigma at the time attached to marrying a non-white. There was no family bible to record marriages and births. Nor was there any record of Harold's bringing a child with him to California after his wife died. But if there had been a child and if that child lurked some-where in the family tree.... It was an intriguing possibility. And apparently there was a way to find out if the rumors were true.

Bert was right in saying it was easy. A sample of saliva and the company would send him a report about his ancestry. And it wasn't expensive.

EARLY MARCH

Several weeks after discussing DNA testing with Bert, Doug had just finished draining and refilling his hot water tank when he heard the usual cacophonous arrival of Bert's car. *Must be below zero with the wind chill*, he thought, seeing that Bert had on his heavy leather coat lined with sheepskin. Bert's attire was as good a thermometer as any Doug had ever owned. Any weather above freezing merited only a jacket in Bert's mind, and only wimps wore that if the thermometer promised better than 40 degrees.

"Ready to put that corner post in for the garden fence?"

"Lemme finish my coffee," Doug said, reaching for his thermos, "then I'll be ready. You want a cup?"

"No thanks. I woke up early; got so much caffeine in me already I probly could jitterbug sitting down."

As if to test that statement, Bert parked himself comfortably on the old sway-backed wicker couch that sat on the porch. The white paint Renee had put on a couple of summers ago was peeling off the arms and back, revealing the light brown of the underlying canes.

"Did you do it?" Bert asked him. "The Dee En Ay stuff?"

Doug hesitated a moment. "Yeah, I did. And I have not one drop of Native American blood. My grandmother was wrong about her dad."

"I knew it!" Bert crowed. "You owe me five bucks."

"If I'd said I did have Indian blood, you'd have said I owed you five bucks," Doug complained. "Hell, I don't remember what we bet." He fished a bill out of his wallet and handed it over. Hoping to distract Bert from more questions, he went on. "Tell you what I do have, though. Would you believe I'm in the ninetieth percentile for Neanderthal genes?"

"Ha! Shudda known." Bert stood up and walked a few paces back and forth on the porch, arms hanging down in a poor imitation of dragging his knuckles. "No wonder you're always out in the woods. Probly more comfortable for you, out in the wild, like. Found any good caves lately?" he snorted.

"You've got it all wrong. The Neanderthals get a bad rap. They weren't really dumb. And my ancestors were likely building shelters with those trees while yours were still swinging around in the branches."

Only momentarily distracted, Bert returned to his questioning. "How 'bout relatives?"

"Naw. Just some really, really distant ones in Minnesota." Doug waved his hand to suggest distance and disinterest. He glanced at Bert, afraid that his overly casual tone might have given something away.

But Bert got up from the couch and stepped down off the porch. "Let's do it."

Doug was relieved. He couldn't tell Bert about the email he had received just this morning—two days after receiving the original MyGenes.com report. One line had stopped him as abruptly and painfully as if he'd run into a closed glass door.

THE HEADING of the email Doug received had been innocuous enough: "MyGenes.com DNA matches." It was what followed that had stunned him: "Good news! You have new DNA matches! 49.3% DNA shared, daughter or sister." *Couldn't be a sister. But...a daughter?* The name of the associated town was shockingly familiar—a bolt from over sixty years ago.

He had another child. *Good news? Good news!?*

He read the email over and over again, in disbelief. *How could this be? There has to be a mistake.* Age 62. No birth date. *Born probably sometime in 1956. If, say, around September, she could quite possibly have been conceived in December 1955.* Her last name, Rausch, rang a distant bell in his brain. *Her husband's name or her father's?* He dug around in the recesses of his memory, finally extracting a name: Tom Rausch. And that made him think of Phyllis.

He flashed back in his mind to the December nights in the backseat of his folks' Chevy when the windows had clouded over from the vigorous activity. And the one night in the cheap motel with the damp sheets and the little space heater. Phyllis with her long blond hair and beautiful hazel eyes. And a small black mole on her left breast he had kissed and called a "beauty mark." They'd dated all his senior year, when he was the football hero and she the Homecoming Queen. What a cliché they had been. He hadn't been that sorry to leave her behind. Still—why hadn't she told him?

But he knew the answer to that. The calls to the dormitory hall phone he had ignored once he was back at college in January. Person-to-person calls; he had told the guys to say he was not there until finally the calls stopped. A letter he had tossed, unopened. His mother had told him Phyllis was dating someone else—Tom Rausch. Wasn't he the guy she'd been with all that fall? Then he heard that Phyllis had married Tom, rather precipitously, and Doug had been relieved that she would no longer be trying to reach him. Phyllis did not appeal to him on any other basis than the obvious one. Sex with her had been both enthusiastic and creative. But he would never have considered marrying her.

His mother had told him about the baby, a girl—but not when she had been born. *Nobody, Mother included, would have suspected the baby was actually mine.* And unless Phyllis had told someone—certainly not Tom—who could have known? Phyllis herself probably didn't know. All that

December, Phyllis had seemingly been on a rotating schedule with her two boyfriends. When Doug confronted her, she just laughed and insisted that Doug was—her term —"numero uno," and told him about all the excuses she fed Tom when she was "unavailable." But then maybe—Doug couldn't really remember after all these years—Phyllis had provided similar convenient excuses when she couldn't be with him. The daughter *could* have been Tom's. Almost certainly Tom must have thought that the child was his when he married Phyllis.

Doug stood up from the computer, walked to the front window, returned, and stared again at the screen, still stunned. To his astonishment, he felt his cheeks damp with tears. *Another daughter*, he kept saying to himself. *A baby*. He pictured blond, curly hair.

Get a grip, he told himself. *That baby you are picturing is a woman—a* middle-aged *woman.*

And she doesn't know you exist.

He doodled a few notes on the pad he kept nearby. He could contact her with a press of the "Contact" button included in the email. *But what could I possibly say? What good would it do?* The last he'd heard from friends back East, Phyllis's husband was suffering from Alzheimer's, and Phyllis herself was very ill. Might have died by now. Better to leave it be.

But another daughter. He had been so disappointed at Renee's decision not to have children. Maybe this newly discovered daughter had children. Maybe he had grandchildren, even a grandson. Someone to take fishing and deer hunting, even at his age. He was still in pretty good shape, despite the heart business. That would be so wonderful; even if a grandson didn't carry on the Holden name, he'd carry on the genes. Again, he felt overwhelmed by a wave of unexpected and foreign emotion. It was almost like grief, the way it gripped his chest.

I'll sleep on it. If I decide to contact her, I'll have to think about that very, very carefully. She must have always assumed Phyllis's husband is her biological father. It's a bit late in life to find out that isn't true.

But wait! If I have this information, that means she did the same DNA test—and received the same report! She now knows that I am her biological father! She must be more shocked than me. Maybe she'll contact me. Or maybe she's embarrassed, or angry, or.... Aw, hell, I don't know what to do.

4

RENEE

arly March

"I've made our reservations," Renee announced to Peter the day after the police informed her of her father's death. "We fly direct to San Francisco and then we'll drive the rest of the way to Dad's, uh, to my place." Although Renee and Peter Jackson had been a couple for over a year now, he had never been to the Holden land in Placer County.

"How long is the drive?" Peter asked.

"About three hours, but almost all of it is on freeways. It's flat and boring through the valley, but once we hit the Sierra foothills, it's really quite pretty."

As they navigated the traffic through San Francisco, Renee could clearly see the distinctive pyramid-shaped top of the building where she had spent so many years practicing law, fighting her way up to partner. She pointed it out to Peter.

"So, should we take a little detour and stop by your old firm? I'll bet they'd be glad to see you."

"Hah! Not likely. Lots of memories, but most of them unpleasant."

"Really? Like what kinds of memories?"

"Oh, you know. Media shit, lots of pressure. One little mistake and your malpractice insurance skyrockets. Lawyer jokes featuring sharks aren't exaggerations; my dear colleagues were always sniffing around for blood in the water. I'm glad to be out of there."

"Is that why you retired so early? You've never told me."

"Yeah, something like that." *No more discussion of my early retirement.* "Hey, there's the sign for the Bay Bridge. I've got to get over a couple of lanes."

Leaving the city, they crossed into Oakland and on up to I-80 through the beginning of the Central Valley. The brown hills always reminded Renee of huge dinosaurs dipping heavy heads down to drink from the Lafayette reservoir. As they climbed out of the heat into the cool Sierra Nevada foothills and neared their destination, Renee pointed out huge rocky mounds along the road, covered with scrub oak trees and manzanita bushes. "We're in Placer County now. You'll see a lot of those, created a hundred fifty years ago by tailings from the big hydraulic jets extracting gold ore."

They passed exit signs for Gold Run and Dutch Flat, evoking the region's history. "My dad's grandmother taught grade school in Gold Run in the early 1900s. I've seen a photo of a little one-room building built on stilts right by the railroad tracks. By that time, people were getting rich on farming, not mining. All her students were children of migrants working the fields. Italians in those days. The children spoke little English and whatever they learned during the school year tended to fade over the summers. We have a few old letters Great-Grandma wrote about her teaching adventures in what were still called gold rush towns, even though the rush was over."

From the interstate, Renee drove the two-lane, winding road, thankful that it was clear of snow. At nearly 4,000-feet elevation, this road was an ice rink in winter. She turned onto the narrow gravel driveway to the house, her rental car barely clearing the trunks of huge hundred-foot firs and pines guarding both sides. The driveway opened to a scrawny lawn in front of the small frame house, Lilliputian next to the giant surrounding trees. She parked in front of her dad's garage-*cum*-workshop and stepped out. The air was fresh and redolent of sugar pines. The scent of home. There were a few scattered patches of snow in the shade.

Fallen branches from the massive black oak trees lay scattered about. Their disposal was probably on Doug's to-do list. *This, all of it*, she thought, looking around, *is now my responsibility. I'll have to find someone to keep it up, do all the little chores Dad actually enjoyed—maintaining the well, repairing the fences.*

The large wood pile at the side of the house sat ready to feed the large fireplace blazes her dad loved. But looking up at the shingled roof, she saw that the chimney was beginning to list a bit drunkenly. *I wonder if he noticed. Probably did, but at his age, not something he could have fixed himself. I'm not sure he had the money to hire someone.* She felt a pang of guilt. *I could have offered help.*

Her father was a talented craftsman; under his hands, polished tables, dressers, and highboys emerged from lumber he cut and planed from his own trees. And he could fix anything. What would she do the next time the well pump broke? What if squirrels claimed squatter's rights in the attic again?

For the first time since she had heard of his death, standing on the land he had loved, Renee really missed him. He hadn't been the most nurturing of fathers, and they had never been close, but he had provided for her after her mother moved out while Renee was in middle school, and he had managed to save enough to send her to college back East. Law school, however, was on her own dime, and it had taken years to repay the loans.

Despite growing up in this house, she had almost nothing in common with her father. His whole life was outdoors: the trees, the birds, the mountains. Hers was "the great indoors"—the law, a comfortable, low-maintenance house with expansive entertainment space, nice restaurants. *This was always Dad's home far more than mine.* And yet she enjoyed the annual summer visits. *I do love this place,* she thought with a bit of surprise at the sense of ownership. *I don't want to sell it—or desert it entirely, the way Mom did. But when I'm gone, then what?*

It was obvious within a few minutes of their arrival at the house that Peter was interested in his surroundings in a way that her ex-husband, Dan, would never have been. Dan would have grabbed a book and settled himself in the ancient balding living room rocker, hardly budging the entire visit. Peter immediately walked around the house, explored Doug's workshop, surveyed the dead stalks in the vegetable garden, and gave the posts supporting the fence around it an exploratory shake. He came inside only when Renee offered to show him maps of the property.

Renee had expected to find the house a mess, dishes in the sink, the bed unmade. After all, Dad had intended to come back after felling the tree. But it was surprisingly neat. The newspaper was on the floor by the rocking chair where he had left it, but his coffee cup was rinsed and on the drain board. And Grandma's old handmade quilt was spread out on top of the bed—as close as Doug ever came to making it.

When Renee spread the maps out on the dining room table, Peter quickly became absorbed. Renee studied him. In an unguarded moment she had confided in her friend Molly Levin: "It's not a perfect relationship, and I certainly don't expect it to be permanent. We come from such different backgrounds—Peter from inner-city Oakland, me from the Northern California woods!" But they had both had professional careers and shared similar interests.

Peter was a good-looking man, his dark skin setting off the white flash of frequent smiles. His nose was prominent ("Roman," her friend Aki had described it) on his pleasant angular face. She relished being able to wear high heels when they went out. Dan had been sensitive about his height. And Peter was a wonderful companion on their travels together. He had a knack for making friends on the tours they enjoyed and could converse on any topic from baseball to the strength of the dollar overseas. People often took him for a former athlete ("Oh, did you play basketball?"), perhaps because of his height but, she thought, more likely because he was Black. People made this assumption so frequently that she now made a practice of introducing him as "Dr. Peter Jackson."

Not that he wasn't athletic. Peter loved skiing, hiking, and pickleball. But despite his enjoyment of the outdoors, he was not a gardener. When a friend had brought him a housewarming gift of potted geraniums, Peter had accepted them graciously and then given them to a neighbor as soon as the gift-bearer was out of sight. "To radiologists," he explained, "things that grow are usually bad." At least one mutual friend thought that joke was macabre, but Renee found it funny.

She enjoyed that incautious sense of humor. Peter was not inclined to worry about what other people thought of him—unless any hint of racism crept into the conversation. According to him, his disdain for tact contributed to his divorce. He had married right out of college, a "colossal mistake," he admitted. He and his wife were so totally different that all they had shared was "youthful lust." The only benefit from the twenty months of marriage was a daughter. Estelle now lived with her partner in New Mexico, and they had recently adopted a little boy.

Too bad Dan and I didn't divorce that quickly. Seven years is a long time to be bored. She had thought being an architect would mean Dan would be interesting. But he didn't like travel or fine dining or theater. Nothing really stirred his soul except perhaps adding a rare Confederate postmark to his stamp collection. Even his work turned out to be repetitious and uncreative. He designed elementary schools exclusively, and she had stopped pretending to be interested after she discovered how little his plans changed from one project to another. "I've married a Roomba vacuum cleaner," Renee had told her mother in one of their infrequent conversations. "Covers the same ground over and over and when he bumps into an obstacle, moves around it." Her mother had put a more positive spin on the situation. "You've married an introvert. He's a good man, but I don't think you're going to be happy together in the long run," she added presciently.

"Because I'm not a good woman?" Renee had asked indignantly. "Is that what you're saying?"

"See, that's why," her mother had said. "You are so quick

to take offense—and to argue! He'll probably put up with it, but I just don't see you two as well matched. You want constant atten—" Sensing Renee start to bristle, her mother had quickly changed her wording. "You like lots of people around you, lots of social life. Dan seems sort of...self-sufficient." *Mom didn't live long enough to see she was right about Dan and me. We certainly weren't well matched.* Renee wondered briefly if the fragile rapport she had begun to allow with her mother after graduating from college would have eventually led to a real reconciliation.

RENEE LOOKED AROUND at the house that her mother had abandoned when Renee was in seventh grade, trying to picture it forty-five years ago. The commercial-grade gray and brown carpet covering the living room now was almost threadbare, while the rest of the floor sported checkered linoleum dating to the Carter administration. Renee eyed it with distaste. *But do I really want to remodel this place?* Thanks to her foresight in putting the huge house south of San Francisco in her name before she married Dan, its sale meant she could afford any changes she wanted. *No need to completely redesign this house like I'm doing in Sunrise Acres, but it needs to be more livable for the summer months Peter and I might use it. And once I get the chimney repaired, we could enjoy a few weeks in winter.* She smiled as she pictured a cozy entanglement of naked limbs in front of a blazing fire after snowshoeing or skiing. She had never felt comfortable inviting Peter here while her father was alive, but now.... If their relationship was going to deepen, he should get more of a sense of her roots.

Peter had been exploring the rest of the house. He

emerged from Doug's bedroom waving a small notepad. "Look what I found next to your dad's old computer. He wrote what looks like 'MyGenes.com' and 'GRANDKIDS???' in all caps with three question marks and underlined about five times. What's that about?"

"Who knows. My folks lobbied for grandkids—at least Mom did." *Why did she say she wanted to be a grandmother when she obviously hated being a mother? If she had liked having children, she wouldn't have abandoned me. Would have taken me with her when she left. Dad blamed her leaving on baby Bobby's death—but she'd had almost six years to get over that before she took off.* "She thought every woman should want children. Well, not me. My friends who have kids?" Renee said. "Always stressed out. One of my friends' kids has food allergies so bad he's impossible to feed. And I certainly would not want to have to rely on some Filipina nanny who might pilfer or get sick and not show up, or...."

Peter didn't wait for the full list of problems with having children. "Don't you want to check out your dad's messages?" he interrupted. "He had a phone, didn't he? Aren't there people who should be contacted?"

"There's a landline phone in the kitchen. But that won't be any use. His mobile probably had messages and emails, but it was smashed when the tree fell on him. I'll send an obituary to the local paper, but most of his friends live around here and Bert O'Shea—he's a neighbor and good friend—has probably already contacted them." Renee paused, let out a deep breath, then continued. "But I really don't want to deal with any of this right now. How about a guided tour of the property?"

They walked down one of the paths to a large clearing. "See those sad-looking apple trees? A hundred years ago or so, this was an orchard, a commercial enterprise of Dad's grandfather that never made any money. Almost all these trees are dead or dying, but there's always a meager harvest. Every fall Dad hauled out the ancient hand cider press and made a few gallons of cider and some apple butter for friends and neighbors, but the rest of the crop just rotted on the ground."

Renee smiled, amused at a sudden memory. "One year a couple of Bert's pigs got loose and gorged on the windfalls—but the apples had fermented. So the pigs staggered around, snorting and farting, 'drunk as lords,' as Doug described it. He loved telling that story and howled with laughter every time."

"Lots of memories here," Peter said. "What are you going to do with this place?"

"I was just thinking about that. I'd like a bigger kitchen. I don't know how Mom managed cooking in a space the size of a shower stall. And of course I need to—"

"I meant long term. You have a wonderful piece of land here—ample water, gorgeous forest, good access to the highway."

"You sound like a real estate developer." Renee's tone was almost accusatory.

Peter laughed. "Sorry. I guess I was looking at it from my perspective, just thinking what inheriting a place like this would mean for people like my family. Generations of city-dwellers by necessity, but loving the outdoors. Maybe *I* should buy it from you. After all, who's going to take care of it after you're gone? If you had kids, it would be different. Hey, how about adopting mine?"

Despite his grin, Renee thought she heard an undertone of desire.

"No interest in adoption," she said lightly. "But maybe I'll remember her in my will."

5

RENEE

Renee had started to unpack, when she heard the crunch of tires on the winding gravel driveway. A small red jeep, topless except for a roll bar, pulled in next to her car. Rod Staley's retriever Honey leaped out and raced to the porch barking happily, anticipating her usual treat from Doug.

Rod was a tall man, a few years older than Renee, with a large mustache attached to a craggy leathered face that women (other than Renee) still found attractive. She stepped outside, closing the door behind her, much to Honey's disappointment. Renee watched Rod's approach with obvious hostility and angrily shoved Honey away from sniffing her crotch. Rod nodded to her and called Honey to his side. "Hi, Renee. Really sorry about Doug. He was a great guy and one of my best friends."

"What do you want, Rod?"

He looked a bit disconcerted by her greeting. "Can we sit down and talk a bit?" he asked, gesturing to the sagging wicker couch on the porch.

"No," she said. She continued to stand outside the door,

arms folded as if guarding the entrance. Rod moved to climb the wooden steps up to the porch, then reconsidered. "What do you want?" Renee repeated.

"Well," he said uncertainly, "I was hoping to talk with you."

"What about?"

"The land," he said, taking off his cowboy hat and using it to gesture widely, taking in the surroundings. His bald head protruded from the collar of his heavy sheepskin jacket like the top of a fire hydrant. A shadow of white stubble ringed the lower half of his head where, if unshaven, a tonsure would sprout.

"Nothing to discuss," she said, and turned to go into the house.

"Hey, wait a minute," he said. "Doug and I had an agreement."

She turned to face him, not at all surprised that he would bring this up. "What kind of agreement?"

"He was going to sell me his land, all 150 acres—the one acre around the house excepted, so you could still live here."

"You can forget that. I'm not selling the land to you."

Rod looked astonished. "You can't still be pissed about my mom's ten acres, are you?"

"I can and I am. I won't let this property go to you. You already cheated us out of the meadowland."

"Oh for…. Renee, be reasonable. I can't believe you're still…. You don't even live here anymore. And Doug agreed. In Dave Elby's office—you know, the lawyer in Colfax."

"First of all, I haven't seen any agreement. Second, you'll need my signature. I'm the heir and I will not agree."

"We didn't get around to a written contract," he admitted. "But Dave was there. He may have even drafted it. Doug and I shook on it. And Doug's word was always good. That's what he wanted."

Renee laughed. "A handshake? That won't hold up in any court. No, you are out of luck, Rod. No sale."

"No one else will offer you that much for the land. No one."

"Maybe. We'll see. I haven't put it on the market. And if I do, I'll advertise all over California. There are a lot of techies in the Bay Area and Silicon Valley with more money than they know what to do with. I could sell it easy. If I wanted to. And I don't, right now."

"You only come up here once a year at most; why not sell?"

"That may change; I have a...friend." As if summoned, Peter appeared in the doorway. Rod appeared startled at the sudden apparition. He backed up a step as Peter stepped quickly across the porch and down the stairs, hand outstretched. Rod shook it warily as Renee continued without pausing to introduce Peter. "We may want to come up for the whole summer. Maybe even during the winter—Peter loves to cross-country ski," she added. As Peter came back up the steps to stand beside her, she linked her arm through his in an obvious statement of their relationship and solidarity.

Rod was not deterred. He replaced his hat and tilted it back a little, giving himself a few seconds to think, but then he addressed Renee again, ignoring Peter.

"Renee, our fathers were friends. And I was Doug's friend, a good friend. I'm telling you...*advising* you as a friend. Sell it to me. We don't even have to get a real estate agent involved. More money you can keep instead of paying a commission. Be reasonable. Are you really going to let a twenty-year-old grudge ruin a good deal? Hell, you can keep the house and spend as much time in it as you want."

"Nice try, Rod. Getting this land won't be as easy as you hoped. You thought I'd be an easier sell than Dad, right?"

"What do you mean? I told you he agreed to sell."

"And then he asked for a delay, right?"

Rod's eyes widened. "He told you that?"

"Yep. Kind of problematic for your plans?"

Rod took a step toward her, his entire body tense and his hands clenched. "What do you know about my plans?"

"Why don't you tell me about them?" From her sarcastic tone, it was clear she didn't expect a truthful explanation.

Rod's shoulders relaxed. "Like I told your dad. Selling some of the firs and pines for lumber. No clear-cutting."

"Well, I'm not as easy a mark as Dad." She fixed Rod with a grim stare. "And you sure as hell won't catch me cutting down any trees in your presence either!"

Rod hesitated. He started to speak a couple of times but closed his mouth in a tight line, looked at her angrily, and then glanced at Peter.

The echo of her own words suddenly gave Renee a vivid image: a great crack that would have signaled the impending fall—a sound that her nearly deaf father probably wouldn't have heard. The sudden horror as he saw the huge pine crashing down. Then Rod standing over him, moving a branch or two aside to ensure he was dead. She felt a sharp stab of grief, a physical fist gripping deep inside her chest and at the same time, fury at the thought that this man in front of her could be a murderer. Trained in the courtroom to show emotion only when it served a purpose, Renee was surprised by tears in her eyes and the wave of emotions washing over her. Seeing Rod momentarily speechless, she quickly tugged Peter by the arm, whirled around, and went inside, slamming the door behind her.

From the living room window, Peter watched Rod's retreat with a bemused expression. "Who was that?"

"A neighbor," she said. "Not a nice one."

"Yeah, my Spidey sense picked that up," Peter said with a smile. Then he asked seriously, "Is he a problem?"

"Not really. Just a nuisance. Like his dog. All bark."

"Huh. Hope you're right. I'm not sure I'd like to tangle with guys who are, what do you say here in the Wild West, 'packing'?"

Renee waved dismissively. "You noticed. Up here, a lot of people carry guns. They say it's for protection against bears, but I think it's just to impress."

"Consider me impressed," Peter said dryly. "Where I come from in Oakland, it's always open hunting season on Blacks. Bears, not so much."

Outside, Rod stood a few moments, glaring at the closed door. Then he said loudly enough for her to hear, "Jesus! That is one stubborn woman!" And something about "another way." He walked down to his car and gestured for Honey to jump in. Then he accelerated up the driveway with an angry spray of gravel, like a dog covering its shit.

Renee watched the jeep disappear around the corner. Despite her comments to Peter dismissing Rod as a threat, she felt a small frisson of fear. He was truly angry. And if buying the land was motive enough to kill Doug, now she was the one who stood in his way.

6

RENEE

Renee pulled on the faded jeans she had left in "her" dresser and a long-sleeved paisley blouse. From the tie rack she used for belts, she selected a wide leather one next to her dad's two ties: one for weddings, the other for funerals. Cinching the belt, she smiled. *Yes! The prong slides right into the old worn hole. No weight gain since last summer. My reward for all the exercise classes and running up and down those bell tower stairs.* She completed her outfit with hiking boots, a lightweight navy fleece, and a broad-brimmed woven straw hat. Prepared for both chill and sun reflecting off the remaining snow patches, Renee decided to walk over to Bert O'Shea's. Bert's house stood on the far side of Doug's land, adjacent to Rod's parcel. Both Rod and Doug often hired him as an extra pair of hands when felling trees, repairing fences, or painting—a chore Doug heartily detested.

"Peter? Want to come meet another neighbor—this time a nice one? I'm going over to check in with Bert O'Shea. He's known me almost all my life and helped Doug with all sorts of work. I may need him to be kind of a caretaker now that Dad's gone. I'd like you to meet him."

As they started walking down the well-worn trail to Bert's cabin, Peter asked, "How come you call your dad 'Doug' sometimes and other times 'Dad'?"

Renee shrugged. "Never thought about it. Depends on how warm and daughterly I'm feeling at the moment, I guess."

"So you weren't very close?"

"He was always pretty...um, reserved. Didn't talk a lot about himself. I don't even know all that much about his life before he married Mom and moved out here."

"Didn't you tell me he grew up on the East Coast?"

Renee nodded. "Outside of Boston. His dad had a small construction company, and Doug worked there on weekends and summers all through high school. But he told me he never considered adding 'and Son' to Holden Construction. He came out here as often as he could, supposedly for vacations—but even then, he helped Grandpa work the land. Dad was in college, finishing his degree in Natural Resources Management when Grandpa died and left him this property. So right after college, Dad moved here, got a job with the California Forestry Division, and stuck with it for forty years."

"And your mom?"

"She left when I was in middle school," Renee said shortly. *She couldn't have left at a worse time in a girl's life. One foot in childhood, still playing make-believe, and the other in teenage life, boys, and weird body changes.* Renee broke away from her thoughts and looked down at the muddy trail leading to Bert's. "Man, I'm glad I wore boots."

Peter, in sneakers, stepped carefully around the soggy areas. The sunlight through the trees dappled the soft cover of pine needles. They passed under a sugar pine whose enormous foot-long cones looked as if they might have spawned a litter of the small ones fallen from neighboring firs. On either side of the path, the blackberry brambles that Doug constantly fought to contain threatened the unwary with thorns on wintry brown stalks.

Renee was conscious of the birdsong around her. "The music of the forest," Doug had called it. When his hearing began to fail, and with it the ability to identify the dozens of birds he knew by sound, he had mourned the loss of bird-song more than human voice.

As Renee and Peter rounded the corner, they could see what Doug had always called Bert's "cabin." It was a grace-less structure that Bert had built on land he rented from Doug for a nominal fee. Its outer walls were heavy plywood painted a muddy brown, punctuated by small high windows. While he was an Edison when it came to anything mechanical, and his prolific garden fed not only the neigh-bors and himself but often the local food bank as well, Bert was not skilled at carpentry. He prioritized function over aesthetics.

Renee had been in his cabin many times. The interior had changed little over the years. As she recalled from her visit last summer, the top of three concrete steps led immediately into a large room constituting most of the house. It served as family room (although Bert was a life-long bachelor), dining room, and kitchen. Variously sized carpet remnants, the most prominent a vintage green shag, covered the floor like scattered pieces of a jigsaw puzzle. The ancient cast-iron wood-burning stove domi-nating the room heated the entire house. She had been surprised to see a large flat-screen television, Bert's only bow to modernity. Facing an overstuffed gray recliner, it owed its reception to the antenna that Bert had somehow managed to attach near the top of an adjacent seventy-foot pine.

Bert was nowhere in sight. As Renee was about to suggest they come back later, she heard his old pickup rattling down the driveway. As Bert climbed out, Renee smiled at his old overalls, covered with so many paint spatters it reminded her of a Jackson Pollock painting. His plain white T-shirt, sleeves protruding from a ragged, heavily padded brown vest, seemed inadequate for the cold. But his tanned, bare muscular arms looked years younger than his wrinkled face. Bert broke into a wide smile at seeing Renee, but suddenly assumed a sober expression as he recalled the reason for her presence. "Renee!"

He turned to Peter and unhesitatingly stuck his hand out, not waiting for an introduction. Nor, Renee noted, did he seem at all disconcerted to find her companion was Black. "Howdy," he said. "Bert O'Shea." The hint of a tattoo peeked from under one sleeve. Renee remembered it was a souvenir of military service, but she wasn't sure which branch. As soon as Peter shook his hand and returned the introduction, Bert turned back to Renee and began expressing his condolences, but she cut him short.

"Bert, I need to find out what happened."

He looked confused. "They didn't tell you? About the tree?"

She shook her head. "No, I mean what *really* happened. Dad wouldn't have gone out there to fell a tree that size by himself."

To her surprise, Bert's eyes filled. "It's my fault. I couldn't go with him. Had an emergency call from that widder in Colfax I alluz help. Doug called me, but I knew I couldn't get back 'fore dark. He was worried that pine could fall on the power line, but I thought he'd wait for me to take it down. God, if only he had!"

"Did Rod go out there with him?" she demanded.

"Heck, I don't know. Doug was thinkin' of askin' him to help, but he must not've reached him, 'cuz Doug was alone when Rod found him."

"Yeah, and just how did Rod *happen* to find him?" Renee asked angrily.

Bert looked surprised at her tone of voice. "Well, Rod said it was actually Honey who found him. Honey runs all over the place, you know. I guess she started barkin' up a storm and Rod thought for a while she'd just treed a raccoon or somethin', but she kept at it, and Rod finally went out to see if mebbe it was that bear that lives down in the gully. And that big sugar pine was down and there was Doug, dead as—" He broke off, embarrassed at his own lack of tact. He glanced guiltily at Peter.

"So nobody knows if Rod was out there too," Renee said.

"You mean when the tree fell?" Bert looked puzzled. "Naw, if Rod'd been there, he'd have put on more guy ropes for one thing, or at least helped with the second cut, and the whole accident wouldn't have happened."

"Unless Rod helped it happen," Renee said.

Bert was shocked. "God, Renee, what're you thinkin'? Rod and your dad were friends. I'm sure Rod was tellin' the truth. He's not a bad guy, just kinda...." He hesitated, massaging one arm with a massive hand.

"Kinda what, Bert?"

"Look, Renee, frankly I don't care much for the guy. We both know that Rod sometimes plays things close to the line. If you'd suggested he mighta tried to suck Doug in on one of his get-rich schemes, like his stupid Christmas tree farm, or cheated someone, I could believe that." Bert turned to Peter to explain. "Rod's family's always been kinda poor. He don't even own the land. His whole family does, and they just let him live there. Anyways, he's always been tryin' to make a buck one way or 'nother offa the land."

Bert paused and looked thoughtfully up the path toward Renee's house. "And he has been pokin' around Doug's property, uh—your property. Probly thinkin' up some way to get rich off it—legal or crooked. But killin' someone? Nah. Rod may be a lot of things, but he's not violent. Never seen it. You shouldn't go around suggestin'.... I mean, why would Rod do anything to hurt Doug?"

"He wants our land. My land. He keeps asking to buy it. Even got Dad to talk about selling."

"I know," Bert said to Renee's surprise. "Last year after the big fires all over the state, Doug was talkin' 'bout havin' at least twenty acres cleared of underbrush, 'specially around the house, cut down on the fire risk. That's a big project. I think he decided it might be easier just to sell most of the land instead. Rod's never done nothin' bad to Doug, even helps out with the trees some, takes good care of his family's property. That was important to Doug. He was slowin' down, you know. What was he, seventy-nine? Eighty? It's a lot of land to keep track of, take care of."

"What do you mean 'slowing down'? Didn't sound that way to me. He was in great shape."

Bert looked uncomfortable; he shifted from one foot to another and wiped his hands on his overalls. "Well, after he got the pacemaker put in..."

"Pacemaker? What pacemaker? Bert, are you saying Dad had heart trouble? When did this happen?"

"Last November.... I thought you knew."

"I...we didn't talk much," Renee said shortly. "And I stayed in Arizona this past Christmas. Bert, good to see you.

We've gotta go," she said hastily and walked off, leaving Peter to shake hands and mumble an awkward farewell.

When he caught up with her, Renee was shaking her head. "Peter, I just don't understand why Dad agreed to sell our property to Rod, of all people. Doug always said he was just the caretaker of the land. If he did sell, he'd want it to go to someone who shared his view. I can't believe that Dad ever thought Rod would be any kind of steward. About seven or eight years ago, he and his brother massacred more than five acres of gorgeous meadow—land that should have been mine. They'd excavated a pond, tried to divert a segment of the creek to fill it, and planted little firs all around it for the 'Christmas tree farm' Bert mentioned. Idiots! The pit wouldn't hold water there—the soil is sandy and drains real quickly. Their great get-rich scheme died along with most of the trees.

"And then there was Rod's stupid Canadian deal. According to Bert, Rod invested in a huge timbered parcel, expecting to sell the trees for lumber. But he didn't do any kind of survey of soft versus hard wood. So, typical Rod, he lost most of his expected profit taking down trees that were good only for pulp. And then he had to sell for pennies on the dollar."

When they reached the front of the house, Renee was still musing out loud. "Dad knew about all those schemes, so I don't understand why he even considered selling to Rod. And where would Rod get the money? Far as I know, he lives off his Army and Postal Service pensions. I suggested Dad delay the sale and see how Rod reacted. If Rod was angry or pushed hard for a quicker sale, we'd know for sure he was up to something sneaky. I'm not sure Dad took my advice, but he said it was a good idea, and when I mentioned Dad's delaying the sale, Rod didn't deny it."

"So that's why you think Rod could have had something to do with your father's death? Because Rod couldn't stand waiting to buy the land? Sorry, but I just don't get it. Did he think if your dad died, you'd be more likely to sell to him?"

"I don't know what he was thinking. Bert says Rod isn't a violent man, but I just can't understand how Dad could allow a tree to fall on him unless someone else guided it or he was somehow incapacitated. And Rod was the one to 'find' him. I told you I'm going to see the coroner about an autopsy. Maybe there's some evidence of foul play. I doubt the coroner will agree to it, but they're holding on to...to Dad's body for another day or two.

"I've arranged for a cremation. Think I'll spread his ashes here among his trees," she added quietly, looking around at the huge oaks. Then she seemed suddenly to recall Peter's presence.

"Anyway," she said with a sharp intake of breath. "I don't trust the Staleys. I wish I knew what Rod's real plans are." She shook her head as she stepped inside the house. "There's got to be some cock-eyed scheme brewing under that ridiculous cowboy hat."

She grabbed the large brown leather purse she had left sitting on the floor inside the door and fished out her car keys. "So, Peter, time to pay a visit downtown, talk to the coroner. Wanna come? I need to find out what really happened."

7

RENEE

The Placer County coroner's office was in a small building overlooking a parking lot in which sat a peculiar freestanding covered island.

"Peter, I'm not sure how long I'll be. I don't have an appointment. Why don't you walk around a bit. This is really an interesting little town—especially the historic part."

"That's okay, I'm in no hurry. I think I'll wait in the car. It's been a while since I've had this many bars on my phone, so I'm gonna catch up on my email and news."

Renee looked around her, concluding that the building had once been a service station and the office occupied the former "convenience store." All that was missing were gasoline pumps outside and a wiener rotisserie inside. This image brought a brief smile that quickly vanished as she entered the office and demanded to see the coroner.

A counter stretched across the front of a room full of filing cabinets and computer stations. After giving her name and a brief explanation of her mission, Renee was surprised when a petite woman in her late twenties emerged from a back door, introduced herself as the coroner, and invited Renee into her office. The woman's dark brown hair had been shaved close around her head below the crown. Contrasting streaked brown and blond hair was pulled up and tied into a topknot. The effect was almost comical to Renee's eyes, the clump of hair sticking straight up, waving like a sheaf of wheat. It wasn't clear if her hairdo was a fashion statement or a practical solution for a woman who needed to avoid hair falling on her work but who also wanted to literally let her hair down for social occasions. The young woman turned to her computer and hit a few keystrokes to bring up relevant files. After a few moments perusing the screen, she turned to Renee. "Could you come with me, please?"

She escorted Renee to the morgue to identify Doug's body. Looking through the glass, Renee was relieved that his face had been spared the worst of his injuries. She nodded and the attendant replaced the sheet over his face. *He looks so old, so fragile, so empty.* She had expected him to look asleep, but instead, he was just...gone. She pulled a Kleenex from her pocket and dabbed at her eyes. After standing in silence for a few more moments, she turned to the coroner. "What can you tell me about what killed him? Didn't you do an autopsy?"

"Ma'am, would you mind returning to my office?"

Once they were both seated, the coroner explained, "There are twenty-five categories of deaths in California that are reported to this office and only four require an autopsy: suspicion of infectious or of contagious disease, death of an infant, or suspicion of foul play."

"Well, I definitely suspect foul play and I want an autopsy."

The coroner looked astonished. "Excuse my bluntness, but your father was crushed by a falling tree. How could that be foul play?"

"I don't believe that he would have been that careless. He was a certified forester, worked for the state for years, felled trees all his life."

The coroner was skeptical. "How could someone make a tree fall on him?"

"It wouldn't be that hard. Not if he trusted someone to help him and that person guided the tree to fall on him."

"And your father would just stand there and let it happen? A tree big enough to cause those injuries must have made a lot of noise when it started to fall."

Renee waved an impatient hand. "Dad was deaf as a cucumber. And I found his hearing aids inside the house on his dresser. He never wore them in the woods—was afraid of losing one. So he wouldn't have heard anything. I want an autopsy."

"I could arrange that," the coroner said, "but I can't justify spending taxpayer money on it. It won't tell us anything beyond cause of death. And that was pretty clear from even a cursory examination. The tree hit him very hard. The wound on the back of his head exactly matches the tree branch size and shape. After your friend Mr. Staley checked that your father was dead and sawed part of the tree branch off him, he took quite a few photos with his phone of both your father and the tree branch, close up. Then he called the sheriff's office, and the deputy took more photos, a 360 video, and also FaceTimed me from the site. It was very clear that the tree branch caused the head wound. How he was so unfortunate as to be right in that spot when it fell—no autopsy will tell us that."

"Staley is not a friend. I still think he arranged the whole thing."

"That's a pretty big accusation," the coroner said mildly. "The evidence doesn't support—"

"To hell with your evidence." Despite Renee's words, she could grudgingly see the logic in what the coroner had said. For a few moments, she considered phoning the sheriff herself. Maybe there could be footprints in the patches of snow at the base of the tree? But from what the coroner said, Rod could easily explain any footprints he left at the scene. What other evidence of an intentional push to the pine could there be?

Renee gave the door a hard shove behind her as she left, but its hydraulic spring deprived her of the satisfaction of slamming it.

When she got back to the car, Peter was concentrating on his phone. She started to knock on the window that he had closed against the cold, but he was frowning so fiercely at the screen that she hesitated. Whatever he was reading was clearly troubling him—no, *angering* him. All she could see through the window was that he was on the website for the *San Francisco Chronicle*. When she hit the window with her knuckles, Peter jumped and then immediately closed the phone.

"Let's get back," she said. "Why are you looking at me like that?" Peter was still scowling. "What were you reading?"

Peter took a few seconds and then said simply, "Something I need to research more. What did you find out from the coroner?"

Renee sighed. "Not a damn thing. Well, it's definitely Dad, not that there was really any doubt." She then repeated what the coroner had told her about the cause of death. "And even if I paid for an autopsy myself, and it showed that Dad had a heart attack, so maybe he couldn't run, it would be a helluva coincidence that the tree fell just that moment. I still think Rod saw his chance and pushed the tree to fall on him." She started the car. "Let's go. One more stop. Funeral home."

AFTER RENEE EXPLAINED to the funeral director that there would be no autopsy, she arranged for the cremation of her father's body. The funeral director was a middle-aged balding man with a rotund shape more suited to playing Santa than an accomplice of the Grim Reaper. He began showing Renee a variety of urns for the ashes or, as he referred to them, much to Renee's annoyance, "cremains."

"I'm going to save you some time," she interrupted. "My dad's *ashes* aren't going into some ornate urn fit for royalty. I'd like a simple cardboard box."

"It's not because of expense," Renee explained to Peter, who appeared shocked. "I intend to scatter his ashes in the pine grove where he died. I think he'd like that, and I know for sure that he wouldn't want me to bury some fancy container that would last for a century in the ground." She hesitated a few minutes. *I guess I could have a headstone put in the cemetery where Mom is buried.* She shook her head. *He'd hate that.*

Peter interrupted her thoughts. "Is that legal...to scatter the ashes?"

"Yeah. It's private property and," she smiled slightly, "as property owner, I can give myself permission."

"How about a headstone?" Peter asked.

"I think the purpose of a gravestone is to mark a place where offspring can come to, uh, to remember the dead, to pay respects. I'm 'it' for progeny, so, what's the point? The pines are his memorials, the land his monument. I will think of him every time I walk the property." To her surprise, the last words caught in her throat and her eyes filled with tears.

Peter awkwardly patted her on the shoulder, but she regained control quickly and turned to the funeral director to make the final arrangements to pick up the ashes from the crematorium.

THE NEXT DAY, Peter and Renee retrieved Doug's ashes. On the drive back from the funeral home, Peter cleared his throat, fidgeted, and opened his mouth several times but closed it without saying anything. Finally, Renee said, "Spit it out, Peter. What's bothering you?"

"I just wondered who else would be there when you spread the ashes. And if we should arrange some kind of, some small, um, ceremony."

"My God, no," Renee said. "There's no one I'd want around. Except...maybe Bert. I'll ask him if he wants to come with me."

After Bert confirmed in a phone call that he definitely wanted to join them, they met in the grove, where the huge pine that had fallen on Doug still lay on the ground. Renee saw where a large branch had been sawed away, but she carefully avoided looking too closely. If there was blood, she did not want to see it.

The box containing the ashes was heavier than Renee

had expected. She opened it and handed Bert a large spoon, arming herself with a similar one. When she offered a third spoon to Peter, he shook his head. "Renee, Bert, I never met him. I think this is something the two of you should do."

There was no breeze, and Doug's ashes fell to the earth. When the box was empty, Bert asked her if she was going to say anything. "No, would you like to?" she asked. She had no idea if Bert was religious or not and what to expect when he nodded.

Bert looked up at the trees in the grove. "Well, Doug," he said. "Guess I'll be joinin' you in not too long. Save me a hot toddy, 'kay?" Then he looked a bit alarmed as a thought appeared to strike him. "If they're allowed where you are, a-course," he amended.

Renee couldn't help smiling at the sentiment—and the love in the old man's voice.

"It was a good send-off," Peter said as he and Renee walked back to the house. "And it was kind of Bert to agree to 'look in on' the house. Until we, uh, until you get up here next."

"Hope it'll be 'we,'" she said. "The blackberries are ripe in late August. Let's come up then."

RENEE RETURNED home with a sense of relief that her life in Sunrise Acres could resume its normal pace. Two days after she got back, she was looking forward to a date she and Peter had arranged before the trip to California. The plan was to have drinks at his place and then dinner at the nearby El Conquistador Hotel. But when Renee arrived at Peter's that evening, he did not look like he was in the mood for fun. When she tried to give him a greeting kiss, he turned his head and said, "Let's go outside." He led her out to his patio, where two glasses of red wine, a bowl of nuts, and another of chips stood on the glass-top table. But before they sat down for their first sip, he said, "Renee, we really need to talk. When I asked you on our drive up to your dad's place why you retired early, you told me a bunch of stuff about negative media attention. I let it go, but now I need to know the truth. Why did you leave Dobbins Howerter?"

The question was so unexpected that she started, almost spilling her wine. "Peter, what...? Come on. I don't want to talk about it. It's water under the bridge or spilled milk or something. Let's just have fun tonight. I've been looking forward to this."

He sat down but almost immediately rose again and started pacing. "Look, Renee. We've been together, what, over a year now and I'm realizing we've avoided talking about something really important to me—how you think about race. I'm beginning to see that we may have a real problem."

"What does that mean?"

"It means I googled you." He continued with barely contained sarcasm. "And I read with great interest about your last case, which, as you know, also fascinated the media. Congratulations, by the way, on winning—or at least not losing—that case. Pretty surprising you managed to get a hung jury, considering the kid who got shot by *your client* was *unarmed*. He rings the doorbell, woman answers and shoots him. Hard to argue it was self-defense. So," he said, his voice rising as he held up both hands when Renee, her face reddening, began to interrupt, "please tell me that everything was on the up-and-up. That this *fifteen-year-old Black kid deserved to die at the hands of some rich white bitch!*"

Renee was appalled. This burst of anger, as well as the

crude language, was so unexpected, so unlike him. "Peter, wait, I can—"

"Maybe that case explains why you took up with me."

"What? What explains…. What are you talking about?"

"Maybe you were feeling guilty about that case when you bailed out of San Francisco. So, just to show you weren't racist, you find yourself a Black boyfriend."

"Whoa, whoa, that case has nothing to do with us and I resent—" Renee looked at Peter's furious face and stopped. "Peter, please…where on earth is this coming from? You've always said you don't play the race card…. But isn't that what you're doing?"

The accusation clearly made Peter even angrier. He stood up and strode away to stand with his back to her for several minutes, staring out at the graveled backyard. When he turned back to face her, he was controlling his temper with obvious effort.

"I think I'll ignore that. It's unfair and, worse, ignorant. You have no idea where 'this is coming from.'" His tone was biting. "None!" he added angrily. "A fifteen-year-old kid, drumming up money for his soccer team. He rings a doorbell and gets shot. The soccer coach dropped off three other kids to canvass that neighborhood. But they were white. Idiot coach! He thought a school uniform would protect the kid."

Renee sat in frozen silence while Peter became increasingly agitated. The words spewed out of him in an uncontrolled flow of rage and frustration. She had never seen him like this.

"That kid could have been my nephew Zeke. A couple of months ago, Zeke got pulled over by some s.o.b. for a broken taillight. He was coming back from camping and the cop looked in the backseat, saw food, including a jar of white stuff that he said looked like drugs to him. Made Zeke take it out and prove it was just sugar. But then the guy spotted a Ziploc bag of weed on the floor and pulled Zeke out of the car, damn near choked him to death. I guess he was lucky he wasn't shot. This was two weeks before Oregon passed the law making recreational weed legal. Two weeks! Zeke got off with just community service and watching a helluvalot of videos about the effects of mari-juana. That's okay; it was good for him to get educated. But it was profiling. Zeke has a beard and dreadlocks. They obviously expected to find drugs. That's why the guy who pulled Zeke over assumed the sugar was cocaine. He never would have even seen the weed if he hadn't been looking for it. And they were absolutely brutal physically—and that I can't forgive."

"Peter, that's terrible. Awful. I'm so sorry that happened to your—"

Peter laughed humorlessly. "Oh, that was just one of many times skin color has almost gotten someone in my family killed. How about my own arrest last month on that bogus looting charge? Maybe I should tell you a few more stories about how the law works for African Americans!"

"But Peter, what happened to Zeke, that wasn't the situa-tion in San Francisco. The homeowner thought the kid was reaching for a weapon. He was a big kid—looked older than he was. She said she felt threatened."

Peter stood over her, his body shaking with anger, his voice rising. "She said she felt threatened? Who told her to say that? That's such bullshit! Where would that kid have a weapon? He was wearing a soccer uniform, for Christ's sake! Soccer uniforms don't have pockets!"

Renee shrank back in her chair from what felt like a physical assault, but her voice was steady and controlled.

"No, but he had a kind of clipboard in his hands. She said she thought he was holding something under it."

"Oh my God. That's how you got her off, isn't it? She *'thought.'* She *'felt threatened.'* Did you tell her to say that? Did you coach her? Did you maybe ask her something like, 'Maybe you thought you saw him reach under his clipboard, right? That's what happened, right?' Tell me the truth, Renee, goddammit! Is that the story that convinced three righteous citizens to hang that jury and get her off?" Suddenly, his shoulders slumped and he said quietly, as if to himself, "Jesus, why do I bother? It's not worth it."

Renee stood up and put down the wineglass she had been strangling in a fierce grip. "I'd better go," she said. "Peter, I've had enough of these personal attacks. Do you really want to ruin our relationship over this?" His accusation had just enough truth to it that she couldn't deny it outright. *Maybe that woman was convincing enough on the stand to persuade those three jurors. We didn't* tell *her to lie, not really.* "I can't help what happened to Zeke—or to you or anyone else in your family. And you're right; I can't really understand how you feel. But you and I've had a lot of fun together. More than just fun. I thought...." She left the thought unfinished. "You said you cared for me. Let me know if and when you can stop lumping me in with all the racists in your life." She opened the screen door and walked through the living room and out the front door.

Peter remained standing.

When Renee got into her car, she was so shaken that she pressed the radio button instead of starting the car. She sat a moment, wondering how the temperature between them had plunged to frigid so fast. It was as if Peter had suddenly ripped off a layer, revealing a raw, bleeding surface she had never seen before. She had taken the reference he once made to "being a raisin in the oatmeal of Sunrise Acres" as wry humor. *But there are so few Blacks here.* For the first time, she realized that being an interracial couple was likely more difficult for him than for her. What did he mean by "why do I bother"? To explain his feelings to her? Was he giving up on their relationship?

PART II

8
———

MIKE LANDRY

Spring 2018 (a year earlier)

Like most newcomers to Sunrise Acres, Mike and Andrea Landry had bought the perfect house only to spend half again the purchase price on shaping their new nest to their personal taste. Inside, walls came down to "let the house breathe," as Andrea put it. The interior décor took on the hues and textures of Arizona: rusts and beiges in the granite countertops, travertine on the floors, and colorful Mexican tiles strategically placed in kitchens and bathrooms. Outside, they cultivated only hardy heat-loving plants and edibles.

After moving in, the Landrys' first year had been absorbed by endless (in Mike's opinion) shopping trips, agonizing over choices among (for him) barely distinguishable floor tiles, paint samples, even cabinet knobs.

Just as the new house began to feel comfortable, Andrea fell ill. Then came months of agonizing doctors' visits, surgeries—seesaw days of hope and despair. Mike and Andrea had thought they had years to join clubs and make friends.

But within nine months Mike was a widower, thousands of miles from his sons on the East Coast and his closest friend, his older sister Frannie in Maine.

A month after Andrea's death, Mike's loneliness was overwhelming. He called the one person who might be able to bring him out of this funk. He pictured his sister in her kitchen as they spoke. He and Frannie shared many Landry family traits: the same red-blond slightly curly hair (now graying), the same straight nose, the light eyes that were blue or green depending on the color of their clothing, the wide mouth and full lips that would have been too feminine on him if he hadn't had a strong jaw. They usually Face-Timed, even though Frannie was prone to multitasking while they talked. She would lay her phone down face up as she emptied the dishwasher or pared potatoes for dinner, with the result that he was often left viewing the ceiling as they chatted. The sprawling water stain there was like a Rorschach ink blot, either a scowling face or a butterfly, depending on his mood. It was dinnertime in Maine, the phone was aimed at the ceiling, and today the stain was definitely not a butterfly.

"Frannie, I've either got to sell this place or get a change of scenery. Every morning when I open the *Times*, I have to catch myself as I turn to tell Andrea about some particularly interesting—or infuriating—article. I'm not only talking to myself, I'm having whole conversations! Very boring ones! Myself and I have the same views on everything from politics to books to food."

He could hear a smile in Frannie's voice. "I think I might worry more if the two of you were disagreeing. But it sounds as if you really need to get away for a while. You could come spend some time here, of course, the way you did last year.

But is there any trip that you think would be fun? Bring a little comfort or even...ah, healing? What's a retired English professor's dream trip?"

Over the next few days, Mike spent some time pondering that question and researching possibilities. He came up with a two-week hiking trip along the west coast of Ireland. Then, only a day or so after returning from that highly satisfactory adventure, he embarked on another, courtesy of a former graduate student. Knowing he was retired, she emailed to invite him to fill in on an emergency basis for a professor at the University of Montana who needed to go on a wholly unexpected maternity leave. "At age forty-three," the professor reportedly said, "you'd think I would have known better than to celebrate an amicable divorce in the company of my ex and a bottle of champagne." Mike had chuckled—and accepted the temporary post.

Mike asked around among acquaintances and several suggested that he contact Molly Levin to help him find a renter while he was in Montana that fall. She was a part-time real estate agent who worked almost exclusively in Sunrise Acres. Ms. Levin turned out to be an enthusiastic woman who was probably described as "perky" when she was younger. Mike met with her only long enough to turn over house keys.

Then he left for Missoula, feeling comfortable that the house was in good hands. He would come back in late December or early January and stay in Arizona at least through the next summer. He could make a final decision about possibly moving back East in the fall.

Despite the inevitable inconveniences of living in graduate student housing (crying babies, miasmas of pot and curry), Mike enjoyed his semester in Missoula. However, when he had taught his last class and had just the final papers to grade, Mike's thoughts turned to home. His renters had moved out in mid-December.

It was time to return to Arizona and face the future alone.

9

—————

MIKE

January 2019

Mike had anticipated that returning to his empty Sunrise Acres house would be difficult, but he had underestimated the pain that Andrea's absence still caused. It had been different in Missoula, where there was no shared experience. Mike had enjoyed the faculty parties, the young aspiring poets and teachers seeking his advice. But now, particularly in the quiet evenings after eight, when Sunrise Acres basically shut down, he tired of watching reruns of *Seinfeld*. He could anticipate the next lines in many of the episodes. ("He took it out?" "He. Took. It. Out!") And he was conscious that the level of Irish whiskey in his bottle was as low many mornings as if he'd been hosting a poker game the night before.

When he looked in the mirror for his morning shave, really looked, the man staring back at him was increasingly unrecognizable. *My neck is turning into a turtle's. Doesn't mean I need to creep into a shell, though.* It was time for a plan, a shift in his mental outlook. Getting older was inevitable, but he intended to follow Dylan Thomas's advice and "not go gentle into that good night." *Not that I'm at "old age" yet,* he reassured himself. *Late sixties is still—sort of—middle age. After all, there are a lot of ninety-year-olds here.*

Later in the year, when everything got more complicated and exciting than Mike could ever have anticipated, he was to think back on this period in his life as an unexciting stretch of days uninterrupted by passion or mystery. Sunrise Acres' small corner of the world was sheltered from violence or even disturbance. Residents were preoccupied with staying healthy, sharing their knowledge where it could be useful, and having fun. Occasional disagreements about a line call in tennis or pickleball were about the only pulse-raising incidents.

During his months of intense grieving, a quiet, repetitive routine was what he needed. But now that time was blunting the sharp edges of his grief, Mike began to think about his life post-Andrea. Maybe he could adopt a pet. In all seasons, people were out walking their dogs, which ranged from dustmop-sized ankle-biters to haughty French poodles. And dogs stimulated the kind of companionable conversations between fellow dog-walkers that babies or small children did in younger communities. Of course, the topics of conversation tended toward diets, doctors, and bond funds rather than diapers and Bitcoin investments. *Probably good exercise, too,* he thought—*all that bending over to pick up doggy deposits.* But having a pet didn't seem likely to deliver the propulsive kick to his rear he needed to recharge his batteries, nor did the prospect of yet another trip. And he was definitely not seeking serious female companionship.

However, he was disconcerted to discover that once his return from Montana became common knowledge, he'd been a widower long enough to be viewed as an eligible bachelor. His determination to avoid romantic entanglements was repeatedly challenged by overtures from three women he christened (but only to Frannie, his confidante) the "casserole ladies."

"The problem is their good intentions are leading to Hell for me," he explained to Frannie. A month or so after he returned, the food-bearers started arriving at his door, with mostly what he thought of as 1950s fare. "The tuna casseroles aren't bad, but I truly despise the things made with Campbell's cream of mushroom soup. And people really do sprinkle potato chips on these concoctions. Yesterday, I got what the bearer called a 'Miracle Whip cake' made with...actual Miracle Whip, you know, like bad mayonnaise. She said her late husband absolutely loved it. I shouldn't admit thinking it, but I did wonder if it was part of his last meal."

Unlike the food Mike had gratefully received during Andrea's illness, the casserole ladies' gifts seemed wrapped in less purely altruistic motives. "They make coy suggestions about 'sharing a meal,' or offer wistful memories of how this had been their late husband's favorite dinner," he told Frannie. "I know they think of me as a hapless male, but you know how I love to cook. And the food they bring is so bland. I like to use spices—not just salt and pepper. If I had a steady diet of what they bring, I'd never use up my smoked paprika or garam masala."

"But they mean well."

"Of course they do. That's what makes it so difficult. And one of the three, Glenda, is as persistent as a housefly and just as eager as one to get into the house."

"Is Glenda the one who comes up with the malapropisms?"

"Oh man," he sighed. "Sometimes I have such a hard

time keeping a straight face. Yesterday she was telling me about a movie—the main character's child dies. 'It was just heart-rendering,' she told me."

"I hope you don't correct her."

"No, I'm a perfect gentleman. I don't even wince. Much."

"Maybe," Frannie said, "that's the solution. Correct her a couple of times and that should do it. I know I hate it when you do it to me."

"That's not helpful, Sis. I don't have it in me to be rude."

She laughed. "My dear boy," she said, sounding twenty years older instead of just three, "how can I help?"

"Give me a strategy. I don't want to lead anyone on, and I don't want to hurt anyone's feelings, but I'm really not in the market for a quote-unquote 'relationship' yet—maybe ever."

"Oh, you will be," she said confidently. "And I know that Andrea wanted you to find someone."

The following morning Glenda telephoned as Mike was finishing breakfast, inviting him to a "songfest with karaoke." "I thought maybe you'd like it. I'll bring over dinner to share and then we could go. Take your mind off of...cheer you up."

"Thanks for the thought, Glenda, but I've never been able to carry a tune. I found out very early in life that the beautiful tones I hear in my head bear not the slightest resemblance to what comes out of my mouth. My first-grade teacher told me to just mime the words after I ruined a Christmas pageant."

That night he reported to Frannie, recounting his efforts to discourage Glenda without hurting her feelings.

"Maybe you ought to give her a chance," she said. "She sounds nice."

"She is," he said. "Very nice. But honestly, it would be horribly unfair to encourage her. I'm an old curmudgeon—

and an English professor-slash-pedant—and I'm just not interested."

"I love you, little brother," she said. "But it's hard to think of you as an *homme fatale*."

"Hey, there's a scarcity principle at work here," he said. "The women, particularly the widows, far outnumber the men, and a lot of those guys are elderly."

Frannie burst into laughter. "Elderly as opposed to what? You mean like you? Youthful? Well," she conceded, "you do still have a lot of hair."

It irritated him a bit that Frannie saw his predicament as humorous. "Come on, Sis. Give me a strategy."

"Maybe," she suggested, "instead of trying to be the anti-social hermit, you should try the opposite tack: make an effort to go out and be seen with a lot of other women."

"That solution might be worse than the problem."

"But more fun."

"Huh," he said. "That could be like the Danes in the Virgin Islands introducing mongooses to control the rats. You remember what happened there."

"I must have missed that one in my Virgin Islands classes, but I assume the mongooses took over. The analogy seems awfully unfair to these nice women."

"Yeah, I didn't mean to be snarky. But the point is: What if I find myself with a dozen Glendas?"

"Poor baby, you should be so burdened," she said. "Give it a try. Pick some nice women who are friendly but don't seem to need a man."

"Lesbians? Nuns?" he asked dubiously.

"Sheesh! Not necessarily. Just women who are not needy, are self-confident—ones who haven't come on to you."

"Well, I did see in our community rag that there's a singles club," he said dubiously.

"So, go to that, pick a few nice self-sufficient women, and maybe go on walks around the neighborhood with a couple of them. Show that you want to play the field."

"This is all too Machiavellian for me," he said. "I didn't play games like that even when I was single and dating. I'm a straightforward kind of person. Maybe I should just be honest with Glenda."

"'It's not you, it's me' kind of talk?" Frannie said skeptically.

"Argh," he said. "I'm too old for this idiocy."

"Apparently not," she said. "Good night, lover boy."

10

MIKE

February 2019

A few weeks after his conversation with Frannie about the unwanted casseroles he was receiving, Mike thumbed through this month's *Sunrise Notes* for the third time, hoping that one of the clubs or volunteer opportunities would seem more appealing than the Singles Club. *Help out in the library? Maybe try woodworking? Line dancing? Is that like a can-can?* A vivid image of himself high-kicking with the Radio City Rockettes suddenly arose, unbidden, bringing a smile. *Do they even still exist?*

"Investment Club" caught his eye. *Huh. Can an English professor learn to speak Wall Street?* Like those of most college professors, Mike and Andrea's retirement accounts were invested with the Teachers Insurance and Annuity Association. Their TIAA portfolio advisor had suggested they consider investing some of their money more aggressively. It made sense, but they'd never gotten around to it. Perhaps the Investment Club would help identify some opportunities.

When Mike got to his first meeting, he recognized no

one among the circle of men and one woman sitting on folding chairs in the small room. The sliding doors looked out on a patio surrounded by a border of agaves, their narrow spikes like clusters of upright sword blades.

"Ah, a new face. Welcome to the Investment Club. I'm Jake Parcell. And you are?"

"Mike Landry. I'm pretty new here and just checking out some of the clubs. I'm mostly here to listen."

"No problem. Chime in any time. And I see Renee has joined us. It's been a while, Renee. We always appreciate a lady's perspective on the market. Welcome back."

Mike glanced over at the tall, youngish woman, who was grimacing—perhaps at the "lady's perspective" reference.

"Mike," Jake continued, "we're pretty laid back, no professionals in the group. We discourage disclosure of personal financial information, but other than that, we mostly exchange investment news and tips."

"Speaking of which...." A very short, trim man with an impressive if incongruous array of tattoos on both arms stood up.

"Ah," said Jake, "our resident startup guru. What gem have you unearthed for us today, Hal?"

"It's called Cytodynamics. Like with any startup, you have to be willing to tolerate some risk, but that's where you can make the big money. This company is small, only a dozen or so employees, but they have a very promising anti-cancer drug in the pipeline. They're just about finished with animal trials, and the marketing guy I spoke to was, not surprisingly, really enthusiastic. They're still accepting Round One investments, but he said they'd be moving to Round Two when they get some more results. I'd be happy to talk to any of you who might be interested after the meeting. I know that most of you are into more conservative stuff," Hal concluded, with a vaguely dismissive glance around the room.

When the meeting ended, Mike joined another man who was standing next to Hal.

Mike extended his hand. "Mike Landry." The other man looked as if he had been assembled from well-worn river rocks. Even his features lacked sharp definition. His bulbous nose tilted to one side as if intending to exit his face. *Former football player,* Mike thought.

"Steve Antonelli. Nice to meet you." He shoved back a shock of white hair falling over his forehead in what looked like a habitual gesture before shaking hands. Standing with feet planted, broad shoulders back and chest thrust out confrontationally, Steve was a physical contrast to Mike. While equally tall, Mike was of slighter build. He had a habit of bending his head down in conversation whenever he spoke with shorter people, and he did so now as he exchanged introductions with Hal, the "startup guru." Catching a glimpse in the reflective window of the pair of them together, Mike thought he looked like a stork addressing a duck. He straightened up self-consciously as Hal introduced himself.

"Hal Avery. Hi, Mike. Steve and I know each other. So, what do you want to know?"

Hal expanded on his remarks from the meeting and Steve peppered him with a number of questions. Mike was content to listen. The more he heard, the more he found himself focusing on the "risk" end of the risk-reward continuum. But it was clear that Steve was very interested.

"What's the minimum investment?" Steve asked Hal.

"Craig Swan, the marketing VP I talked to, says they would accept investments of twenty thousand and up, with a guaranteed option to invest in any future rounds, including any IPO, which of course would be months or, maybe, years away."

"Twenty grand, huh? Can you text me the contact info for this Craig Swan? Sounds like quite an opportunity. I'm ready to take the plunge," Steve said.

Mike thanked Hal and shook hands again with both men. *Too risky for me*, Mike thought as he left. *If the stock market tanks, you can lose a good chunk of your investment, but with a startup, you could lose every cent. And if twenty grand is just the ante for the First Round, what would it be for Round Two? And Three? I sure hope Steve knows what he's getting into.*

March 2019

It took a few weeks for Mike to succumb to Frannie's pressure and check out the Singles Club page on the Sunrise Acres website. Looked innocent enough, and they got group tickets for concerts and plays and made some trips. In fact, there was one coming up that looked pretty interesting: up to Sedona, with a stop in Phoenix. Mike mailed his membership dues and signed up for the trip.

When he arrived at the Activity Center, a large bus was idling in the parking lot. It appeared almost everyone had already boarded. Mike climbed in, glanced around, and noted that there were a number of couples, two or three single men, and the rest single women. Most of his fellow passengers ignored his arrival, but a couple of the women sitting alone looked up and smiled. Thinking of Glenda, he walked by somewhat nervously. *This is like boarding the high school bus the first time.* He was relieved to recognize the real estate agent who had rented his house for him, Molly Levin, sitting by herself, and asked if he could sit next to her.

Molly was an attractive woman in her mid-sixties, he guessed. She was small and slim, with short dark brown hair. His clichéd image of a real estate agent was that of a blonde wearing a lot of makeup, flashy jewelry, and driving a Cadillac, but everything about Molly was understated—light makeup and small silver hoop earrings. She flashed a warm, welcoming smile that erased a decade from her age, and patted the seat next to her. They chatted a bit about his house, the renters, and the current real estate market, but as soon as the bus started up, Mike pulled a book from the backpack at his feet. Maybe she would think it rude, but he had used this ploy on airplanes to avoid conversations that could veer into the personal, and he definitely was not ready to get into that. To his relief, Molly fished around at her feet in an open woven red-and-black straw basket with handles, retrieved her own book, and started reading.

Their first stop was the Musical Instrument Museum in Phoenix. Mike hadn't done any homework prior to the trip and had envisioned a converted house with a few old violins and harpsichords. Instead, he regretted that the group could spend only two hours in the enormous modern museum with over 15,000 instruments from nearly two hundred countries. He spent ten minutes by the angklungs of Indonesia, amazed that shaken bamboo reeds could sound so much like a chorus of wind instruments.

When they got back on the bus, everyone went to their same seats, as if assigned. "Would you prefer the window this time?" Molly asked. "When we get near Sedona, the views are pretty remarkable."

"Thanks, but I can see fine from here. And this way, I can also help the driver—keep an eye on the road ahead."

She smiled politely at his attempt at humor. "And what

will you do if you see an obstacle in the road or a deer crossing or something?"

"Scream helplessly, I suppose. And brace for the crash."

"Well, be sure to let me know before the impact," she said, turning back to her book. They read in sociable silence until they began to see the famous red cliffs and rock formations of Sedona.

"No wonder the ancients thought this area is holy," Mike said. "That group of rocks over there looks like a group of giant pilgrims carrying bundles, frozen in place."

"Aha," Molly said. "Are you also a cloud whisperer, or do you only interpret rock formations?" Mike was amused at her easy familiarity.

"Just rocks. But I'm not alone. The guidebook says visitors will see a teapot, a cathedral, and a ship."

After checking into their hotel, the group members were given their choice of afternoon activities: a "Pink Jeep" ride to various off-road sites, shopping in the main tourist district, or a hike around Cathedral Rock, one of the most famous of the red rock formations. Mike and Molly both chose the hike. It was a self-guided trail, and the group was instructed to be gone no more than two hours. They had walked about a half mile on a winding dirt trail through the scrub, twisted junipers, cacti, and a couple of dry creek beds, when there was a startled cry toward the end of the line. A heavyset woman, her face red with exertion or sunburn, had fallen with one leg twisted under her and her woven straw hat askew. "Maude!" Molly ran back along the path and squatted, helping her to sit up. Maude's white shirt was covered with the red earth, but there was no blood either on the shirt or on the leg that she painfully straightened.

"Would you like me to help you stand up?" Mike asked.

"No hurry, Maude," Molly said. "Just when and if you are ready."

"I don't know if my leg will take my weight," Maude said fearfully.

"Molly, if you get on her left side to steady her, I can lift her," Mike said. Molly looked at him a bit dubiously but nodded. It was harder than he had expected; she was almost a dead weight and did little to help.

Once on her feet, she tried gingerly to put weight on her leg. "I think I can walk, but I need to get back," she said.

Molly slung an arm around her waist. "I'll go back with you. We can call and get someone to pick us up at the trailhead."

"I'll go with you," Mike offered.

"No, I will," another woman said. "Better if you go on with the rest of the group. They might need help if anything else happens."

Mike stood in indecision.

"Yes, please come with us," another woman begged. Mike caught Molly's eye and she nodded.

Without further incident, the group finished the hike and joined the others at dinner in the hotel restaurant. To Mike's slight disappointment, Molly sat with Maude at one of the small tables reserved for their group; Mike ended up at the largest table, hearing about vortexes and the healing crystals purchased by one of the men, who introduced himself as Phil. "Sedona has all these unique vortexes," Phil explained. "The natives aren't the only ones to consider it a very holy place. Along some of the hiking trails, where the vortexes are especially strong, people have built hundreds of small cairn towers, piling up to nine or ten rocks. They're like miniature stone forests. And Sedona is the very best place to buy healing crystals."

The club leader stood to announce a very early start the next morning and to urge everyone to retire early. They would visit Ro Ho En, the Japanese Friendship Garden in Phoenix, before lunch and then head home. Mike used the interruption to excuse himself.

At the Garden, Mike found himself watching Molly as she hovered solicitously over Maude, linking an arm through hers as they walked slowly around the koi pond. When they got back on the bus, Mike hurried to help Maude up the bus steps and asked how she was feeling. "Better," she said, "but I'm sure developing some gorgeous bruises on my hip." She and Molly settled into the front seat.

Mike thought of what he would tell Frannie. *All right, I've found one apparently self-sufficient woman who definitely did not come on to me.* The man who now shared his seat ignored the hint when he took out his book. It was the crystal collector, Phil. Mike's polite expression of interest when Phil showed him one of his purchases had raised Mike in his eyes to a fellow enthusiast. He regaled Mike with descriptions of the different types of crystals and their varied beneficial effects. Mike had a devilish desire to ask if there was one that cured volubility. The thought made him smile, which of course merely spurred Phil on.

He glanced up the aisle at Molly. Her head was tilted toward Maude's, intently listening. *Huh,* he thought. *I didn't rate that kind of attention.* He ignored the small imp sitting on his shoulder who reminded him that he had been the first to take out a book.

After lunch, everyone headed for the same bus seats, but to Mike's relief the group leader suggested that people "might wish to swap seats" so that everyone had a chance to "sit in a different part of the bus." Molly relinquished her front seat to one of the other men, and when she headed back in the bus, he scooted over and invited her to sit by him. "It's over the wheel," he warned her, "but not too bumpy."

"It doesn't bother me," she assured him. They exchanged views about the Garden, its serenity, the skills of the Japanese in balancing plants, rocks, and water, but then she took out her book again, forcing him to do the same. "Hope you don't mind," she said. "I'm a bit talked out—highly unusual for me!"

"Not at all," he lied.

Then, just before they got off the bus, he made a mistake that kept him up most of that night, replaying what he should have said—and not said. He started out all right: "Is Maude going to be okay?"

"Uh-huh, physically," she said. "But it's a hard time of life for her. She was widowed just a few months ago and now her children are begging her to move near them."

"I guess being friendly with people like that is good for business, right? A house on the market?" He thought he was being humorous, but the look she gave him quickly dispelled that fantasy.

"You make me sound like some kind of vulture," she said. "Preying on the vulnerable." She picked up her basket and moved to the very back of the bus where there were several rows unoccupied.

He sat, feeling miserable, wondering how to apologize. Everything he thought of saying to her seemed totally inadequate. "I didn't mean..." would inevitably lead to her asking what he *did* mean. Telling her that he thought he was being funny left him open to the totally accurate charge that he had a very lame sense of humor. Every gambit he thought of she was able to brutally counter in his imagination. *What an oaf! Jerk!* When they pulled into the Activity Center, he fairly ran off the bus and stood in wait for her.

"Molly," he said, "I am so sorry; that came out all wrong and I am an ass."

"Apology accepted," she said coolly, leaving Mike with the distinct impression that it actually wasn't. And that she concurred with his self-assessment.

"SO MY VENTURE into the Singles Club was a disaster," Mike told Frannie, concluding his tale of the Sedona trip.

"Doesn't sound like it. Seems like you met at least one interesting woman."

"And totally alienated her. Guess my attempts at humor don't always land the way I intend."

Frannie sighed. "Nope, often with a thud. But. Do you want to get to know this woman, Molly Levin, better?"

"I'm not sure. I told you, I'm not really looking for any kind of serious relationship. But I do enjoy the company of women, and of the women I've met here, I do find her the most...interesting."

"So, why don't you ask her over for dinner? Make one of your ethnic specials, like chicken tikka masala, or that Hungarian paprikash. Makes my mouth water just to think about them. Go easy on the hot spices."

"No way! That would make me a casserole guy, luring women with food. But...I'll see if she comes to the Singles Club movie night."

But to Mike's disappointment, Molly did not come to the showing of *The Shining*—a film he had seen when it first came out. He wasn't that eager to see Jack Nicholson's rictus again but found it awkward to get up and leave.

When he saw her at pickleball a few days later, it was impossible to get her alone for another apology. There were at least fifteen people milling around, waiting for their turn at the next free court. Mike noted the position of Molly's paddle, with the obligatory name label, and surreptitiously moved his own back so that he would be in the foursome when she next played.

As they walked onto the court, he tried again to apologize. "Molly, I'm so sorry. You have not forgiven me yet."

To his relief, he received a small smile in response. "In a confrontation, they say people have an impulse toward fight or flight. For me it's always flight. I'm not a fighter. That's why I walked away."

"Does that mean we aren't likely to win if we're partners?" he asked, hoping that he wasn't making another mistake in teasing her.

"Oh no," she said. "When it comes to pickleball, I never retreat!"

Mike discovered that she had not exaggerated. Molly was an aggressive and obviously experienced player. When she partnered with her friend Renee, they were almost impossible to beat, no matter who was the opposition. Mike and Molly played as partners a number of times over the next couple of weeks, mostly paired by luck. Mike was inordinately pleased when once he saw Molly move her paddle back in the waiting line in order to partner with him. But she never stayed for more than three or four games, so they only talked while waiting for a court to open up. And there were always other players standing around, so it was far from private.

Still, he was a bit surprised at how much he looked forward to those brief encounters.

"EVERYONE STANDS AROUND and socializes while we're waiting for the next pickleball court to open up," Mike told Frannie one evening. "So I'm spending a fair amount of time chatting with Molly, but it's always very superficial. People talk about the weather, grandchildren, pets—nothing of substance. So," he concluded a bit wistfully, "I don't know much about Molly at all."

"Dear Abby," Frannie pretended to read a letter. "My sixty-seven-year-old brother is afraid to ask out a woman he's attracted to. What would you suggest I tell him? Perplexed in Maine.

"Dear Perplexed," Frannie continued. "Tell him he's old enough to figure it out himself. Or you could remind him that life is short and give him a kick in the tush."

Mike laughed. "Okay, okay. Ouch. The kick just landed. It's just...well, I'm out of practice. Haven't asked a woman out since...God, the days of Watergate! And I'm honestly nervous—not only about sticking my neck out, but getting it chopped off if she turns me down."

"She won't," Frannie predicted. And then she added with a wicked chuckle. "But good luck!"

MOLLY LEVIN

Later in March

One of Molly's favorite volunteer jobs was escorting orientation tours of Sunrise Acres. When she arrived to lead her last tour of March, three people were waiting to climb into the stretch golf cart the volunteer "ambassadors" used for the tours. Her passengers were a couple in their mid-seventies and a single woman, considerably younger. The wife was tall and lanky, with hair dyed a rather incongruously youthful red blond, quite a bit of makeup (*she'll give that up here eventually*, Molly thought), and a broad-brimmed sun hat with a colorful blue and red scarf tied around the crown and draping gracefully down her back. Her husband (*or at least companion*, Molly mentally corrected herself—they wouldn't be the first to cohabit here without being married) Molly pegged as ex-military. Well over six feet tall, he stood very erect, shoulders back, his gray hair only a bit longer than a crew cut. He wore jeans and a dark blue T-shirt emblazoned in red "Wilderness Travel"—a souvenir from some exotic excursion, no doubt.

"I'm Molly Levin; I'll be your guide on the tour of our wonderful community. I'll explain things as we go along, but feel free to ask questions." As she began to ask for introductions, she was interrupted.

"I'm Mary," the older woman said, "and this," with a brief wave in his direction, "is Roger." She then launched immediately into a detailed explanation of the reasons they were "only just now" getting to the orientation, although they had moved in the previous week. "I couldn't begin to tell you all the problems we've had," she said. Then she proceeded to explain said problems at length, while the others stood patiently around the golf cart. Molly found herself envisioning a jumble of black letters and words cascading from Mary's mouth and wondered how to cut off the stream long enough for the other woman to introduce herself and for Molly to get them all into the cart.

The single woman was short, a bit on the chubby side. Her arms in a sleeveless peach blouse and legs in khaki shorts were so white that Molly considered offering her some of the sun block she always carried in her purse but decided to wait until later in the tour when the need would be obvious. It was an unseasonably warm day for March, and newcomers tended to underestimate the damage the sun could inflict on unprotected skin. The woman's round face was balanced on her stocky shoulders like an under-sized beach ball beneath a tall beige cowboy hat that failed to fully contain a mop of very curly dark hair. Her lips curved in an amused smile at Molly's obvious discomfort with Mary's monologue. In desperation, as Mary had now moved on to describing the scourge of pack rat nests under the hot tub, Molly finally simply thrust her hand out to Roger.

"Roger, is it? Welcome," she said cheerfully. His wife sputtered to a halt, shook her head, and pursed her lips with annoyance.

Molly turned to the other woman, who shook her hand and introduced herself: "Elizabeth Rausch, but everyone calls me Betsy."

"What brings you to Sunrise?" Molly asked.

"Ah, I'm just renting for a few months. Checking things out for maybe something more permanent."

"Unusual for someone to start renting in late March," Molly observed. "The weather's great right now and into early May, but June can get pretty, um, challenging."

"Yeah, I've heard that. But I can probably stand it. I may even stay through July; the owners say I can extend if I want."

I'll bet, Molly thought. *They'd be lucky to get a renter to stay through July.* "Well, it does get pretty hot in the summer, but as you'll find out in this orientation, there are tons of activities all year round." She eyed Betsy with interest. *Maybe a potential client for a house sale if she can stand the summer heat and I can counter Mary's complaining.*

The tour took over an hour and a half. Molly drove through a couple of neighborhoods but spent most of the time showing off the community amenities: the hobby center with rooms devoted to wood carving, jewelry making, stained glass, pottery, and model trains. "Many of the snowbirds have flown away by now," she said. "So there are fewer people here, but they'll be back in the fall when it cools down." She took them to the three swimming pools and the golf course. They passed the bell tower, from which the quarter hour was just sounding. "Highest structure in Sunrise Acres. It's our community logo. And right next door is the heart of the community, the Activity Center. Any of you like dancing? Western, ballroom, line?"

Molly noticed a moue of distaste from Mary, but which one of the dance options kindled the response was unclear. "Or if you like to play cards, like bridge or euchre, or there's mahjong.... And this auditorium is where we have educational lectures." Her passengers were beginning to wilt in the noon heat. Summer was previewing itself. Mary had taken her hat off and was fanning herself vigorously. Betsy emptied the last few ounces in her water bottle. "The gym is air-conditioned," Molly said, pulling up in front of the building. "Would you like to go inside?" No one moved. Interpreting their lassitude as lack of interest, Molly added, "And you can see the tennis and pickleball courts from here. I'll leave those for you to explore on your own." She took them back to their starting point in front of the Administration Building.

"I'm exhausted just thinking of all I could and should do here," Betsy said. "I'd like to get in shape, lose a few pounds, and it looks as if I'll have no excuses not to."

"Well, if the gym doesn't appeal, you might consider the hiking club or the pickleball club. Both are very popular," Molly said. "And you may have noticed all the bicycles. A lot of us bike and use golf carts more than cars to get around. The supermarkets are a bit far for biking, but we have banks, hair salons, a drugstore—all within walking or easy biking distance."

Roger made his only comment of the entire morning. "And a funeral parlor," he observed morosely. Molly wasn't sure how to respond to that. But Mary didn't appear to have heard her husband. She seemed to be getting her second wind.

"Roger and I play a good game of tennis," she said. "I

hope there are some level 3.5 or 4 players here. Back in Wisconsin we played in county tournaments...."

"I'm sure you'll find some enjoyable competition," Molly said, hoping to stem the flow of more verbiage. "How about you, Betsy?"

"I'm not much of an athlete."

"If you'd like to learn pickleball, the club does teach beginners. I don't know the schedule, but one of my neighbors, Renee Holden, is real active in the club—does some of the mentoring for beginners. I could ask her what days and times the beginners meet."

Betsy looked up sharply. "That would be terrific. Maybe I could give pickleball a try. Could you introduce me to Renee? I'd love to meet some other women," she added.

"The exercise and craft classes are good places to get to know people. But I'll get a few of the women I know together for a meet-and-greet," said Molly.

"That would be great. Thanks."

"Fair warning," Molly said. "We'll all try to convince you to buy a home here. I'm a real estate agent, but most of my girlfriends are the true saleswomen. They all love it here and take more pride than I do in recruiting residents. I'll try to protect you from the worst of the onslaught."

Betsy smiled. "I just got through selling my mom's house, so I know what home owning entails. I hope I'll never accumulate as much junk as she did, but for right now, renting and using other people's stuff suits me fine." She gave a small wave and walked away.

Mary and Roger had started toward the parking lot when Mary stopped and turned to Molly for a last question. "What about crime here?"

Molly thought immediately about what she had heard just this morning. An elderly woman had been caught stealing all the toilet paper from the ladies' rooms in public areas. Molly had a mischievous impulse to recount the heinous crime but decided she would rather not invoke Mary's predictably voluble commentary. She gave her standard answer instead: "A lot of people don't even lock their doors. Sunrise Acres is virtually crime-free."

13

BETSY RAUSCH

Earlier in March

Just a few weeks earlier, Betsy Rausch had been back in her hometown in Massachusetts, selling the family home. Her mother had died, and her father had departed mentally while physically existing in what people euphemistically called a "memory unit." There was no point in keeping the old house.

Thanks to being in a nice neighborhood with decent schools, it had sold quickly. The buyer, Betsy recalled, seemed to be mentally knocking down walls and remodeling at the final walk-through. But to prepare for that day, Betsy had the depressing chore of clearing the house of fifty-odd years of detritus. *I should have insisted Mom sort through some of this while she still could.* Everything was so disorderly. And shabby. As a child, Betsy had sat in this same heavy upholstered furniture. Who had pink toilets anymore? Or Formica countertops? She had trashed the obvious junk and hoped the upcoming "estate sale" might clear out most of the rest. *Ha! Some estate! Well, somebody might buy this stuff.*

A friend had suggested that she delegate the whole

chore to professionals. "Let them decide what to keep and what to toss." But Betsy had gritted her teeth and done it all herself. The fact was, she didn't want to spend the money.

In retrospect, given her startling discovery during the final sorting and cleaning, she had been smart not to follow that advice. It took her most of a week to doggedly work her way through the rooms, finishing with her mother's bedroom. Once the closet was bare, only the bed covers and the contents of the antique dresser remained. But on Saturday, as she started emptying drawers, she heard the downstairs back door open.

"Yoo-hoo—hi, door was open." Sandy Shotland, a friend she had offered a 10 percent commission to help her sort and display what was saleable, entered the kitchen. Sandy worked at the same plant nursery as Betsy, but usually at the cash register rather than out in the greenhouses and fields. Betsy didn't envy her the cool sales room and light physical labor. Tending to the new plants, answering questions, and helping customers with their selections was a welcome trade-off for boring indoor work.

Sandy was a plain woman, her brown hair covered with a blue bandana as if she were anticipating dusty work. At the nursery, she favored bright blouses and skirts—reds and yellows, accompanied by strings of bulky beads. But today she had on jeans, a plaid men's shirt, and her son's heavy wool cardigan sweater emblazoned with the local high school basketball team's panther logo. The two women finished tagging the larger items in the living room and moved the small ones to the garage where they had set up card tables, some borrowed from neighbors for the day. A bank of clouds was slowly sliding like an awning across the sky, closing off the blue. No snow was forecast, but it was still winter, and Betsy went upstairs to retrieve a padded red jacket to wear over her sweatshirt.

The first customer arrived a full hour before the sale was advertised to start. Betsy recognized her from the self-styled "antiques" store downtown, Life's Treasures, locally known as "Life's Trash."

"Hi, Monica, we don't have everything laid out yet," Betsy said, hoping to discourage her from continuing to pick up and scrutinize items off the tables.

"Oh, that's okay." Monica waved a gloved hand languidly. She was dressed warmly but much more stylishly than the other two women, in a full-length black leather coat with a fur collar and high-topped boots that clung to her calves. *Prada—either genuine or decent knockoffs. Her shop must be doing well. Or her husband's auto business,* Betsy thought.

"I've already been looking at the stuff out here. I can tell at a glance if there's anything I want. And I'm mostly after furniture. Okay if I look inside?" Without waiting for an answer, Monica mounted the stairs from the garage into the kitchen and disappeared into the house.

"But, hey..." Betsy sputtered.

"Oh, let her look," Sandy said. "Maybe we can unload that huge armoire. I'll keep an eye on stuff out here." Betsy followed Monica into the house.

Monica walked through the downstairs rooms hastily, barely glancing at the old stuffed chairs and sagging couch. She similarly dismissed the dining room set. Only when she entered the upstairs bedroom did she break stride. She homed in on the old dresser that had belonged to Betsy's grandmother—probably even her great-grandmother. As a child, Betsy was forbidden to put anything on it or touch any of the drawers. The striated white marble top supported an oval mirror framed in carved walnut. Three lower drawers in front bore brass swag pulls, dulled with age. On each of the dresser's curved sides a door fronted a shallow cabinet.

Monica stood looking at it for a while, caressed the marble with her hand as if testing its smoothness, and then turned to Betsy. "I could take this off your hands," she said with studied casualness. "Unless these are fake doors and there are no cabinets behind."

So it's a genuine antique, Betsy thought. *And worth a lot. Whatever she offers, triple it.*

"How much?"

"Inherited from my great-grandmother," Betsy said quickly. "Very old and valuable."

"Uh, say one-fifty?"

Betsy recalculated. She'd only been in Monica's store once, but she didn't remember any high-quality pieces of furniture. She decided on a gamble.

"Actually, I thought I'd put a picture on eBay."

Monica looked dismayed. "Oh no, don't do that. I know someone right here in town who would likely buy it. For the right price," she added hastily. "And only if it's solid wood throughout. I'd need to see the inside of the drawers and the backs of the side cabinets—make sure no one has substituted pressed board." She pulled at a drawer. It opened a few inches, revealing a solid mass of underwear and old nightclothes that, escaping their confinement, bulged out like rising bread dough.

"If you'll empty it out entirely," Monica said, "I'll give you...um, two hundred fifty dollars and I'll have Winthrop come get it right now."

"Eight-fifty." For a moment, as Monica hesitated, Betsy thought she had lost her bet.

"Seven hundred."

"Okay." Betsy dumped the dresser contents onto the bed, heedless of possibly soiling the old handmade pink-and-green quilt bedspread. Later she wondered if she would have missed the most important item in the dresser, had Monica not insisted on examining the back panels in each side cabinet.

Because stuck against the back corner of the left-hand cabinet was a small diary. Monica impatiently pried it free of the panel to which it had adhered over time and threw it on the bed on top of the pile of clothes, old bank books, and receipts. Betsy turned the diary over in her hands as Monica telephoned her husband to come get the dresser. The cloth cover, dirty and a bit mildewed, was imprinted with violets and unidentifiable yellow flowers—a style Betsy thought her mother would have disdained as "frou-frou." Some pages, wrinkled and stuck together, bore witness to an unintended bath decades ago. Betsy began to skim the first few entries. The first page read "PHYLLIS'S Diary, Private!" Each block letter in the name sported different colored ink. In the early pages, the rounded juvenile script included tiny circles dotting the *i*'s. Betsy could hardly believe her mother had ever written these pages, given her adult handwriting— crabbed and almost illegible. When she looked more closely at the dates carefully entered at the top right corner for each entry, Betsy realized her mother had written it during high school. *Maybe the diary will help me understand why Mom was so intensely private, so cold. Maybe she even wrote about my birth.*

The storage location of the diary also intrigued Betsy. Why had her mother not stowed the diary in the boxes labeled "memorabilia" that held Betsy's childhood drawings, the Mother's and Father's Day cards she had composed, her complaining letters from summer camp, and photos of herself when she was still a skinny girl with hair so curly it looked like a small animal had camped out on her head? Why had her mother put the diary in this out-of-the-way, almost secret dresser compartment?

Just as she was about to dive into the contents, Sandy called her from below to come help.

THE REST of the morning of the estate sale was frantic, even with two of them staffing the tables and collecting cash. The hours went by in a blur of responding to questions, making change, and negotiating. Toward noon, a beat-up pickup pulled up at the curb. A tall, gaunt man with cheeks so hollow it looked as if he was deliberately sucking them in climbed out. He wore overalls and a long-sleeved shirt, apparently the same vintage as the truck. A tow-headed young man waited in the passenger seat.

The older man stood beside the truck for a moment looking around, and then headed for the folded wheelchair leaning against the side of the garage. "Does it still work?" he asked.

Betsy wasn't sure what he meant. "It's not electric or anything. No motor."

He just looked at her. "Can I open it out?"

"Sure."

He opened the wheelchair, looked carefully at the brakes and footpads, and then turned around and sat in it. He propelled himself a few feet and only then looked at the yellow sticker with the price on it: $125.

"How about seventy-five bucks?," he said. "It's for my son," he added, indicating the young man in the truck with a tilt of his head. "Motorcycle accident."

Betsy shook her head. "It's worth more than a hundred twenty-five."

"Mebbe," he acknowledged. "But I can't pay more than a hundred. That's all I got. Really."

Betsy shook her head again. "Sorry. One twenty-five."

The man looked angry and then his face wilted. He walked back toward the truck, shoulders slumped.

"Betsy!" Sandy said. "Surely we can—"

"If I'm going to give stuff away," Betsy said, "I'd rather give it to a real charity and get the write-off. If I price that wheelchair at four hundred dollars, I'd get a tax break of about one-fifty."

Sandy's mouth pursed in disapproval. "Hell! I'll make up the difference." She turned and ran down to the curb, waving her arms. "Wait!" she yelled. "Hey, Mister...."

Betsy flushed angrily and walked back inside the house while Sandy completed the transaction. She waited until the end of the afternoon to berate Sandy. By four o'clock, few items remained unsold, and Betsy took the "Estate Sale" sign down. Sandy sat sorting bills by denomination. Betsy watched with mixed emotions. She had been pleasantly surprised by the sale of things she had expected to relegate to the trash. But she was still annoyed at Sandy. "That wasn't your decision to make about the wheelchair."

"What do you care? I said I'd make up the difference and I will. It's only twenty-five bucks, and judging by the condition of that truck, I'd say that's a lot more money to him than to us."

"Jesus, what a bleeding heart. For all you know, he's got a Mercedes back in the garage. You are so gullible. We should never have priced that wheelchair so low. I shouldn't have let you talk me into it."

"Yeah, and for all you know, his son is a permanent

cripple and his wife has cancer! You're being a chintz! We made more money today than I would have ever expected from all that ju—stuff."

"Well, you really embarrassed me," Betsy said. "And we may have sold a lot, but I'm still going to have to just give away plenty."

Sandy did not look at her but concentrated on painstakingly turning the bills so that George, Abe, and Old Hickory all faced the same way.

Betsy watched her for a few moments as the silence grew between them until it felt like a solid physical barrier. "Look, Sandy," Betsy blurted. "That was everything. I'm not getting any more cash out of Mom's stuff." Resentment roiled her stomach as she thought of the elegant Georgian home Sandy would return to, paid for by two salaries, one of them unnecessary. Sandy's stockbroker husband probably earned ten times what she did at the nursery.

Sandy looked up from her task, startled at Betsy's tone. "Haven't you sold this place?"

"Sure, but look at it. I couldn't get top dollar. It's not exactly going to keep me in roses."

After Sandy left, Betsy made herself a cup of coffee and sat down at the wood-veneer kitchen table, noting absently as she did that it was covered with white circles where careless diners had put wet or hot dishes. *Not worth much money anymore, damaged like that. No wonder no one gave it a second glance. Another tax deduction. No need to look for a coaster for my coffee mug.*

The day had been tiring. She couldn't face a lot of cleaning. Betsy had left the diary in a kitchen drawer, emptied of the miscellaneous spatulas and wooden spoons, most of which had miraculously sold. *Now let's see why Mom went to so much trouble to hide that diary.*

That little book was the engine on the train of events that propelled Betsy to Arizona.

BETSY HAD OPENED the diary near the beginning. It was filled with references to dances and gossip about various teachers. And she had been surprised to see how catty her mother sounded at that age!

Miss Coolidge wears the most ridiculous blue eye shadow.... I can see the outline of her girdle....

Many of the entries were about boys, and clearly her mother had not consulted a dictionary for spelling. Probably thought no one would ever read her scribbles.

Luke is lushous. He sat by me at lunch today in the cafateria; he is really the cats meow way cool??.... David Stanhope asked me to the prom, even tho I'm only a sophmore. What a laugh! As if I'd ever go with him—anywhere. He walks like a duck.

Betsy skipped ahead a couple of years to her mother's junior year. The handwriting matured, the spelling improved, and the entries were increasingly about a boy whom she referred to as "12." (Was this the "lushous Luke"?) Her mother referred to other people by initials or nicknames (Sparks, Bubbles, Pencil). *Why all the code? Maybe Grandma was a snoop?* However, 12 was the only one with a number as a pseudonym.

I really love 12.... If he loved me half the way I do him, he'd go to college here instead of out in Michigan.

Angry and despairing entries filled the next few pages.

He won't go here. Football and forestry are too important. He says we can make it work long distance. I know him. He won't. He'll go off with some college girl. I hate him!! He says his parents want him to break it off with me. That's just an excuse. I hate them!!!!

And then a page stained with splotches of smudged ink. *Tears?* She felt a wave of compassion for the seventeen-year-old girl who had written the words.

He won't change his mind. I love him so much. Oh, God, how can I bear this? I can't live without him!!!!!

However, the teenage high drama seemed to subside over the next few entries when Phyllis began writing about "T"—possibly Betsy's father, Tom.

T is so kind. He's been really good to me. Saw House of Wax with him last night. Creepy! He asked if he could kiss me! What a sweetie.

There were more entries about dates with T—movies, a dance, a beach party down by the river.

And then 12 reappeared.

12 is home for Christmas. Called me as soon as he got in town. God, I still love him. Had to lie to T so that I could go to the quarry with 12. He must still love me, the way he acted. Maybe I can talk him into transferring back here to Tufts or B.U.

But then a single page, uncharacteristically undated. It was difficult to discern all the words, so many were blotches of smeared ink, but Betsy thought she had deciphered:

He's gone. No use. He's a jerk. How could he [a few indecipherable letters] **xxx *with me and then xxx me again. I should never xxxxx...***

Then, clearly and firmly written, and for the first time, one full, actual first name:

Tom is worth three of him.

It was the last entry.

Betsy stood with the diary in her hands for a few minutes and then turned to the box of memorabilia, which she now pored through with heightened interest. She found her parents' wedding invitation, a small album with photographs of the modest ceremony, a scallop-edged paper napkin embossed "Phyllis and Tom" in silver script, and even an envelope with a few grains of rice from those thrown by friends at the newlyweds when they emerged from the church. They had married on March 17, 1956, three months before Phyllis was to graduate from Woburn High School.

Betsy found her own birth certificate—September 20, 1956, a little over six months after the marriage. That explained her grandmother's comment one time that Betsy was "a preemie" and her mother's swift warning, "Mom!" Only six or seven at the time, Betsy interpreted her grandmother's odd tone of voice as meaning that being a "preemie" was bad. When she was old enough to understand the term, she thought she must have misinterpreted her grandmother's sly tone. *After all, it was hardly anyone's fault that I was born early.* She looked again at the birth certificate: seven pounds three ounces. No wonder her grandmother used the term *preemie* sarcastically.

Counting back from her birth date, she realized she must have been conceived around Christmas. At a sudden thought, she gasped audibly. What if.... She opened the diary again. The last page was not dated, but it had to have been written at the end of December or maybe even in early January, when college students returned to their campuses. *Is it possible that I'm actually 12's daughter? If Tom isn't really my father, that could explain why I never felt I fit into the family mold. Who was 12? Could the number 12 mean he was a high school senior when Mom first started seeing him?*

High school yearbooks. 12 was a year ahead of Mom. Maybe I'll see some resemblance to myself when I find his picture. She had stacked the yearbooks in a corner, intending to put them in the trash—all except the year her mother graduated. She wasn't sure why she was keeping even that one. Maybe Kevin would be interested someday, or if he and Carole ever gave her a grandchild, that child might. There was no one else who would care. Her only sibling had died of measles as a toddler, and her parents either had given up trying for children after that or her mother had miscarried. She remembered several times when her mother was mysteriously bedridden during Betsy's grade school years.

She fished her mother's junior yearbook out from the pile and looked at the photos of the senior boys. No Lukes or Lucases. So "lushous Luke" must have been in a different class—and wasn't 12. She was disappointed that she could not see any resemblance to herself in any of the young men, although a couple had curly hair like hers and it appeared in the black-and-white photos that several had light eyes—maybe blue like her own. She thought about her mother's friends. *Was there anyone who knew Mom in high school?* Phyllis's best friend had been Shirley Thompson. She pulled out her mother's address book and called Shirley. After a few minutes commiserating and chatting, Betsy asked her if she knew whom Phyllis had dated her senior year in high school.

"Good heavens!" Shirley laughed. "That was over sixty years ago. I didn't even live here then. Why on earth are you trying to find that out?"

"Just curiosity. I found an old diary of Mom's and she mentioned dating someone she called 'Twelve,' whatever that means." Betsy hesitated, knowing that further questioning would seem odd, but she decided to ask anyway. "Do you know any of Mom's friends who might know? Someone she might have gone to school with?"

Shirley said nothing for a few moments. The question obviously puzzled her. "I'm still not sure why you want to know. She dated Tom before they married, I know that, so whoever that Twelve boy was, he couldn't have been very important—she probably went out with him before she met Tom."

She started to correct Shirley but decided it would be unwise to let anyone know her mom apparently was dating two men at the time that Betsy had been conceived. Her mother was dead, and Tom's Alzheimer's had progressed to the point that he didn't even recognize her, so there was no point in arousing suspicions. She wished Shirley well, made a half-hearted invitation to stay in touch, and disconnected.

Betsy went back to sorting or trashing the residue from the sale. All the while, her thoughts kept returning to the diary, and the question of 12's identity, like probing the sensitive gum around an aching tooth. How else could she identify him?

What if 12 or a sibling or child of his has done a DNA test? And I did one and found him that way? But suppose I did find him—what on earth would I do about it?

14

———

STEVE ANTONELLI

ater in March

Standing in the living room of their Sunrise Acres home, Steve Antonelli ended the call he had been on and turned to his wife of forty years with a triumphant smile.

"Julie, that was the news I've been waiting for." Just two months earlier, Steve had acted on a "hot tip" in the Sunrise Investment Club and plunked down a sizeable chunk of their 401(k) in a startup. *Now it's time to raise the bet. And convince Julie it's the right move.*

Julie sat down on the aqua-and-rose patterned couch that divided the living room from the dining area. She positioned a rose-colored cushion behind her back as she awaited the details. It was obvious to Steve that she did not share his enthusiasm. She crossed her knees under one of the tie-dyed muumuus she always wore at home and settled back, arms crossed.

"As you could probably tell, that was the marketing guy from Cytodynamics, Craig Swan. They just got the results from their animal trials, and they are amazing. None of the monkeys died, and the tumors in almost half of them have actually shrunk. They're submitting the results to the FDA and want to start human trials ASAP. Julie, I think this is it! Since we're Round One investors, we're eligible for second-round funding. And then—IPO, baby!"

"Second-round funding?" Julie asked hesitantly. She frowned. "What does that mean for us?"

"It means the more we put in now, the more we'll get when they go public."

"I know what an IPO is. But how much can we afford? How long until we get our money back?"

"Money *back*, are you kidding? We're looking at three, four, maybe ten times our investment. Think, I don't know, Google or Facebook or something. Those guys who were there at the beginning and all their pals are billionaires now. And we've got enough to hang in there in the meantime. We can take out a second mortgage on the house—interest rates are low. Julie, this is as close to a sure thing as we're gonna get. Even before the animal trials, my buddy Hal from the Investment Club, who put me on to this company in the first place, said he thought this could be a big deal, and Craig just confirmed it."

"Steve, we just finished paying for the new kitchen...."

"Julie, for Christ's sake, just show a little appreciation for once in your life! I finally find a way to ensure our future, and all you can do is complain. Jesus!"

"Honey, I'm not complaining. I'm just.... Why do we need to take risks at this time in our lives? We have plenty. We—"

Steve was not to be distracted. "We do not have 'plenty.' We haven't planned a trip since last year's cruise. We haven't bought a new car in three years. We...."

Julie's frown deepened as Steve paused.

"In fact," he said, "speaking of new cars. I am so bored with our Camry. That is a truly boring car—"

Julie interrupted. "I like our boring car. It's easy to drive and park, it's comfortable, it gets me everywhere just fine."

"Julie, It. Is. A. Boring. Car! You're not driving—you're just steering." Steve was grinning now. "I want a car like the one I learned to drive on."

"Steve, what.... Have you...."

"Relax. I'm just telling you I'm thinking of doing some things for me. And for you too, of course," he added hastily, seeing her unhappy face. "Why don't you buy some new duds. You said you felt underdressed when we went on the cruise. Spend some money. Get something fancy—something that screams 'expensive'—or at least 'classy.' But right now I'm calling Craig Swan back."

15
——————

MOLLY

Early April 2019

The room in the Activity Center had been carefully arranged. Two rectangular tables had been shoved together to form a square in an obvious effort to make the meeting of the Sunrise Acres Renovations and Improvements Committee seem like a chat in someone's dining room. As a committee member, Molly had been dreading the meeting all week. She had seriously considered manufacturing a sudden illness or urgent consultation with her doctor. *This is going to be messy. To Renee, this meeting is just a short inconvenience with a predetermined outcome. For Steve and Julie, it's a terrible prospect; they have so much invested in that house—both emotionally and financially.*

Six people were arranged around the tables. Steve and Julie sat along one side. Julie was a small woman, with a round, almost wrinkle-free face. She wore her gray hair long, in a simple blunt cut, pulled today into a haphazard bun secured at the crown by a red pincer-style plastic hair clip. Her flowered blue denim shirt fell loosely over gray slacks tapering to black Abeo sandals. She was a head shorter than her bulky husband, who wore a long-sleeved Western shirt over his jeans. Molly thought Renee was an elegant contrast to both of them in her white slacks and a light-weave beige-and-white silk top.

Molly and the other two committee members sat together. They had just met privately to discuss how the meeting should be handled, and Molly did not expect it to go smoothly. Tony Featherstone and George Carpenter, the committee chairperson, had clearly just returned from the links, judging from their golf shirts and shorts. Tony, tall and thin, perched on the forward edge of his chair, leaned back, and sprawled his long legs under the table. Molly, dressed in black jeans and a T-shirt celebrating the Pima County Food Bank, took the remaining seat and crossed her feet at the ankles, hands in her lap, feeling intensely uncomfortable. Friends with both Renee and Julie, Molly was wishing she had joined the Library Committee instead of the RIC. Maybe, now that Renee had inherited her father's house in California, she would be less focused on renovating the one here in Sunrise. But knowing Renee, and aware of her animus toward Steve, Molly was pretty sure Renee would not back down.

George's face was two-toned. His white forehead, where his hat had fended off the sun, was a startling contrast to the rest of his face, an all-season brown deep enough to suggest incipient mummification. He signaled the beginning of the meeting simply by placing an orange folder on the table, but spoke formally. "Okay, everyone's here. This is a special meeting of the Renovations and Improvements Committee, so we can dispense with the approval of the last meeting's minutes. As a courtesy, I invited Renee and Steve and Julie here to address the committee following our decision to approve Renee's petition to extend her family room at the back of her house. We found that the extension was in compliance with our bylaws and that pending approval of paint colors and revised patio design, her project could go forward. Steve? Julie? I know you still have concerns. We've all read your request to revisit the decision about the project, but the bylaw is very clear, so I'm not really sure what can be done. But you insist..., uh, requested a hearing. So you have the floor, then perhaps Renee could respond."

Steve was red-faced, but not from sunburn; a vein pulsed in his forehead, a simmering teakettle about to whistle. "Look," he said, his gaze going around the table to Renee and the members of the committee in turn. "We bought that house because of the view—the desert and mountains." Then, staring directly at Renee: "You put that extension in, you cut off more than half our view. Bylaws be damned, it's not fair!" His voice, which he initially made an obvious effort to control, increased in volume and shrillness as he pleaded their case. "We've just finished a two-year renovation project: new kitchen, new tile floor, new picture window to see the mountains. We moved the fireplace to a different wall so it wouldn't block the view. We even built in a permanent window seat. Do you have any idea how much that cost? And, now what's our view going to be? Your friggin' house!" By now, Steve had lost all semblance of control.

George held up a conciliatory hand. "Hey, Steve, let's keep it civil...."

His plea only made Steve angrier; Julie put her hand on Steve's arm and started quietly sniffling. "Civil!" Steve yelled, rising from his chair and shaking off Julie's hand. "Tell *her* that!" He jabbed a stubby finger at Renee. "THIS. IS. NOT. FAIR!" He punctuated each word with a slap on the table, causing everyone to jump. "I know where this is all going. You're gonna take her side again—the committee is supposed to be neutral! She has no right to do this. We have rights too!" He leaned over the table, continuing to point in Renee's face.

George stood up, his own voice rising. "Steve, please, sit down."

"Steve, look," Renee said. "The committee made its decision based on the bylaws. As long as my extension stays within ten feet of the property line, I have every right to build out. The committee agreed to hear you out, but no one said the decision would be changed."

"You think this is settled?" Steve yelled. Suddenly, he lowered his finger as if he'd just had a thought. His voice was quietly menacing. "Well, it sure as hell isn't! We are not going to be walked over like this! Come on, Julie." He turned away from the table but swung back to deliver a final salvo at Renee. "You are going to regret this, Renee. I can promise you—you are going to be sorry you screwed us."

George and Tony sat like stunned fish, mouths agape as Steve stormed out. Molly slowly shook her head and continued to stare at her lap. Then she looked up quickly at Renee, whose expression was one of anger and...was that fear? Julie dabbed a tissue at her eyes with one hand and grabbed her sweater from the back of her chair with the other. Then, with a quick apologetic glance at George, she trailed hastily after Steve.

"Wow," George said quietly.

Tony attempted a weak joke: "We're going to need hazard pay for this job."

"*You*," Renee said. "How about me? That sure sounded like a threat."

~

Two days after the RIC meeting, Molly answered the door-bell to find Julie Antonelli on her doorstep. Molly thought furiously for a few seconds about how to avoid the desperate plea she knew was coming. *Why the heck didn't I resign from the RIC before the conflict between Renee and the Antonellis grew from a spark to an inferno?* Her mind flashed to the old grue-some practice of executing felons by tying their limbs to four horses driven in different directions. Okay, so getting tugged in opposite directions by friends wasn't exactly the same as being drawn and quartered, but she still felt tortured. She sighed inaudibly, collected herself, and stood aside, motioning Julie in with a smile.

Before she could offer a drink or even a seat, Julie launched into the expected passionate entreaty.

"Molly, I thought you were my friend! Couldn't you have spoken up for us at the RIC meeting? It just seemed so unfair that everyone took Renee's side. We've made a lot of renovations to take advantage of the view. We certainly don't want to look out our new window at that extension of hers. And losing the mountain view will cost us a lot of money when we sell someday. You're a realtor, for God's sake, you know that! In fact, you're the one who told us how much losing the view takes away from the house value."

"Julie, I'm really sorry. I didn't have any choice. The committee was just following the HOA rules, and you knew what the decision was before you asked for the meeting. It was just a courtesy to hear you out."

"Okay, but can't you do something? You're Renee's friend. Can't you persuade her to back off? Just talk to her, please. She won't give me the time of day. Just says she has a right to do it. And I think she really hates Steve. I know he can get, well, emotional, but he can be really sweet."

Molly hesitated. *Sweet Steve Antonelli?* "Julie, you know

Renee. I don't think anything I could say would change her mind."

Julie chose to regard Molly's words as an offer. "But you'll try?"

Molly closed her eyes but said nothing, mentally slapping herself for giving Julie the slightest opening to expect some action or, worse, some better outcome.

Julie rushed to fill the empty air, hope seemingly revived. She sat down in the nearest chair. "I love my house. Maybe even as much as the one in Prescott."

Molly eagerly seized on the change of topic. "That's where you lived before moving here, right?"

Julie appeared caught up in her memories of the Prescott home. She stared out the window, but it was clear she was not looking at the street out front. "We had almost five acres of land, a great view, eight fruit trees," she said dreamily. "We designed and built that house, and it had every feature we'd ever wanted."

"So why did you leave? It sounds wonderful."

"It was, it was. But then Steve's fight at Yavapai College...." Julie stopped abruptly. She almost stood, then sat down again, looking at Molly's face with an unspoken plea.

"I've only driven through Prescott," Molly said easily. "Pretty country. But didn't you get snow there?"

Julie's eyes filled. She gave Molly a look of pure gratitude. "Not much," she said, her voice choked with emotion. She swallowed hard and went on in a more normal voice. "Our peaches and cherries loved the winters. We had more fruit than I could can or make into jam."

"Speaking of food," Molly said. "How about a piece of coffee cake and a cup of tea or that mocha coffee mix you like? I still have some of it."

By the time they each had a mug in their hands and were seated at the kitchen table, Julie seemed relaxed enough to chat about their joint volunteer work on *The Sunrise Notes*, the monthly community publication. "Good thing you know how to run that software," Molly said. "If you left it to Aki and me, we'd have digital soup."

Julie chuckled.

She didn't mention Renee again.

After she left, Molly sat for a few minutes thinking about Julie's inadvertent revelation. What kind of fight had Steve gotten into? An argument or something more...physical? If the altercation had led to Steve's dismissal, as Julie's words suggested, then it had to have been more serious than a mere disagreement. If Steve had a history of fighting, it would cast a different light on his words at the RIC. Was he more of a real threat to Renee than the committee members believed?

16

RENEE

April 2019

Arriving home a bit after nine o'clock from Pilates class one morning, Renee was greeted at the door by Jessie, her black and white border collie–Lab mix, tail wagging. Giving Jessie a perfunctory pat on the head, Renee told her, "Cool down, girl. We'll go out for a walk in a bit; let me relax for a few minutes first." She sat down in the armchair in the family room with the day's newspaper, but Jessie followed her in and pushed an insistent snout under the paper. "Okay, okay. How about if you just go out and pee in the patio rocks first and then we'll walk in a bit." Hearing the word "walk,"Jessie looked at her hopefully, but obediently went out when Renee pushed open the sliding door.

The back area was barren of foliage, the earth scraped in preparation for construction. Renee watched Jessie, thinking she'd want back in almost immediately, given that there was nothing of interest outside. To Renee's surprise, Jessie loped over to a spot by the back fence and started drinking out of a small brown bowl. It took Renee a few seconds to become alarmed. That wasn't her bowl. She hurried over to find Jessie eagerly lapping up a yellow-green liquid. "Jessie! No!" Renee grabbed Jessie's collar and hauled her away from the bowl. Holding the bowl out of Jessie's reach, Renee brought it to her nose. It smelled sweet. Renee started to pour it out on the gravel, but then realized she needed to know what it was. She hurried inside and thrust the bowl into a Ziploc bag, where the remaining liquid flowed to the bottom. Then she called the veterinarian and explained that she had found Jessie drinking this odd-colored liquid.

"What do you mean by 'odd-colored'?" the receptionist asked. When Renee described the color, the receptionist was alarmed. "Bring her in immediately. And bring the bowl if you have it."

When she arrived at Dr. White's animal hospital, the receptionist called the doctor's assistant, Rona, who took one whiff of the Ziploc bag and announced to the other three people waiting with their pets, "We have an emergency here, folks. We'll get you in just as soon as we can—but please be patient; if this were your dog, you'd want us to take her in immediately."

Renee lifted Jessie with some difficulty onto the vet's examining table. Corralling fifty pounds of living, uncooperative creature was different from lifting weights. Dr. White smelled the contents of the Ziploc. "Ethylene glycol. Antifreeze," he added for Renee's benefit. "Renee, we have to get this out of Jessie's system as fast as possible. Rona—hydrogen peroxide and the charcoal. I'll draw blood."

While Renee patted her dog and spoke calmly to her, the doctor quickly shaved a section of her foreleg and drew blood. He handed the tube to Rona as she came in with several bottles. "Tell the lab what she drank," he directed.

"They'll know to check kidney function." Then he turned to Renee.

"Okay, Renee, this is going to get messy," he warned. "Help me hold Jessie."

It took both of them to hold a squirming and bewildered Jessie as the doctor shot almost a half-cup of hydrogen peroxide down her throat.

"Now let her stand," the vet said. "She's going to—" Before he finished speaking, Jessie threw up copiously into a hastily positioned bucket.

"That's antifreeze?" Renee asked, looking at the yellow-green liquid pouring out of Jessie's mouth. "Like in a car radiator?"

"Yep. Dogs love it because it's sweet. They'd rather drink it than water. Cats won't touch it, but dogs will eat or drink anything."

Renee bridled a bit at the apparent slight to her beloved canine but resisted the retort that came to mind. She needed the vet's full attention.

Once Jessie appeared to be finished vomiting, Dr. White directed Renee to help hold the dog again while he pumped activated charcoal down Jessie's throat.

"How much do you think she drank?" he asked Renee.

"Maybe a quarter cup? It's a small bowl, but I really don't know how much there was in it. I got to her and stopped her pretty quickly."

"Where was the bowl?"

"Just inside the fence on my back patio."

"How would someone get to your patio if there's a fence?"

"Easy enough. My house backs up to a stretch of desert that's common land, and there's a hiking and equestrian path maybe fifty yards or so from the back of the patio.

Anyone could have slipped the bowl through the bars in the fence anytime this morning while I was out, or last night, for that matter. I usually walk Jessie just before bedtime and I don't let her out back when it's dark anyway. We've had rattlesnakes out there. She'll be all right, won't she," Renee said, more a statement than a question. The alternative didn't bear considering.

"We have a good antidote to give her," Dr. White assured her. "She should be fine. But we'll need to keep her here for at least four days. We'll put her on IV fluids and monitor her kidney function. That's what's dangerous. The ethylene glycol attacks the kidneys, lessens the ability to filter or condense urine—so the kidneys fail. It's a good thing you saw her drinking and got her in here right away."

"I had no idea," Renee said. "I guess this stuff is pretty easy to get."

"But who would do that to a dog?" Rona asked indignantly.

"I can think of at least one person," Renee said grimly.

"Did you see the article about someone on the West Side poisoning coyotes with antifreeze? It was in the local paper about two or three days ago," Dr. White said.

"I don't read that idiot rag," Renee snapped.

"I find it useful for local news," Dr. White said mildly. "Anyway, that article might have given someone the idea."

WHEN RENEE RETURNED from the vet's office, leaving a groggy Jessie behind, she immediately marched next door.

Julie Antonelli answered, clad in jeans and a billowing T-shirt—obviously her husband's—instead of her usual tie-dyed muumuu.

Renee tried to control her anger, but her voice was tight, and her fists were clenched at her sides.

"I need to talk to Steve."

Julie turned to get him, but Steve was already emerging from the back of the house. As always, when facing aggression, he went on the attack.

"Now what?"

"I have a veterinarian's bill for you," Renee said, her voice rising a notch, thrusting a piece of paper at Steve. "And there will be another one in a few days."

"Huh?" He took it and read it with a blank expression. "What's this got to do with me?"

"It's what you owe me for trying to poison Jessie. She almost died. And if you ever pull a trick like this again, I'll make sure you regret it."

"What are you talking about? Poison your mutt? How? And why?"

Julie stood by, nervously bunching up and clutching the tails of her T-shirt in her hands on both sides. "Renee, I don't think we understand..." she started.

"*You* may not," Renee interrupted, "but I'm sure Steve does. Though I don't see how killing an innocent dog would make me change my mind about my house extension. Just revenge, right, Steve? Just want to get back at me, right?"

"Wait just a minute here. You're making a serious accusation. What makes you think I've tried to hurt Jessie?"

"Somebody put a bowl of antifreeze through the fence in my backyard. Who else would do that?"

"Is that what poisoned her? Hell, anyone could have done that, and I can think of several people who might have liked to. Admit it, that dog's a menace. How many times has she bitten other dogs? Got you kicked out of Puppy Park, right? The Morrisons' poodle had to have stitches in the ear

Jessie damn near tore off. If Jessie had bitten a person, she'd have been put down by now."

"That stupid poodle attacked Jessie."

"And how about the incessant barking? I'm not the one who complained to management most recently. There's a lot of people who would like to get rid of Jessie."

"Nobody has complained as much as you and I can't see even Mary Morrison trying to poison any dog."

Steve shrugged. "If you're so sure I did it, prove it. If you go around accusing me without any evidence at all, I'm not going to take it sitting down."

"I have the bowl!"

"And you can prove it's ours? Real distinctive, is it? One of a kind? Maybe an antique Ming Dynasty bowl?"

"You know it isn't. But I still may be able to find out where you got it," Renee said.

Steve's laugh was a short, humorless snort. "Ha! Good luck with that! You're as much a menace as Jessie. Now get the hell out of my house!"

17

MOLLY

pril 2019 (One week later)

A week after Jessie was poisoned, Renee called Molly. "I feel as if my life is falling apart." Her voice cut out on the phone and Molly knew it wasn't because of a bad connection.

"Need a 'cuppa'?" Molly and her women friends in Sunrise had discussed more than once the apparent reliance of the British on a cup of tea in times of stress, even as bombs fell on London. Suggesting a "cuppa" had come to mean an offer to cheer someone up.

"Got anything stronger?" Renee's feeble attempt at levity seemed forced.

"We can put anything in the cup you like," Molly said. "Your house or mine?"

"I'll come over," Renee said, then perhaps belatedly realizing she hadn't asked before, "unless you're busy."

"No worries. I just came back from grocery shopping, so the rest of the morning is wide open."

"Thanks; I really need some advice."

Renee asking for advice? Now that's something new! Molly

wondered for a moment if Renee really did want something stronger than tea, but it was unlikely at ten thirty in the morning. She filled the teakettle with filtered water and turned it on.

But Renee started talking the moment she got inside the door, waving off Molly's offer of the drink.

"Molly, read this email exchange with Peter, please, and help me think what to do. Start at the bottom—last week." She thrust her phone at Molly and only then sat down at the kitchen table.

The email thread was long. Molly scrolled down to the first message, dated five days earlier, and read the exchanges in chronological order.

To: Retiredatlast1964@gmail.com

Dear Peter,

I've started to call you half a dozen times since our argument. And I've gone out to get into the golf cart to come over to see you at least 4-5 times. But every time, I've been afraid you are still angry and that I wouldn't be able to handle it if you blew up at me again. And I admit that I'm still upset myself. I feel as if you are blaming me for doing the job I was hired to do and that the firm required of me. What could I have done—resign from the firm?

Renee

Molly looked up at Renee. "I think you need to give me some background," she said. "What did you and Peter argue about?"

"It was silly, really. About my last case in San Francisco. I told you it was what got my house torched."

"I know some people were mad about the verdict, but I don't know much more than that."

Renee took a big breath. "Okay, let me start at the beginning. This could take a while. Any chance I could have one of your coffee packets instead of tea?" Renee explained how she had caught the case, the way she had defended the homeowner, the hung jury and how the D.A. had declined to retry, the media coverage, and finally, the firebomb attack on her home by a small angry mob. "Peter chooses to see my defense as...as, well, immoral. Racist even. And because of what's happened to him during his life, he is really angry at me. Just read what he wrote." Renee's eyes filled and she looked around the kitchen. "Kleenex?"

Molly pointed wordlessly to a box on the small built-in desk in one corner of the kitchen and returned to reading the emails.

To: R.Holden@spear.net

Hi Renee,

No of course I wouldn't have expected you to resign. But as I see it, you must have coached that woman to lie. Did you have to do that?

Peter

Molly looked up: "What lie?"

"She said she felt threatened by the kid and was defending her home. Maybe she wasn't really lying, but... well, most of the jurors probably thought she was, because the kid was fifteen, just holding a clipboard, and he was in his team uniform. So they didn't think she could have really felt threatened. But three jurors held out, and the jury couldn't reach a unanimous verdict. And because the kid was Black...." Renee spread her hands in a gesture suggesting her meaning was obvious.

"I see," Molly said thoughtfully. "So Peter thought you must have coached her." She looked down at the phone again.

To: Retiredatlast1964@gmail.com

Peter,

What I was required to do was to act as a defense lawyer. That was my obligation. I didn't tell her what to say, but there was really only one possible defense, and she knew it. Our managing partner handed me the case; I didn't think I had a choice. Apparently that decision makes me a bad person in your eyes. I regret that, truly. I admire and respect you and we've had a terrific time together this last year.

Renee

To: R.Holden@spear.net

Renee,

I'm trying to see this from your point of view, but couldn't you have recused yourself? Does a lawyer have to defend someone who has committed an atrocious crime?

Peter

To: Retiredatlast1964@gmail.com

Yes. If a lawyer recused herself every time she thought her client could be guilty, or she simply dislikes the client, or thinks the client may be lying to her, or the crime itself is awful—well, most accused people would have to defend themselves. And unfor-

tunately there are quite a few probably innocent men on death row whose lawyers didn't formally recuse themselves but they might as well have, given their weak or nonexistent defense arguments. Don't you want your lawyer to do his best to defend you from that stupid looting charge?

Renee

To: R.Holden@spear.net

Point taken.

Peter

MOLLY LOOKED UP, astonished. "Peter was accused of looting? When he was young?"

"No, believe it or not, just a month or so ago when there was that protest march in South Tucson and some guys took things way too far. Peter was trying to *stop* the looting, but the police arrested him because he was in the middle of it all. And a shopkeeper got injured. Not seriously."

"I had no idea. That's absurd—as if Peter would need to loot stuff."

"Yeah. I'm sure the charge will get dropped once all the evidence is in. But it's put Peter even more on edge. So I... well, just read the next ones."

To: Retiredatlast1964@gmail.com

Thank you. But I do want to prove to you that I have learned something both from being with you and from that awful case. Your own arrest gave me an idea. There's a nonprofit outfit in South Tucson that supports lawyers defending people of limited means. I contacted them to find out how I might help, and they asked me to join their Board. I accepted the invite.

    Renee

To: R.Holden@spear.net

    Huh. White liberals to the rescue!

    P.

MOLLY LOOKED UP AGAIN. "OUCH!" Renee just nodded and motioned her to continue reading.

To: Retiredatlast1964@gmail.com

    That's offensive and nasty. And egotistical. And racist.

To: R. Holden@spear.net

    Wow. I hit all four buttons at once.

    P.

"THIS THE LATEST ONE? "Molly asked, looking at the time displayed on the message.

"Yep. I really don't know how to respond. Looks as if I'm damned in his eyes no matter what I do. He's letting his past destroy our future."

They sat in silence for a few minutes. "Can't live with 'em," Molly said softly, thinking of her own complicated relationships in the past.

"I *can* live without 'em," Renee said, refusing to complete the cliché. "But," she went on, "I really don't want to break it off with Peter. We're good together. Or we were, before he found out all the details of my case."

"I don't think emails are the way to handle this," Molly said. "You need to talk it out face-to-face."

"Do you think that smiley face in his last email is a kind of opening? I really don't know how to interpret it. Could be sarcasm."

"Only one way to find out. Go see him."

Renee shook her head. "I'm really reluctant to make the first move, to tell you the truth."

"Yeah, well, I shouldn't be giving advice anyway," Molly said ruefully. "I'm not good at relationships—at least not romantic ones."

18

MOLLY

One afternoon after they had played pickleball together in the morning, Mike called Molly with an invitation to dinner. Molly's acceptance came with one stipulation: "It has to be Dutch treat, okay?" *Keeps it more like a friendly outing. Not a date,* she assured herself.

The restaurant was small: ten tables inside. But the space was doubled by a patio surrounded in heavy plastic hangings to keep the cool in or out, depending on the season. The interior décor featured murals celebrating Italian wines and wineries. But when Mike deferred to Molly to make the decision, she opted for outside, where there were fewer patrons. Once they were seated and handed menus, Molly slipped into her Sunrise Acres ambassador role and asked the usual ice-breaker questions.

"Mike, I understand you're from Michigan. I have to ask, why Arizona? Why Sunrise?"

"Well, like most people here, I suppose, Andrea and I were tired of northern winters. We had visited Tucson once and liked it. We aren't—weren't—Florida people. And the idea of a quiet adult community with no crime or violence was appealing."

Molly cocked her head very slightly, lips parted as if she was thinking of speaking, but she looked away and remained silent.

Mike picked up on the hesitation. "What were you going to say? I thought all the crime was south of here, where there are gangs."

"No, you're right; there's no serious crime. A few burglaries. But we've had a few pretty heated neighborhood disputes. Mostly territorial—a neighbor cutting down a tree where they shouldn't. That kind of thing. Even seniors can have short fuses. And people don't leave their former lives entirely behind. For good or bad, they bring their pasts with them."

"Huh. So no retired Mafia bosses or Witness Protection refugees I should look out for?"

Molly smiled. "They're probably all in Florida, so good decision not to retire there! But, seriously, I don't want you to think Sunrise is Eden. We've had some pretty nasty confrontations. I always hear about them because of the volunteer work I do. You'd be surprised at what sets people off."

A tall, slender young woman with a large assortment of earrings piercing the circumference of her ears, plus a ring in her eyebrow and a red crystal stud in her nose, introduced herself as Carla, set down warm focaccia, and took their drink orders. Mike asked for a run-through of beers on tap.

After the drinks were ordered and their meals selected, Molly glanced pointedly at Mike's left hand, where a narrow untanned band of skin circled his ring finger. "I finally took it off," he said. "Just last week."

"Hard, isn't it? I moved here right after Max died," Molly said after a pause. "Wanted to downsize and, well, it's been over five years, but I do remember what that first year is like. Adjusting to being alone...." Her voice trailed off. Behind her, through the plastic barrier, a sunset burned the desert sky. A small gust of wind separated the plastic panels, causing a few fiery streaks to slant through the gap, lighting one corner of the table.

"In fact," she said, "it took me over a year to put my ring aside." *Don't think I'll mention that the major reason for wearing it was to fend off lonely men—not because I was so attached to it. Or how I threw its mate—Max's—into a river.*

"You don't realize how happy you are," Mike said, "until it's all taken from you."

She rearranged the napkin in her lap. "Uh-huh."

"What did Max do?" he asked.

For a startled moment, she didn't realize he was asking about Max's profession. "Uh, he was a sales rep for Eli Lilly. Traveled a lot." *Especially to Pittsburgh.* "The pharmaceutical industry is pretty cut-throat. Max brought a lot of that home with him, particularly after dealing with prospective clients who were being wooed with competing products. The ones who hinted at some sort of kickback scheme really pissed him off, and Max wasn't the sort of man who wanted to talk it through when he got home. He'd just head off to what passed for his man cave and stew. Oops, TMI. Sorry."

Before Mike could respond, Carla returned and set their salads in front of them with deliberate care. She turned each plate to a precise orientation probably dictated by the chef for maximum visual impact. Mike and Molly exchanged an amused glance, neither of them seeing any difference in appeal. By then the moment for Mike to commiserate had passed.

Molly mischievously gave her plate a quarter turn before starting to eat. Mike grinned at her. "Rebel! You're messing up the presentation."

They ate in silence for a few minutes before Mike went back to the topic of spouses. "If you don't mind talking about it, how did Max die?"

"He was killed while out jogging." She paused for a few minutes, reaching out to reposition the salt and pepper shakers from the center to the side of the table. "He had just finished with...with a client in Pittsburgh and was staying overnight with a college friend who lived in the suburbs. Brent—his friend—said that Max went out for a run before dinner. It was dusk and I guess the area is sort of out in the country, so Max was on a winding two-lane road. Knowing Max, I'm sure he was well off onto the shoulder, but some guy came around a bend too fast and.... Next thing I knew, a state policeman knocked on my door. Ten o'clock at night; I was almost in bed. I couldn't believe it; had to call his parents and his sister." She would never be able to erase from her brain the sound of his mother's anguished keening. "And, of course, Megan—our daughter."

She toyed with the salad, pushing leaves around the plate.

"Did the driver stop?"

"No. No skid marks. They never caught him—or her. The tiny part of my brain that entertains conspiracies wondered if it had anything to do with his job, but the big part said nah, just some idiot or drunk. Wrong place at the wrong time." She absently moved the salt and pepper back to the center of the table.

She paused, but as Mike seemed to be trying to think of what to say, she continued, determined to finish the topic and move on.

"Max's sister and Megan arranged the funeral. I don't remember much about it at all; I was in a fog." *A fog of pure grief, then. The anger came later.* She pulled back to safer territory in her memory. "My parents are observant Jews and were unhappy the service was in our Unitarian church. But I was relieved to skip the Kaddish and sitting shiva."

"I'm so sorry you went through that," Mike said softly. He started to reach across the table as if to touch her hand but pulled back. "It's such an awful experience. Andy, our younger son, just hated the condolences. People don't know what to say, so they say dumb things. Like 'At least she won't have to go through old age.' Or assuming you have the same religious beliefs as theirs about the afterlife, 'gone to a better place' and such. I know those people have good intentions, but..."

"I know," she said. "I think people want to say something comforting, but 'At least he didn't suffer' was not exactly consoling. How the hell would they know? *I* don't even know. In fact, he probably did." Her voice caught. *Despite it all, I hate to think of his dying alone like that. And in pain.* She swallowed before saying, "And then I'd get the Christian messages. But that's okay. As you said, those folks mean well. But my Megan was really upset about a couple of unbelievably insensitive comments, like 'Why was he running on a road?' And 'Joggers need to be more careful.' She really gave the guy who said that hell. But there were anonymous idiots who made even more horrible comments on the internet.... And people really shouldn't say 'I know how you feel' unless they honestly do. Megan told me, 'It's a shitty club, but I don't want to talk to anyone who doesn't belong.'"

"I like Megan's phrasing," he said with a smile. "My kids

would agree that people who haven't lost someone precious to them can't really empathize."

Carla provided another welcome interruption, returning to remove the salad plates and present the entrees. Again, she caressed the plates into position as if they were paintings to be viewed. Looking at her long fingers, Molly wondered if she was perhaps a musician or an artist in her other life.

"Buon appetito!" Mike said.

After Molly had sampled her salmon and Mike his *tagliatelle à la Romana,* he returned to Molly's earlier comment.

"So you were raised Jewish. I thought maybe you'd married into the religion."

"No, in fact I kind of married out of it. Max's family was not at all observant and we ended up going to the Unitarian church I mentioned, in Cincinnati. My folks weren't too happy. As Max used to say, he looked good on paper—nice Jewish boy—and then he took me out of the religion."

"Does Megan follow Jewish traditions?"

Molly's lips curled in amusement. "Megan got her religious education in the Unitarian church we attended—very different rituals, to say the least. Both my sister and brother are still very much involved in synagogue, so when Megan and her cousins were growing up, they had to coach her when we visited my folks. Megan liked to show off for her grandparents when she'd learned some Hebrew phrases or could participate in some of the rituals. But no bat mitzvah —another disappointment for my folks."

"Both your parents are still alive?"

"Yep. They still live in Illinois—Edwardsville. My dad taught history at Southern Illinois University for more than thirty years."

"Aha, another academic. But you didn't follow in the parental footsteps."

"Oh no. I had a bookstore when Max and I lived in Monfort Heights—right outside of Cincinnati. I thought of starting one up here, but it was hardly the time to compete with Amazon. A friend of mine talked me into getting a real estate license. Not that it's a full-time job, thank God. I rarely have clients outside of Sunrise Acres, but there's enough business right here to keep me as busy as I would ever want to be. I could retire entirely, but I do enjoy working with people and I'm genuinely enthusiastic about Sunrise, so it's not a chore to sell homes here."

She smiled, a bit embarrassed. "It strikes me that I'm doing all the talking here. It's your fault of course, being such a good listener. But now it's 'grill Mike,' time."

She saw a slight wince cross his face at her characterization of his questions. *But I did feel a bit as if I was being interrogated.*

"Tell me about your family," she suggested. After he had told her about his two sons and their careers, he asked about grandchildren. Molly pulled out her phone and showed pictures of Clara and Teddy. Mike reciprocated with photos of grandson Grady with his parents. "They say all babies look like Winston Churchill," he commented, handing his phone over to Molly. "But I think Grady looks more like Yul Brynner in this one. I should get a more recent shot; he's two now—actually has hair and a definite personality."

"Wow, Yul Brynner. That sort of dates us, doesn't it? Loved him in *The King and I*," Molly said.

"Ever been to Thailand?"

"No, Max and I tended to stick more to Europe on our trips: England, Germany, Austria...."

"How about Ireland?"

"That was on our bucket list, but we never made it."

"I hadn't either until just last summer, right after...after the service for Andrea. I was in a serious funk, and my sister pretty much forced me to think of doing something special, a big splurge just for me. I found a tour operator named Con Finnegan in Galway—his name alone sold me—and a couple of weeks later I was hiking along the western Irish coast, staying at nice places, enjoying the company of my fellow adventurers, and developing a serious fondness for Irish beer and whiskey."

"That sounds like a great decision. Any particular highlights? I don't know much about Ireland," Molly said.

"Well, do you want the quirky or the amazing?"

"How about quirky—sounds intriguing."

"Okay. The last few nights we stayed at what Con described as a 'shabby chic' hotel in this little town of Dingle. First of all, Dingle is truly small, but it has over fifty pubs! And the prize for most quirky has to go to my favorite —Jack's Pub and Hardware Store."

"You're kidding!"

"Nope, you walk in the front door, and on the left is a full bar, every stool taken at two o'clock in the afternoon. On the right, floor to ceiling, tools, screws, and nails. More stools, all occupied—but with beer drinkers, not guys planning their next DIY project."

"Guess you have to be careful ordering a screwdriver there!"

Mike chuckled politely, but Molly got the distinct feeling that beer drinkers would consider that a sissy drink. But all he said was, "Never tried! Now, tell me about one of your trips—quirky, amazing, or just fun."

They continued exchanging trip stories over coffee for

him, tea for her, both of them loath to bring the evening to an end. At last, significant glances from the wait staff alerted them to the silence in the rest of the now deserted patio.

Molly was quiet on the drive back to her house. *Was this a date? Would he expect a good-night kiss?* She felt an unaccustomed awkwardness.

When Mike pulled up in her driveway, she had her hand on the door handle and her seat belt released by the time he put the gear in park. "Um—great night," she said. "I'll see you on the pickleball court!" She fairly leaped from the car, giving him no time to react.

Mike then backed the car up to shine the headlights on her walk, which was unlit. Once she had the door open, she waved and vanished inside.

Several days later, Mike called Molly to set up another date. "It was a lovely evening," she said, "but I'm in charge of the Pickleball Club dinner coming up and I'm going to be really busy. I need to ride herd on the caterers to be sure they bring the right equipment—last time they didn't even bring hot plates to keep the food warm. And we have to figure out table decorations, how to decide which tables go to the buffet first..." Her voice trailed off as she realized she was explaining too much. "Um, let me call you if things look under control," she ended lamely. They said an awkward good-bye and she clicked off the phone.

Maybe I'm being a bit unfair. I probably shouldn't have gone out to dinner with him in the first place. But I can't let him think I'm interested in him as a...as anything more than a casual friend.

19

———

MIKE

Mike stared at his phone. *What the heck was that? Too busy because of a pickleball party? And after our dinner last week, she couldn't have left the car faster if she'd been propelled by a slingshot. Yet I'm sure we both had a good time that evening. Heck, we were having so much fun we closed the joint.* His first reaction was to feel baffled, then to be peeved. He hadn't felt this way since college when Susanna Gooding (*can't believe I still remember her name*) had given him the brush-off. *But maybe I did something wrong?* Well, the pickleball party was the weekend after next. He decided he would wait until then, in case she really was swamped.

His resolve to bide his time while he waited for Molly to call lasted only a few days. *How much time does it take to set up a Pickleball Club party? Why is she ignoring me? I'm not eighteen anymore; I can take rejection—I think. But I need to know why she's blowing me off.* The problem with growing old, he thought, is that the road ahead is shorter than the road already traveled. *No time for inertia.*

He debated how to contact her: *another phone call? Email?*

Text? Show up on her doorstep? He thought of calling Frannie for advice and laughed at himself for his own insecurity. He recalled her words, "kick in the tush." *Okay, same sentiment but more elegantly put, Shakespeare's Henry V famously encouraging his troops on the eve of the battle of Agincourt: "Once more unto the breach, dear friends, once more." That strategy had worked out well for old Hank.*

Reminding himself that Henry not only decisively won the battle with the French but also won Catherine as his wife, Mike decided on the boldest move: to show up on Molly's doorstep. However, he would not go empty-handed. At the restaurant Molly had commented on how much she enjoyed the focaccia, so Mike looked up a recipe for a no-knead version. It did look surprisingly easy and conveniently produced two loaves. He'd try one first and if it was good, bake the other for Molly. He topped his with sea salt, some dried Italian herbs, and a sprinkling of fresh rosemary from his garden and was pleased with the result. He was therefore confident that the second loaf would be good enough to present to Molly. *Who can refuse warm, homemade bread?*

Mike drove to Molly's house, the bread wrapped in a clean cotton dish towel. He'd leave it on her doorstep if she wasn't home. She'd likely know who it was from. It occurred to him that he was turning into a casserole widower. Food as bribery for companionship. He almost turned around at the thought. *I'll know how she feels when she sees me. If she looks disappointed, I'll back off.*

When Molly opened the door, to Mike's relief she looked both surprised and delighted. Mike found himself tongue-tied. "Uh, I made bread. It's just out of the oven." He handed it to her and then closed the screen door as if he would leave.

"How lovely! Come in, Mike. Can we have a slice now while it's warm?"

He sat at the kitchen table, watching her move gracefully around the kitchen, pulling down small plates, and setting out butter and olive oil. Her kitchen had warm cherry cabinets and a spacious granite island in the middle. The granite was alive with movement, swirls of what he thought of as Arizona colors: rusts and earth tones. Molly's small family room held two large black leather recliners and looked out on a surprisingly large back patio with a fountain composed of three metal saguaros of varying heights. A cactus wren was perched on the tallest one, drinking from the stream of water that bubbled out the top and cascaded down the sides. Birds of various colors and sizes competing for seeds were attacking a hanging bird feeder, their frantic pecking knocking many seeds to the ground. *The doves and quail should appreciate that,* he thought.

"Would you like some coffee?" Molly asked.

"No thanks," he said, assuming that it would likely be supermarket fare. "I won't be staying long, and I don't want to trouble you." *Remember, she's a tea drinker. Single for five years. Argh, it could even be instant! So sayeth the coffee Nazi.*

"No bother," she said, turning on the electric teakettle. *Uh-oh, bad sign.* "I have these little packets of instant from Starbucks and my coffee-drinking friends tell me it's not too bad." She opened the cabinet above the counter and fetched down Earl Grey tea and the coffee, which had been packaged in single servings.

Crap. It was a measure of his eagerness to be accommodating that he smiled, accepted the cup of boiling water, the coffee packet, and a spoon. "I'm sorry, I don't have any cream," she said. "I do have milk, but as I recall, you take it black anyway."

"Right," he said. So she had noticed how he ordered the coffee at the restaurant. Good sign?

She cut off several fragrant slices of bread and placed them on the plates, along with a small saucer of olive oil. She sat down across from him at the table.

He didn't know where to begin, but she saved him the trouble. "Mike, you're wondering why I didn't accept your invitation," she said.

Thank God, a direct woman. "Yes," he said simply.

She looked down at her tea for a second or two, then nodded slightly to herself as if she had made a decision. "Mike, I really, really enjoyed the other night."

"Then why—" She held up a hand.

"Let me explain," she said. "Andrea passed on barely a year and a half ago. From all you've told me, it was a very happy marriage." She paused again, and this time he was quiet.

"A lot of people—especially men—who lose a spouse enter right away into a rebound relationship—and those are temporary. I don't want to be your rebound...whatever. I have to admit that I did have that kind of relationship after Max died. An old friend of ours who had lost his wife two years earlier courted me. I was really lonely, and Kirk was a terrific support; I had known him for years and he was Max's best friend. He called me every night while I was working through the grief. He gave me hope for the future. And Kirk was so good with Megan—really helped her too. But, in the end, I realized it wouldn't work and I ended it. And I hurt him. I cancelled a trip with him I had agreed to go on and I told him honestly it would be a mistake to plan a future together.

"It wasn't fair of me to even let the relationship start. I really regret it—the hurting, not the ending. So I just don't think it's a good idea for us to start seeing each other...like that," she concluded.

He stared at her. Of all the things he imagined she might say, this hadn't occurred to him. "Wait a minute. Are you telling me that because we had a really good time together, it might mean I'm attracted to you because I need a rebound...person?"

"I'm not saying you *need* that exactly; I'm just saying that you are very vulnerable right now. I know that from experience. You do want companionship. And to be blunt, I don't want to get hurt the way I hurt my friend."

"Molly," he said, reaching across the table and seizing both of her hands. "I don't know how to convince you to take the risk, but I'm not so lonely that I must have romantic companionship. What if...." He paused. "What if we agree to just enjoy each other's company, no romance, and see where it goes? I'll not pressure you in any way, I promise."

"Let me think about it, please," she said, drawing her hands back from his grasp. "You would just move on to someone else, so it's not really you I worry about. Oh," she said with a small laugh, "that didn't sound very nice. What I mean is—"

"You want to be careful," he finished. "I understand. I doubt that will be a problem! My sister assures me that I am far from irresistible." He grinned.

20

BETSY

Late April

"Hi, Betsy, it's Molly Levin—from your Sunrise tour last month?" To Betsy's pleased surprise, Molly was following up on her offer to introduce her to some women friends. "How about coming to a no-host happy-hour gathering day after tomorrow at the golf club restaurant I pointed out? Just a couple of my women friends and neighbors. We call it a hen party. Don't know if that's sexist or not—you'll have to ask Aki—she's the one who named it."

"That's so nice of you," Betsy said. "I didn't really expect you to do that."

"We all love an excuse to get together over a glass of wine," Molly said. "The Hole-in-One is really the only restaurant in Sunrise. Nothing fancy—bar-style food, but cheap drinks during happy hour. And it gets crowded early, so is four thirty okay?"

"That's perfect. Can you fill me in a little on the other women? Is one of them the Renee you mentioned to me?" Betsy asked, careful to keep her tone casual.

Molly talked briefly about Renee and Aki, but said, "They can both tell you more. Though Renee's not real forthcoming about her law career."

The women gathered at an outdoor table where they could sit in the sun, avoiding the chilly breeze. They all wore hats and sunglasses. Betsy had traded the cowboy hat she had worn on Molly's tour for a more practical sun hat. Mustard yellow, it had an asymmetrical brim, very deep on the sides and shallower in front. She could see her reflection in the window of the restaurant. With her curly dark hair sticking out above and behind her ears, Betsy thought she looked a bit like a sheep dog that had gotten a lopsided bucket dumped on her head. She took it off, deciding, *Getting sunburned is better than looking like a misfit.*

Molly introduced Betsy to Renee ("lives across the street from me and knows all about the pickleball mentoring") and Aki ("is in a bunch of the clubs"). "Betsy," Molly explained, "is renting here for three or four months. Let's see what we can do to persuade her to move in permanently!"

"You'll love it here in Sun*set* acres," Aki said, smiling at her own play on the name. "We came just for a couple of days to visit friends and we've been here now, um, five years."

Ignoring the hint about aging, Betsy picked up on Aki's use of "we," and made an assumption. "So you came with your husband," Betsy said. "Probably makes a move easier. I'm divorced."

"So is Rausch your ex's name?" Renee asked, before Aki could respond.

"Nope. I went back to my maiden name."

"So did I," Renee said, nodding her head in approval.

"And he hasn't been in the picture for a long time," Betsy

said. "I'm a confirmed renter since the divorce, but I still have a lot of stuff, and I just spent weeks clearing out my mom's house before selling it. So the thought of moving by myself is enough to give me a migraine."

"That's why God created moving companies," Renee said. "And don't listen to Aki. She's our resident comedian. Not all of us are preparing to greet The Reaper. Lots to do to keep us fit. And don't worry about being single, either. Both Molly and I came alone, and we love it here."

Betsy studied Renee, who looked considerably younger than any of the other residents she had met. The planes in Renee's face were sculpted; she had a generous mouth and large hazel eyes perhaps just a bit too close together for conventional beauty. *She looks a bit hard*, Betsy thought. *But she'd been a lawyer, according to Molly. Probably she had to be tough.* Her blond-streaked brown hair was cut shoulder-length in what Betsy assumed might still be called a "page boy," but the hairdresser had feathered the sides into wings that curved in and framed her face. Her hands were beautifully manicured. A delicate red pattern on the forefinger nail of each hand overlaid the pink abalone-shell sheen on all the nails. Expensive. Betsy could not help contrasting this elegant look with her own. *Hair design by Cheap Cuts*, she thought derisively, *and nails by Betsy.*

"You're not really alone," Aki said to Renee. "You have Peter."

To Betsy's inquiring look, Renee explained. "Peter Jackson—a, um, special friend." She waggled her eyebrows suggestively, to the laughter of the other women. Molly shot Renee a questioning look. Renee shook her head slightly and, Betsy noticed, gave a subtle thumbs-down on one hand.

"Peter is one of the youngest eligible bachelors around,"

Aki said. "Renee snared him practically the first day she set foot in Sunrise." Aki was small, with porcelain, almost translucent skin. Her contrasting shoulder-length blue-black hair was pulled back into a ponytail under a simple white sun visor. Her petite size and smooth face made her seem closer to Renee's age, Betsy thought, than the others at the table, as did her oversized oval sunglasses.

"But I'm totally single," Molly said. "Lots to do here without a man. Although," she added thoughtfully, "there are some bachelors—and widowers—around. I rented out Mike Landry's house for him while he was away teaching for a semester. He's a retired professor."

To Betsy's eyes, Molly was softer looking than Renee, and older, but equally slim and carefully groomed. Her beautiful smile displayed white, even teeth and her lively presence made her seem younger. Her dark brown hair (*had to be dyed*) was cut short and feathered back over her ears. Heavy bangs fell off to one side in a wave that she pushed back when it threatened to fall in her eyes. *That hair would be easy to take care of*, Betsy thought—*not like my tangled mop.*

"What's Mike Landry look like?" Aki asked. "The name doesn't sound familiar."

"Um, tall..." Molly started.

"...dark and handsome?" Aki interrupted.

Molly laughed. "Nope, kind of sandy-red-graying hair. And blue eyes. Sort of handsome, I guess."

"Do I detect a note of interest?" Aki asked.

Molly held up both hands in protest. "In Mike? Not for me. I swore off dating years ago. And even if I were in the market for male companionship, he's too.... I've just played pickleball with him a few times. I only mentioned him because we were talking about bachelors." To Betsy's ears, the comment seemed deliberately casual.

"Molly tells me you might want to learn pickleball," Renee said, transparently veering away from the topic of male companions.

"To tell you the truth, I don't know anything about the sport," Betsy admitted.

"Have you ever played tennis? Racquetball? Badminton?"

"A little tennis back in the Dark Ages," Betsy said. "I was terrible at it. Sorry, no racquet sports for me. Maybe bocce?"

"Well, give it some thought. If you change your mind," Renee said, "I'll be the assigned mentor this Thursday, helping a bunch of beginners. It's a lot of fun. We play on a small court, a fourth the size of a tennis court, with a sort of Wiffle ball, and always doubles, not singles. So it's a great social way to get some exercise. Or you could run up and down the stairs at the bell tower—much more fun than the StairMaster in the gym. I try to do it at least once every other day for five or ten minutes." She patted her thighs. "Quads of steel."

"And maybe she'd also like to go to Billy's exercise class or Pilates," Aki suggested.

"The Pilates might be a bit much if you haven't been doing a lot of exercise," Renee said, openly assessing Betsy's figure.

Betsy took no offense. "Right you are. Do you go to any classes that would be easier for a beginner?"

"Maybe Billy's Sweat and Move class," Renee said. "There's actually a fair amount of exercise in it also, but not nearly as much as the Pilates."

"And no teeny-boppers in tight spandex outfits and tattoos like in most exercise classes downtown," Aki chimed in. "The music covers the sound of knees popping. We're all into sags and bags; gravity is the enemy of the people. If only we could shed our skins like snakes do and find a new, youthful me underneath," she added.

"Anyone too young for Medicare is a pseudo teeny-bopper around here," Molly said. "That means you, Renee," she added with a teasing smile. Renee acknowledged the comment with a slight smile and tucked her hair back behind her ears under her woven straw broad-brimmed hat.

To Betsy, the gesture seemed like preening. *She loves the compliments,* Betsy thought. *She's like royalty, acknowledging her ladies in waiting. Or maybe I'm just jealous....*

Just at that moment, Renee turned to her. "So, Betsy, where's home for you?"

"I grew up in Massachusetts."

"Really, where?"

"Woburn. It's outside of Boston."

Renee looked astounded. "You're kidding. That's where my dad grew up. Did you know anyone in the Holden family?"

Betsy shook her head. "Maybe my parents did—my dad ran the local hardware store; he knew most everyone in town. Renee, what brought you to Sunrise? Molly told me you were a lawyer in a big California firm. Sounds like quite a switch."

"Well, I'm a Western gal by birth—brought up in California. And I'd had enough of the Silicon Valley go-go culture. You'd think it's the only place in the world that has lots of startup companies. Guys wear black mock-turtleneck T-shirts because they think it makes them look like Steve Jobs—entrepreneurial and creative. Cocktail parties are all about who has the biggest, um," she glanced around and adjusted her language, "venture capital investment. And they are such hypocrites. Talk big about saving the environment when really they're more concerned about 'plane money'—to buy their own jets."

The waitress, a harried-looking middle-aged woman with a streak of dark roots parting her dyed blond hair like an asphalt highway, plopped a glass of wine down in front of Renee, Aki, and Molly. Betsy noted uncomfortably that she was the only one to order beer.

Renee took a sip of her wine and continued: "I was going to move to Phoenix at first, but it's all cement, artificial turf, and freeways. And then some friends persuaded me to come here, just the way you have, Betsy, to rent for a couple of months. It's cooler than Phoenix, and I love all the outdoor sports. And I was really surprised at how much 'cultchah' there is: lots of theater and music downtown."

"And rodeo," Aki chimed in, affecting a Texas twang. "And gun shows! Don't forget gun shows!"

Betsy wasn't sure whether Aki's enthusiasm was genuine or ironic.

"Yeah, kind of an interesting mixture of old and new West," Renee summed up. "And I was more than ready to retire."

"Kind of early, wasn't it?" Betsy asked.

Renee looked surprised at the question. "Kind of, I guess," she said hesitantly. "But a lot of the clients were A-holes and many of my partners were bigger ones, so...sold my house in Atherton and...." She paused. The others looked at her expectantly. But she was finished talking about her past. "So here I am!" She pointedly turned to Betsy. "But what made you decide to rent here, Betsy?"

A DNA test, Betsy thought. But she stalled a response by taking a sip of beer. She set the bottle down and wiped a wet ring off the table with her napkin. "Long story," she said finally. "I'll tell you another time." She turned to Molly.

"And how about you?"

"The weather was a big draw for me," Molly said. "I'm not the athlete Renee is, but I love being able to play pickle-ball and bike anywhere in the community all year round. Ohio winters can be brutal. I had a bookstore back there, but I find I really prefer working in real estate. No employees, no boss, so it's a lot less stressful. I don't work full time, but the market here in Sunrise Acres alone keeps me busy."

Betsy turned to Aki, but she looked at her watch and apologized. "Oops, gotta run. Another time. Great to meet you, Betsy. Welcome."

"I'm off too," Renee said. "Meeting friends for dinner." She grinned, handed Molly a five-dollar bill, "for my share," and was off.

"Do you have to leave too?" Betsy asked.

Molly shook her head. "One of the perks of being single is dancing to one's own tune. So, what else would you like to know about Sunrise?"

"Tell me about Peter and Renee," she said. "Sounds kind of serious. This may sound like a dumb question, but I'm just finding my way around a place that's only for, uh, seniors. Do people here get married? Is Renee likely to marry Peter?"

"Oh, heavens! My crystal ball clouded over years ago. There are a surprising number of romances in the old town, but not many of them end up in marriage, and I really couldn't tell you about Renee and Peter."

Molly's response seemed evasive. Betsy wondered about the thumbs-down Renee had signaled to Molly when they were discussing Peter. But obviously Renee didn't intend for Betsy to see the gesture; a direct question would be rude. "Renee seems so...glamorous," she said. "And athletic. I've only just met her, but she seems funny. And nice."

"You sound a bit surprised," Molly said, smiling. "You'll find people tend to have extreme reactions to her—both positive and negative. She speaks her mind. She's also very competitive. In exercise class, she pushes herself to do more reps than anyone else. And she's a terror on the pickleball court—if there's any doubt about whether a ball hit to her is in or out, she'll almost always call it out. Makes people mad—and she doesn't exactly avoid confrontation. Criticism just rolls off her back, maybe because of all her work as a lawyer. Argument was her profession.

"However, she can be very generous with her friends and charity causes like the library and The Nature Conservancy. She has a real passion for the land. Newcomers may not see it at first, but there's amazing diversity of both plants and animals in the desert and a lot of us in Sunrise want to keep it that way. I got to know Renee when she and I served on a committee to stop the state from putting a big electrical substation on a parcel of open space adjoining Sunrise Acres. Renee's legal and negotiating skills are responsible for getting it moved a few miles away where it doesn't affect any communities."

"I would think a guy would have to be pretty special to attract her," Betsy said.

"Well, Peter is very smart and easygoing. Usually," she amended, her eyes shifting away from Betsy's face for a moment. Then she looked back and hastily continued. "He's about her age, maybe a couple of years older. Another early retiree. And they're both well off, so they can do things together that cost money."

"Such as?"

"Oh, like tours, ocean cruises. I think the trip they went on last fall was one of those Viking river cruises in Europe.

And I know they have season tickets to the theater, symphony, and opera during the winter."

"Wow, that does sound expensive."

"Yeah, but you know there are lots of things to do right here in Sunrise that don't cost much at all: lectures, dances, free movies, all the clubs. And during the winter, there are visiting musical groups. You don't have to be rich to have fun." A siren sounded nearby, startling them both.

"Fire or police?" Betsy asked.

"Likely a fire truck. The fire station right here in Cactus Heights responds to all sorts of emergencies—from heart attacks to falls. Sometimes the police help out. But there's virtually no crime."

The bold statement was reassuring, but Betsy thought it sounded automatic. *She's a real estate agent,* Betsy reminded herself.

21

BETSY

A few days after the "hen party," Betsy looked at herself in the mirrors lining the walls and closet door of the bathroom in her rental and sighed. *What kind of masochist puts that many mirrors in a room where you'll be naked? Especially in a retirement community! I look like a marinated prune—wrinkled and fat at the same time. But if I'm going to integrate into the community....* She put on her loosest shorts and headed for her first Stretch and Move exercise class.

Looking around at the participants as they gathered in small groups and chatted before class, she was reassured. Gardening and walking had been her only "exercise" and she knew she was not in good shape. But these women (plus a few token men) were almost all older than her, some, she estimated, by at least twenty years. *I shouldn't have much trouble keeping up with them.* But then the instructor, Billy, began snapping out commands and the women around her, all regulars, fell into robotic responses. The changes in position were swift and demanding. Betsy's heart rate was rising alarmingly. *So much for keeping up. A few of these classes and*

I'll either be in tip-top cardiovascular health or dead. Seeing Renee, Betsy moved in her direction.

Billy clearly thought of himself as a Marine drill sergeant, minus the cussing. He alternately berated, cajoled, and scolded the participants. "Come on, folks," he yelled. "This is an *active* adult community, remember? Mountain climb!" On that command, the group converted into a kind of can-can, each kicking vigorously toward the ceiling. "Joyce," he called out, "get that leg higher!"

If he calls me by name, I may die on the spot. Apparently Betsy's face broadcast her alarm. Renee glanced at her and grinned. "Don't worry. He doesn't know your name. And you can keep it that way!"

The exercises varied from mild arm thrusts to martial kicks and lunges. "HOO—AHH!" Billy yelled, in drill sergeant mode. Betsy had positioned herself behind Renee, not only to have a model to follow, but also because Renee's height offered shelter from Billy's eyes and the agony of seeing herself in the large mirror covering the opposite wall.

"Grapevine!" Billy yelled. The initiated flowed to the right with a one-two, step behind. *Why is this a grapevine?* Betsy kept glancing at the clock. *Have we really been going for only forty minutes?*

The worst exercise came almost at the end of the hour— the dreaded "plank." Betsy watched the white-haired woman next to her, over eighty for sure and probably closing in on ninety, hold the difficult pose for the full minute, while she herself flamed out at twenty seconds. To Betsy's dismay, Renee was even more impressive. She switched to a side plank, raising one toned leg in the air while holding the rest of her body off the mat with one arm. "I'll never be able to do that!" Betsy exclaimed in despair.

"Try it on just your elbows first—easier. Hey, some of us

are going out for coffee after class," Renee added, with no indication of breathlessness. "Wanna come?"

"Sure."

Molly moved her mat next to Betsy's when several of the women left at the end of the "sweat" part of the session. "Now you know why us regulars call Stretch and Move 'S and M'—Billy's sadism, our masochism," Molly whispered. "Saw you watching Renee. Wrong model. Next time you should come over next to me. Or Julie. Much, much less intimidating!"

"Which one is Julie?"

"Oh, that's right," Molly said. "She wasn't at the hen party because Renee was, so you haven't met her yet. Julie is the petite gal in the pink warm-up suit. She and Renee, ah, don't get along."

With ABBA playing quietly in the background, Billy now assumed the role of yoga coach, guiding the group through relaxation and stretching exercises. Despite this welcome change, by the end of the ninety minutes, every muscle in Betsy's body felt like overcooked pasta. She was tempted to skip the coffee hour, but it was another opportunity to get to know other women—especially Renee. And Betsy was flattered to be included. It was sort of like being invited to sit at the popular girls' lunch table in high school. *Not that I ever was.*

What a disappointment I was to both parents, Betsy thought as she lay relaxed on her mat. *To Dad because I have the athletic abilities of a sea slug. To Mom because dressing me in stylish clothes, however inexpensive, always felt like Halloween. I am built for frumpy.* Phyllis had constantly lectured Betsy on improving her looks. "You want to always look your best," her mom had said, looking at her round face, too-short nose, and too-small mouth with an almost audible sigh. "So don't come out of your bedroom in the morning without lipstick." What little discretionary money they had could be spent on clothing but not books, hair coloring but not computers. And both parents had favored boys. *At least I gave them a grandson. No granddaughter could have had the place in their hearts that Kevin did.*

Maybe it will be different living here, she thought, looking around at the immobile bodies. *Nobody seems to care what you look like, and I can see they don't dress up much. Who can be glamorous at these advanced ages? Maybe Renee—but then she's still young. And so far, at least, she seems open to being friends with me. And that is definitely good.*

22

RENEE

Early May 2019

When the phone rang a few weeks after the fraught email exchanges with Peter, Renee snatched it up without looking at the caller ID, hoping it was Peter offering an apology. She still had not taken Molly's suggestion to make an overture herself. To her disappointment, the voice on the line was Rod's. She considered hanging up on him but figured he would just call back and leave a long voice mail. The phone service was set up to allow deleting of voice mails only after the entire message had played. *Gotta get that changed. But until I do—might as well get the conversation over with.*

"Hey, Renee, glad I caught you. I just wanted to let you know that I talked to Dave Elby—you know, the lawyer I told you about. He'd be willing to testify in court that your dad and I did have an agreement."

"Rod, he's a very bad lawyer if he let you think that a verbal agreement would stand. Or maybe he's just ignorant of real estate law in California. All real estate transactions must be in writing, signed and accepted by both seller and buyer. Period."

Rod sounded a bit frantic. "But it's what your dad wanted! What if I raised the offer ten percent? Or maybe—"

Renee hung up.

Her phone rang again almost immediately, and Renee was relieved to see Molly's name on the caller ID. "Thank goodness it's you," she said.

"Who did you expect?"

"Rod Staley." Renee explained Rod's repeated attempts to buy the land. "He gave me the same spiel when Peter and I were out in California. He's like a mosquito—annoying, persistent, one of those useless creatures that make you wonder if God got distracted when He was working on His animal kingdom."

Molly laughed. "Sounds like a delightful character. Swat-worthy. Come drown your problems at happy hour this afternoon; I'm getting the gals together at the Hole at four thirty. We're all eager to hear about your renovations."

THE CONVERSATION that afternoon was a typical blend of exchanged stories about incredibly talented grandchildren, odd occurrences at volunteer activities, and house crises such as computer failures in refrigerators! Who knew refrigerators could be rebooted? But Renee's house makeover was of interest to everyone, not only because of the Antonellis' continuing complaints about her house extension, but also because of how ambitious—and expensive—the whole project was.

"Are you planning to redo your landscaping also?" Betsy asked.

"Yep, I'm doing the Full Monty, inside and out. But aside from the family room extension that's been so delayed because of Steve and Julie's objections, the inside is pretty much done. And now that the extension is finally approved, I can begin to plan the outside."

"Um," Betsy said hesitantly, "I've worked in landscape design for over twenty years now. If you would like some free suggestions...."

"Can't beat the price!" Aki said.

Renee looked a bit dubious. "I know," Betsy said with a smile, "you're thinking you'll get what you paid for!"

"Hey, don't sell yourself short," Molly said. "Show Renee those photos you showed me of the landscaping you designed around that mansion. She's really good," Molly continued as Betsy searched through pictures on her phone.

"Here's a big job I just finished in Massachusetts," Betsy said, handing the phone to Renee. "Of course, the plantings out here are totally different. But I've visited a couple of big local nurseries, and displays at the Botanical Garden, and I think I have a sense of what works in the desert. And if you don't like my suggestions, I won't take it personally. People's tastes differ."

Renee was busy scrolling through the numerous photos on Betsy's phone. "These are really wonderful," she said. "Very artistic. Okay, if you really mean it, how about coming over on Tuesday to take a look at the place?"

23

BETSY

Betsy was thrilled that Renee had invited her to look over her existing plantings and make suggestions. It was an opportunity both to get to know Renee better and to challenge that part of her brain that loved designing attractive, functional landscapes. As she drove over to Renee's house, her mind went back to the project she had completed just before coming to Arizona—the pictures she had shown Renee of the Harrison mansion and its grounds. Mrs. H. redid her landscaping as often as she changed husbands—every two or three years. One reason Betsy had enjoyed the Harrison project so much was the unlimited budget. The triple diamond ring on Renee's right hand suggested a similar lack of cost constraints.

Despite her lack of formal landscaping credentials, Betsy was good at her work. Mrs. Harrison's project had been challenging, but when she had declared herself happy with the final design, Betsy's fingers had fairly itched to get started with the planting. She never minded getting dirty; she loved working outdoors and the feel of loam between her fingers. Her mother had never understood that. Nor had

Dad, for that matter. They always referred to her as a "gardener" when speaking to their friends—never a landscape designer. They didn't seem to appreciate what she could create, the care with which she selected everything from bulbs to gravel.

Thinking about all the money Mrs. Harrison had spent, Betsy mused: *What must it be like to be rich, to travel whenever you want, buy what you want, even destroy a perfectly good landscape plan every couple of years out of boredom? Mom and Dad never had enough money to go anywhere. Just an occasional weekend in Maine or Cape Cod. There was that one trip to Branson to take in the shows, but they complained endlessly afterward about how much it set them back. Maybe if I had finished college, I would have had enough money to finance a trip for them. But a college degree is no guarantee of a good-paying job, of course. Kevin isn't exactly making a mint, even though I made sure he finished college—barely. Good thing he and Carole don't have children; traveling with a band is a gypsy life. They couldn't afford kids anyway. If I could make more money....*

But it was time to think about Renee's project. Betsy parked in the driveway, took a quick look at the front plantings, and rang the doorbell. *It wouldn't hurt her to offer to pay something for my time. I certainly won't refuse if she does.*

"Coffee? Water?" Renee offered after greeting her at the door.

"Water would be great, thanks."

Handing Betsy a bottle of Fiji water, Renee said, "Okay, let's get to it. This may be a waste of your time, because I'm not real interested in maintaining a garden. And most of what I've inherited looks pretty crappy. I'll probably just get rid of everything."

"I see what you mean," Betsy agreed, looking around at the plants in Renee's front yard. "There are some pretty pathetic specimens, but you might want to keep the lantanas. They'll give you color most of the year, and they don't need much water. Renee, I don't want to be pushy, but you have such a beautiful house, and you said you plan to entertain. Don't you think some nice plantings, interesting boulders, and maybe a few attractive pots would be really inviting? That big saguaro could be the centerpiece and we could play off that."

"I didn't realize boulders could be 'interesting.' But, yes, I'm certainly keeping the saguaro." Renee gestured at the towering cactus. "I'm told they're quite expensive, the big ones, and grow very slowly. I figure this guy, given his height and the fact that he has arms, must be a hundred years old. Seems appropriate in a place like this," she added with a smile.

"I thought your house was only twenty-five years old," Betsy said.

"It is, but it's illegal in Arizona to take down mature saguaros. Builders have to conserve as many as possible or pay a hefty fine. Either this one was already here, and the builders worked around it, or they brought it in when it was already mature. I trust it wasn't purchased from a saguaro rustler."

"I've heard of cattle rustlers," Betsy laughed, "but how do you rustle a saguaro?" She pictured the Marlboro man galloping on horseback, twirling a lasso. The vision disintegrated with Renee's decidedly less romantic explanation.

"Guys dig them out of the desert and sell them. Totally illegal, of course, but there's a market for cut-rate specimens. Anyway, maybe I'll want to put in another one."

"But you said they're expensive."

"They are," Renee said with a dismissive shrug.

"Okay, so if you're concerned about maintenance, maybe I could work on a xeriscape design."

"Meaning...?"

"Basically, native plants that need very little or no water."

"I'm not really overly concerned with my water bill. Japanese gardens are great, but if I'm going to do this, I want more than gravel and rocks."

"Oh, of course," Betsy assured her. "Cacti, some succulents, maybe a few grasses. A couple of mounds out front with a dwarf citrus and maybe a desert willow to give a little shade. Meyer lemons are easy and attractive, and a little unusual. The area will be beautiful. And very low maintenance."

"Well," Renee said dubiously, "it's really good of you, Betsy, but I don't know.... I'm not sure I'm ready to make decisions yet. Maybe I'll get the extension out back started first. I'd like you to go ahead and draw up some designs for the front yard, but I insist you bill me at your usual rates. I don't want to exploit our friendship."

Our friendship. Betsy smiled. "How about a barter? I lend you my expertise and you give me some legal help." Seeing Renee's look of consternation, Betsy added hastily, "Nothing serious. It's just that I've never had enough money to bother writing a will and now that I have a little from the sale of Mom's house, I thought maybe I'd have one drawn up, for my son Kevin's sake. It would be pretty simple, believe me. I don't have much to leave him."

Renee shook her head. "You'd definitely get the worse of that bargain. I'm a litigation lawyer. I wouldn't trust myself to write a will!"

"Shows how much I know. So you have to pay someone else to do your legal work?"

"Yeah, I have a friend in California who helped me rewrite my will when I married Dan. Then after the divorce I had him take Dan out. Now that I have property in Arizona, maybe I should find a local lawyer. If I do, I'll let you know. But if money's an issue, you can probably find a perfectly adequate form on the internet."

Huh. A lawyer without a current will? That's surprising. But shoemaker's children go without shoes.... "Okay, thanks. So... back to landscaping. Do you want me to look out back as well?"

"Well, I cannot do much out there until the extension is finished, but I'd like your advice about what kind of hardscape to put down. I've got a couple of pallets of bricks in the back to replace that metal fence with a solid wall, but now whatever I choose for the deck has to look good with the bricks. I've got samples of flagstone, slate, and pavers."

"Not flagstone," Betsy said as they walked around the house toward the back. "Not if your guests drink red wine. Even if you start with a good sealant it stains like carpeting when the sealant wears off. Slate is nice—or maybe a different kind of brick pavers to complement the wall. Usually, though, you'd want something with a different texture. Let me have a look at the space and the samples."

ONCE RENEE AGREED TO PROCEED, it took several meetings and a few weeks' time to arrive at a final landscaping plan. But by late May, Betsy had overseen the placement of two "interesting" red rock boulders and most of the plantings out front, including the Meyer lemon tree. The two women were admiring their work when a small white convertible slowed and pulled up at the curb. Betsy looked at it curiously and at the tall man with the cowboy hat and dramatic mustache unfolding himself from the driver's seat. When he stood and rounded the car, Renee's lips compressed into a tight straight line.

"Rod! What the hell are you doing here?"

"I came to see you, of course. My daughter lives in Phoenix," he added, as if that fact would somehow explain his presence.

"How did you get my address? I don't give it out to anyone."

"Your dad gave it to Dave Elby when we met with him and made the agreement about the land."

"Rod, there is no 'agreement,' and if you came to talk about buying my land, you can just get right back in the car and head back up to Phoenix."

"Renee, you owe me at least a few minutes to hear me out."

"I don't owe you squat! I gave you your 'few minutes' in California. Are you hard of hearing or just stupid? I. WILL. NOT. SELL. TO. YOU!"

"I'm not the one being stupid here. I've offered you at least fifty percent more for that land than anyone else ever will. I'll leave an acre around the house...."

Renee's fists were clenched at her sides. "Get off my property. Leave or I'll call the police on you for trespassing."

"Come on, Renee, don't be like this. I'm standing on a public sidewalk. You can't call that trespassing."

"You're harassing me."

"This lady is a witness," he said, indicating Betsy. "Did you see me harassing her?" Not expecting an answer, he continued. "I haven't done anything but ask you to listen to a very lucrative offer. You're going to regret not taking me up on it."

"Is that a threat?"

"Of course not. It's a statement of fact. If you are her friend," he turned again to Betsy, "try to talk some sense into her." He walked back to the car and stood by the driver's side. "I'm not giving up, Renee. You'll come around, or, well..." he said over the top of the car, shaking his head. He got in, flipped a U-turn, and headed back toward the highway.

Renee stood on the pavement watching the back of the car until it disappeared around the corner. "Asshole!"

She turned back to Betsy, who was open-mouthed at the encounter. "Sorry you had to witness that...idiot who doesn't know when to quit," Renee said.

"I know it's none of my business, but can you tell me what's going on with him?"

"He's just a jerk who's trying to buy my land. I may sell some of it eventually, but never to him. His mother cheated my grandma out of the only part of the land I really wanted. His whole family's a bunch of scumbags."

"He seemed awfully determined."

"Well, so am I. He'll get that land over my dead body. The more he bugs me, the less inclined I am to even consider his offer. Forget him. Let's figure out where that desert willow should go. I'm not sure I like the idea of it right by the window. Won't it get too big?"

24

MIKE

May 2019

"Okay, O Wise One, what do I do now?" Mike was FaceTiming with his sister Frannie. After several more fruitless tries to invite Molly out—even with assurances that the invitation was friendly rather than romantic—he was stymied. "It's not like Molly's totally blowing me off. But boy, talk about looking for a woman who's not needy. I've definitely found one. Molly continues to be friendly, invited me in when I brought her some home-made bread, seems to enjoy playing pickleball with me and chatting between games, but she seems convinced that I'm ready to plunge into a 'rebound' relationship, and she doesn't want to get hurt."

"Well, she's probably right to be skeptical." Mike could tell Frannie was folding laundry; her phone was displaying the laundry-room ceiling fan. "Recent widowers do tend to find a new love quickly—and those relationships often turn out to be temporary. Ask any grief counselor."

"I'm not that recent," Mike protested. "And if I'd been desperate for a companion, you remember Glenda." *Man, that would have been* very *temporary.* Frannie's phone was now apparently bouncing in the laundry basket on top of the folded clothes, making Mike a bit dizzy. He decided to stop looking at his screen. "I really enjoy her company—makes me face forward more than back."

"Hmm. Tell me about your invitations."

After Mike had recited his attempts, along with Molly's deflections, Frannie offered a suggestion. "Those were all for an evening out. Too much like a romantic date. Try for a hike or an informal lunch somewhere."

"What if that doesn't work?" He recognized a plaintive tone in his voice. *God, I sound like a lovelorn teenager.*

"It's good practice," Frannie said cheerfully. "You'll be better prepared for the next time you find someone you want to date."

"Ugh. I doubt I'll want to try again. When I fall off a horse, I *don't* want to get back on. I want to take up a different sport."

BUT TO MIKE'S DELIGHT, Frannie's suggestion worked. Molly was agreeable to casual daytime outings. They visited Tucson's famous Desert Museum, its name giving little hint of its actual combination of extensive zoo, art museum, and educational programs. Early morning, they hiked the trails in nearby Catalina State Park and drove down to Tubac to explore the shops full of craft work. And they occasionally had brunch or lunch at the Hole-in-One—always Dutch treat.

One such day in May, they chose a seat outdoors on the covered patio, hoping they would spot some wildlife such as mule deer, javalinas or, if they were fortunate, the bobcat family that had been promenading on the golf course recently. By late afternoon it would be far too hot to eat outdoors, but in Arizona's famed "dry heat," it was pleasant enough for an early lunch. The overhead fans created a mild breeze that gave the illusion of cool.

Keep it casual, Mike warned himself. He felt as if he was trying to befriend a skittish puppy. They chatted amiably about the success of the pickleball party, the most recent warnings from the "Neighborhood Pride" committee about removing "weeds and tree debris" in yards, and local hiking trails. The most predictably edible item on the menu at the Hole-in-One was their hamburger, and both Molly and Mike had ordered that with a shared side of sweet potato fries.

As they were finishing, Molly leaned over the table to Mike and spoke quietly: "See that guy at the next table, tall, bald, mustache?"

Mike stole a quick glance. "Uh-huh."

"I saw him just a half hour ago talking with Renee outside her house when I was watering my houseplants. Think Peter has a rival?"

Mike smiled. "He's a little old, I think, but I don't know. Why don't you go ask him?"

She waved a hand dismissively . "Okay, okay. I know people think I'm nosy. But I've never seen him around before. Obviously, I couldn't overhear their conversation, but Renee looked tense. I thought maybe he was an old flame. Betsy was there too, though, so maybe he was talking more to her. I wonder if he's thinking of moving here. I think I'll go say hello—part of my job as a community ambassador, you know. And, hey, as you once reminded me," she winked, "I can always use another sale."

Before Mike could react, Molly grabbed her purse,

slipped out of her seat, and approached Rod, hand outstretched.

"Hi. I'm Molly Levin. Are you a friend of Renee Holden's?"

Rod looked up, startled at Molly's sudden approach, then rose and hesitantly took the extended hand. "Uh, well...not exact...um...," he stuttered.

"I saw you talking with her outside her house this morning," Molly explained, ignoring his discomfort. "I live right across the street from her. I, uh, just happened to be at my window," she added awkwardly.

Rod had finally recovered enough to be coherent. "Rod Staley. I was a friend of her late father."

"Doug? I was so sorry to hear about his death. Renee really needs her friends right now, and I thought maybe that's why you were at her house." Rod glanced at his unfinished meal and, obviously flustered, remained standing and speechless, wadding his napkin in his left hand.

Mike was following the exchange, both amused and impressed with Molly's chutzpah. He wondered if he should intervene and rescue this stranger, but he knew Molly's genuine friendliness and interest in others usually compensated for her puppy-dog behavior. And, as he knew from his own professional dealings with her, she knew Sunrise Acres better than anyone.

"I hope you'll be staying here for a while," Molly persisted. "It's getting toward the hot season, of course—but we have three swimming pools and loads of indoor activities."

"I'm just passing through. Mostly visiting my daughter in Phoenix."

"Well, if you ever do consider renting or buying here, I hope you'll let me help you," Molly said, pulling one of her ubiquitous business cards from her purse and handing it to him. "Lots of rentals right now. And we're at least five degrees cooler here than in Phoenix. Nice to have met you."

He took the card and stuffed it into his shirt pocket. "Uh, thanks," he said, waving at the waitress who was clearing a table on the far side of the patio. He mimed scribbling a signature. She nodded and went inside to get his bill.

Molly returned to her seat. "Well, that was a bad idea. I wonder why he seemed so antsy. I barely got his name. Am I that intimidating?"

"No comment," Mike said. "But I don't think the poor guy got to finish his lunch."

"Pooh. What was so scary? And," she added in a whisper, "I think he's the one Renee compared to a mosquito, said he was trying to buy her land. Guess he's not a rival to Peter. But he's quite attractive, in a Western sheriff sort of way. Maybe romantic potential for Betsy?"

"Matchmaking is a hazardous hobby, as a zillion movie versions of *Emma* can attest. As far as Peter is concerned, he seems pretty well ensconced in Renee's affections."

"You and your big words!" she said with a laugh. "But you're probably right. They took that riverboat trip in Europe together last fall, so I'd be surprised if they weren't, ah, 'sconcing.' But," she added more thoughtfully, "they've had some...issues lately. I texted Renee a few days ago, asking about Peter, but she texted me back just two words: 'I tried.'"

"Meaning?"

"I'm pretty sure she means that she took my suggestion to try to talk to Peter face-to-face instead of emailing back and forth. Sounds as if it didn't work. I'm not sure they're still a couple."

25

MIKE

Early June 2019

Mike's morning began just before dawn. He ground his beans (mail ordered from Stumptown), carefully measured the proper amount, fed it into the French press, and poured in the water. At 2,500 feet above sea level, water boiled at 207 degrees, Mike was pleased to discover—exactly the right temperature for perfect coffee. While the coffee steeped, he walked out to retrieve the morning papers. Often, he saw Mr. and Mrs. Gutowski (*Goronski? Grabowski? Ought to look it up in the Sunrise directory*) out for their morning constitutional. Mr. G. shambled along determinedly down the middle of the street, devoid of traffic at this hour, escorting some sort of terrier of similar age in doggy years. Mrs. G., meanwhile, glancing at her Fitbit, was doubling or tripling her mileage by slaloming back and forth across her husband's path.

Mike and Molly's relationship had evolved into easy companionship. In keeping with his promise not to push romance, Mike had been arranging activities with Molly during the daytime. But when June arrived, the weather forced a change in their routines. By afternoon, the dry wind from the south felt as if some godlike hand had opened Heaven's oven door. Mike was surprised that the wind didn't scorch the leaves off the plants. The nonnative ones in his garden, despite their drip irrigation, drooped by mid-afternoon, their broad leaves hanging down like exhausted dogs' tongues.

After a particularly ill-advised mid-morning hike in the desert, they realized they needed to adapt to the natural rhythm of the Arizona seasons. Mike suggested that for exercise they could continue to play pickleball a few mornings a week—no later than seven o'clock—but perhaps a couple of evenings watching movies in the air-conditioned comfort of their homes would be a nice change of pace. Mike volunteered to bring a DVD of one of his favorites.

As Mike confessed to Frannie after a week of his and Mollie's new routine, he was "remarkably inept" at guessing Molly's taste in movies. His "favorite," *Babette's Feast,* was a French film with subtitles. Only after he had suggested the musical *Oliver!* for the next movie did Molly confess that his first choice had worried her. "She thought I was going to be too high-brow—her words, not mine—and academic for her. I think she was fearing art films from Uzbekistan."

Frannie had laughed. "She doesn't know you very well yet, does she? Tell her about your passion for *Breaking Bad.* That should prove your brow is low. Or scare her off," she added.

Mike and Molly decided to take turns selecting a series or movie to watch. Tonight was his turn to choose. He showed Molly the case for the DVD displaying the names of the primary actors: Julia Roberts, Dennis Quaid, and Robert Duvall. The title was *Something to Talk About.* "I vaguely remember seeing it when it came out. I think it's kind of funny. And top actors."

They settled in on Mike's couch and he cued it up. Just over ten minutes into the film, he realized that Molly had stopped helping herself to popcorn and had moved away from him. When he turned to her, he saw her face was rigid with discomfort.

"Molly? Are you okay?"

"Mike, I'm so sorry, but I really don't want to watch this. I didn't know what it was about, or I would have said so sooner." She got up from the couch and moved toward the chair where she had set her purse when she first came in.

"Okay." He hit the pause button. "Molly, wait. Where are you going? I'll find something else to watch. Please—what's going on?"

"I, I...look, please go ahead and watch it. It's got top actors, uh—I am being...I'm sorry. I'm ruining your evening. I just can't...even now, it...and I don't know...you might..."

Mike stood and held both of her arms, turning her to face him. "Molly, please, whatever it is."

She started to pull away, but he held her. "No flight this time, okay? You can tell me. Please trust me...."

To his surprise, her eyes overflowed. "Trust!" she repeated, her voice a ragged sob. "Trust! I'd like to. I'd really like to trust you. But how can I? I was sure I could trust Max. I would have staked my *life* that I could trust him. And he betrayed me, Mike. He destroyed my trust."

"I'm not Max," he said firmly. "Whatever he did to you, I can promise you I will never do. Never."

She didn't seem to hear him. "And Kirk knew about it. He knew about it and still he...he said he was in love with me."

"Kirk? The guy who was your...what you called your

rebound lover? The guy you...went with after Max died? I thought you said...."

"Oh, Mike, I'm so sorry." She sat down heavily on the couch and fished a Kleenex out of her pocket. "I didn't tell you the truth about Kirk. Or at least not all of it." She struggled a moment with her voice, but when she finally spoke, her words were calm. "I told you that after Max died, I...I thought I could...I thought Kirk and I could be happy together. That was the truth. Kirk thought he was in love with me. That was true. But I didn't tell you why I broke it off. I might have married Kirk, began seriously thinking about it—but then I found out he knew Max had been unfaithful. It wasn't a one-night stand. It went on for more than three years. And Kirk knew the whole time. He and Max were good friends. But Kirk was supposed to be my friend too. He said he tried to talk Max out of the affair. Maybe he did, I don't know. But he should have made Max be truthful with me. They both lied to me.

"Three years, Mike! Kirk said he hadn't told me because he didn't want to hurt me. But he hurt me more by lying. Much more. I didn't suspect a thing until the police finally got Max's phone back to me a few months or so after...the accident, along with other personal stuff he'd been carrying. That's when I found all these texts—mostly to her, but some to Kirk as well. The three of them, they killed my love for Max, and they killed my ability to trust.

"This woman...." She gestured to the television set, where Julia Roberts's face filled the screen, frozen in place where Mike had hastily stopped the video. "She's a victim, a sucker. Just like me."

Mike sat down beside her and took her hand. "So when you said you didn't want to be more than friends...."

"I wasn't lying about the rebound danger, Mike. It's real,

especially for widowers. I couldn't be sure that you wouldn't suddenly realize that I wasn't Andrea and never would be. But besides that, Max and Kirk left me afraid to trust what anyone says. People lie."

"You mean *men* lie, right?"

"Not just men, of course. But maybe it's part of the excitement, the temptation... between...between...."

"Lovers," he said bluntly.

She flushed. "Romantic partners," she said awkwardly.

"Molly, may I tell you a few things about myself?" He didn't wait for her nod. "I've had a lot of opportunities in my career to be unfaithful. College girls just discovering their freedom from home. Graduate school women who would close the door behind them when they came in for an office meeting with me. Workshops and conferences with lots of female colleagues who confided in me over drinks about unhappy marriages. Was I ever tempted? Yeah, maybe a time or two. But I soon realized that for whatever reason— God, upbringing, Darwin—I'm totally, inescapably monogamous. You must have noticed that ever since you and I met, I have not been seen with another woman. *Despite Frannie's advice.* And face it, even were I so inclined, my libido isn't what it was when I was twenty."

She settled back against the couch cushions.

"But don't get too comfy," he said with a grin. "Doesn't mean I'm a eunuch. Or that I don't find you almost unbearably attractive. I just won't...um...jump until invited."

Molly cocked an eyebrow in his direction, but with a slight smile.

He stopped, hearing an echo of his words in his head: *"jump until invited." Foot-in-the-mouth time again,* he chided himself. "Um, that was kind of presumptuous of me. Assuming I might be invited sometime."

At that moment, the television switched over to scroll through various screen savers of nature scenes. Molly switched it off and turned to him. "I'm being foolish," she said. "Renee says that Peter is letting his past destroy their future. I don't want to do that. My turn to be presumptuous." She leaned over and, to his astonishment, kissed him lightly on the lips. Hers were warm and soft. His body responded with an alacrity that surprised him. It had been so long.

"Please, ma'am," he said with a serious face. "Could you presume again?"

She laughed and delighted him by snuggling into his arms for a more prolonged kiss. In his mind he heard an echo of Frannie's words after Andrea's death: "There will be joy again."

26

MOLLY

id-June 2019

Molly and her daughter talked at least once a week. It was easier in the summer because Arizona didn't observe daylight savings time. As a result, Oregon and Sunrise Acres were in the same time zone. In the winter, Portland was an hour earlier—just enough that Molly had to keep in mind the change in dinner and bedtimes for Megan's two children. Sometimes Molly read to her grandchildren before they went to bed. She knew all the classic children's books from her years running the bookstore. She especially liked Susanna Leonard Hill's lively books and FaceTime allowed her to share the illustrations, but now that Clara and Teddy were older, Molly had moved on to "chapter books."

When she had missed two opportunities to read, Megan grew suspicious. "Mom, what's up? You've mentioned this Mike guy three times now. That's the most I've ever heard you talk about a man. Are you two, um, dating?"

"Nothing serious," Molly assured her. "He's just a friend

I've been spending some time with. He's a rather recent widower."

"Oh-kay," Megan said dubiously, drawing out the word. "So tell me about him."

"Well, oddly enough, he kind of reminds me of your grandfather."

"In a good or bad way?"

Molly laughed. "Both. He's a retired professor, so he's kind of like Dad—an academic, fussy about how people misuse or mangle English, although Mike's even worse than Dad on that score. Have to be really careful about your 'lies' and 'lays.' But he's also a lot of fun to be with. He's smart, loves to read...."

"Children?"

"Yes, he has two grown sons. And I met them at the memorial service for their mom last year. They seem very fond of their dad. It's a close family."

"Jewish?"

"No, but you know your dad and I were never observant, so that's no barrier. And Mike certainly doesn't care."

"Barrier to what? Sounds as if he's more than a friend. I assume your relationship is platonic at your age, but Mom, come on, seriously, are you thinking of marrying this guy?"

Molly felt her face flush; she decided to address the last question rather than the comment about a platonic relationship. "Good heavens, no! I'd never want to go through losing a spouse again. I just mean...I don't care that he's not Jewish and he doesn't care that I am. It's a nonissue. I'm just enjoying the companionship. He plays pickleball, likes theater, movies, travel. And the fact that he had a long and apparently very happy marriage...." Molly drifted off, realizing she was just reinforcing Megan's concerns.

"Huh. Maybe I'd better come down and check this guy out."

"You know I'd love to have you all visit. But not in June and July. It's too hot. And definitely not to check Mike out. Hey, did I ever come to college to check your friends out? Double standard here?"

"Just want to be sure some old guy isn't searching for someone to nurse him through his twilight years."

"Oh my gosh. Maybe you had better come see for yourself. Mike is a few months younger than me, and in better shape. He bikes and hikes and...he's not one of these guys whose hair is receding while his stomach advances."

"Okay, okay. I'm backing off. Send some photos. And...if the relationship isn't platonic—I heard you pause when I said that—at least don't get pregnant."

Molly burst into laughter. "Who do you think I am —Sarah?"

"Well, If I recall my Bible correctly, she was ninety when she had Isaac," Megan said. "Besides, I just couldn't resist the opportunity to return the advice you used to give me." Molly could hear the wicked smile in her daughter's voice. "Oops, I just heard a crash in the living room. Talk to you in a couple days. Love you!"

She clicked off. Molly was left amused at Megan's initial assumption that old folks' relationships were obviously platonic, but also feeling confused: *Where* is *this relationship with Mike headed?*

27

MOLLY

ate June 2019

"Let's go out on the patio and watch the action," Molly suggested. She and Mike were just finishing dessert at Molly's house, when they heard low rumblings heralding the approach of the first big thunderstorm of the summer's monsoon.

"When I first arrived in Arizona," Mike said, "and kept hearing people say how eager they were for the start of 'the monsoon,' the only image that evoked in me was daily downpours in the jungles of India."

"Well, there are times when it seems some giant water bucket has been upended in the heavens. And occasionally we get hail as big as ice cubes. I guess you were gone a lot of the summer last year, so you may not have gotten the full monsoon effect yet."

"I do remember the lovely drop in temperature after we'd been roasted alive in June."

"But now we get an end to our famous 'dry heat.' Did you hear Bob this morning at pickleball griping about the humidity?"

"Yeah, he should try the East Coast. My boys tell me that where they are, both heat and relative humidity are in the nineties."

The awning they sat under was beginning to flap with mounting winds like a bird preparing to launch. The clouds had been ballooning all afternoon, expanding from marshmallows into towering black behemoths. If they were lucky, torrents of rain would fall, turning dry washes into raging rivers, reviving parched desert plants and inhabitants. The storms themselves were usually short-lived but spectacular, with hundreds of lightning strikes that could torch the seared mountains. And aside from the hazards of wildland fire, the sound-and-light show made for dramatic entertainment.

Molly was dog-sitting for Renee. Jessie was decidedly unenthusiastic about the monsoon storms. Torn between the delights of tummy and ear scratches if she stayed outside with her humans and the safety of indoors, Jessie had already crawled under the bed, seeming to anticipate the louder, scarier thundering to come.

"Look at the lightning reflecting off the clouds to the south," Mike said. "Mother Nature's semaphore. How's your Morse code?"

"Aha! I knew you were a cloud whisperer! What's she saying?"

"I think, 'Here I come.'" They sat in silence, sensing the drama about to unfold. The seconds between lightning flashes and peals of thunder shortened until a simultaneous blinding flash and tremendous stroke of thunder startled them into whooping and laughing. Even the roof overhanging the patio was little protection from the cascading, wind-driven rain and leaves that followed, plus a smattering of hail. They scurried back inside, a bit damp but exhilarated.

Molly had earlier cued up a movie of her choosing, one without subtitles.

But they never got around to watching it.

THE NEXT MORNING, Molly woke up a bit groggily and stared at an unaccustomed sight: the dancing patterns of morning sunlight on her bedroom wall, filtered through the leaves of her mesquite tree. It was late! What had happened to her five o'clock canine alarm clock? She sat up, a bit worried. "Jessie!" Renee's dog came bounding into the room and put both paws on the side of the bed. A quivering rump and a tensing in Jessie's back legs announced the dog's intention to launch a forbidden leap onto the bed. "No, Jessie. No." Jessie slunk back down, disappointed, and began vigorously licking the foot Molly had stuck out of the covers in anticipation of needing to track Jessie down. "Ugh." Molly hastily withdrew the now thoroughly wet foot back under the covers. "Yeah," she said, "thanks for the kisses, but...shoo!" She flapped a hand at Jessie, who ran off toward the kitchen.

Kisses.

Now completely awake, Molly thought about last night's wonderful human kisses. And...she turned quickly and saw that the other side of the bed was rumpled but empty. Her heart plunged. Mike had gone home while she was asleep. *What did that mean?* She glanced around the bed, hoping for a note, but there was none. It had been...so perfect last night, so natural after the excitement of the storm. She had been so worried about revealing her no longer beautiful body to him, worried that no man could possibly desire her anymore. She hadn't been with a man since that one night months after Max died—the abortive rebound relationship she had warned Mike about. Maybe she had scared Mike off with her obvious enjoyment of his caresses, her enthusiastic, rather vocal responses during lovemaking. But he had made her feel wanted again and he had said she was lovely, and it had been so long.... Could it be over already? She thought again of the fear she had expressed to him that she would be a temporary rebound lover. If she was not, why had he run off? She felt tears pricking her eyes.

But then Jessie came running back in, with Mike in close pursuit. "Did she wake you?" he asked solicitously. "I was trying to let you sleep in."

Molly felt herself close to tears again, but this time from relief. "No," she said, glancing at the clock. "I woke up without Jessie's help. But it's late. I'd better take her out."

"Already done," he announced proudly. "We made the rounds while you snored away."

"Did I really snore?" Molly could feel her face reddening.

"Well, not loudly. Gentle little susurrations. Almost imperceptible." He grinned. "Maybe you were sleeping so soundly because of some unaccustomed exercise last night." His grin widened.

Molly was tempted to tease him back, maybe about using another big word, or asking how he knew the exercise was "unaccustomed." But she decided to just bask in the pleasure—and relief—she was feeling. *We had a wonderful time last night. And he's still here.* Besides, she thought happily, she did feel a bit, um, exercised in some tender places.

"Anyway, madam," he said with a bow, "breakfast will be served as soon as you are ready. Your tea water is hot, but I didn't presume to ladle out the right amount of tea to steep. Your refrigerator is a bit 'poor,' as my son Andy used to say when he was little and thought there wasn't enough food in ours. However, Jessie and I visited my house and brought provisions, including coffee for me. So, there's pancake batter, or you could have an omelet, or both! Oh, and there's fruit and homemade granola. Or we can dance."

Molly looked at him quizzically. "Dance?"

"I confess to being a bit giddy. I feel like a teenager. Last night was...wonderful. I was a bit, um, nervous."

She grinned. "Never would have known it. I hope there will be more evenings like it."

He bent over to kiss her lightly. "There certainly will be if I have any say in the matter. Frannie will be delighted."

Molly was alarmed. *Just how much does he confide in his sister?*

Mike hastily explained. "No details, I assure you. Just that I'm...really happy. Last year, when I was pretty low, she kept telling me, 'There will be joy again.' I think she deserves the chance to say, 'I told you so.'"

28

MIKE

As Mike parked in Molly's driveway a few days later, he was hailed by a guy across the street who was washing a classic Mustang. "Hey, Mike!" The man dropped a chamois cloth into a bucket and walked across the street, hand outstretched. "It is Mike, isn't it?"

Met him at the Investment Club, Mike reminded himself. He couldn't think of his name. *Could be Bob; most every man here is Bob or Dave or....* Just in time, he remembered. "Hi, Steve," he said, pride in retrieving the name making him sound more enthusiastic than he felt.

"Hey, come take a look." Mike was tempted to shake hands and quickly retreat inside. But that would be rude. He could afford to spend a few minutes talking—and, he thought, probably admiring the car.

Sure enough, Steve was eager to show off his purchase. "See what my investment in Cytodyamics bought?"

"You've already gotten a payout?"

"Well," Steve admitted, "not yet; but we're really close to an IPO."

Mike ran an appraising hand along the fender of the car. "Is it a 'sixty-eight?"

Steve beamed. "You know your cars, huh? Yep, this baby is a 1968 GT 390 fastback coupe. Same one Steve McQueen drove in *Bullitt*. Not the same car, of course—but same model. I don't think there are many of them left. I got this one cheap from a widow up in Tempe. The guy who was restoring it had a heart attack."

"How much work does it need?" Mike asked, trying not to sound skeptical.

"Aw, not much. A little body work, a little engine tuning. I haven't really given it a serious workout yet—just drove it down here and around town, and it seems to run okay. And it's got a built-in anti-theft device." He chuckled. When Mike didn't react, Steve spelled it out for him: "Stick shift! Most car thieves are young guys—wouldn't be able to drive it!" He laughed.

Mike smiled politely.

Steve wasn't finished crowing. "And I sold our old Camry for almost half of what I bought this for. Got a real deal there, too. I think the dealer wanted our car for his daughter, 'cause she's moving, and he was in a hurry. He gave us $17K for it—better than Blue Book."

"So you got this for $34K, huh?"

Steve looked sheepish. "Uh, well—a few thousand more than that. But," he added enthusiastically, "when I get through with it, it'll be a work of art. I'm going to paint it fire-engine red, drive it to some of those classic car rallies."

"Your wife into cars?" Mike asked curiously.

"Julie? Naw. She can't handle stick shift. Only automatic. Far as she's concerned, a car has only two pedals. I keep telling her, she's not really driving—just steering. And that is boring as hell. But I've ordered a nice little Ford Escape for her, be in at the dealer's in a couple weeks."

Mike took his farewell and crossed the street to Molly's. She was standing behind the screen door waiting for him and watching the exchange.

"How does Julie feel about this purchase?" Mike asked, once he was inside.

"She's not happy. She told me at exercise class that she's already worried about the amount of money he's put into some startup. Now he's bought this car that she can't drive, and she'll have to bike everywhere for at least a few weeks."

29

STEVE

Only a few days after Steve purchased the Mustang, he sat in front of his computer, willing the spreadsheet to give him a different result. *If only,* he thought—the saddest two words in the English language.

How could he have been so stupid! There was no Cytodynamics! No Craig Swan! It had all been a scam. The emails, the official-looking reports, the phone calls urging him to take advantage of the "extraordinary opportunity" to invest in Round 2. When he had tried to call Swan, the number had been disconnected.

When he called his Investment Club "pal," Hal Avery, Hal was apologetic but philosophical. Yes, he had neglected to mention that his information on "Cytodynamics" had come from a cold call from Swan, followed by emailed documents that seemed legit. He had, in fact, decided not to make an investment himself and had failed to tell Steve that. "Steve, I hope the Feds catch up with those crooks, but they're probably laughing their asses off in Moscow or Nigeria or some other place out of reach."

Steve had kept the magnitude of his "investments" in Cytodynamics from Julie, who had always trusted him with their finances, so she had been stunned when he admitted his folly and said that their entire financial future was in jeopardy. *We're going to have to economize radically—and downsize.* The thought brought a clutching pain in his chest.

We both love this house. Maybe spent too much on the reno-vations, but Julie is so happy here—happier than I've seen her since Prescott. She keeps saying how great the kitchen is set up— every time she opens a cabinet or uses the island.

He took another despairing look at the spreadsheet. *If we can sell before Renee's damned extension cuts off the view, we'll have enough for a small house somewhere. But no more new car every three years, no more cruises.*

The Mustang was in the garage, and it was drivable, but it appeared it needed a lot more work than he had thought. He'd never get what he'd paid for it. *That widow in Tempe conned me as well. Idiot!* He'd canceled the order for Julie's new car, but the Camry had already been sold. They'd have to buy another used car. *Shit.* Could he ask Julie to try to return the clothes he'd let her buy as a sop for his own impulsiveness? *Shit, shit, shit!*

As if he had conjured her up, Julie came into his little office with a plate of sandwiches and the suggestion that it was still cool enough to eat lunch outside.

"I'm not hungry," Steve said impatiently.

"Honey," she said quietly, "I know what's happened to our nest egg. You told me it was bad. You don't need to try and hide the details. It's my problem too. What if I went back to work? Every company today needs IT help."

"Julie, damn it, let me figure this out. That's a stupid, ridiculous idea. You're sixty-four and your skills are way out of date. Companies today are getting into web design and artificial intelligence and all sorts of stuff you know abso-lutely nothing about. If anyone goes back to work, it will have to be me."

"But you're almost seven years older. And even if some high school were desperate for a chemistry teacher, you don't have a teaching certificate anymore. And—" She stopped abruptly.

Steve knew she was thinking about the other deterrent to anyone who considered hiring him. *Damn my temper. Although that history teacher at Yavapai College was way out of line.*

"I know, I know. Oh God. Please, Julie, just let me...." Steve closed his eyes, put his head down, and clenched his fists. She put the sandwich down on his desk beside the computer display and left the room noiselessly.

If I'm careful, set up one or more annuities after we sell the house.... He hadn't believed the first real estate broker he asked about the "view premium" in pricing the house, but he trusted Molly Levin, and she had said the same thing. Losing a big chunk of that view, to say nothing of having construction next door for six months—maybe longer—would lower the price at least $35,000—maybe more. And worse, the noisy, messy construction for the frigging exten-sion would make it hard to even find a buyer. *Damn Renee! Damn that rubber stamp of a committee and its stupid and unfair rules! Maybe a lawyer could get some kind of injunction? But lawyers are expensive, and Renee is a lawyer herself. She'd figure some way around any legal assault.*

Last night, when he had lain awake listening to Julie's even breathing, he had thought of all kinds of stupid, unlikely schemes to delay construction. Could he find some higher state or even federal authority to back him? Maybe he could create a fake archaeological site by planting some shards of Indian pottery. Or a human bone? Where the heck would he find one? He was practically ready to donate one of his own. Maybe an endangered species? He had snorted loudly enough at that thought to cause Julie to partially wake and turn over. *Yeah, sure, a special species of termite found only next door. Come on, think,* he kept telling himself as he tried to go back to sleep. *There has to be a way to stop her.*

RENEE

Early July 2019

Renee's doorbell rang. She was surprised to see her next-door neighbor standing on the doorstep. It was unlikely to be a social call.

"Oh, hello, Julie," she said with little welcome in her voice.

"May I come in?"

Renee stepped aside and led the way to the kitchen table. "Water?" she asked—the automatic offer of Sunrise Acres residents during the hot months.

"No thanks." Julie sat gingerly on the straight-backed chair, staring down at the table. It was an uncomfortable seat, and she shifted uneasily but said nothing. Her discomfort was clearly more than physical.

After a few moments' silence, Renee asked, "Why are you here, Julie?" Renee had a pretty good idea. She had sometimes referred to Julie as "the sad sack" to her friends, and the encounter with the RIC had done nothing to change her opinion. She steeled herself for a teary appeal.

Julie took a deep breath. "Renee, I want you to understand why this extension you've planned is such a big deal to us. I need to tell you something in confidence. Can you keep it to yourself?" Renee nodded. "For sure?" Julie appealed.

She's like a small child, Renee thought. *Next she'll ask me to cross my heart or pinky swear.* But she didn't have the heart to voice the sarcastic comments that came to mind. "Yes, Julie, I can keep whatever you say a secret. Assuming it's not illegal," she added with a smile.

Julie ignored the attempt at humor. "Oh, no. But if Steve found out I told you, he'd...he'd be very angry with me. Very angry," she repeated softly, as if to herself.

"Okay, Julie, I promise I won't tell Steve. Or anyone else. Spit it out."

Julie looked relieved. "Early this year, Steve put almost all our savings...." She trailed off and started over. "We've made some bad investments. Someone at the Investment Club told Steve about this drug company startup. It sounded so legit—I saw the reports they sent. But," Julie paused and the next words burst out in a passionate torrent, "it's a total scam! They took all our money! Cytodynamics doesn't even exist!" She went on in a quieter but despairing voice. "The guy who suggested it to Steve at the Investment Club didn't even invest himself. But the point is, we're...."Her chin began to quiver and Renee could see she was close to tears.

"The point is?" Renee prompted, hoping to forestall a downpour.

Julie nodded. "The point is...we're...." Her voice lowered to a near whisper. "We're broke. Or close to it. We have to sell the house." Her voice wavered. "We *love* our house." She made a visible effort to calm herself before continuing. "We have to cut expenses and find a cheaper place to live. We know we'll never get back all the money we've put into our place, but Molly said...Molly said that once your extension cuts off part of the view of the desert and the view of Pusch Peak entirely, we won't get nearly as much as we need. Views are important to buyers. So that's why Steve is so...upset. His blood pressure is sky high. Every day he spends hours on the computer just looking at what's left of our savings and he's so.... I can hear him muttering to himself, cussing. Even talking about trying to find a job. At his age!

"If you could just wait until next winter to start construction? We can't sell during the heat of the summer. Molly says fall is the best time to put it on the market. Please, Renee. You are taking thousands of dollars off our house value—tens of thousands. Just postpone?" she pleaded.

"Julie, I appreciate your problem, I really do. But with all the entertaining I do, I just have to have a bigger living area, and there's no other way to create that space. And it would cost *me* thousands to wait. I have a contract for construction and because it's during the summer, I got a pretty good deal. The contractor plans to start in the next couple of weeks. He isn't going to just wait for six months. I'll bet Molly is exaggerating anyway. Not all buyers care that much about a view. And have you forgotten when I asked *you* for a favor—to agree that I could raise my fence to six feet? The Bowers on my other side had no objection. The height it's at now is a risk for Jessie. Coyotes can jump that high, you know."

Julie's brimming eyes finally overflowed. She pulled a Kleenex from her pocket. "Oh, Renee, I've never seen Steve this desperate. I'm not very good at asking for favors, and I know we haven't gotten along recently, but I'm pleading— no, begging you. Just a few more months."

"I'll think about it," Renee said, moving toward the door. "But," she warned, seeing Julie's face light up with hope, "I wouldn't count on it. I'm sorry Steve is so upset." *That's his problem for being a stupid investor.* "This really is your problem, not mine," she emphasized just as they reached the door. "I have the legal right to do this."

"'Legal' and 'right' can be very different things," Julie said quietly as she left.

PART III

31

RENEE

July 9: Day One

At seven fifteen, just before sunset, Renee's phone alerted her to an incoming text. It was from Peter:

Meet me at tower at 8 tonite. Watch city lights come up & stars come out. Have something to discuss.

Renee felt both excited and a bit apprehensive. While she took a quick shower and dried her hair, she puzzled over Peter's text. *Well, this is out of the blue after months of silence. Has he finally forgiven me?* It sounded serious, even romantic, the way he mentioned the lights and the stars. *Am I ready to forgive him? Get back together?* She considered telephoning him to probe a bit what to expect. But this kind of overture, with its romantic overtones, was unusual for Peter even when they were together, and she didn't want to spoil his surprise. If he'd wanted to talk on the phone, he would have called. Faintly in the distance, the bell tower sounded the quarter hour.

She wondered what to wear. *Something better than my usual shorts and T-shirt. But not something too dressy or presumptuous.* She quickly laid a couple of different outfits on the bed. Now with only ten minutes to get there, she settled on a black low-cut blouse and a pair of flowing black-and-white-patterned pants that always elicited compliments. She grabbed her favorite silver necklace off the dresser, added a pair of large silver dangling earrings, and dashed for the door. *Car or golf cart? Golf cart*, she decided. *Given the cut-through past the gym building, it will be quicker.*

She was about to pass Molly walking in the opposite direction when Molly waved her down. "Hey, I recorded an oldie-but-goodie movie. Cary Grant. Want to watch with me or.... Wow, you are all dolled up....You have a hot date?"

"Thanks," Renee said. "I'd like to, but in fact I *do* have a hot date! Damn!" Thinking about Peter's text, she realized she had left her phone in the recliner where she was reading when she got the message. *No time to go back and get it now.* With an apologetic wave to Molly, she sped off to her rendezvous at the bell tower.

"Turn your lights on!" Molly yelled after her.

RENEE PULLED her golf cart into the parking lot next to the gym and dance studios. She fairly bounded up the tower's two flights of stairs, curious and a bit eager to hear Peter's news. Reaching the top landing, she called softly, "Peter?" There was no response, and now she could barely make out a lone form leaning casually over the railing, mostly obscured by the stairs leading up to the actual bell chamber. "Um, hi. Sorry." Again, there was no response. Just a lonely stair climber backlit by the city lights on the horizon. Confused, she paused, wondering if she should wait for him here, despite the unwanted company, or go back down. He had been very specific about the time to meet and now it was a couple of minutes past eight. Could she have mistaken the "tower" in his message? What other tower was there? Still distracted, she began to slowly descend. Maybe he was late, or perhaps he just didn't want an audience for whatever he intended to say to her, and once he saw someone else up there....

She didn't finish the thought. As she reached the lower landing and was moving toward the final flight of stairs, a heavy blow struck the back of her head. She fell to her knees. A second blow was delivered on almost the same spot. She crumpled to the landing, and she felt a strong shove on her back. Barely conscious, Renee toppled down the left side of the stairs, sprawling on the pavement below.

As she flickered in and out of consciousness, she heard a dog bark as if from a great distance. And then a male voice, even farther away, asking something.... She tried to focus, but she was still tumbling, tumbling. "Ee-urr?" was her last utterance as darkness enveloped her.

32

JOSE VILLEGAS

The alert from the 911 dispatcher came in shortly after eight o'clock on the evening of July ninth. In their patrol car, Detective Jose Villegas and Sergeant Sarah Partridge listened carefully: A woman had fallen down the stairs of the bell tower in Sunrise Acres and was seriously injured. The dispatcher described the 911 caller as almost incoherent with the fear that "the woman was dying." Villegas radioed that they were seven or eight minutes out and were responding, and confirmed that the nearby fire station had been alerted. Partridge turned on the flashers and siren and they sped toward the center of the Sunrise Acres community.

When they pulled up in the parking lot by the bell tower, Villegas saw that the fire truck was already in position, close behind the staircase. The truck's floodlights were illuminating the scene at the base of the tower almost like daylight, the powerful beams bouncing off the walls of the nearby buildings and shining into the faces of the people gathered around. The fire crew must have just arrived, because two young men and a woman were running from the truck toward the base of the tower. The detective and sergeant approached the bloody scene, Villegas well ahead of Partridge, whose ample waist was encumbered with the usual equipment in addition to a holstered gun: handcuffs, radio, baton, pepper spray, taser, flashlights, gloves and, multi-purpose tool. Villegas couldn't help thinking she looked a bit like an upright, ambulatory toolbox.

As he approached the tower, he could see a man in a tracksuit holding a phone in flashlight mode and kneeling by what appeared to be a body at the foot of the stairs. The victim was lying on her back and an ominous halo of blood spread from behind her head. When the three members of the fire crew reached the kneeling man, he stood up, moved aside, and said, "Thank God you're here!" The knees of his sweats were wet with blood. *Must be the guy who called 911,* Villegas thought.

"Move back, please," Villegas said loudly to the onlookers. "Give the paramedics room." People in the gathered crowd obediently shuffled a few feet back. An EMT whom Villegas recognized from the scene of a hit and run he'd worked a few weeks earlier took charge. While the EMT looked considerably younger than the other first responders, Villegas knew he was highly trained and could be relied upon to do anything that could be done for the victim.

Villegas turned to Partridge. "Denise, start getting the names and phone numbers of these people. Ask that guy in the tracksuit if I could have a few words." He moved a bit further aside to give the EMT space, then watched carefully as the first responder checked the victim's condition.

The EMT checked for airways, breathing, and circulation, then knelt by the unconscious woman. "Ma'am, can you hear me?" He repeated the question, but Villegas could see that there was no response. The EMT bent close to her face and reported to the other two first responders and Villegas that she was breathing shallowly, even as he checked the carotid artery. "Weak pulse," he added. "No arterial bleeding, but severe head injury."

The female member of the trio told him, "I've called for the ambulance."

The EMT nodded. "Be sure they bring a C-collar and backboard with straps. Tell them we've got a fifty- or sixty-something-year-old female, unconscious, shallow breathing, weak pulse, heavy bleeding from back of the head." He then placed one knee on either side of the victim's head and one hand on either side of her jaw, stabilizing her head.

Villegas asked, "Has anyone gone up the stairs yet to see whether there's an obvious reason for her fall? Something to trip over?

"Not yet," the EMT said.

"I'll do it," Villegas said. He turned his phone to flashlight mode and walked slowly and carefully up the stairs, swinging the flashlight back and forth and filming as he went. Because the floodlights came from behind the tower, the stairs were dark. At the first landing, he saw a large pool of blood and copious spatter on the side posts. He paused to take careful close-up video.

At the top of the next flight, he saw no blood. He scoured the dark corners, looking for a purse or a phone, and as he headed back down to the first landing, he could see nothing that an unwary person descending could have tripped over.

"Any indication that she tried to catch herself?" he asked the fire crew.

"Not even a scraped hand," the lead EMT said. "Had to have been unconscious when she fell."

This was no accident, Villegas realized. *This poor woman was viciously attacked.* He felt a chill at the thought and, he was embarrassed to note, a bit of excitement. As first detective on the scene, he would be the lead on this case, in charge of any police involvement. He called the dispatcher and requested two additional detectives and the crime scene unit.

When he rejoined the group of responders, Partridge waved to him, indicating the man he wanted to interview. After introducing himself, Villegas verified, "You're the one who called nine-one-one?" The man nodded. He was composed, but his hands were shaking.

"Is she alive?" he asked.

"Yes, and thanks to you, she's being helped. So how long ago did you find her?"

"I didn't find her. That lady over there with the dog did. She screamed and I was just coming out of the gym, so I ran over and...." He swallowed hard, as if words were physically stuck in his throat.

"Was she conscious when you got there? I see," Villegas gestured at the bloodstained pants, "that you tried to help her."

"I didn't move her at all," he said nervously. "I knew not to do that. Could be spinal injuries; one jostle and you could make someone into a quadriplegic." He choked up again. "I just tried to tell her she wasn't alone.... I thought...I thought she was dying."

"Did she say anything?"

When he nodded, Villegas immediately turned his phone recorder on. "Go on, please."

The man looked a bit surprised at having the phone thrust at him, but then he said, "She tried to say something twice and I got my ear right down by her mouth, but I don't hear that well and she was struggling to breathe. The first time, it sounded like 'puh.' And the second time it was different—sounded like 'ee-yuh' to me. But that can't be right. I'm sorry."

"Not easy to be a Good Samaritan. But thank you," Villegas said, putting the phone away. After confirming that Sergeant Partridge had the man's contact information, Villegas asked her to see if the woman with the dog could wait a few minutes and talk with him.

The ambulance arrived with two more people. "Went back for the collar," the burly driver said, apparently explaining why they had been delayed.

The paramedic from the ambulance helped the fire crew EMT slide the cervical collar under Renee's head.

A siren announced the arrival of a black-and-white Cactus Heights PD Ford Tahoe, and Villegas walked over to brief the occupants. Detective Denise Weatherby stepped out. She was a tall, attractive woman. Although she wore no makeup and pulled her light brown hair back severely into a ponytail, her appearance caused a quiet ripple of comments among the onlookers. She was joined by a second detective, Terry Rasmussen, whose large bulk caused the car to seem to shrink in comparison when he stepped out. "The reason I asked you to come," Villegas said to the two detectives, "is that I'm calling this in as an assault. It's quite apparent that the victim was unconscious when she fell. The EMT found no broken or even scraped wrists and hands, so no attempt to break the fall. I'd think medical event, but there's a big pool of blood on the landing. Maybe she passed out at the top and hit her head then, but there's also significant blood spatter, so it's unlikely this is an accident scene. I've called for the CSI team."

The three detectives conferred briefly, then Weatherby addressed the bystanders. "Please don't anyone leave without giving Sergeant Partridge your name and phone number. Hey, I mean everyone!" she shouted at a thin man in shorts and a T-shirt who was walking toward the gym. The man stopped and reluctantly turned back.

"I just got here," he protested.

Weatherby ignored his complaint except to say, "It will just take a minute of your time."

Weatherby and Partridge began blocking off the sides of a rough circle with crime scene tape, leaving the back open where the first responders were preparing to transfer Renee into the waiting ambulance.

All five of the first responders gathered around the unconscious woman to do a "log roll." The lead EMT was still holding her head, while two gripped her shoulders and two her hips and legs. The paramedic counted "one-two-three," and they expertly rolled her to her right as the man on her left side used his free hand to position the board against her back. Again on the count of three, they rolled her carefully back onto the board. Then they lifted her, board and all, onto the stretcher and into the back of the ambulance.

Villegas could foresee hours of investigation ahead. The small police force would be stretched, and most officers had little experience with violent crimes. It was going to be a long night, maybe a long week. "Terry," he said to Detective Rasmussen, "I want you to leave immediately for the hospital. The victim'll almost certainly be going into surgery. They'll bag her clothes, but I want you to ask the surgeon to look for any debris in the area of the head wounds—save them if possible. We might get lucky and get some sort of fragments that will identify the weapon used. Have them bag anything they find. Finally, I want you to have the surgeon contact you as soon as they have any idea if and when she might be able to talk. Sarah, did you get all the names and numbers of the bystanders? Good. Text them to me, please."

The Fire Department crew members were packing up their equipment when a third squad car arrived with two uniformed cops. The onlookers were bombarding the paramedics with a chorus of questions. "What happened?" "Is she alive?" "Did she have a heart attack?" "Will she be okay?" "Why is there crime scene tape?"

"She's in good hands," the fire crew EMT said. "They'll have her on oxygen and start treating her on the way to the hospital. And the tape is routine for any serious accident. Lots of details to record, so it's important not to disturb the scene."

Villegas motioned Partridge over and spoke softly. "Sarah, move that crime scene perimeter out a few more feet. Once the crowd disperses, I want you to search the immediate area for a weapon." Anticipating her likely question, he held up his hand. "Any kind of weapon—a hammer, a rock, something pretty heavy—but it will likely have a lot of blood on it."

He walked over to the woman with the little dog. "You found her?" he asked.

"Well, really Tory did. I was walking him and when we came around that corner over there, Tory started just barking his head off at those bushes. I thought it was probably a squirrel and pulled him away, but then he started barking again and just dragged me over here," Tory's owner said proudly, gesturing to the victim.

"Did you hear her say anything?"

"Oh no. I was kind of screaming and Tory kept barking. Then," she indicated the man in the bloodstained sweat suit, "that guy came racing over and got down on the ground with her. It looked like he was talking to her but I couldn't really get that close, 'cause Tory was still barking and jumping around."

"Do you know her name?" At the woman's head shake, Villegas turned to the rest of the group standing around, impatient to leave now that the drama was over.

"Anybody know the name of the woman who...um, fell?" The bystanders looked at each other, and a white-haired woman in a lavender and pink workout suit raised a hand tentatively. "I've seen her at exercise class. I think her first name is Renee, but I don't know her last name. We hardly ever use them here."

"Anyone else? Anyone know Renee's last name? No? Anyone hear her fall? See anyone around or anyone leaving?" There was a collective shake of the head. "Okay," he said with a sigh. "We'll be contacting each of you tomorrow. Maybe you'll remember something in the meantime. Thanks very much, you can go now."

While they waited for the crime scene crew to arrive, Villegas turned again to Tory's owner. "I'd like a formal statement from you, ma'am. Could you come to the station in the morning? We can pick you up if you'd prefer."

"Certainly. If it weren't for Tory," she said, "I could have walked right by her."

THE CRIME SCENE investigators arrived shortly after Villegas finished with the witness. Villegas briefed the team, introduced them to the first responders, and left them to do their jobs. "Okay, Denise, let's figure out how the victim got to the tower," he said, walking toward the parking lot. A dozen or so cars remained scattered about in the lot like so many chess pieces in an interrupted game, but only two golf carts sat in the designated spaces near the buildings. "Let's try the carts first," Villegas said. As they were checking the registration numbers, a man in workout clothes, one of the onlookers at the tower, approached one of the carts, looked curiously at the plainclothes detective and the uniformed officer, and said, "This is mine. Okay if I take off? I gave my phone number to the other officer." After noting his name, Villegas waved him away just as Detective Weatherby closed out her phone.

"This one's hers." She indicated the remaining cart, with distinctive tiger stripes down the sides. "Renee Holden, 2435 Stonegate."

"Let's go, Denise. *Tempus fugit*. We need to get to her place, talk to anyone else living there."

Villegas entered the address into his phone's GPS and they both climbed into the police car. As she backed around to head out, Weatherby paused a moment, then asked, "Hey, Jose, what's with the Latin—it is Latin, right?"

"Sorry, Denise, old habit. Yeah, it's Latin. 'Time flies.' Hammered into me by a Catholic education in Phoenix. The nuns taught me well, maybe too well. And at one point, I was headed for the priesthood."

"Is it like Tourette's syndrome? Can't help it? No offense."

Villegas chuckled. "None taken. No, I don't think so. Sometimes it's just the first way a thought occurs to me." He was studying the phone GPS. "Take the next right."

"Wow, quite a switch from priest to cop!" Weatherby said as she swung the car around the corner.

"Not as much as you might think." He glanced up from his phone and gestured. "Left at the stop sign."

"So what made you switch?"

"Ah, that's a story for another time. Left again—this is her street."

As they drove down Stonegate, scrutinizing the faintly lit house numbers, Villegas said, "No keys and no phone found with Ms. Holden. I grabbed the golf cart key, but I was hoping for a remote garage door opener in case there's nobody home. If we're lucky, she left the front door unlocked. Or maybe there's an entry code. We need to find her phone immediately to locate next of kin. From what the EMT said about her injuries, this could very well turn into a murder investigation." It was getting late, and they didn't use sirens, but their flashing lights brought out several neighbors as they pulled up in front of 2435. Villegas rang Renee's doorbell, but there was no answer except a burst of furious barking. They tried the door. Locked.

"She must live alone; no one could sleep through that racket." They walked around to the front of the garage. "Yep, here's a keypad," Villegas said. "Let's see if anyone has a door key or code to the garage door. In communities like this, neighbors often have them."

Weatherby nodded. "I'll start over here," she said, indicating the right side of Renee's house. Villegas headed to the left and rang the bell.

After a few moments, a large, rumpled man, his white hair wet and plastered against his head, came to the door barefoot and in a light green terry-cloth bathrobe. He looked very wary. "I saw the lights. What's going on? Why are you here?"

"Sir, pardon the interruption. I'm Detective Villegas, Cactus Heights Police," he said, showing his badge. "And you are?"

"Steve Antonelli. What's happened?"

"Mr. Antonelli, do you have a key to Renee Holden's house or code for her garage door?"

"No," he replied, with a mirthless chuckle, "I certainly don't have either—wouldn't want one, but why? What the hell's going on?"

Ignoring the questions—and the attitude—the detective asked, "Do you know if anyone else around here does?"

"I don't know. Maybe my wife knows. Oh hell," he said, turning his head toward the back of the house. "She just went to bed. I'll see if she's still awake."

A minute later, Steve returned to report, "Molly Levin would. She lives over there," pointing across the street. "She's Holden's friend—takes care of Jessie when Renee's gone."

"Jessie?"

"Her friggin' mutt. The one barking its head off right now—as usual. But what's going on?"

Villegas again ignored his question and headed across the street. "Denise," he called. "I think we've found someone who can help us." Weatherby turned from her conversation with the neighboring Bowers, both of whom had come to the door, excused herself, and joined the detective at Molly's door. The house was totally dark, but the doorbell button was illuminated. Pushing it, they heard the first few notes of Beethoven's Fifth, then after a few minutes, a sleepy female voice: "Just a minute."

Molly came to the door in a short bathrobe, feet bare and her cheek creased from sleep. Her eyes widened at the sight of the two police officers and the flashing lights of the cruiser in Renee's driveway.

"What's going on? Was there a burglary? Is Renee okay? Why are you here?"

"We understand you are a friend of Renee Holden's."

"Yes?"

"Do you have contact information for her next of kin? There doesn't appear to be anyone home. Does she have a husband or...."

The question seemed to jolt Molly wide awake. "Next of kin! No, she doesn't have a husband. Oh my God, has something happened to Renee?"

After a glance at Villegas, who nodded, Weatherby said, "Ms. Holden has had an accident."

"Oh no—with the golf cart? How bad? Is she—"

"No, no," Weatherby said hastily. "She's alive, but she's pretty banged up. It's just standard procedure to let her family know. Do you have telephone numbers for them?" Villegas pulled an electronic tablet out of his pocket and poised his fingers above it.

Molly shook her head. "She doesn't really have any family left. Her father just died. She's divorced, no children; she's an only child."

"Maybe her mother?"

"No, she died last year. Honestly, I don't know any next of kin. Her friends are her family. Oh!" she gasped. "Does Peter know what's happened?"

"Peter?"

"Her...I guess you'd say, uh, boyfriend."

Villegas paused, his fingers still poised above the tablet. "What is Peter's last name? Does he live here in Sunrise Acres?"

"Peter Jackson. Yes, he lives over on Desert Palm Street—1853, I believe."

"Are you sure Ms. Holden has no one else we should notify?"

"Well, she and I've talked about family, so I'm pretty sure she doesn't have any close relatives. Do you have her phone?

Maybe she'd have someone I don't know about listed in her Favorites."

"As far as we know, she didn't have a cell phone with her. I assume she has one?"

"Oh sure. That's weird. She didn't have it with her?"

"Not that we found," Villegas clarified. "Could she have left it at home?"

"I suppose so," Molly said. "She seemed in a terrific hurry when I saw her."

"You saw her? When? Did she say where she was going?"

"No, just that she had what she jokingly referred to as a hot date. She was dressed up and in her golf cart, and was in a big hurry. That's why I thought she'd had an accident in the cart. And because she didn't have her headlights on. It was just a couple hours ago."

Villegas made notes. "Can you be a bit more precise about the time? And place?"

"Okay, but then will you please tell me what happened and how badly she was hurt? A few minutes before eight, I was walking home and she passed me in her golf cart, headed toward the Activity Center. I invited her to come over for a drink and a movie, but that's when she said she had a date. I don't know that she meant that literally," Molly added hastily, looking at Weatherby typing into her electronic tablet. "Maybe she was going to a club meeting or something."

"At eight o'clock at night?" Weatherby sounded skeptical. "I thought everything closed up around here by eight thirty or so."

"Not always," Molly said. She waved her hand at the question as if it were a distracting gnat. "Now. Please. Is Renee okay? Where is she?"

"She's at St. Anne's," Weatherby said. "She'll be.... She's being taken care of."

Villegas asked, "Do you have a key to Ms. Holden's house?"

"No, I use the garage keypad, but...," Molly said tentatively.

"If she left her phone here, we need it; as you say, it could help us locate family. Could you let us in, please?"

"I'd better go in first. Jessie—her dog—knows me."

"Thank you," the detective said. "Sounds like a plan." He then muttered something to himself and Weatherby's eyebrows rose in question. "Jose, ah, did you just say 'coffee can'?"

Villegas smiled a bit apologetically. "Sorry. I said *cave canem,* 'beware of the dog.' I hate big barkers."

"I'll get dressed," Molly said. "Can you tell me what's happened? Can you at least tell me that much?"

"If you could help us get into the house?" Detective Villegas persisted.

"Yes, yes, of course. I'll hurry." She returned a few minutes later in jeans, a T-shirt, and sandals, hastily shoving her phone into a back pocket.

As they approached the garage, Jessie's barking grew more frantic and they could hear her pawing at an inside door. The two detectives looked at each other warily.

"I'll go first," Molly said. "She's not at all dangerous if she knows you."

"Be my guest," Villegas said with a slight smile.

Molly opened the garage and then, cautiously, the door from the garage leading into the house. "Jessie, Jessie," she said. "Quiet, girl. It's okay," she went on in a soothing voice. "It's okay." She slipped inside through the narrow opening, turned on the hall light, and called back, "I'm going to put her back in the garage. She's not real fond of strangers. I'll close the garage door and you can come in through the front."

Molly opened the front door for the two police officers. Jessie's now muffled barking continued.

"Let's see if she left her phone here," Villegas said. "If we don't find it quickly, I'll put a trace on it. Could you turn on some more lights?" He and Molly went into the bedroom.

"Wow, she really was in a hurry," Molly said. There were several piles of clothing on the bed and a towel on the floor. "She's usually very neat." There was a charging station next to the bed, but no phone in it. The detective went into the bathroom and looked around but emerged with a head shake.

"Looks as if she was reading out here," Weatherby called from the family room. She indicated a book open and upside down on the seat of a large black leather recliner. "Here it is!" she said triumphantly, pointing to a black iPhone half buried in the seat cushion.

"Ms. Levin, would you mind retrieving that phone?" When Molly looked puzzled, Villegas explained. "You have access to the house and therefore presumably have Ms. Holden's permission to come inside. You aren't bound by the same rules we are. We have to be very careful we don't violate the laws governing search and seizure. So until such time as we are issued a warrant, you, and only you, are her agent."

"Okay," Molly said. She picked up Renee's phone and examined it. "It probably opens with face recognition. You might have to take it to the hospital and have her look at it."

Villegas shook his head. "Not sure that would work, given her injuries. But I'll call the hospital to check." While he placed the call, he heard Weatherby giving Molly a carefully curated account of what had occurred—that Renee had been found at the bottom of the bell tower steps, unconscious. To Molly's agitated questions about why Renee was in the tower and how she had fallen, Weatherby just kept repeating that they did not know.

Villegas finished his call. "The nurse said it would be impossible for us to put the phone in front of her face for several hours. And even then, she'll be heavily bandaged, so forget face recognition." He turned to Molly. "I don't suppose you know Ms. Holden's password?"

"I could try 'Jessie.' I'm pretty sure it's *i-e*, not *y*," she mumbled to herself as she worked the keyboard. She shook her head as the phone remained closed.

"Guess we'll have to get a warrant," Villegas said. "But I'll leave the phone in your possession in the meantime. Please keep it someplace safe."

"Wait! I know she kept a list of passwords. We talked about that once, whether to use an online app for all passwords or not. I guess you could say we're both old-fashioned—prefer a written list, but in our own kind of code. I'll bet it's in her desk."

She led the two police officers into Renee's study. The desk was a beautifully preserved polished oak antique, with a sliding partition that rolled down to cover a series of cubicles at the back, and a writing surface that slid out, complete with an old-fashioned leather desk pad and gray ink blotter. A shallow drawer ran across the front.

"Wow, a rolltop!" Weatherby exclaimed, earning a bemused glance from Villegas.

Molly looked quickly through the drawer, but it contained nothing but pencils, pens, rulers, and scissors—no papers at all. Next she started sorting through the five cubicles, working from left to right. She pulled out a sheaf of papers from the first cubicle and started to hand it to Weatherby, but the detective shook her head.

"I'm afraid you'll have to handle these for now, ma'am."

Villegas and Weatherby watched Molly hopefully while she systematically searched the cubicles, but she announced there were only old bills, some Christmas cards, and some flyers for various tourist destinations.

"Nothing," she said. "But she has a list of passwords! I know she does."

"Can you think of any other place she might have kept her passwords?" Weatherby asked.

"Wait. Maybe...." Molly lifted up the desk blotter, revealing a typed sheet, covered with handwritten notes and cross-outs.

"That it?" Villegas asked.

"Looks like it." Molly set the sheet down on the desktop so they could all see it. "This is all in her own code."

Villegas could see that each entry included an abbreviation for the account or, in some cases, URLs for websites.

"These must be hints to help her remember the password," Molly said. "And I guess these x's indicate the number of letters or numbers."

"Do you happen to know who 'Doug' is?" Villegas asked. "A lot of these mention him—'title to Doug's favorite song,' and 'Doug's saying about pine knots01.'"

"Yes, that's Renee's father. She often refers to him by his first name," Molly said.

"And he just died, you said?"

Molly nodded, continuing to run her finger down the list. There were also references to book titles, such as "World's best romance novel03," and proverbs or sayings. "WW's line about daffodils123." Villegas assumed the password was constructed from the first letters of the phrases.

Other hints suggested a single word was the password. "Mom's best friend01."

Molly ran a finger down the list of accounts to "Verizon." "Here," she pointed. "That has to be her phone." There was an account number, and after it the password hint: "Shkspr evil sister1."

Both detectives looked puzzled.

"I'm pretty sure the abbreviation is for Shakespeare," Molly said, "but I don't understand the hint. If he had a sister, I have no idea who that is. Let me google it." After a quick search, Molly announced, "Okay, Shakespeare had two sisters, but it doesn't say anything about one of them being 'evil.' Maybe the hint refers to someone in Shakespeare's plays?"

Villegas sighed. "Guess we'll need a warrant after all," he said. "I had hoped we could get a contact for the hospital tonight."

"Wait, I know someone who might be able to figure it out," Molly said. "Mike Landry; he's a retired English professor. He knows a lot about Shakespeare. I'll call him." Villegas started to protest, but she had already punched in a number.

"Would you put that on speaker, please?" Villegas asked.

After a couple of rings, Mike picked up. "Who is this? If this is a damn robot I'll…"

"Mike, it's okay. It's Molly. I'm sorry If I woke you, but I have to get into Renee's phone, and I'm trying to guess her password."

"But why the heck do you—"

"Mike," Molly interrupted, "please. I'll explain later, but right now I need your expertise as an English professor. If we fail, the phone probably locks up after a few tries. We've already tried one."

"Who is 'we'? If it's her phone, where's Renee?"

"Mike, I'm sorry, but it's kind of urgent. I'll call you back in a few minutes and explain everything."

She read out the hint to him. He agreed that "Shkspr" almost certainly meant Shakespeare. "Not the witches," he mumbled. "Weird but not evil." Then he said, louder: "Try 'Regan.' Not the president. You know, from *King Lear*." He spelled it out.

Molly started to enter the digits but stopped suddenly. "It can't be 'Regan.' There are seven *x*'s followed by a one. Mike, is there a seven-letter evil sister?"

Mike mumbled, "*G-o-n*.... Okay, hmm, the other evil sister in *Lear*—well, maybe not evil so much as grasping...."

"Mike, please, who was the other sister?"

"Sorry. Try *G-o-n-e-r-i-l*."

Again, the obnoxious screen shake that indicated failure.

Villegas started to turn away to call a judge for a warrant, but Molly held up her palms. "One more try," she whispered to the detectives. "Mike, I might only have one more try."

"Sorry, I'm fresh out of evil Shakespearean sisters."

Then Molly turned to the page again. "Wait. Some of these clues have 'lc' and others 'uc' before them. The Verizon clue says 'lc.' Could that be 'lowercase'? I spelled 'Goneril' with a capital *G*. Let me try it with all lowercase."

The phone opened to Messages.

"Mike, you are a genius!"

"Now can you tell me what the heck is going on? Why am I having to dredge up Shakespeare characters in the middle of the night?"

"Mike, I'll call you right back, I promise. I just have to finish with the police here."

"The police!" His startled exclamation was cut off as she ended the call.

Molly was staring at Renee's phone with a puzzled look on her face. Weatherby and Villegas crowded in on either side of her.

"There's a text from Peter." She turned the phone so the two detectives could see the message:

Meet me at tower at 8 tonite. Watch city lights come up & stars come out. Have something to discuss. At the bottom was "sent from Peter's iPhone."

"Guess that answers your question about why Ms. Holden was at the tower," Weatherby said.

"We'll have a word with Mr. Jackson," Villegas said. He started for the door, but Weatherby stopped him.

"What about the Favorites on the phone? Ms. Levin could help us with those."

Molly touched the Favorites button. "There aren't many here," she said. "Me, Peter…"

"That's probably Jackson, right?"

Molly nodded.

There were a couple more names of people Molly identified as Sunrise Acres residents. "But I'm not sure who this 'Bert' is. Renee did mention talking with a neighbor in California. It's the same area code as her dad's. So that's probably who it is."

"Not a relative, then?" Villegas said. He read the number on the screen to Weatherby. "It's too late to call tonight, but try first thing tomorrow, tell him about Ms. Holden's *accident*, and see if he knows of anyone else who should be notified."

"Will do," Weatherby said.

"Thanks again for your help," Villegas said to Molly, heading for the door.

Correctly interpreting that as her exit cue, Molly started to follow. "But what about Jessie?" she asked. "I can't leave her in the garage. I guess I'll take her home with me, unless you think Renee will be back tonight."

"Unlikely," he said.

"I need to take all of Jessie's stuff," Molly said. "Her bed, food, toys...and I'll need to get back in to water the plants. Will that be a problem?"

"Can't see that it would be. There's no one to object. Mr. Jackson doesn't live here, right?" At Molly's head shake, he continued out the door.

"I'll lock up," Molly said. "Too much stuff to take tonight. I'll just grab a couple of cans of dog food and Jessie's bed and get the rest tomorrow."

As the detectives pulled out of the driveway, Villegas looked back to see a very large dog dashing out of the garage and instantly relieving itself on a patch of gravel. *If dogs could talk,* he mused, *this one would be saying "ahhhh."*

VILLEGAS

It had been almost three hours since the assault on Renee Holden when Detective Villegas rang Peter Jackson's doorbell. After a few minutes and a second ring, a light went on toward the back of the house. When he arrived at the door a minute or so later, Peter's bare feet poked out from a pair of jeans, and he wore a plain white T-shirt. He turned on the porch light, leaned on the screen door jamb, and peered at the two police officers.

Weatherby gave Villegas an involuntary startled look. Villegas betrayed no emotion at the appearance of a tall, scowling Black man. "Mr. Jackson?"

"Yes," Peter said groggily. "And it's *Doctor* Jackson. What's going on?"

"We'd like to talk with you for a few minutes."

Peter glanced automatically at his bare wrist. "What time is it?"

Weatherby looked at her phone. "Almost eleven."

"How about waiting until a decent hour?" Peter's voice had a definite edge.

"Sorry it's so late, sir, but It's about Renee Holden."

Peter's eyes widened. "Renee?" The significance of two police officers showing up at his doorstep that late at night seemed to have suddenly hit him. He opened the screen door and stepped back, now fully alert, his scowl instantly replaced with alarm. "Is she okay? What happened?"

"If we could come in?" Villegas asked.

"Of course, but please...why are you here? Has something happened to Renee?" Peter looked frantically from Villegas to Weatherby.

~

"Let's all sit down," Villegas said, motioning to the living room chair and couch.

Peter sat down heavily in the nearest chair, a black leather recliner that belched under his weight. "Please," he said again.

At a nod from Villegas, Weatherby opened her notebook. "Dr. Jackson, can you tell us how you spent this evening?"

"Tonight? Poker game. With friends. What has this got to do with Renee? For God's sake, you're scaring me. Tell me, is she okay? What's happened?"

Villegas pulled out his notes. "We just saw Ms. Holden's phone," he said. "At seven fifteen tonight, she received a text from your phone. Detective Weatherby, would you please read it to Dr. Jackson?" As she read the brief message, Villegas focused on Peter's face.

When Villegas got to the signature, Peter looked totally bewildered. "What the hell? I didn't send that."

"Would it be all right with you if we could see your phone, sir?"

"Sure. You'll see I didn't send any texts to Renee." Peter

returned from his bedroom with an iPhone. He turned it on, held it to his face to open, and handed it to Villegas, who scrolled through the texts and then silently handed the phone to Weatherby, who scanned the recent texts, then returned it to the other detective.

"Dr. Jackson, with your permission, we'd like to hang on to the phone for a while," Villegas said.

Peter looked stricken. "You're taking my phone?"

"Sir, we cannot compel you to surrender your phone. We are asking your permission."

"Well, what if I refuse?"

"And why would you do that?"

"Because it's my phone! How long could *you* go without…. It's got everything…." He looked at their grim faces and his shoulders slumped in surrender. "Never mind. When will I get it back? How long will it take your people to figure out that I never sent that text?"

"Thank you for your cooperation. I will ask that they expedite. Maybe a couple of days? I'm sorry, but I'm afraid I have to ask you for your access code, Dr. Jackson. I promise you that it will be kept confidential, but when we return the phone you should of course change the password," said Villegas.

Peter waved his hand in dismissal. "Okay, okay. But what about Renee? You can't just sit here and ask me questions without telling me what's happened. She's…very important to me." He took a deep breath and asked shakily, "Is she…? " He couldn't finish the question.

"No, she's alive," Villegas said.

Rather than reassuring him, the cryptic response alarmed Peter more. "She's hurt? Badly?"

Villegas continued to ignore his questions. "Tell us about the poker game you were at."

"No, damn it. I'm not answering any more of your questions until you answer mine," Peter said angrily. "What's happened to Renee?"

"Okay," Villegas said. "She's had an accident. She fell down the stairs at the bell tower and she's been taken to St. Anne's."

"Wait...the tower? She went to the tower?" Peter shook his head as if to clear it. "That message," he said. "She thought I sent her that message." He sat staring at them without focusing on their faces, apparently struggling to put the pieces of the puzzle together. "And she fell...." He sat silently for a few moments, then suddenly straightened up in the chair. "That's why you wanted to know where I was earlier. You think I was there at the tower? That I saw her accident?" His face cleared as he appeared to see the logic in their questions. The two policemen's faces showed no reaction.

"I wasn't there," Peter said. "Our poker game started about seven thirty—maybe a bit later—and I got home about ten and went straight to bed."

"How do you explain the message from your phone?" Villegas asked.

"I can't explain it, except to say that I didn't send it. We haven't been..." Peter paused before continuing, "I couldn't have met her there—I was playing poker. So why would I ask her to meet me? And if you think I did send it, and then deleted it, well, you have my phone. Your technicians can confirm that I didn't delete a message."

"Thanks, we'll be sure to have them to do that," Villegas said. "Now, who else was at the poker game? Contact info?" Peter retrieved his Sunrise Acres directory and gave Villegas the names, phone numbers, and addresses. The detective recorded the information in his tablet.

"Would they be able to swear that you were there the entire time?"

"Sure," Peter said. "Now, I've got to get to the hospital. Renee will need me."

Villegas stood. "They won't be able to let you see her," he said. "You aren't family, right?"

"No, but I've got to be there. She doesn't have any family. They'll have to tell me something. She'll tell them to let me in." Peter rose. He walked to the door and held it open in an obvious invitation to bring the interview to a close.

Villegas and Weatherby both stood but made no effort to leave. "Just to be sure. You did not leave the poker game for any reason, for any length of time—and these three men will confirm that."

"Yes, yes," Peter said impatiently. Then he stopped as if struck by a thought and seemed to be about to speak. He shook his head slightly and closed his mouth.

"Yes?" Villegas prompted him. "Something you forgot?"

"Yes. I just remembered," Peter said quietly. "I was supposed to bring the beer, so I drove home to get a couple of six-packs."

"In your car?"

"No, my golf cart. But I was gone for just a few minutes, and what difference does it make? I didn't send that message, I wasn't at the tower, and I didn't see Renee's accident. I'm not a witness. I have to go!"

Villegas and Weatherby exchanged a significant look. "What time was that?" Villegas asked. "When you went to get the beer?"

Peter was opening the door again. He gave an exasperated sigh. "I don't know exactly. Soon after Hal Avery arrived, and we realized Jerry only had a couple of bottles. Maybe about eight o'clock or so? Look, I really can't help you and I have got to get to the hospital. You said St. Anne's?"

"We'd like you to come down to the station tomorrow morning," Villegas said. "It's pretty late now, how about eight o'clock?"

"Why? I told you I wasn't there, I don't know how she fell. I can't help you."

"Tomorrow morning at eight, sir," Villegas said firmly. "Shall we send a car for you?"

"Hell no, I can find my own way." Peter closed the door after they left with almost a slam.

"Just out of curiosity," Weatherby said to Villegas as they got in the cruiser. "Why did you tell him it was an accident?"

"I wanted to watch his face," Villegas said. "And did you see it? He looked relieved when he thought he was being asked about witnessing an *accident*. Maybe he thinks he got away with assaulting her."

"If they're a couple," Weatherby offered, "why wouldn't she know that he was playing poker and couldn't meet?"

Villegas smiled. "Good question. I hadn't thought of that, but you're right. Let's be sure to ask Jackson about that tomorrow. See just how much of a 'couple' they are. Just buddies or—"

"Friends with benefits?" Weatherby contributed. "Jose, are we going to check with these three guys about when Jackson was away from the poker game?"

"Yeah, but we can put that off until tomorrow. I'll get Sarah Partridge to help me interview Jackson again at eight o'clock. We need to push him on that alibi. Denise, how about if you interview the poker players." He looked at the list on his pad. "Jerry Saperstein, Hal Avery, and Marek Novotny. When you talk to them, push a bit. See if you pick up anything. Seems pretty convenient that running out of beer coincided with the time of the assault." He spelled the names for her and texted her the addresses. "You know what to ask."

"Sure," Weatherby said. "When Jackson left and how long he was gone."

Villegas nodded and turned to get out of the cruiser before wheeling back to add, "Oh, and be sure to ask each of them if he recalls what Jackson was wearing, both before he left for the beer and when he returned."

"Hey, Jose? I got it." The "I've been a detective longer than you" was implied. But Weatherby's tone was typically mild; it was clear she hadn't taken offense.

Villegas gave a rare smile and shook his head. "Sorry, Denise. Guess that's what you'd call micromanaging."

Weatherby chuckled. "Maybe that's what *you'd* call it. But if Rasmussen pulled that kind of shit with me, he'd get a more colorful response. Now, I would never call *you* a bossy prick...." She drove off toward the station.

Villegas stared after her, wondering where the fine line lay between giving too many and too few instructions to colleagues. He knew he was inclined to be "detail oriented," according to one of the many psychological profiles he'd undergone both for seminary and the police academy. But how could he be sure the other members of the team would think of all the items on his mental list? And if they didn't, wasn't getting the investigation done right more important than skirting around tender egos?

And speaking of tender egos, Jackson was as prickly as a desert cholla. I wonder how many African Americans there are in Sunrise. Darn few, I'll bet. So Jackson would stand out. I don't know if that makes us suspect him more—or less.

34

______

MIKE

July 10: Day Two

It took Mike a couple of hours and half an Ambien to get back to sleep after Molly called to explain the distressing events: Renee's accident, the decoding of Renee's phone password, and the strange text from Peter. Consequently, Mike didn't arrive at Molly's house until almost ten the next morning to haul Jessie's supplies from Renee's garage.

"Thank you, Mike. Renee buys dog food in Costco sizes —huge bags of dry food and cases of cans," Molly explained. "I may not need it all here, of course, but I got the feeling from the police that Renee is going to be hospitalized for quite a while, and I don't want to trot back and forth across the street every time I need to feed Jessie."

"Is there any word on Renee's condition?" Mike asked.

"I called first thing when I got up this morning. All the woman answering the phone would tell me was that she had been brought in last night and was still there. But she wouldn't give out any information about her condition except to family. I pleaded for more, and she transferred me to a nurses' station, but no luck there either. 'I'm sorry, can't talk to non-family, blah blah.' I briefly considered posing as a sister, but I was afraid she'd call my bluff."

"Then how are we going to find out anything? Peter won't get any further than you did," Mike said.

Just then Molly's landline phone rang. She hesitated. "I don't recognize the number, and it's usually junk on this line, but maybe it's about Renee." She picked up and switched to speaker so Mike could hear.

Peter didn't let Molly get past "hello." The words poured out. "Molly, have you found out anything about Renee? I have to use this damn burner phone. The cops took mine. I spent hours at St. Anne's and nobody would tell me anything. I thought maybe someone with a less, uh, tropical complexion might get some information. Are you home? Of course you are. Sorry, too much coffee."

"No, Peter, I didn't get anywhere either. Listen, Mike's here. Can you come over? You sound like you need some TLC."

"What I need is answers. And someone to vent on. You wouldn't believe what the cops have just put me through. I'll be right there."

Peter arrived unshaven and pale with fatigue. His red golf shirt was heavily wrinkled and there was a long brown stain down the front. The hand holding the cup of decaf coffee Molly offered him was trembling and his eyes were bloodshot.

"The cops woke me up last night practically at midnight, took my phone, and then ordered me to come down to the station for more questioning, at eight this morning, before I'd even had breakfast. And no one— nurses, doctors, cops—will tell me how Renee is," Peter said angrily. "I kept telling them at the hospital that I'm the closest thing to family that she has, but they keep citing HIPAA at me."

"I know," Molly said. "They did the same with me. I get that they have to protect people's privacy, but you'd think that act would make allowances for close friends when there's no family. I'm going to try again later. Peter, I got bagels. Please eat something."

While they ate a desultory meal, Peter continued to vent. "Last night, the way they talked, I thought they wanted to talk to me in case I saw Renee's accident. But this morning—hell, they acted as if I'd pushed her! And I guess Renee's still unconscious, so they can't ask her any questions. That's about all I could get out of them about her condition. I mean, I don't see how they could suspect me of doing anything last night, even if they're clueless enough to think I'd ever hurt her. I was sitting in for Brett on the Tuesday night poker game from about seven thirty until around ten. But this detective Villegas kept going over and over the same ground, questioning me about where I was every minute and even why Renee didn't know I was at the game.

"I wasn't about to go into details about our breakup, just kept telling him that we haven't exactly been keeping close tabs on each other lately. Anyway, I don't normally play Tuesday night. Brett's wife got stung by a scorpion just before dinner last night. She moved some boards in the garage without gloves and.... So he called me from the ER, begging me to substitute at the last minute. It's not fun to play poker with just three guys, so Brett was feeling bad about not going. I explained all this to the cops—at least three times."

"No breaks?" Mike asked.

"I dashed home to get some beer," Peter said. "When

Brett asked me to sub for him, maybe he mentioned that it was his turn to bring it, but it didn't register at the time."

"When did you go get the beer?" Mike asked.

"I don't know exactly. Pretty soon after we started playing, when we realized there were only two or three cans in the fridge. On a night like that, even with air-conditioning everyone was thirsty. Maybe eight or eight fifteen. The police kept pushing me about that—how long I was gone. Couldn't have been more than twenty or twenty-five minutes or so, maybe eight to ten minutes each way in the golf cart. The beer was right in my garage refrigerator. I didn't even have to go into the house. They asked a lot of idiotic questions, like did I have a cooler in the car. I think that detective was trying to trick me by asking about the car. But I told them I used the golf cart, and no, I didn't use a cooler. This morning, they went out and looked over the golf cart. And then they came to the house and searched the car. Not sure what they thought they'd find. I could have made them get a warrant, but that would have just made them more suspicious. They kept harping on that damn text to Renee. I didn't send it; it couldn't have come from my phone. I had it with me all night. I showed them the phone—no text messages sent since about four o'clock yesterday afternoon, when I texted my grandson. But they took the phone. Guess they thought I'd just deleted it. It just makes me so angry. Frigging police! I'm so damned worried about Renee.

"Why would I possibly want to hurt her? I know, we've had this big argument, but.... Oh God, how stupid I've been! Molly, she must have told you? We had this awful row. My fault. I just wouldn't listen, too wrapped up in my.... What if...what if I don't get the chance...." He buried his head in his hands.

"Hey, don't think that way," Molly said. "She's strong;

she'll come through this. And since you didn't send the text to her phone, the police'll be able to confirm that. You can't permanently delete messages without leaving a trace."

"Then who did? And how could it come from my phone?"

"It didn't," Mike said. "Someone could have sent it from a different phone or even from a computer and made it appear it came from your phone."

"That's possible?"

"'Fraid so," Mike said. "It's called 'spoofing,' and it's not that hard. There are websites that show how to do it. We were talking about it at a book club meeting a few months ago when we were discussing a new book on cybercrime."

"Actually," Peter said, "that makes me feel a little better. Not that someone tricked Renee, but that it wasn't my fault she was at the tower and had the accident. But the police better have someone confirm it wasn't me who sent it or I'll sue their asses. And I want my damn phone back! I know how they operate."

Molly shot Mike a puzzled look at Peter's last comment. "Uh, what do you mean?" Mike asked.

"I've had plenty of dealings with police before," Peter said. "They jump first and look afterward. See what they expect to see. And believe me, when you're Black, that's all they see—what color your skin is. It's been that way all my life. When I was sixteen, just got my license, I was driving my dad's new Chevy, delivering a quilt my grandma had finished for a lady in this posh neighborhood. All big custom-built houses, big green lawns. In Oakland, for God's sake! Nobody skimped on water in those days, if they were rich. Anyway, I rang the doorbell and stood there on the porch while she looked through the window and decided whether or not to answer the door. I held up the quilt so she could see it and she called out, 'Leave it on the porch swing,' as if she was afraid I'd jump her if she opened the door. So I was in a pretty piss-poor mood leaving the house. And then, as I drove away, was a few doors down the street, this police car comes up behind me and blasts the siren for me to pull over.

"The guy all but accused me of casing the houses, asked me why I was driving so slow, called me 'Boy.' When he told me to get out of the car, I kind of lost it and said something about it not being against the law to drive slowly as far as I knew—unless you were Black.

"That made him furious. He slammed me up against the car so hard it cracked a rib. God, I can still hear his voice right up against my ear. I won't even tell you some of the things he said—some of the grossest threats I've ever heard, called me a nigger, of course. He said he could shoot me right there for resisting arrest and no one would even blame him.

"Now these cops here have got it in their heads that I attacked Renee and they won't let go. They probably aren't even looking for whoever did this. And they'll pounce like a cat on a bug if they find *anything* in a background check...."

"Well, maybe the police have gotten a bit less racist since...." Mike's voice trailed off as he saw the disgusted and disappointed look on Peter's face. "Look, we know you wouldn't hurt Renee," he said hastily, "and I'm counting on Molly to find out how she's doing. Molly will find someone who knows a nurse or someone in the hospital. She's really good at getting information." He gripped Peter's shoulder reassuringly for a moment as they walked to the door. "Maybe the spoof was supposed to be a joke or something and she fell accidentally."

Peter shook his head, unconvinced. "You didn't hear

them. They're certain she was shoved. And if I find out who did it...," he added angrily as he wrenched the door open and strode to his car.

MIKE WATCHED Peter's tire-screeching departure. *Man, he is in bad shape*, Mike thought. *A lot of anger, a lot of guilt—what if she doesn't make it? No wonder he feels like hell.*

When Mike got back inside, Molly was standing with her phone up to her ear, looking dumbfounded. She held up a finger, asking him to wait. Then she said quietly, "Thanks," and put the phone down, shaking her head in disbelief. "You are not going to believe what the nurse I finally got through to just told me."

"Tell me," Mike said.

"I asked about Renee, and as usual she said they couldn't tell me anything—could only tell family. But when I said that she didn't have any family, only friends, the nurse corrected me. She said Renee does have family, that the doctor talked with her sister just a couple of hours ago and that I should get the report from her. I was incredulous, and I told her she doesn't have.... Well, anyway, the nurse was a bit miffed. She said something like, 'I know that's what her friends who've been calling say—no family. I'm surprised you don't know about the sister. She lives right in Sunrise Acres.' I couldn't imagine who she meant, so I just asked. She said, 'Her name is Betsy.' I could hear a few keystrokes on her computer. 'Betsy Rausch!'"

"What the heck?"

"Betsy must have done what I was tempted to do— pretend to be a family member to get some information. But

I would have expected her to tell me. I'll call her and see what she found out."

"Wait a sec," Mike said. "Maybe we should think a little about this. First of all, how did she find out about the accident so fast? And then why would she pretend to be a family member?"

"Yeah, I was wondering the same thing about how she found out. Has the news spread that fast? I'll have to ask her about that and also why she'd lie to the hospital—not that I wouldn't do the same thing if I thought I could get away with it! But I suppose she just wanted to get information about Renee's condition. I thought I was the queen of chutzpah here, but Betsy has me beat."

"Okay, but why sister? Wouldn't she have to prove it?"

"I wouldn't think so. How would you prove you were a family member if you had a different last name? I think you probably just have to sound convincing. I still think I could have done it myself, but I'm a really bad liar, especially in person. My face turns red."

"Nice to know," Mike said with a grin. "Okay, I guess we can just ask her. She may be mad that we know about her little subterfuge, but the important thing is to see what she found out. I told Peter I thought you could get some info."

Molly put the phone on speaker as she called, and told Betsy that Mike was also in the room. When she explained the reason for the call, Betsy sounded angry.

"I didn't expect the nurse to tell everyone about me! Seems as if that should be private."

"I was tempted to try the same thing," Molly said, "but I wouldn't have been as convincing. So, how did you find out what happened?"

"Oh, uh, I was at the gym early this morning and people were talking about the big scene with the police and ambulance and everything last night. But nobody really knew anything. So I went to the hospital to find out."

"Well, what did they tell you? Peter is going crazy with anxiety, and so are we."

There was a pause at the other end of the line before Betsy said, softening a bit, "She's in bad shape. She's in a coma—induced, I think. They had to operate for a subdural hematoma."

"Oh God, no, that's horrible! A coma? We were really hoping for better news. What's the operation for? Removing a blood clot?"

"I don't think so. From what they told me, it's a big bubble of blood and it was putting pressure on her brain, so they needed to drain it. She's in the ICU and no one is allowed to visit. They wouldn't let me even look in."

"How long will she be in the coma?"

"A few days at least. They'll know more this afternoon after some tests they're doing."

"They'll let you talk to the doctor?" At the short "yes" in response, Molly added, "What if they find out you aren't really her sister?"

"That won't happen," Betsy said firmly.

35

VILLEGAS

This meeting is unlikely to go smoothly, Detective Jose Villegas warned himself as he walked toward the squad room where the Holden case team of four was to meet. He mentally reviewed possible sources of incoming artillery. Villegas knew he needed to project a careful balance between his authority as the lead detective in the case and his lack of seniority. Sarah Partridge was unlikely to challenge, as she was a relative newcomer to the Cactus Heights police force and a patrol officer. But both Rasmussen and Weatherby had been on board longer than Villegas and both were also detectives.

Weatherby and I worked together reasonably companionably last night, although Denise did make it clear she resented my reminder about checking if Jackson changed clothes. But if ill winds blow, they will come from Rasmussen. I know he dislikes me, and it seems personal. Villegas was tempted to believe Rasmussen's attitude originated from a bias against Hispanics. *Or gays. Or gay Hispanics?* He caught himself. *Watch out for the chips on your own shoulder.*

Maybe, he smiled to himself, *you're looking for bias when it's just that you're obnoxious in some way.* That thought in turn brought to mind his husband's reminders about a tendency to be self-critical: "Remember, Jose—the Catholic order you almost joined didn't encourage either hair shirts or self-flagellation!" No matter the source of the animus, Rasmussen was sure to resent the less experienced upstart being put in charge of an important case. *Well, I can't change that, even if I wanted to.*

The squad room used for training and meetings was too large for such a small team, but Villegas's cubicle was impossibly small and the one conference room was too often occupied to count on when needed. Personnel were so scattered these days because of forest fires and protests that the squad room was rarely used. And it had the advantage of lots of wall space for charting progress in the case.

The officers filed in, Partridge predictably first and, just as reliably, Rasmussen last. They set up folding chairs from the large rack in one corner. The room showed the wear of the almost four decades since the station was built. The walls had been recently painted an off-white, but the pale-yellow floor tiles were chipped and cracked in many places and the grout was almost black from years of traffic. A yard-wide band of newer, mismatching mustard-colored tile ran along one side under the windows, where some long-forgotten repair had necessitated taking up and replacing the floor.

As the four officers settled in, Villegas started populating with photos the large bulletin board that ran ten feet along one wall. He had cleared the board of all notices, including some that were curling and yellowing, the detritus from old HR initiatives, announcements of promotions, and some long-solved—or abandoned?—cases.

In the center of the expanse, he pinned up a photo of

Renee before the attack—one Weatherby had found on the Sunrise Acres Pickleball Club website. Weatherby had enlarged the full-length shot of her in front of the court net, paddle raised to her shoulders. The ball cap covering her hair—looked like she was a San Francisco Giants fan—was pushed back slightly, revealing her face. But the day must have been cloudy, because she was barely squinting. She was relaxed, smiling broadly, almost laughing at the camera —a very attractive woman, vibrant, fully alive. Villegas murmured a short benediction as he secured the bottom of the photo with pushpins. *She will need everyone's prayers to survive.*

Not for the first time in his chosen work, he thought about the debates he and his young colleagues in seminary had had about the nature of evil. It was not an abstract concept to him anymore. The task before him was a heavy cloak wrapped around his shoulders, weighing him down. He thought of the passage from Ecclesiastes: *And some there be, which have no memorial; who are perished, as though they had never been; and are become as though they had never been born....*

It is up to me to find justice for this woman. I will not forget you until I find it, he vowed to her portrait.

To one side of Renee's photo he put up a photo of Peter Jackson, obtained from the same website. The others watched him in puzzled silence. To Villegas's surprise, Weatherby was the first to challenge him. "Uh, Jose, I set up a SharePoint website for us, you know. We can use that as a kind of central repository—photos, interviews. It'd be much more efficient to put stuff in there."

Rasmussen snorted. "Yeah, like we'd run out here every time we wanted to add something to the case files."

"No, I'm not a complete Luddite," Villegas said. "The

SharePoint site will be our main, uh, repository. I've already posted the notes from Denise's and my interview with Jackson. But SharePoint gives us a kind of linear view of the case —hard to keep in mind an overall picture of the people involved and their relationships. If we are given more officers to help, they can come in here and get an overview at a glance." This assault was already the most serious crime Cactus Heights had seen in several years—and Villegas was mindful that it could soon become a murder case. *And I want us to keep a vivid picture of our victim in mind.*

Weatherby looked skeptical, but said nothing more.

Rasmussen was more vocal. "So who's going to keep the church bulletin board up to date?" he asked sarcastically.

Villegas turned his back on the group, wondering if the snide emphasis on "church" meant Rasmussen's antipathy had something to do with Villegas's Catholic faith. He very deliberately shoved a pin into a second enlarged photo of Renee Holden, definitely not smiling in this one, but unconscious and bleeding, sprawled at the bottom of the bell tower stairs. "I will," he said quietly.

He turned back to Rasmussen. "Terry, what did you find out at the hospital?"

A few seconds passed. "Ah, I caught Ms. Holden's surgeon just before she went in to relieve the pressure of a…" Rasmussen made a show of scrolling down on his tablet to retrieve his electronic notes, "subdural hematoma. There were some fragments of what looks like brick in the hair they shaved off before her operation." He glanced up from the tablet. "The crime scene guys found similar hair and fragments on the stairs she fell down. I sent the one from the hospital to the lab and they'll get back to us, probably sometime today, but it looks like a brick was the attack weapon."

"We didn't find it at the crime scene," Partridge added.

"Okay." Villegas absently scratched the side of his head, looking at the board. "Potential suspects." He pointed to the photo of Peter. "Peter Jackson. Denise and I interviewed him in his home last night and Sarah and I talked with him again here this morning."

Villegas started to review why Jackson was a person of interest but Rasmussen waved him off. "Yeah, Denise told me about Jackson's text on Ms. Holden's phone."

"Of course, he denied sending it," Villegas said. "And it wasn't in his Sent file. But we have his phone, and the lab will determine if he just deleted it."

"Pretty dumb move, if he's the guy who shoved her down the stairs," Rasmussen observed.

Villegas ignored the interruption and continued. "We inspected both his car and golf cart this morning, again with his permission, took swabs, no blood residue. Denise has been looking into his alibi."

Weatherby took up the narrative. "His alibi is a poker game with three other players, but he'd gone home, allegedly to get beer, right around the time of the assault."

"Let's hear about what the other players had to say. Denise, did you get hold of the host, Jerry..." Villegas checked his own electronic notes with a sly sideways glance at Rasmussen to make sure he saw the use of the tablet, "Saperstein?"

"Yeah, caught him just as he was about to tee off on the Sunrise course," Weatherby said. "He confirms that he forgot he was low on beer. 'Senior moment,' he said. Jackson said he was supposed to bring some and forgot, and volunteered to go back and bring a couple of six-packs. Saperstein said he wasn't sure how long Jackson was gone, but thought it was about twenty, twenty-five minutes—time enough for three or four hands. He was on a hot streak, said with only three players the games went fast. Said his quarters were piling up." Weatherby glanced around at the others with a grin. "Guess he doesn't have senior moments when he's winning."

Villegas cleared his throat discreetly but deliberately. "So, his point was that Jackson couldn't have been gone too long?"

"Um, sorry. Correct. Jackson got back, they played poker and drank beer until about ten, when the game broke up."

"Sheesh! A poker game that ends at ten o'clock?" Rasmussen laughed. "What kind of game is that?"

"A game for people who get up at five a.m. in the summer," Villegas said. "Remember, this is *Sunrise* Acres." He continued, "Did Saperstein have any recollection of what Jackson was wearing? Any chance he changed clothes?"

"I asked, but he said he really wasn't paying attention to his clothes. Said his focus had to be on his cards. Apparently, Jackson is a helluva poker player. Saperstein said they'd all be broke if Jackson was one of their regulars. 'Really smart and bluffs like a pro,' according to Saperstein."

"Hm, interesting," Villegas said. "Did you get to the other two guys?"

"Yeah, Avery and Novotny. They said about the same thing. Jackson was gone about twenty minutes, came back with cold beer, they didn't notice anything different about his clothes."

"Did you pick up any vibes that any of these guys might not be telling the whole truth?" Rasmussen asked.

"Well," said Weatherby, "Saperstein was nervous, of course, being rousted by a cop while he was on the golf course with his buddies, but no. He looks a lot older than Jackson, probably over ninety. Amazing he's still golfing. I just don't think he has it in him to make up an elaborate story, particularly given his 'senior moments.' Same with Novotny and Avery. Aside from a little nervousness, they both cooperated, seemed on the level. And unless they talked to one another beforehand to get their stories straight, which I sincerely doubt, they were pretty much in agreement."

"One more thing," Villegas said. "I have a recording I'd like you to hear. The guy who called the nine-one-one in said Ms. Holden tried to tell him something before she passed out entirely. Here's what he thought he heard." Villegas turned the volume on his phone high, and the team members clustered around.

"She tried to say something twice and I got my ear right down by her mouth, but I don't hear that well and she was struggling to breathe. The first time, it sounded like 'puh.' And the second time it was different—sounded like 'ee-yuh' to me."

"'Pee-ter!'" Rasmussen said. "That's what she was trying to say."

"Could be 'puh-lease,'" Partridge said. "She would be asking this guy to help her."

Rasmussen scoffed. "Damn clear to me. She's telling us who attacked her."

"Seems to me," Weatherby said slowly, "even if she was trying to say 'Peter,' doesn't mean much. She was planning to meet him. Naturally, he'd be top of her mind."

"Okay," Villegas said. "I'll upload it to the team site and we'll keep after Jackson; we need to know more about him and his relationship with Ms. Holden. Denise, that'll be yours. Check for priors, of course, but also any other background info that might be useful." Weatherby nodded.

"What if our vic dies?" Rasmussen asked bluntly. "Would Jackson inherit?"

"We can't be sure until we find a will," Villegas said. "I assume she has one. Would be kind of odd for a lawyer not to. But she and Jackson aren't married and live separately, so he's not likely to be her heir. And he's well off himself. If she died intestate and without relatives, it's my understanding that the state gets everything."

"So unless he's in the will, he'd have no incentive to do away with her," Partridge commented.

"Right. At least no financial incentive. We do need to see that will."

Rasmussen pulled on one ear and shook his head. "Plenty of other reasons to try and kill a girlfriend."

"Is that the voice of experience, Terry?" Weatherby teased.

Rasmussen didn't take the bait. "Just.... This guy's alibi looks too pat. And he's no dummy." The big detective got up and lumbered toward the door, throwing his final comment over his shoulder. "I still like him for it."

36

MOLLY

July 11: Day Three

"Mike!" Molly glanced at the Caller ID on her ringing phone. "It's that Detective Villegas I met night before last—the one who's been harassing Peter. Should I answer?" They were sitting on his back patio under the awning after lunch, eyeing a particularly promising black cloud and considering a rain dance to encourage some more precipitation.

"Sure, pick up," he said hastily.

"He wants me to come down to the station as soon as possible," she said after clicking off.

"I'll go with you. If you don't mind," he added after a moment.

Good catch, Molly thought. *Without that little addition, I might accuse you of typical male overprotectiveness.* But her response gave no hint of her internal musings.

"Fine with me. He said he wanted to get more 'background' on Renee and thought I could help, since I'm one of her best friends. Maybe we can convince him to lay off Peter."

THE CACTUS HEIGHTS police station was a one-story stucco building, its architecture harkening back to the days of a smaller town and modest construction budgets. Its mauve paint blended in with the surrounding buildings as unobtrusively as a chameleon. Only the large sign above the doorway revealed its identity. Inside, however, visitors would be swiftly disabused of any notion that they were entering a commercial establishment. The receptionist, whose name tag identified her as "Maria," sat behind a sliding glass window that faced the door. She checked a list and nodded pleasantly at Molly.

"Right on time," she said approvingly. "But," she looked at Mike, "I don't think Detective Villegas is expecting anyone else. Is this your lawyer?"

Molly gaped. "My lawyer? Why would I need....We're just here to give some background information about Renee Holden's accident."

"Sorry," Maria said to her before turning to Mike. "You are...?"

"Mike Landry. We're good friends of Renee's—and we think we can be helpful to Detective Villegas."

"Let me just check," Maria said, reaching for the phone.

"Good thing she asked you," Molly whispered. "I couldn't have told her you were a good friend of Renee's—at least not without turning beet red at the lie. You hardly know Renee!"

"He'll see you both," Maria announced, just as a large man came through the front door. He was dressed in an open-necked black shirt and a wine-colored sports coat so straining to contain his muscles that he looked like an overripe eggplant threatening to burst. "Detective Rasmussen," she said to him. "Could you take these visitors to Detective Villegas?"

Rasmussen did not look pleased at the request, but he nodded. "Sure." After Maria buzzed open the metal door to their left, Rasmussen pointed down the hall: "Third door on the left." He did not offer to accompany them but wheeled about as if on parade and walked back out.

"Are all the police that big?" Mike asked, looking after Rasmussen with something like awe.

"No, you'll see. I met Detective Villegas night before last," Molly reminded him. "He's a little shorter than you. Nice looking."

When they entered the hallway, Detective Villegas stuck his head out of the detectives' room and waved them in.

"Thanks for coming down," he said, heading down the aisle between cubicles. "Would you like some coffee? I can't really recommend the Mister Coffee brew," he added. "It's melted the braces off some of our young overnight guests. But we do have an espresso machine given to us by a grateful citizen. And I believe I'm the only one who's figured out how to use it." He paused a moment to receive their response to the offer, but both declined. The cubicle he directed them to was small, barely large enough for his desk and two straight-backed chairs. The walls of the cubicle were bare except for one photo of him shaking hands with a tall man in police uniform and a military crew cut who seemed to be congratulating Villegas.

"You have holding cells here for your, uh, overnight guests?" Mike asked, looking over his shoulder at the other doors in the hall.

"Our holding cells are over there," Villegas said, gesturing vaguely over his shoulder. "Drunk tank and the occasional bar fight loser. Or winner. Anyone in serious trouble gets transferred to the County, usually within twenty-four hours. Crime here is mostly property damage or loss. Parties. Kids."

"So," Mike said, "not a lot of major crimes?"

Molly shot him a warning glance. Detective Villegas might see the question as implying an inability to handle this case.

Villegas's response sounded a trifle defensive but was offered in a pleasant tone. "We're a small but well-trained unit, and we keep up to date. We're cross-trained, so we can cover for each other. You're basically right, though—this terrible incident is unusual for Cactus Heights."

Molly intervened to change topics. "I...we are both very concerned about Renee, and I was pleased to get your call. We want to help any way we can. Between the two of us, we can probably answer questions you have about Sunrise Acres. And, of course, about Renee. And if we can't, we'll know someone who can."

"Well, I appreciate that. Since you do know the community—and Ms. Holden—so well, you could save us a lot of time."

"So accidents like Renee's are unusual?" Molly asked.

The detective hesitated and Mike jumped in. "The 'terrible incident' wasn't an accident, was it?"

"What makes you think that?" Detective Villegas sat up straighter, looking like a bird suddenly spotting prey.

Ignoring the detective's question, Mike said, "Detective Villegas, as you say, we know the community, we know the people—or can easily find out about them. For example, it might take you a while to find out how athletic Renee is; she has good reflexes. Seems odd that she didn't catch herself by the railing if she tripped or stumbled."

Molly could see neither confirmation nor contradiction

in the detective's laser-like gaze. To her discomfort, Mike pressed on. "And you've been grilling Peter Jackson. Why would you do that if it were an accident?"

The policeman said nothing.

At least he isn't kicking us out, Molly thought.

Mike continued, "So, are you treating this as an accident, or...?" His voice trailed off.

Detective Villegas looked at them, his face still giving away nothing. Finally, he asked, "If you think it wasn't an accident, you must have some suspicions about who had a motive to harm Ms. Holden."

"Not really," Molly said, shifting uncomfortably in her chair.

"I think you do," Villegas said, turning to Mike.

"It's not so much that we have a bunch of likely suspects. Neither of us likes the idea of pointing fingers at anyone," Mike said. "But we do think you need to look beyond Peter. He loves Renee and has no motive that we can think of to hurt her." Mike stole a quick glance at Molly, who continued to look steadily at Villegas. "He's really concerned about her."

"And?" Villegas persisted, a suggestion of irritation creeping into his voice. "Allow me to rephrase. Who dislikes her? Who might have it in for her? Who benefits from her death? *Cui bono?*" Mike smiled, but Molly found the detective's Latin disconcerting. At their continued silence, each looking at the other to speak, Villegas, with a small but audible sigh, continued: "Let me ask you this: Has Ms. Holden had any arguments that you know of with anyone in the community?"

Mike and Molly both smiled. "Yes—quite a few. She's a bit, well, prickly, argumentative," Molly volunteered. "She's had little spats with other people. But nothing worth talking about. Disputes at pickleball, that sort of thing." *Not exactly the whole truth,* Molly thought a bit guiltily. *Pretty big spats with Peter and with the Antonellis.* But she didn't want to bring those up for the police to seize on.

"Yes, well, our Sergeant Partridge and Officer Kurtz might attest to Ms. Holden's, ah, argumentativeness," Villegas said.

Seeing blank looks, Villegas explained. "The police officers who informed her of her father's death." He continued. "Any serious disputes? Arguments that might have escalated?"

"Not really," Molly answered. "Although her dog, Jessie—you remember her from last night—was deliberately poisoned."

The detective's chair squeaked as he sat forward. He picked up an electronic tablet from his desktop. "Who did that? When?"

"No one knows who," Molly said. "It was two or three months ago. Anybody passing by could have put the antifreeze within reach. Renee's property backs up on open common land and her rear fence is just bars."

"Did she suspect anyone?"

Molly and Mike glanced at each other. Looked away simultaneously, as if choreographed. Neither of them spoke.

"Look," the detective said, now obviously exasperated, "if Ms. Holden really is your friend—and it seems that you, Ms. Levin, are perhaps her best friend—don't you want to find out who did this to her?"

Mike leaped on the detective's slip. "So it definitely wasn't an accident."

"No," Detective Villegas admitted reluctantly. Then his tone became more aggressive. "Now please stop being so... cautious or protective, or whatever, and help us identify people who might have a motive. You say you know the community, know the people. Give us some names. We aren't the Gestapo here, you know. We won't assume anything, and we can be very diplomatic with the taxpayers. But Peter Jackson is our only lead at the moment, and it's pretty clear that you don't think it was him."

"It doesn't make sense; Peter has no motive to hurt her," Mike persisted. "Won't Renee be able to tell you soon who did this?"

The detective hesitated, seeming to weigh how much to reveal, then shook his head. "She may be able to eventually. But they've put her in a coma to help her heal and the doctors say even when she is brought out of it, she may not remember anything. Trauma victims often don't, especially with head injuries. Look, you came down here to help, right? So please help!"

"Okay," Mike said. "As long as you understand we aren't accusing anyone. Renee has a long-standing disagreement with her neighbors Steve and Julie Antonelli. They are very unhappy with her plans to extend her family room out six feet; the extension will cut off some of their view of the mountains."

"And they need to sell their house," Molly chimed in. "Her extension will definitely lower the value of their property a lot. We had a very unpleasant meeting of the HOA committee that reviews architectural changes. The committee—I'm on it—had approved Renee's proposal and invited Steve and Julie—the Antonellis—to a meeting to present their case for reversing the decision. The meeting was really just a courtesy, since everything conformed to the HOA guidelines and the Antonellis don't have a legal leg to stand on. But things got really heated and Julie left in tears. Renee took it pretty well—she's a retired lawyer and I guess lawyers are used to confrontations. But Steve said—yelled, really—some things that sounded like threats to her, and frankly, to the committee as well. And he was that upset even before they knew they were going to be forced to sell. According to Julie, Steve blew all their savings on a phony startup and now they're broke—so their situation's a lot worse than at the time of the meeting."

Detective Villegas recorded the names in his tablet. "What kind of threats did he make?"

"I don't remember his exact words. Something to the effect that she would regret pushing ahead with the extension. We sat there kind of flabbergasted after the Antonellis left. We all thought his behavior was awful but that he's just a blowhard. Renee wasn't so sure. After all, someone poisoned Jessie. And Renee thought Steve had done it. Not that there's any proof that he did. Uh, at least nothing we know of." She glanced at Mike as if for confirmation and he nodded.

Villegas knew how to use silence. He just sat and looked at Molly, waiting for her to continue.

"Mike and I agree, whoever assaulted Renee could easily be someone from Renee's past. As you said, she was a lawyer," she added, as if it were obvious that all lawyers made enemies.

"Anyone you can think of?" Villegas asked.

"No," Mike said. "We didn't know Renee before she moved here, so couldn't say..."

"Rod Staley," Molly interjected. "He had a big argument with Renee, and Betsy witnessed it. She said Renee was furious with him. It had something to do with her land in California. She has a big spread somewhere north of Sacramento. He was pressuring her to sell it to him."

Mike looked at her curiously. "Who are you talking about?"

"Remember when we were at the Hole-in-One and I went over to talk to that good-looking guy with the mustache?"

"Yeah, I remember when you interrupted his lunch," Mike said with a smile.

"Oh pooh, he was almost finished, and I just introduced myself and gave him my card. But he did have that argument with Renee—I don't know how serious."

"Hitting Renee over the head strikes me as a rather poor way to convince her to sell," Mike said.

"Maybe he was hoping...." Molly's voice trailed off.

"That she wouldn't recover?" Mike finished for her. "What good would that do him?"

"Tell me about this argument," Villegas said.

"I was inside my house, watering my African violets on the windowsill, so I couldn't hear anything," Molly explained. "But you remember, my house is right across from hers, so I could see them clearly. Just from the body language, I thought they were arguing. Renee looked furious. It was brief. Then he got in his car and drove off."

"I don't suppose you got a license number."

"Gosh, no. It's not like he was committing a crime."

"Any idea how we could track Staley down?"

"Not that I can—wait, didn't you talk to that guy Bert in Renee's Favorites list on her phone? If I was right that he was Renee's dad's neighbor, maybe he would know Staley?"

"Good idea. We'll follow up with him." Villegas stood, thanked them, and extended his hand. They were clearly being dismissed.

"Jeez, what have we done?" Mike mused as they left the station. "When we went in, we only wanted to let him know that Peter couldn't possibly have hurt Renee and give him some general knowledge of Sunrise. Now, twenty minutes later, we've handed him two new—what do they call them on the cop shows—'persons of interest.' If they find out what we've done, our asses will be grasses around here."

"Thank you for not bringing up the problems Peter and Renee have been having. That would just make them focus more on Peter. What do you think of Detective Villegas?" Molly asked as they pulled into her driveway.

"Well, any guy who brews his own espresso can't be too bad. Seriously, though, he does seem sharp."

"Yeah. Not exactly the hard-bitten cop we see in TV shows," Molly said. She cocked her head thoughtfully. "What the heck does that mean, anyway? Hard-bitten? Who bit them?"

Mike laughed. "Sometimes your mind goes off in totally unexpected directions. But in a good way!" he hastened to add.

"Glad to afford you some amusement," she observed wryly. "But did you notice how he's dressed? Neat pin-striped shirt. You could chop celery with the crease in his pants. I'll bet his wife sends him out every morning like that."

"I'm not so sure he's married. Or at least not to a woman. I get the feeling he plays for the other team. I didn't see any personal photos in his cubicle. Just that one picture with another cop—looked like a formal occasion."

"Maybe cops aren't supposed to have them."

"No, I saw lots of pictures and kids' drawings in the other cubicles we walked past. If he is gay, maybe he doesn't advertise it."

"Hey, this is the twenty-first century. Nobody has to hide in the closet anymore," Molly said.

"No, but a lot depends on who you work with. That big detective built like the Incredible Hulk— Rasputin or something?"

"Rasmussen."

"Yeah—he wasn't exactly Mr. Rogers with us. Hope he's friendlier with his colleagues."

Molly started to get out of the car, hesitated, and then turned back to Mike.

"Mike, there's one thing I didn't tell the detective. About Steve. It's probably nothing, so I didn't want to bring it up. But Julie said something once that makes me think Steve had been in serious trouble up at Yavapai College. That's where he was teaching just before he retired. I can't remember exactly what she said, and the only reason I remember it at all is that she was clearly upset she'd let something slip. We were talking about why she and Steve moved here and she was bemoaning leaving Prescott. She loved their house there, fruit trees, great view, and so on. I asked why they left, and that's when she said that they really had to after Steve had that fight at Yavapai. After she said that, she looked stricken—really scared and kind of confused. I thought she was trying to decide whether to ask me to keep that secret or to pretend she'd never said it. So I kind of quickly changed the subject, asked her more about Prescott. And she seemed very relieved. We never talked about it again. But if he had some argument with someone at the college that was serious enough to make him leave...."

"I wonder whether it was just an argument or whether 'fight' meant fisticuffs."

"No clue, but obviously I can't ask her about it."

"Why not?"

Molly shook her head and gave him a "don't be dumb" look, lips pursed. "Even if I could ask her, which I can't, she'd never tell me anything damaging to him. She's as loyal as a, a...cocker spaniel."

"I guess we could find out what happened."

"How?"

"I'm pretty sure one of my grad students from Michigan got a faculty position there a couple of years ago," Mike said. "If I still have her email, I could maybe contact her."

"But if she's new there, she wouldn't know about something that happened, what, five or six years ago?"

"No, but she might know someone on the faculty who would. I'll check it out."

"Go easy," Molly said. "I don't want to cause more problems for Steve—or Julie—than they already have."

37

VILLEGAS

"I just met with two residents of Sunrise Acres," Detective Villegas announced to Rasmussen, Weatherby, and Partridge, whom he had called into the squad room. "One of them, Molly Levin, is a good friend of Renee Holden's and appears to function as a kind of town crier." At the uncomprehending looks on the faces around him, Villegas translated: "A human intranet. She's a real estate agent, specializes in listings in the community, sits on a lot of committees, volunteers a lot. She and her friend, Mike Landry, teed up two other possible suspects, Steve Antonelli and Rod Staley. I'll get to these guys in a minute, but first let's talk about Jackson.

"Levin and Landry say Jackson and Holden are in an exclusive relationship. Both are likely very well off. She's a retired lawyer and the Sunrise Acres directory lists Jackson as a retired radiologist. So no obvious motive. Then there's the time window. Jackson would have had to drive to the bell tower, attack Ms. Holden, then somehow get all the blood off of himself, unless he found time to put on a protective suit and dispose of it, retrieve the beer from his house or maybe from a cooler in his car or golf cart, and arrive back at the poker game, all in twenty to twenty-five minutes."

"And how could he have known there wouldn't be enough beer?" Partridge said.

"If that excuse hadn't come up so conveniently, he could have been prepared with another reason to be gone from the game," Rasmussen observed. "Forgot he left the stove on, or needed to make a call—or any number of other possible reasons to leave for a few minutes."

"Yeah, maybe," Villegas said. "But we couldn't find blood in either his car or golf cart. Still, let's do a background check on Jackson, see if there might be something hinky in his past."

Villegas summarized what Molly and Mike had told him about Rod Staley and Steve Antonelli, adding, "and apparently the Antonellis' financial situation has gotten a lot worse since he made the threats, telling Ms. Holden she'd 'be sorry' during the HOA committee meeting." He turned to Weatherby. "Denise, I want you to go after Antonelli's and Staley's backgrounds as well as Jackson's. Get as much information as you can. Any priors, of course, but also relevant news items. And get their fingerprint files; it's possible, of course, that one of them might not ever have been fingerprinted, but highly unlikely these days. And I want you to do the same for Renee Holden. She's divorced, so you'll also need to find out if she's used a married name."

"Jose," Weatherby interjected, "I already got that from Ms. Holden's father's neighbor, Bert O'Shea, when I called him the morning after the assault. Her married name was Sanford."

"Good. Did you get anything else from O'Shea that would help us?"

"Not that I could see—except that he's known her a long time, so he might be a good source for more background. We didn't talk long. I didn't tell him it was an assault, nor how seriously hurt she was. Let him assume it was an accident. He was very concerned and asked to be informed of her condition. I explained we couldn't really do that, since he's not a family member. I wrote it all up and posted it on our SharePoint site. Of course, when I spoke with O'Shea I didn't know that Staley was a neighbor, so I only asked about Holden."

"Okay. From what we've been told about Ms. Holden's 'prickly' personality, it's beginning to look like she may have quite a few people who'd want to hit her over the head." Villegas paused, a bit uncomfortable that he had sounded flippant. He glanced repentantly at the photo of Renee he had put up and went on, choosing his words more carefully. "We're looking for anything that would give someone, either here or in California, a motive to assault her. We still don't know if the perpetrator intended serious injury or murder."

"Not many people could be expected to survive those blows to the head and then the fall down the stairs," Rasmussen observed. "I think it's pretty clear the intent was murder."

"Probably," Villegas agreed. "But she was apparently in good physical shape, kind of an exercise fanatic. She may yet survive.

"Next, we need to check out alibis for Steve Antonelli and Rod Staley. Denise, after I get your background reports on them, we'll conduct informal interviews in their homes. I'll do Antonelli in the next day or so. We're pretty limited in what we can legally do in a casual setting, so we'll very likely have them down here for something more formal, especially as we get more information. Antonelli lives here in Sunrise, so there's less urgency on him than Staley.

"Terry, you go after Rod Staley. He lives in California, but apparently he's been staying with a daughter in Phoenix. He's been down here to see Ms. Holden at least once recently. Telephone first," he said, handing Rasmussen a hard copy of his notes from his meeting with Molly and Mike, including the phone number, "and if he's in Phoenix, get Del Washington from the night shift and the two of you go see him. I want to know why it was so important to come all the way down here to talk with Ms. Holden."

"Tonight?" Rasmussen didn't look pleased.

"Yeah, I know it's late, but we want to lock down Staley's alibi, if he has one, before he goes back to California. I don't think we have the budget to send you out of state. *Carpe diem*, or what's left of the *dia*. Use the flashers and you can get to Phoenix in less than ninety minutes. And ask to see his rental car. Whoever hit Ms. Holden had to be covered in blood. Jackson let us check out his vehicles, so let's hope Staley's cooperative as well. If he refuses, that will tell us something. Take pictures."

"Shit, Jose," Rasmussen said. "I won't be back for hours. Can't it wait until tomorrow? Or maybe Washington could handle it alone, since he's on night shift."

"You're the detective," Villegas said. "And for all we know, Staley's flying back to California in the morning."

Rasmussen looked as if he'd like to continue objecting, but Villegas had turned away from him.

"Guess we won't be able to use luminol," Rasmussen said as he headed toward the door. But Villegas stopped him.

"No, we'd need a warrant for that," Villegas agreed. "It's unlikely any of our suspects would give us permission to spray for blood residue. Luminol really stains. I didn't even bother asking Jackson. I was just happy he let us do a visual and swab. If Antonelli agrees, we'll look at his car and golf cart when we interview him."

"How about Ms. Holden's ex? Should I check him out too?" Weatherby asked.

"Sure. Check him out, but I'm less interested in his background than what he might be able to tell us about Renee Holden. Clues from her life likely provide the clues for her... for the attack.

"That's it for now. Terry, good luck with Staley." He waved a dismissal and turned to his typed statement of the woman who had found Renee. Judging from appearances, she didn't look to be capable of lifting a brick, much less hitting someone with it. And she had a yappy dog with her —not a good accessory for a vicious crime. So they could eliminate one person from suspicion. The blood on the guy who tried to help her was only on his knees. If he'd been the assailant, it would have been all over him—especially on his shirt. *We can probably eliminate the rest of the onlookers for the same reason—no way a blood-covered person could have blended in. Laudate Dominum,* he thought. "Praise the Lord," he murmured to the empty room. *But reducing the number of suspects in a crime this public won't help us much. Back to the basics: motive and opportunity.*

JULY 12: Day Four

"How did it go with Staley?" Villegas asked Rasmussen. The case team was meeting the morning after Rasmussen had driven up to Phoenix to interview Staley.

"He was cooperative. Del and I asked to speak with him

alone. Told him we were talking with everyone who had had any recent interactions with Ms. Holden. He seemed to accept that explanation for my driving all the way up to Phoenix to see him. Didn't ask much about what we called 'the accident.' We chatted about how he spends his time in Phoenix versus California and he volunteered that he'd attended a Diamondbacks game by himself at Chase Field the night of the assault."

"Hold on," Villegas said. "So he *volunteered* an alibi?"

"Yeah, at the time I thought I was pretty lucky. I was prepared to keep pushing him until we got to the time of the assault. But you're right, it was...unusual. When I joshed him about going alone, he said he invited his son-in-law," Rasmussen checked his notes, "Jack Parrish, to go with him, but that Parrish pleaded too much work at the last minute and didn't go. The way the D-backs' season is going, I don't blame him for bailing. But later on while I was looking over the car, Del talked to the son-in-law separately about how come he didn't go to the game, and Parrish told Del a somewhat different story."

"Different how?" asked Villegas.

"Parrish partially corroborated Staley's story but said his decision to skip the game wasn't really last-minute. He said that he had told Staley that morning that he wasn't going. Staley showed me a ticket stub for the game, but of course he could have gone in through the gate and right out again."

"So in addition to providing an alibi out of the blue, there's an inconsistency," Villegas said. "Not enough to take it to the next level, but we can challenge him on it if we get enough to bring him in. Go on, Terry. Sounds like you were able to check out the rental for blood residue?"

"Yeah, I kinda asked him real casually if it would be okay if I took a look at it. He had no problem, although he asked what I was looking for and I had to make up some shit about dirt samples from Cactus Heights versus the Phoenix area. He didn't buy it, just sorta smirked, but he didn't stop me. Told me to knock myself out. Seemed to find it kind of amusing. I looked it over as best I could with him looking on —big Toyota SUV, so lots of interior. No guarantees that I didn't miss something, but nothing obvious. After I'd checked the brake and accelerator with a flashlight and a magnifying glass, I asked him for a drink of water, to give me time to wipe a section of each of them down real quickly to see if I picked up any blood. Nada. But the swabs are in the evidence bags, just in case the lab wants to go over them. He's been in Phoenix all week, so he could have driven down. There are no toll roads between Cactus Heights and Phoenix, so no E-ZPass records for his rental. If he's a hot suspect, we could maybe get a warrant for the car to check mileage, but he could always say he'd driven around a lot, just not down here."

"Does the rental have a GPS? Could we check for destinations?" asked Villegas.

"It does, but we'd probably need a warrant. Privacy issues. He'd likely use his phone's GPS anyway, to get him to Sunrise Acres," Rasmussen replied.

"Did you ask him about why he was talking with Ms. Holden?"

"He seemed pretty open about it, wants to buy her land in California. Said she's hardly ever there and now that her dad's died there's nobody to take care of it."

"Any idea why they might have argued about it?"

"Nah, we didn't get into that. We were more focused on his alibi. So after we left his daughter's place, Del and I drove over to Chase Field to see if there was video coverage of the gates. There's some at the main entry gate—none at the exits, apparently. But we only checked that out with the night security guy, who was either half drunk or on something. It was like talking to a three-year-old. We need to follow up with someone who can handle words with more than one syllable. He did finally show us Tuesday night's tape of the entrance, and I told him to hold onto it, but I don't know how much good it would do us. Unless we can spot Staley going out right away, we can't blow a hole in his alibi. He told his daughter he was going to grab a burger somewhere, then head to the park. The game ended around ten forty-five, so he could have driven down here, leaving the stadium at five-thirty or so, and been back to Phoenix in plenty of time. Could have listened to the radio broadcast on the way back in case we asked for details on the game. But Del is going to call the security office up there when the day manager is in, see if the rent-a-cop was right about no coverage of exits. And that's about it," he said, checking his tablet. "I'll enter it in the files."

"Hold on," said Villegas. "You say he had a ticket stub? Did you ask to see it? And did you take a photo of it or write down the seat number?"

Rasmussen looked annoyed at the oversight. "Crap. Yeah, I see where you're going. He did show me a ticket stub and it was the right date. You're thinking we could maybe find the people on either side of him. Guess I was sleepier than I thought."

"Not too late, maybe. Give him a call and tell him to save the stub. We'll need to see it. He could take a picture of it and text it to us. I don't see how he could fake something like that. Then we can see if we can locate the fans on either side. Probably it would only pay off if they were season ticket holders. Otherwise, they could have gotten their tickets online or anywhere. Still, time's passing and we're not exactly hot on the trail of our victim's assailant, so maybe we'll get lucky."

Rasmussen seemed eager to make up for his oversight. "Of course, on one side of him the seat would be empty because his brother-in-law didn't go to the game. How about people behind him? Or at the end of the aisle where he would have to crawl over them to get in and out?"

"That sounds like a lot of work for very little likely payoff," Villegas said dismissively. Noting Rasmussen's sullen expression, he added, "But we may have to eventually go that route. We'd need to get some recent photos of Staley to show around. Now, you said that Staley was cooperative and seemed almost amused with your questioning. So, either he knows that you're treating him as a suspect and he has nothing to hide, so he's just being genuinely cooperative..."

"Or he's our assailant, but he feels confident that he's covered his tracks and we won't find anything. He seems like a smart guy. The only hole in the story is Parrish's contradictory account of why he didn't go to the game."

"I agree. But we can't get Del Washington involved in any follow-up. You'll have to do that yourself, Terry."

The directive obviously annoyed Rasmussen. "Dammit, Jose, why don't you get us some more help? The three of us can't do it all."

"Four," Partridge pointed out quietly.

"Yeah, whatever," Rasmussen said impatiently. "But it's up to the case lead to get the resources we need."

"The captain said she couldn't give us any more bodies. Guess we'll have to work smarter." Villegas winced at his own words. *Lord, what a cliché.*

Rasmussen was quick to point it out. "Je-sus! Got any

more bumper stickers for us?" He shook his head and sat down heavily in one of the metal folding chairs.

"I'm going to talk with the captain about getting some overtime," Villegas said, then looked at Weatherby expectantly. "Denise? You're up. Did you turn up anything interesting on Staley?"

"Not really. Sixty-six, divorced. Enlisted in the Army a couple of years after the Vietnam War ended, served stateside. Honorable discharge, retired as a sergeant after twenty years. Probably a decent pension. Then moved back to Placer County in California, where he had a home and some land. Worked for the Post Office just long enough to get another pension before he retired a few years ago. One traffic citation in 2013. Ran a red light. That's about it."

"There's got to be more here," Villegas said. "The alibi's really weak, particularly since he lied about why his brother-in-law didn't go to the game with him. And what's with Holden and him arguing about his buying her out? Just another example of her being prickly, or is there more to it?"

Weatherby ignored the rhetorical question and moved on, glancing at notes on her iPad. "However...." She looked up at Rasmussen. "You're going to love what I found on Jackson. Seems our guy has a record and it's right in Tucson!"

Rasmussen all but purred. "Knew it," he said. "What's the charge?"

"Disorderly conduct." Rasmussen looked a bit disappointed that it was just a misdemeanor.

Villegas rolled his hand in a "get on with it" gesture.

"Back in February," Weatherby continued, "Jackson was involved in a skirmish with a shop owner in South Tucson. It was during that Black Lives Matter protest march. The chief sent some of our guys down to help with it. Anyway, Jackson got swept up with a bunch of the protesters who were rioting, breaking windows, stealing stuff. He claims that he was actually trying to stop the looting and that the shopkeeper attacked him, thinking he was one of the looters. Jackson says he was just defending himself. Pretty effectively, it turns out. The shopkeeper definitely got the worst of it."

Rasmussen snorted.

"South Tucson PD has sort of put it on the back burner," Weatherby continued, "so Jackson's case has been dragging along. His lawyer is trying to get hold of some body cams and more surveillance video that he says will prove Jackson's story is right and he's innocent."

"Why would a guy as rich as Jackson steal stuff he could just buy?" Partridge said. "Doesn't make sense. And why would he be all the way down in South Tucson?"

"Maybe to buy drugs," Rasmussen suggested.

"He's a doctor," Partridge protested. "If he wanted oxy or something, he could write a prescription."

"Not for street drugs," Rasmussen said. "You can't write a prescription for White Lightning, or Blow!"

Villegas held up his hand. "Whoa. We're getting into all sorts of speculation here. The simplest explanation is that he was down there as part of the BLM protest. Why bring drugs into it? Denise, since the charge is local, why don't you talk to the arresting officer and see how strong the case is. I tend to agree with Sarah that it seems kind of odd that Jackson would be looting. Now, what did you find out about Antonelli?"

"Antonelli's results started out routine," Weatherby said. "Retired chemistry teacher at Yavapai College up in Prescott, married for umpteen years to Julie Antonelli, blah blah. Then it gets interesting. In 2012 he got arrested on a simple assault charge for decking a patron at a restaurant bar in

Tucson. Got the charges knocked down to disorderly conduct when he pled guilty and the guy who was assaulted told the prosecutor that he wouldn't testify, maybe because he was embarrassed that he got flattened by a senior citizen."

"Nothing before or since then?" Villegas asked. Weatherby shook her head. "Okay, what did you turn up on our victim?"

"Renee Holden is quite interesting," Weatherby reported. "Getting info on her was not nearly as straightforward as I had expected. No criminal record; again, just a couple of traffic violations—speeding in her case. But she's made an effort to fly under the radar the last couple of years."

Weatherby scrolled through her iPad. "I'll give you the Cliff Notes version. She practiced law under her married name, Renee Sanford, in San Francisco." Anticipating Villegas's likely question, she held up her hand. "I haven't checked out Sanford, her ex, yet." She continued her narrative: "Ms. Sanford was partner in a big firm. Her last case made quite a splash. She was defending a woman who shot and seriously wounded a kid who showed up at her front door, collecting money for his sports team. The defendant claimed she felt threatened, tried to invoke the California 'castle' law about defending your home. But apparently you can only defend your castle against an actual intruder in California. The kid who was shot said he never pushed his way in, as the shooter claimed. He later died of his wounds. The fact that he was African American made it particularly newsworthy. The kid was only fifteen, dressed in his soccer uniform, and it looked like a pretty clear manslaughter at least. Anyway, Sanford/Holden got a hung jury and the DA decided not to retry it. But Sanford and her firm caught hell in the press. And that's not all. A few days after the trial, her own castle in Atherton got firebombed. I guess some of the Black kid's buddies didn't appreciate Ms. Sanford's performance. She was at home at the time but wasn't hurt. Luckily, the fire was pretty minor. But then she started getting grief from her neighbors. Atherton is one of the richest suburbs in the U.S. People there take a dim view of their town's being a target. Then she quit her law firm, decided the easy life awaited in Arizona. She had divorced Sanford in 2013, but didn't go back to her maiden name until she moved here about eighteen months ago, shortly after her fifty-fifth birthday. I've posted three articles about the case from the *San Francisco Chronicle* on SharePoint."

"Oh, great!" Villegas said. "Yesterday we had three possible suspects and now it sounds as if we may have a couple dozen more." He sat in silence for a few minutes. "Well, we really don't have the manpower to go after the California connection now." He smiled weakly. "You know the old joke about the drunk looking under the lamppost for his lost keys because the light was best there. Let's look at our local suspects first. I'll start by interviewing Mr. Antonelli in his home. If he agrees, we can check out his vehicles at the same time. Sarah, you're with me again. Give him a call and see if he's available around eight or nine tomorrow morning."

"What should I tell him? Does he even know about the 'accident'"?

"Just say that Ms. Holden was injured and we are talking with neighbors and other people who knew her to get more information. Keep it vague. If he asks questions, say that I'll explain more when we talk with him. And, Denise, keep doing your magic with the databases and the internet, and include the ex-husband.

"Terry, if you're not too wiped after last night, we need one more thing: Before our next meeting, see if you can time how long it takes to travel from where each of our suspects presumably was at the time to the tower."

"Car and golf cart both, I assume," Rasmussen said with a sigh.

"Yeah. Our guy was likely in a hurry, so I'd push the posted speed limit a bit. It's twenty-five to thirty-five on the roads between the tower and Antonelli's or where Jackson was playing poker."

"Okay—once for car and once for carts. Golf carts that can top twenty-five can't be sold legally, and I doubt anyone has souped-up models here. In fact, I'll bet Antonelli's and Jackson's carts are older than they are. Probably can't go over fifteen."

"While you're at it," Villegas added, "keep an eye out for a good place along any of those routes someone could toss a brick covered with blood and probably tissue and hair as well."

"If Staley's doing the tossing, could be anywhere along the interstate between here and Phoenix." Rasmussen grinned. "Another reason to hope it's one of the local guys. My money's on Jackson."

38

VILLEGAS

July 13: Day Five

"I don't see how people can live in houses that look so similar," Partridge said as she and Villegas stepped out of the cruiser to approach the Antonelli house. She looked around with a slight air of disapproval. "Don't visitors get lost trying to find the right one? Or even the owner, if he had a bit too much to drink? Every house is one of the same three colors, same Southwest stucco, a tile roof, gravel and brick out front, shoulder-to-shoulder with a neighbor—I hope to heck I don't end up living in a place like this."

Villegas smiled. "You could do worse, Sarah. My folks live in a retirement community like this in California. They love it. They like having neighbors nearby. And everyone manages to make their house individual.

"Huh. Now there's something you don't see often around here." Villegas pointed to a green octagonal sign prominently displayed near the sidewalk: *Poop happens. Just not here, please.* "Guess some dog owners haven't been picking up well enough."

Several large colorful Mexican pots with ferns and cacti lined the portico of the house, and there was a porcelain tile on the wall: *Mi casa es su casa.* "Bet his wife put that one up," Partridge whispered to Villegas as he rang the bell.

Villegas chuckled, but said quietly, "Open mind, Sarah, open mind. And we need to be very careful about our questions. He's not officially a suspect yet." They waited a few minutes and Villegas knocked on the door. When there was still no response, he asked Partridge, "You did confirm this appointment, right?"

"Twice. Yesterday, and this morning I left a reminder."

A few more minutes passed. *He's keeping us waiting on purpose,* Villegas thought. Steve Antonelli finally opened the door and stood aside for them to enter. He wore peach-colored Bermuda shorts, a knit shirt with narrow matching stripes hanging over an ample belly. "Have a seat."

The house interior seemed totally at odds with the Southwestern theme outside. The living room and adjacent dining room floors were covered with light cream-colored carpeting. Heavy rose and cream draperies, held back with gold braid ties, hung to the side of the floor-to-ceiling windows and fell to the floor with extra length spread out luxuriously over the carpet for several inches. A colonial brass chandelier with green shades hung over the mahogany table. Two tall glassed-in cabinets held displays of rose and cream china. Two large white hassocks seemed intended for additional seating space, but Villegas and Partridge eyed their button-decorated surfaces and pleated skirts uneasily. They looked not only uncomfortable but vulnerable to the slightest dust or dirt that an unwary sitter might deposit.

Whoever decorated this is still mentally in the Midwest or Northeast, Villegas thought. After momentarily standing indecisively, he strode to the couch and sat on one end. He immediately regretted his choice, as he sank into the soft cushions, leaving his legs so cocked that his knees were nearly at eye level. He found himself looking up at everyone, including Sergeant Partridge, who had selected one of the hassocks as a perch. *Should have had Antonelli come down to the station*, Villegas thought ruefully.

The sergeant took her phone out and set it on the coffee table. "Mind if we record our conversation?" she asked innocently. "I'm a terrible note-taker."

Steve eyed the phone with distaste but didn't protest as she turned it on.

Villegas adopted an informal, chatty tone. Recalling Molly's mention of Jessie's poisoning, he started with the sign out front. "I see you've had some trouble with dog owners not picking up after their pets?"

The observation unleashed a torrent. "They just don't give a damn. Let their beasts shit all over the yard. And they say they've picked the turds up—but I still have to go hose down all the spots. And they're so self-righteous. Want to tell you all about how they 'rescued' these mangy things." He emphasized the word with air quotes. "What a ridiculous description. What marketing genius came up with that term? When I was growing up, we never said we 'rescued' the dogs or cats. Cats caught rats and dogs chased foxes or announced trespassers.... They sure as hell weren't rescued! Of course, I grew up on a farm and I don't think of animals as pets. We couldn't—had to eat our pigs, our chickens, our—"

"Horses?" Villegas interjected, smiling.

Steve frowned. Apparently, it was not a subject for levity. "People treat their dogs and cats better than they do humans. 'Put them to sleep' when they're old. Hell, I'd just put them out and let the coyotes take care of them. Nature's way." He looked at Villegas and then Partridge as if expecting agreement.

"Of course, pets could also be disposed of with poison," Villegas noted.

Steve looked startled. "Who the hell have you been talking to? I suppose Holden told you she thinks I poisoned her precious mutt."

Steve's wife, Julie, had been hovering in the hall, and she chose this moment to interrupt somewhat nervously. "Would anyone like coffee? Or a glass of water? I just baked some biscotti." She was wiping her hands on an aqua-and-rose-colored apron she wore over baggy jeans.

Villegas shook his head a bit impatiently, leaving Partridge to decline politely.

"Julie," Steve said, "for God's sake...." Julie retreated back toward the kitchen but stayed in the hallway. "I didn't poison the damn dog. Didn't die anyway," he added, as if that were an additional vindication. "I thought you were here to talk about the accident. What's the dog got to do with that?"

"Oh, Ms. Holden's fall is exactly why we are here," Villegas said casually. "Could you tell us about your relationship with her? She's your next-door neighbor, right?"

"My relationship," Steve repeated sarcastically. "I'd say 'cordial,' wouldn't you, Julie?" He threw the question over his shoulder to his wife, who was still standing in the hallway. She didn't respond.

Villegas said nothing but just looked steadily at Steve.

"Oh, for God's sake!" Steve exploded. "I'm sure Holden's given you a song and dance about how everything she's planning on doing is perfectly legal. But look outside. See how we have a great view of the entire mountain range? Well, when she builds her extension—see where her fence is? The extension would go halfway out to that fence—would cut off most of our view of the mountains. And we moved the fireplace just so we could put that big picture window in."

Villegas stood, using Steve's gesturing as an excuse to extract himself from the embrace of the couch, and walked to the windows.

"And Molly Levin, you know—the real estate agent—says cutting our view will take the price of our house down maybe as much as thirty-five grand," Steve continued. "Holden doesn't need that much space. She lives alone, for God's sake. Says she needs the room for 'entertainment,'" he said, emphasizing the last word derisively.

"Does she need your permission to do that?" Villegas asked innocently.

"Hah!" Steve grunted. "She should, but she doesn't. The committee in charge is a bunch of spineless idiots who don't give a damn about our rights. Even Molly—and she knows what it'll cost us."

"We heard there was a rather heated meeting about Ms. Holden's plans," Villegas said carefully.

"Yeah, well, you haven't heard our side of it. So how bad was her accident anyway? Maybe she'll be out of commission for a while?"

"Would that be a good thing?"

"Hell, yes." A quickly stifled gasp came from the hallway.

"No reason to be a hypocrite," Steve said irritably, aiming his comment toward the hallway.

Villegas began circling the issue of Steve's alibi. "When did you hear about Ms. Holden's accident?"

"Hell, I don't remember. I knew something had happened when you came to the door looking for a key to her place, but I didn't know what. Probably Julie told me when she heard about it. Right, Julie?" He again threw the question over his shoulder at the hallway.

"Four nights ago—Tuesday?" Villegas prompted.

"Naw, couldn't have been then. That's when it happened, right?"

At Villegas's nod, Antonelli continued. "Must have been a couple of days ago. Julie's the one who keeps up with gossip. Julie?"

Still in the hallway, Julie edged closer. "Yes," she said. "I heard about it from some of the women."

"No one called either of you that night?" Villegas asked. Partridge shot a puzzled look at the detective, who was still standing, his face as unrevealing as that of a Buddha statue.

"I was here all night; never heard the phone ring."

"And you?" Villegas turned to Julie.

"No," she said. "No phone calls. We were both here all evening."

"Just the two of you?"

Steve looked very annoyed, and then apparently decided to be amused instead. "Well, we did have a sex orgy with some of the neighbors," he said.

"Steve!" Julie said indignantly, still in the hall but stepping closer to the group. "That's not funny. No, no one else was here," she said to Villegas. "Steve was on the computer and I was reading."

Villegas smiled at Steve. "Sounds a bit less exciting than your version," he said pleasantly. "Just a quiet evening at home, then. Neither of you went out?"

"No," they said almost in unison.

"Well, thank you very much for your time," Villegas said. He started toward the door and then stopped to address Steve. "This has been very helpful. I wonder if you could find time to come down to the station tomorrow morning, say eight o'clock, just to confirm all this, so we can write it up and have you sign it."

"What the hell! She recorded it all," he said, gesturing toward Partridge. "I've already told you everything I know."

"It's just routine," Villegas said. "We have to have you review and sign it."

Antonelli regarded him for a few long moments. "Am I under arrest?"

"No, of course not."

"Then I think I'll come down at my own damned convenience—if at all. And that won't be tomorrow. I'm busy all day."

"All right," Villegas said. "Give us a call when you know your schedule. But let's make it within the next couple of days." He stood and headed for the door before pausing. "Oh, and just one other thing, since we're here. Would you be willing to let us take a look at your car and golf cart before we go?"

"What the hell for?"

"Just routine. We're trying to cover all our bases."

"Don't you need a search warrant for that?"

"Not unless you object. Assuming you have no reason to...." Villegas allowed the words to hang in the air.

"Oh, all right. I don't have anything to hide. But I don't have a golf cart. Don't play golf. The car is in the garage. Be careful of the finish; I just polished it."

Julie led them to the door to the garage. She stood in the doorway, watching as if she feared they would steal something. Sergeant Partridge climbed into the car and, using a flashlight and magnifying glass, examined the accelerator, clutch, and brake pedals, snapping a few photos and swabbing a small section of each.

After placing the swabs in evidence bags, Partridge

joined Villegas in the squad car. "You kind of danced around the alibi. Couldn't you just ask him what he was doing during the time of the attack?"

"It's better in these informal interviews on the subject's home turf if he volunteers where he was," the detective explained. "That way, no lawyer can get the recording thrown out because we made him self-incriminate without Mirandizing him first. If we get enough on Antonelli to arrest him, then we'll read him his rights and push hard on the alibi. Right now, all we have is motive and probably opportunity. We can ask more direct questions when we get him down at the station. Including about that 2012 assault charge Denise found. We'll see how Mr. Antonelli explains that."

39

MIKE

Nothing's ever as easy as it sounds, Mike thought. He had been optimistic about locating the email address of his former student now teaching at Yavapai College, but his computer had choked on several years of saved communications. A search for her name in his email files ground away for a minute or two, only to spit out "no results." *Damn. Must have deleted it. Well, more than one way to skin a javelina.* Yavapai was a small junior college in Prescott, Arizona, and its list of faculty was short. There she was: Emily Broadhurst, teaching business communication. He recalled her senior thesis was about portrayals of women in Shakespeare's tragedies. If there was a connection between Lady Macbeth or Desdemona and creating business memos and PowerPoint presentations, it did not spring to mind.

Before writing or emailing her, he found a recent yearbook online and noted those teachers who had taught at Yavapai for at least six or seven years. They'd be the ones Emily could introduce him to.

He was rather pleased with himself when he succeeded

in talking a woman in the Registrar's office into giving him Emily's phone number—which was not available in the faculty roster—by explaining Emily was a former student whom he needed to contact urgently.

Now for a bit of subterfuge. What possible reason could he have for talking to Steve Antonelli's former colleagues about the man? Doubtful he could pose as a prospective employer—Steve was too old. Thinking back to when he had met Antonelli, Mike decided that the approach to his delicate mission would be that he was considering partnering with Steve in a nonprofit venture and wanted to talk to former colleagues.

Emily was delighted to hear from him. After he was caught up on personal news (another baby on the way already?) he told her about his fictitious startup, trusting that if by chance she ever tried to find out about it in the future, he could just say that it had fallen victim to inadequate funding. But he hadn't given enough thought to the details before he called. He hadn't even named it or given it a cause.

"What's the name of this new venture? What's it about?" she asked.

Caught off guard, Mike looked wildly around his living room for inspiration. The portrait of his grandson rescued him. "Um, it's designed around an online literacy course for children under six."

Her enthusiasm was embarrassing. "Oh, what a great cause. What's it called, and should I enroll Dana in it? She's just four."

He imagined his creative muse cowering in a corner, covering her eyes at his palsied imagination. "Um, well, we're considering several names. Uh, that is, we're thinking of having a contest to name it."

"How exciting. Will there be a prize for the person who suggests the winning name?"

Argh. When do I stop digging this hole?

Desperate to crawl out of a deepening chasm, he feigned an appointment he needed to get to. "But before I run, could you tell me which of your colleagues would likely talk to me about Steve?" He identified several of those he knew to have been there long enough. Fortunately, Emily offered to pave the way with an introduction.

When he hung up, he had two revelations. First, don't go into a session when you're going to have to lie without having practiced; and second, lying makes one sweat—a lot!

By the time he called Emily's colleagues, he had a few more details about his fictitious startup straight in his mind. And fortunately, he could truthfully say where he had met Steve. But his explanation seemed to puzzle them anyway. The environmental studies professor was skeptical: "What does Steve's teaching here have to do with a business arrangement?"

Mike winged it. "Well, the whole purpose of the venture is to help children—sort of like teaching?" Mike could hear his voice go up at the end, as if he himself questioned the connection between the new venture and college teaching.

This is hard work, Mike thought. *I'd never make it as a private investigator.* Although at least then, he'd have some actual authority. The electronics professor did say that Steve had left "under a cloud," but refused to say more and referred Mike to the guidance counselor. And that's where he "hit pay dirt," he bragged to Molly later, adopting what he assumed would be the proper language for the clever sleuth he was beginning to consider himself.

"It turned out," Mike told Molly, "that the guidance counselor's husband, who had coached athletics in addition to teaching history, got in a big argument with Antonelli over some budgeting issue, and the disagreement turned nasty. And physical. According to the guidance counselor, the teachers' lounge was trashed. She's still very unhappy that her husband wouldn't take it to the police. Apparently there were no witnesses to the argument, so it was a 'he said–he said' as to who started it. Both men were fired. But according to the counselor, her husband left with a good reference, so it's pretty clear that the school thought Antonelli was at fault. She said Steve had 'poor impulse control,' which I presume is psych talk for flying off the handle. In fact, she assumed the reason I was asking about him was because Steve had gotten violent again. She said she would no more go into business with him than with a pregnant rattlesnake."

"Pregnant?" Molly questioned.

"Yeah, I didn't follow that one up to find out what she meant. Maybe pregnancy makes them unusually cranky?"

"Or maybe a pregnant snake is capable of creating more destruction. You know, loosing all those venomous babies around."

"Huh. Maybe. But I'll tell you, it's a weird image to carry around in your head." Mike shook his head. "I'm afraid I'll think of it next time I see Steve Antonelli."

"Think we should tell Detective Villegas about what you found out? Certainly makes Steve look a more likely suspect than Peter."

"Okay. I'll give him a call."

But when he telephoned the police station, he was told Detective Villegas was out and Maria directed him to Detective Rasmussen. When Mike said he had some news about Steve Antonelli's past to give Villegas, Rasmussen insisted that he was a member of the case team and could receive any relevant information. At first, he sounded very skeptical that Mike had anything of value to provide. But after Mike recounted the gist of his discovery, he could tell that the detective began to take him seriously. He had to explain exactly whom he had spoken with at Yavapai and to review the conversations as verbatim as his memory allowed.

"So, you'll pass this along to Detective Villegas?" Mike asked.

He rather expected some congratulations or at least a mild expression of gratitude for his detective work, but Rasmussen just grunted noncommittally and said an abrupt good-bye.

40

VILLEGAS

July 14: Day Six

Captain Linda Dubrow had summoned Villegas for an "update on the case progress." She was on the phone when he entered, and she motioned him to take a seat on one of the modern leather and metal chairs that always seemed ready to fold itself in on him, like a Venus flytrap.

Dubrow's office was prime real estate in the police station, a coveted corner room, flooded with sunlight from windows on two sides. Dubrow had inherited it from her predecessor, who had expired just before Dubrow transferred to Cactus Heights from Tucson. Villegas had come to appreciate the captain's intelligence and dedication to the job. Nonetheless, there was a certain amount of resentment that she had been brought in from the outside, depriving the lieutenants of an opportunity for advancement. As Villegas waited for Dubrow to get off the phone, he observed with some amusement the large, unhappy ficus plant next to his chair that had been the innocent recipient of that resentment: sodas and the swill that passed for coffee being repeatedly but surreptitiously dumped in it. The captain decorated her space with colorful rugs and photos of her two children—one of them posed with her ex-husband. Although gossip had him absconding with his comely dental hygienist as the cause of a bitter rupture in the marriage, Villegas knew that the divorce had in fact been both mutually desired and amicable.

The captain finally put down her phone. "So, Jose, bring me up to speed on the Holden attack."

Squinting a bit against the sunlight, Villegas summarized the investigation to date, including what the team had uncovered about Peter Jackson, Rod Staley, and Steve Antonelli.

"It sounds as if Staley and Antonelli both have motives," Dubrow observed. "Staley wants her land and Antonelli is mad as hell at her for blocking his view and lowering his property value. But Antonelli is the more likely to resort to violence. Have I got it right?"

"Well, both of them have threatened Ms. Holden, according to witnesses."

"What about Antonelli's history of assault?"

Villegas nodded. "Seemed like a typical barroom brawl."

Dubrow's looked confused. "Bar? No, I mean Antonelli's assault against the other teacher, when he was at Yavapai College."

"Antonelli's assault against...where did you hear that?"

"From a member of your own team—Terry Rasmussen. He told me about how that civilian, the man who lives in Sunrise Acres...Mike somebody, somehow talked to someone at Yavapai and tracked down Antonelli's history there." Dubrow sat back in her chair. She said nothing for a long minute, seemingly assessing Villegas's surprise. "Jose, what the hell? How come I know about this before you do?"

Villegas sat immobile, frowning and looking down at the floor to the right of his chair as if some explanation were written there. His jaw was tight with anger as he took in the insult of Rasmussen's going around him to report to Dubrow. He wasn't sure how to respond without either excoriating Rasmussen or seeming weak.

"You shouldn't," he said shortly.

"Do you want me to—?"

He interrupted her with a wave of his hand. "No. I'll talk with Terry. I'm not sure why...," he said through clenched teeth. He took a deep breath and blew it out in exasperation. "I'll handle it."

Dubrow looked down at the ballpoint pen she was holding in her right hand, tapping it lightly against her left. She hadn't dismissed him; she seemed to be considering what, if anything, to say. "Okay," she said finally, looking up at him. "Terry is...a good detective, Jose. Not necessarily easy to get along with, but smart. He'll be a great asset to your investigation, if you can..." another pause as she selected her words, "get past this. You need to be in control of your team."

Villegas nodded sharply and stood to leave. "Got it. I will. We will. Get past it."

He walked slowly back to the detectives' room and his cubicle, considering how to handle this breach in police norms. Rasmussen's actions were a rather clear taunt. As his initial anger waned, he decided to address the challenge directly—but as objectively as possible.

Why wait? He walked to Rasmussen's cubicle, entered without knocking on the side panel, and sat down. Rasmussen was at his computer; he hit a last key and swiveled around to face Villegas.

"I've just met with the captain," Villegas said levelly.

"You gave her information that would have been good for me to know before I met with her, and certainly before I interviewed Antonelli yesterday. And you haven't posted it on our SharePoint." He looked at Rasmussen steadily. Neither man spoke for a long minute or two."Why?" he asked finally.

Rasmussen had been prepared for an angry attack. He seemed surprised at Villegas's temperate tone. He pursed his lips and rubbed a hand over his mouth as if stifling a response. "Dammit, Jose," he said. "Being lead detective doesn't make you God. You can't ignore Denise and me. We've been working cases a lot longer than you."

When Villegas said nothing, Rasmussen continued: "I know I screwed up by not getting that ticket stub from Staley, but...." He shook his head. "I just got pissed off at the way you tell us every little friggin' thing to do. 'Be sure to take pictures. Check for blood in the car.' Christ!"

They sat in uncomfortable silence for a few minutes, and then Villegas stood and turned to leave. Then he changed his mind and sat down again. "Okay," he said. "You're being honest with me. Let me return the favor. If Denise were running the case and did exactly what I've done, wouldn't you react differently?"

"Maybe," Rasmussen said, and looked surprised at his own candor. "But," he added after a moment, "she *wouldn't* do exactly what you have. We'd make more decisions together."

"So you're saying it's not personal."

To Villegas's surprise, Rasmussen chuckled. "Of course it's personal. You drive me friggin' nuts!"

Villegas forced a smile. "Yeah, well, I guess you're not alone." He stood again. "How about if I agree to be...um... less dictatorial, and you agree not to go behind my back."

"If being less *dictatorial,*" Rasmussen emphasized the word, "means being less of a prick, I'm in." He extended his hand. "For now," he added with a slight smile.

AN HOUR LATER, Villegas had gathered the team in the squad room. "I just met with Captain Dubrow. Because of the seriousness of the crime, the chief wants me to report directly to Dubrow, who will keep the chief in the loop.

"Any questions?" Villegas looked around the room, but seeing only head shakes, he put up a projection of the SharePoint site on the screen. Weatherby was sitting on the edge of her chair, holding her iPad up, waving it for attention. Villegas looked grim. "Denise, I hope that flying tablet means you have some progress to report."

"Maybe it's progress. Lemme start with Peter Jackson. I talked with the guy who arrested him, along with several others also arrested for the looting. Guess who helped him get his car out of lockup, by the way—Renee Holden. Anyway, two of the guys arrested with Jackson told his lawyer that Jackson was telling the truth. Not surprising— they were 'brothers.' But according to Jackson's lawyer, the shop owner's—guy named Nguyen—own surveillance cameras back up Jackson's story. I saw the footage. You can see Jackson pushing his way from the back of a bunch of guys smashing windows to the front and gesturing, trying to talk them down—actually grabbing the arm of one. Then Nguyen comes flying out and tries to slug them both with a baseball bat. Jackson grabs the bat and uses it to shove Nguyen in the chest and he falls back through the broken window."

"Sure sounds like self-defense; a baseball bat's a serious weapon," Partridge observed.

"Even if used to shove someone," Rasmussen retorted. "How badly did Jackson hurt Nguyen?"

"Lucky for them both," Weatherby said, "Nguyen didn't get seriously cut up on the broken glass. Probably had a beaut of a bruise on his chest. But so far, he's still ID-ing Jackson as one of the looters. The hearing's coming up, but Jackson's lawyer is convinced he's going to walk. Says some police body cam footage he's seen will show self-defense even more clearly."

"But Jackson isn't the only violent guy among our suspects," Villegas said. He started to explain and caught himself. "Terry, why don't you go over what you found out about Antonelli from our local senior citizen sleuths."

Rasmussen's knowing grin at Villegas caused Weatherby and Partridge to exchange a puzzled glance, but they snapped to attention when they heard that Antonelli had more than one assault in his history.

"Why wasn't this reported?" Partridge asked.

"Probably," Weatherby mused, "the college didn't want the publicity. Maybe I should follow up? You know, officially? Maybe get a signed statement from the other guy in the fight? I don't want to rely on what some civilian—Landry, right?—found out."

"Damn amateurs," Rasmussen muttered. "Father Brown and Miss Marple tag-teaming."

"Well, you did ask me to get more resources," Villegas said dryly. Then, as Rasmussen looked ready to detonate, Villegas held up a hand. "Joke, Terry." As Rasmussen shook his head but subsided, Villegas continued, "Look, Yavapai's a three-hour drive each way; we may need a statement sometime in the future, but let's wait a bit. We could probably get someone on the local force there to help us."

"Holy sh...," Partridge said, her exclamation dying off. "What's with these old guys getting into fights anyway? Somebody giving out testosterone shots?"

"Maybe they've heard that 'sixty is the new forty' so often, they believe it," Weatherby said.

41

BETSY

July 15: Day Seven

When Betsy called, she was all business. "Molly, are you home?" When Molly confirmed that she was, Betsy did not wait for an invitation. "I'll be over in five minutes," she said, and hung up.

When Betsy showed up, she ignored Molly's immediate plea for news about Renee's condition. "I need to get into Renee's house, and the police told me you have the code to the garage."

"Why do you need to get in?"

"The hospital needs to know if she has a living will and if so, who has power of attorney. They don't even know if she has a lawyer."

Molly gasped. "Oh my God, does that mean she's gotten worse?"

"No, she's still in a coma. I'm assuming she has copies of everything in her home office. Or if she doesn't, I can maybe find out if she has a lawyer and if the lawyer's office has papers."

"I'll come with you," Molly said.

"Thanks, but I'd rather you didn't. I don't need help."

"But you really shouldn't go alone," Molly said in a surprised tone. "We could be witnesses for each other, in case—"

"In case what? Some jewelry goes missing? You've got the entry code, so you'd have more opportunities than me."

Molly flushed. "No, of course no one would think that. But...well, actually," she said, her voice betraying some resentment at Betsy's attitude. "Yes. We have no idea who's in charge of her belongings while she's hospitalized, or who...would...." Her voice trailed off.

"Inherit if she dies?" Betsy said bluntly.

The flush on Molly's face deepened. "It's horrible to even think that, but I just think, until we know who's in charge, we should be very circumspect. Be sure no one could accuse, um, could criticize.... I know the hospital thinks you're next of kin, but when they find out you aren't, that would put you in a really precarious ethical—"

"But I am," Betsy interrupted. "Next of kin. I really didn't want to have to show this to anyone around here, but I thought you might not want to give me the code, so here, take a look." She handed Molly a printout of the email from MyGenes.com.

Molly skimmed it. "What is this?" She read the brief DNA report, her face registering confusion and then surprise as she read it a second time. Betsy watched Molly's face, remembering her own astonishment when she first received the report back in February.

THAT COLD LATE WINTER DAY, Betsy recalled, she had decided on a takeout salad and canned soup for supper. She had just thrown a few dried cherries and cranberries in with the usual mixed greens when she heard the alert from her computer in the next room, signaling a new email. She almost decided to wait to look at it until after eating, but her curiosity got the better of her. *Lordy, I'm as addicted to that little ding as Pavlov's dogs.* But when she glanced at the sender, she was glad she hadn't resisted the pull. The message was from the DNA testing company she'd sent her saliva sample to, MyGenes.com. She scanned the initial part of the report that showed her heritage as mostly northern European. No big surprise there. But then...

The report showed she shared 49.3 percent DNA with seventy-nine-year-old Douglas Holden, from some place named Dutch Flat in California. "Sibling or parent."

She stared at the screen, reading and rereading the words. *Sibling or parent.* Was Douglas Holden the "12" her mother had written about in her diary? The one who had broken her mother's teenage heart? She grabbed from the desk the yearbook she had searched before. Why the number 12? Suddenly she made the connection. Athletic teams. She flipped through the varsity teams, skimming the names below the photographs. Basketball, soccer...football...Doug Holden! He was standing in the back row in the middle. She bent over the book, looking closely at the small image. But was he "12"? The numbers had to be on the backs of their uniforms. She turned the page to photos of the football team in action. And there it was: a shot of him throwing a pass, the number 12 clearly visible on his back. The caption read, "Quarterback Doug Holden hits wide receiver Chick Evans with the winning touchdown pass." She had found "12"—and he was certainly too old to be a sibling. He was her father! This was incredible news. She was too excited to sit any longer. She stood and paced about her tiny living room. This could explain a lot about her relationship with her parents.

And the news opened up so many possibilities for the future. After living as an only child all her life, with parents she was never close to, she now not only had a different father but probably half-siblings. A real family. People who might well have more in common with her than Tom and Phyllis had. Why hadn't she done this DNA testing before her mom died? Did her mom even know that Tom wasn't the father? Did Tom know? Even if Tom were coherent enough to understand, she certainly couldn't raise the topic with him now.

So, what next? The fact that the report alerted her to Douglas Holden meant that he had also conducted the DNA test. And so he must know about her. Why hadn't he contacted her? Betsy noted the "Contact Douglas" button in her email. Douglas Holden would have seen something similar in his. Obviously, he didn't want to interact with her. Or maybe he had done the test a long time ago and she wouldn't have been identified on that early report. *Wait a minute. I just now got the email from MyGenes.com, so he would also have been notified about the same time. Maybe he's just as conflicted about contact as I am. Or...maybe he already knew about me and has been keeping it a secret.*

This was all too confusing. She needed to compose a message to him—something nonthreatening. She honestly didn't want to disrupt his life. But there were so many exciting implications. Cousins and aunts and uncles for Kevin. Douglas Holden had not only an unknown daughter but a grandson. He should be told about Kevin. Maybe he would be willing to get to know Kevin, even if he didn't want a new daughter in his life.

That night she felt as if she was skimming the surface of

sleep, never really diving down into unconsciousness. At three a.m., she gave up trying and sat down to write Douglas Holden. She composed draft after draft of a message. Finally, she decided that brevity was critical; they could get acquainted by phone or maybe even in person if he were willing. So she wrote simply: *I learned about you from a diary my mother kept. She clearly loved you. I have a son, your grandson. I don't want to impose on you in any way, but could we talk sometime on the phone?*

Before she could reconsider, she hit the Send button. Again that night, she could hardly sleep. Every time her in-box chimed, she raced to the computer to see if it was a return message. But there was no response. Several days went by and her initial euphoria changed to near despair. He did not want to connect with her. She felt rejected—again. At age sixty-two and a mother herself, she certainly shouldn't still long for a parent, but she did. And what if she had half-siblings? Maybe they would be willing to get to know her.

After waiting in vain to hear from Douglas Holden for almost a week, Betsy thumbed through the yearbook again. Scrutinizing his senior-year photo, she wondered what he looked like now. It suddenly occurred to her that maybe she could locate a recent photo through the internet. The MyGenes report had included a town with his name. Perhaps there would be an item in a local paper. At the very least, she could find out more about him. She entered "Douglas Holden" and "Dutch Flat CA" into the search engine.

What came up was as stunning a disappointment as the MyGenes report had been a revelation: an obituary. Douglas "Doug" Holden had died ten days after she submitted her saliva to MyGenes.com—barely enough time for her sample to have been processed and for him to be notified electronically of her existence. He probably had never even seen that he had a daughter. He certainly had never seen her message to him.

She told herself that it was unreasonable to feel so dispirited. After all, she'd only known about him for less than a week. She should be no more unhappy than she had been before she found him. But she couldn't help feeling a big loss. Just one more disappointment in a life filled with them.

Reading the obituary carefully, she saw that he was survived by a daughter, Renee Holden, of Cactus Heights, Arizona.

So she did have a half-sibling. Only one, apparently (unless her randy old dad had more than one fling). Betsy wondered what this half-sister was like. Was she married? Divorced? The fact that she had kept—or returned to—her maiden name suggested a certain independence of mind. Would she welcome Betsy as a relative or would she reject her? *I'm just not the kind of woman other women like*, Betsy thought. *Not even my own mother. Joel's family never warmed to me either,* she thought, remembering how distant her ex-husband's sisters had been, no matter what overtures she had made. Still, maybe Renee Holden would be different. Betsy could not resist googling Cactus Heights. Population a little over 35,000. The obituary had not included an address, of course. Even if she wanted to contact Renee Holden, how would she find her?

She tried a simple Google search. Of the thirty or so Renee Holdens who turned up, she could eliminate most immediately on the basis of race, age, or even gender. (One little boy was going to go through life explaining his name!) But of the three possibilities, none lived in Arizona. Puzzled as to how Renee could have eluded Google, she decided to invest with an organization that "guaranteed" to find any person for what seemed to her a rather hefty fee. After all, she already knew the hometown for the Renee Holden she sought. That should make it easier. She didn't have a birth date, but she could narrow it down to a range of ten to fifteen years, given the marriage date for Doug in his obituary.

The response she got the next day was brief: Renee Martha Holden married in 1999 to Daniel Sanford. Divorced 2013. Changed last name back to Holden in 2017. The address she was given was in an over-fifty-five community called Sunrise Acres in Cactus Heights, Arizona.

She had the same dilemma that had stymied her with Douglas Holden. *Should I contact her out of the blue? Call her up and say, "Hi there, I'm your half-sister, born of a teenage love affair between our dad and my mother. You are the only family I have left. Let's go get a pedicure together and bond!" No, this is even worse than with Douglas Holden. Given the difficulty I had in locating her, Renee Holden pretty clearly is not interested in a public presence. She may not welcome being found.*

Betsy looked up Sunrise Acres on the Web. It was a community of about two thousand homes. The website described an "active adult" community. The photographs looked great: swimming pools, all kinds of card games and hobby clubs, tennis and pickleball.... *What the heck is that?* An idea had formed. What if she visited there and met Renee—kind of checked her out before telling her they were sisters? Maybe there were short-term rentals in the community?

She searched the Sunrise Acres website. There were houses for rent by the month. With the money from the sale of her mother's house, she could afford a few months.

But how could she arrange to meet Renee Holden? And if she could, how should she reveal their relationship?

"OKAY, Betsy, I see it's your DNA, but...." Molly read out loud: "Forty-nine-point-three percent...with Douglas Holden." She looked up, startled. "That's Renee's dad!" She read on: "Sibling or...*father? Doug* Holden is your—"

"Is *my* father also."

Molly just stared at her. "Why didn't Renee...?"

"She didn't know until I told her—just last week."

Molly looked as if she had just been tased. "How could she not know?"

"It's a long story. In brief, Douglas Holden had an affair with my mother just before she married my...married Tom Rausch. They were just teenagers. I don't think anyone knew for sure that I was Douglas Holden's daughter until I found out through that DNA test. My mom must have figured either Tom or Douglas could have gotten her pregnant, but never said anything. I can see why—it would have devastated my...Tom. But Douglas died before I could contact him."

"So that's why you came here...." Molly's voice trailed off as she tried to think about the implications.

"Look, Molly, other than my son, Renee is my only living blood relative, and I wanted to get acquainted before I sprang the sister thing on her. I've heard that kind of revelation can go horribly wrong—resentment and rejection. I wanted to get to know her as a friend. That way, if we liked each other, it wouldn't be an awful shock—or terribly disappointing. And if we didn't, well, maybe I wouldn't even let her know I'm her sister. I haven't had much luck with female friends and my mother and I had a very…I guess I'd charitably call it a 'rocky' relationship. I didn't need another bitchy relative."

"How did she take the news?"

Betsy's face hardened as she repeated sarcastically, "How did she take the news?" Then she told Molly.

"Anyway," she finished, back to all-business mode. "Now you know the whole story, and I need that code. Please." She took out her phone, ready to enter the numbers.

"Betsy, I'm really sorry, but I can't just give the house code to you," Molly said. "The police said that since Renee has given me access to her house, I have responsibility. Even they can't go in alone without a warrant. So I'm afraid I'll have to accompany you." At Betsy's grimace, Molly continued, "Betsy, can't we make this friendly? I'm just trying to do the right thing, the legal thing. Let's look for that stuff together, okay? Now, tell me what we're looking for."

Betsy hesitated again. "Legal documents," she said. "For the hospital." When Molly still looked blank, she continued. "Like a will."

"A living will—a health-care proxy? One of those that says 'do not resuscitate' or assigns a power of attorney to make health decisions?"

Betsy nodded impatiently. "Yeah, or…any other kind of will."

"An estate will?"

Betsy didn't answer the question. "Let's go," she said, heading across the street. As soon as Molly opened the door to Renee's house, Betsy announced, "I'm going to start in her office," and walked in that direction.

Reluctantly, Molly joined in the search. There were several dozen files in the drawers of Renee's desk and some green cardboard boxes holding upright files in the garage.

They also found a number of three-ring binders holding various papers, mostly medical records and brokerage reports. Betsy would have liked to linger over the financial records, but with Molly looking over her shoulder, she felt inhibited. She was able to see impressively large sums next to account numbers, however. Renee was indeed wealthy. One large black binder held newspaper clippings about Renee's career, but neither woman spent any time looking through that.

After a couple of hours of looking, they were both tired, dusty, and thirsty. Betsy declined Molly's invitation to come to her house for a glass of water or cup of tea and drove off.

42

MOLLY

Once inside her own home again, Molly immediately called Mike. "Mike, I just had a very interesting—and kind of disturbing— discussion with Betsy. I'm not sure what to do with the stuff she told me, if anything. I'm stuck between...between..."

"Scylla and Charybdis?" Mike offered helpfully.

"What? What the heck are you talking about? Hey Mike, Planet Earth calling. I need some serious help here. Don't go all English prof on me."

"Sorry. What happened?"

Molly explained being presented with the DNA report, Betsy's insistence that they search for legal documents, and her belligerent attitude.

"So, what did you mean when you said you were stuck between..."

Molly exhaled audibly. "I told you that Betsy was quite annoyed."

"I believe the technical term is 'pissed.'"

"Okay, yes, but more than that, she was just...different. Not at all like herself. Or at least the way she was around me before. She was curt, even kind of, um, abrasive. I know that the hospital would like to know who to consult with about any decisions, but it just didn't seem like that was the only reason she was so eager."

"Huh. So you think maybe if there isn't a will or a designated health-care proxy, Betsy could be appointed one, as her closest relative?"

"Yeah, something like that. And that's not all. I asked Betsy how Renee reacted to the news and when I finally got her to tell me, it wasn't at all what she had hoped. Not sisterly, to say the least. So, Mike, what should I do with this information about their relationship? Betsy's my friend, and I'd like to keep it that way, but given we didn't find a living will, if she might be put in charge of making decisions about Renee's treatment..."

"Then," Mike finished her sentence, "Detective Villegas should be told."

"I guess. The hospital already knows. Maybe that's enough. But what if...what if..."

"I think you should call Villegas," Mike said. But when Molly dialed the number she'd been given for the police task force, the line went to voice mail for Detective Rasmussen. She left a brief message to call her back.

THE INTERACTIONS with Betsy and the fruitless search of Renee's house for "any kind of will" had left Molly exhausted. She almost didn't pick up the phone when it rang. Given all the sales and political calls from humans, to say nothing of robots, she was inclined to let calls from any unrecognized phone numbers go to voice mail. She remembered with amusement a conversation she'd had a few months earlier with an aggressive financial salesman who had called numerous times and left increasingly pushy—and long—messages. Finally, she picked up the phone and asked him to cease calling. "It's no use," she said. "I just don't answer junk phone calls."

"Junk!" he had exclaimed indignantly. "This is not a junk call."

"Allow me to explain," she said politely. "Did I call you?"

"No, of course not," he said.

"Did I ask you to call me?" Silence; he could see where this was going. "That, sir, is my definition of a junk phone call—one that I didn't ask for and don't want to receive. Now, please put me on your do-not-call-because-she-will-never-answer list. Please." Dial tone.

Still, in the era of cell phones, it was hard to know if the caller was someone in Sunrise Acres. So many residents, especially the seasonal residents, were still using a cell phone with the area code of another state. And suddenly she recognized the area code: 916, same as both Renee's father Doug's and the mysterious "Bert" in Renee's phone Favorites. She picked up.

"Ms. Levin?" The voice was unfamiliar.

"Yes," she said cautiously, already regretting picking up. Maybe this was a sales call after all.

"Rod Staley. You won't remember me, but you gave me your card when we were eating at the Hole-in-One in Sunrise Acres a month or so ago."

Molly's mind immediately invoked an image: tall, mid-to-late sixties, luxurious mustache. Good looking. "I remember you, Mr. Staley. I have been accused of ruining your lunch there. What can I do for you?"

"My lunch was fine. But I'm trying to reach Renee Holden. I've been calling her all day and have left messages, but she hasn't gotten back to me. And now her voice mailbox is full. I know she was in some sort of accident a few days ago because a couple of cops drove all the way up to Phoenix to ask me questions about it, but now I'm thinking it must have been more serious than I thought. Anyway, I remembered that you said you lived across the street from her, and I thought you might be able to tell me how she's doing. Or maybe that friend of hers—Peter something—would know? Do you have his phone number?"

Molly took a deep breath. "Uh, Mr. Staley, I'm really sorry to tell you this, but Renee's accident was very serious."

"Jeez, is she going to be okay?"

"She fell down some stairs in the bell tower here in Sunrise last Tuesday and she was pretty badly hurt. I can't tell you much more because the hospital won't release information to any non-family members." Realizing that he might have some useful information that no one else did, she asked, "Do you know of any relatives?"

He was quick to respond. "No, she's divorced, and her mom died a year or two ago, her dad just a few months ago. She doesn't have any kids and she's an only child herself."

No news there. "That's what we all thought. But it turns out she has a half-sister."

"What? She never said anything about that to me. I can understand she would never tell me, but Doug? I can't believe that he wouldn't have said something to me in all the years we've been friends. Are you sure about this half-sister? With all the scams going around, it seems anyone can claim anything. It just doesn't add up. Doug and Candy married right out of college. I'm almost positive Candy hadn't been married before. You're telling me she had *two* girls?"

Molly hesitated. How much should she reveal? It wasn't really her place to explain.

Rod jumped into the silence. "So, this so-called half-sister knows about the accident?"

"Yes, she's staying right here in Sunrise. And she could tell you more about the whole situation—how it happened that she and Renee have the same father."

"Whoa, wait a minute. Are you telling me that this half-sister is *Doug's* kid? What the hell?"

Molly was feeling increasingly uncomfortable. "I think it would be best if you talk directly to the sister. Her name is Betsy Rausch. I'll give you her cell number." Struck by a sudden memory, she added, "Actually, you've met her. She was with Renee the day you, um, stopped by Renee's house. You know, the same day you and I met. Betsy can also tell you how Renee is doing."

Rod continued to sound stunned by the information. "Doug has another kid?" he said wonderingly, as if to himself.

After giving him Betsy's number, Molly hung up, relieved to have passed the responsibility on. *So the police did follow up on my suggestion and questioned him. But they obviously didn't tell him how seriously hurt Renee was.* She did wonder fleetingly why he seemed more interested in Betsy than Renee. *I hope it was okay to give him Betsy's number.*

July 16: Day Eight

As the morning wore on, Molly was increasingly impatient for Detective Rasmussen to return her call. She paced around her living room, holding her cell phone and glancing at it every few seconds as if she could force it to ring. After watching her make a cup of tea that she allowed to cool without tasting, Mike finally said, "Okay, enough.

Let's just drive down there and find out if Rasmussen picked up your message."

At the police station, they checked in with Maria and asked for Detective Villegas. Maria made more than one call and suggested they take a seat on a grubby bench against the wall across from her window. At another bench to their right sat a young woman—just a teenager really. She was bent double, her head resting on plump knees, her hands behind her in handcuffs. Her face was hidden by a rat's nest of dark hair that spilled over her head in greasy shanks, old dreadlocks grown frizzy. Her bright pink blouse was completely open in back, punctuated by a black bra strap that pushed the flesh on either side into parallel rolls.

Neither of us is here really by choice, Molly thought, looking at her, *though you less than me, for sure.* The bench quivered as Molly moved restlessly, stood, and then sat again.

"Second thoughts?" Mike asked.

"No. Well, maybe. Won't they find out about Betsy from the hospital? I really don't feel good being the messenger." But just as Molly had decided to leave, Maria came out from behind the partition and asked them to follow her. Molly stood indecisively and then nodded to Mike and they went with Maria, who escorted them to a small conference room across from the detectives' suite where they'd met Villegas previously. After a few minutes, Villegas entered, accompanied by Rasmussen and a very pretty, athletic thirty-ish woman who Villegas introduced as Detective Weatherby.

"I was going to return your call," Rasmussen said, almost accusingly.

Molly blushed. "I know. I apologize for rushing down here, but...I wasn't sure anyone picked up the voice mail...." She looked at Mike.

He was less apologetic. "We have some information about Betsy Rausch that you should have, if you don't already."

Villegas gestured a silent invitation to go ahead.

"Betsy is Renee Holden's half-sister," Molly said bluntly. Villegas's face, as always, was impassive, but the other two detectives exchanged startled glances and then spoke simultaneously.

"How...? What do you mean?"

Villegas intervened. "Ms. Levin, perhaps you could start at the beginning and tell us how you know this."

Molly told them about Betsy's wanting to get into Renee's house and about seeing the DNA report. "It's kind of a weird story. Betsy and Renee's father had a teenage fling with Betsy's mother over sixty years ago...."

"Sixty-two years ago, to be exact," Mike said, taking up the thread of the story. "And apparently no one knew that Betsy was the result—not even her own mother, because she was also seeing the man she married shortly thereafter."

"And Betsy didn't know either, until she got the results of the DNA test," Molly added. "Douglas Holden—her biological father—had done the same test, so they both found out that they shared about half their DNA."

Detective Weatherby opened her laptop. "You saw the report yourself?" At Molly's confirmation, she asked her to spell Rausch and started typing.

"Apparently," Molly continued, "when Betsy told Renee last week, she didn't react the way Betsy hoped."

"Ms. Holden didn't know?"

Molly shook her head. "Douglas Holden died a few months ago. As far as we know, he didn't tell anyone."

Villegas sat immobile, his body relaxed but his

unblinking eyes fixed on her face intently, waiting for Molly to say more about Renee's reaction.

Rasmussen shifted uneasily in his chair, but he followed Villegas's lead and was silent.

The only sound in the room was the quiet tapping of keys as Weatherby followed her own line of questioning down electronic paths.

Molly mentally sifted through what Betsy had said, worried how a verbatim report would sound and considering whether to soften the tone. Unfortunately, she remembered Betsy's exact response very well when asked how Renee had taken the news.

Betsy gave a short, bitter laugh. "First she accused me of lying to her. Which I never did. I just didn't tell her the whole story within the first five minutes of meeting her. How the hell could I do that? And then when she cooled down a little, she just...blew me off. Said it made no difference in her life and shouldn't in mine. Like it was nothing. Didn't matter."

To Molly's embarrassment, a single tear angled down Betsy's face. She brushed it aside absently. "I should have known," she continued. "I've never had a decent relationship with any woman. I thought...I hoped because we got along so well...." She didn't finish what she had hoped.

Molly decided on a very abbreviated version of the conversation for the police: "Betsy said that Renee, um, blew her off."

Rasmussen finally spoke: "So Ms. Rausch was angry at that treatment?"

"Not so much angry as hurt, I think," Molly said carefully.

"How about your search in Ms. Holden's house. Did you find the legal documents you were looking for?"

Molly shook her head. "No; Renee didn't lock her files,

so we were able to look through everything, but we didn't see anything resembling a living will. If she has one, it's not in any obvious place."

"How about an estate will?"

Molly again shook her head. She considered whether to tell the detectives about Betsy's reaction to the fruitless search. Rasmussen had been watching her face carefully.

"I guess Ms. Rausch was disappointed," he ventured.

"Um, no. Not at all."

He nodded as if she had confirmed a private speculation. "Pleased?"

Molly felt her stomach clench. How should she answer that? In fact, Betsy *had* seemed pleased. Molly had been surprised and puzzled. While she hesitated, she was rescued from having to answer by Villegas.

"I surmise that Ms. Holden is pretty well off," he observed. "Retired lawyer, renovating her house here extensively?"

"Yeah, successful lawyer, used to live in Silicon Valley; she's pretty well off. You're thinking of inheritance, if Renee should die," Mike said. "*Cui bono*?"

If Villegas was amused or impressed with Mike repeating his Latin back at him, he betrayed nothing. His face was as blank as a just-washed whiteboard.

Molly's face mirrored conflicting emotions—alarm, guilt, and fear as she saw how quickly the police seized on the motive for attempted murder. She questioned the impulse that had brought her to the station. "Oh, I didn't mean...! Betsy came here just to get to know her sister. Aside from a son, she doesn't have any other family. I just thought...because we didn't find a living will...you should...." She looked at Mike wildly, overwhelmed by a sense of betrayal and a desperate desire to leave. She half stood, but Villegas waved her back into her chair.

"When did Ms. Rausch move here?"

"I don't know the exact date, but sometime in late March. She's just renting for a few months," Molly explained. "When she got the DNA test results, she first tried to locate her biological father, Douglas Holden, but he had died in a recent accident. So when she found out she had a half-sister living here, she pretty much immediately drove cross-country to meet Renee. But," she added awkwardly, "Betsy would be the best person to fill in details."

After asking Molly to repeat her observations, the detectives let them go, with the request that they call again if anything new occurred to them.

Once the door closed behind them, Molly said, "If Betsy was unhappy with me before, she'll be ready to kill me now."

As she heard her own careless words, she blanched.

43

VILLEGAS

It had taken a couple of pointed phone-call reminders, but Steve Antonelli had eventually agreed to come down to the station to sign a statement. When he arrived a few minutes after four o'clock just after Molly and Mike left, Maria escorted him to an interview room. Detective Villegas and Sergeant Partridge watched through the one-way observation window as Steve looked at the sparse furnishings, the table with two chairs on one side, and a single chair opposite, obviously designated for the interviewee. He paused, smirked, and selected one of the two chairs intended for the police.

"Looks like our guy wants to play games," Villegas said to Partridge. "Let's see if we can turn the tables on him." He then whispered some instructions to the sergeant.

When Villegas and Partridge entered the interview room, they did not react to Steve's choice of seating, but shook hands, and Villegas took the seat next to Steve. "Thanks for coming in," Villegas said. "You remember Sergeant Partridge," who nodded and took up a position directly behind Steve.

Steve shifted in his seat and looked nervously over his shoulder.

Bet he regrets choosing that seat, Villegas thought with carefully hidden amusement.

"I need to let you know that our conversation is being recorded," he said casually.

"I thought I was here to sign a statement."

"Yes, it's not quite ready. When it is, they'll bring it in to us. In the meantime, I'd like to clear up a few things."

"Such as?" Steve asked belligerently.

"Apparently there was a rather heated committee meeting with you about Ms. Holden's extension."

"So?"

"We've been told that Ms. Holden felt you had threatened her."

"Threatened! I didn't threaten her. Who says I did?" He shifted his chair a few inches away from Villegas, with another backwards look at Partridge.

"Mr. Antonelli," Villegas said, "as I recall, the night of Ms. Holden's fall, when we came to your house looking for a key to her house, you were just getting out of the shower."

"What makes you think that?"

"The bathrobe and wet hair."

Steve stared at him a long moment. "Okay, Sherlock. So what? Is going to bed clean a crime now?"

"I wondered if you had perhaps just returned home. Your neighbors—and your wife—were all already in bed."

"I already told you, when you came to my house. I was home. On the computer. All evening. You and her," he said, turning to point accusingly at Partridge. "You said you were talking to people on some list because of her accident. And I told you we didn't know anything about it. What's going on? Why do you care where I.... Wait a minute! You think someone *arranged* her accident?" He stood and took a step toward the door. "And you think I had something to do with it? This is, this is…harassment. I wouldn't have agreed to talk with you if I'd known you were going to accuse me—"

"No one is accusing you," Villegas said calmly. "We just need to know where you were that night during that time period."

"Well, I don't have to tell you squat," Steve said. "And I think it's time for me to leave."

"Before you do, we are also interested in hearing about your history of assaulting people."

Steve's face reddened. "What are you bringing that old news up for? That wasn't my fault. Guy got in my face, I pushed him—not even hard—and he fell over a stool. It wasn't assault. If I'd assaulted him, he'd have been in a lot worse shape. His wife made the charge—and he dropped it once he woke up enough. Stupid woman! And anyway, the prosecutor dropped the charge down to disorderly conduct."

"Have you been involved in other fights like that?" Partridge spoke for the first time.

Steve rounded on her. "It wasn't a fight! If it had been a real fight—" He stopped, apparently realizing he was not helping himself.

"The other guy would have been in worse shape," Partridge finished for him. "But if we were to look further into your past, would we find you'd had some 'real' fights?"

"Not since college. And even then, there were just a couple…uh, minor altercations. Why the hell are you digging into my past? What is this, the Inquisition?"

"No racks, no thumb screws," Villegas said mildly. "But maybe you could tell us more about the disagreement you had with Ms. Holden about her building project."

"And maybe I couldn't! I know my rights. I don't have to tell you anything. I don't even have to sign that statement." He opened the door and walked swiftly down the hallway toward the parking lot.

"So, what did we learn?" Villegas seemed to be musing out loud more than asking.

But Partridge responded anyway. "He reaffirmed his alibi on tape, such as it is. And he certainly seems to have a temper. He thinks we only know about the assault reported to the police. Why didn't you bring up the fight with the guy at Yavapai?"

"I would have if he hadn't skipped. But you notice he lied about having no other assaults in his history. We may have learned as much about him from that deliberate lie as we would have from hearing his side of the fight with the history teacher." *Although I doubt he's cornered the market on lying for this case.* "He's still high on my list of suspects; we'll keep after him."

44

VILLEGAS

July 17: Day Nine

When Villegas was summoned to the police chief's office, he knew he was going to be grilled about his failure to close the case. Robert Barajas, a Marine veteran, did not believe in micromanagement. He expected his detectives to take the initiative. He would concern himself with the "big picture," attentive to strategic and, frequently, political imperatives. But he still kept up with investigations and would want to hear about their progress.

Before Villegas even had a chance to acknowledge the chief and Captain Linda Dubrow, who was already seated, Barajas began speaking. "I just got a call from St. Anne's." Villegas took the chair next to his captain, across from the chief's desk. Behind the desk was a tall Scandinavian bookcase displaying mementos and photos. One was a framed studio family shot; others showed the chief at various ceremonial occasions, shaking hands, cutting a ribbon, presenting a medal or shield, manning a shovel at a ground-breaking ceremony. Barajas tilted back in a comfortable-looking desk chair that complemented the modern décor.

"Renee Holden is unlikely to be roused from her coma," he continued. "She's on life support and her doctor said there is almost no brain activity. They will monitor her, of course, but they aren't optimistic that she will recover consciousness. In fact, if life support were removed, it's likely she would die very soon."

He paused and looked at their faces to be sure they grasped the significance of that statement. "The moment that plug is pulled, it's not attempted murder anymore. It's a homicide investigation. And from what you've told me, it was clearly premeditated."

Mierda. "So much for interviewing the victim, then," Villegas said, shaking his head.

The chief continued as if Villegas had not spoken. "I assume you know how many murders we had in Cactus Heights last year."

A glance at Dubrow confirmed that the missile was aimed at him, not her. "Yes, sir," Villegas said. "None."

"And the year before that? And the year before that?" The chief didn't even stop for a response. "Right, none. And now guess where Mayor Harcourt's mother lives."

"I'm guessing Sunrise Acres," Villegas answered uncomfortably. *Only the chief could get away with playing this game.*

"Correct." The chief skewered Villegas with a laser glare. "Now where are you in this case, Jose? Do you at least have a suspect?"

"Four, actually," Villegas said. *Plus a bunch more in California.*

"*Four?* For God's sake, can't you narrow it down?"

"We were hoping that the victim would be able to help us do that. Her doctor thought that when they brought her out of the induced coma, she might be able to talk. He was going to call me as soon as she was awake. But now that she may never wake up...."

"She never gave you any info at all?" Dubrow asked.

"None. She's been unconscious the whole time since she was found."

There was a heavy silence before Chief Barajas spoke again. "The media is going to be all over this. I asked the hospital to hold off on telling anyone about her condition, but once she dies, we can expect calls from the local papers asking what we are doing to protect little old ladies from a killer."

"This murder attempt was intensely personal," Villegas said, "not some random assault. Renee Holden was lured to that bell tower by someone who wanted her, and only her, out of commission. The 'little old ladies' can rest easy."

"Try telling that to the mayor. Weapon?" Barajas asked.

"It appears to have been a brick. We think the assailant hoped we would assume the blows to the head came from the fall on the brick stairs. Detective Rasmussen accompanied the ambulance that transported Ms. Holden to St. Anne's. The docs bagged her clothes and some brick fragments embedded in her scalp. Those are now in the lab with Brandon Liao's team."

"Any chance at all that it really was an accident?" the chief asked hopefully.

Villegas sighed. "None. The crime scene unit says the blood spatter pattern was definitive. The fall contributed a lot to her injuries, but two blows to the head were the starting point. The first one probably drove her to her knees on the landing and the second sent blood everywhere. She then fell down the stairs or was pushed. The blows were hard enough to have killed her, the surgeon said, but she was in very good shape for a fifty-seven-year-old woman and she might have survived those blows if she hadn't fallen down the stairs."

"So what have you got, Jose?" Captain Dubrow asked. "Besides the blood spatter, what did your crime scene team turn up?"

"Not a lot," Villegas confessed. "Some more brick particles from the impact, jarred out when she fell down the stairs. They are almost certainly from the mur...from the brick she was hit with. Those went to Brandon also. And one blood smear from the sole of someone's shoe. I went up the stairs to check there were no other victims or obstacles that might have tripped her, but I took a lot of care about where I stepped. So it's possible, even likely, that the print is from the assailant's shoe. But it's so partial, we can't even tell how big the shoe was."

"Please tell me you've got an idea where to find the brick," Chief Barajas said, clearly exasperated.

"Well, it wasn't left at the scene. We searched the area very thoroughly. Frankly, I'm not very optimistic that we will ever find it, but we haven't given up. Could have been tossed anywhere out into a wash or buried. We'll have the lab analyze the brick particles, of course, but aside from establishing whether the brick used was the same as the ones in the tower stairs, I don't think we'll learn much from that analysis. Unless, of course, it was a very distinctive brick and we could track its source." *That would be nice*, he added to himself. "And a brick is unlikely to retain fingerprints. But Brandon Liao says there might be traces of the attacker's DNA, assuming no gloves."

"When the chief is through with us, Jose, brief me on alibis for the four suspects," Dubrow said.

The chief sighed heavily. "Once Her Honor hears about

this, she's going to ask for all sorts of extra protection for Sunrise Acres. And that will just pull resources off from solving the murder."

Resources, Villegas thought, *means me.* He didn't bother to correct the chief that it wasn't yet a murder. That thought reminded him: "If Ms. Holden continues in a coma, with no brain activity, who decides if and when to pull the plug?"

Dubrow answered. "Her family, I guess. Did she have a living will? A DNR?"

Villegas said, "This is where things get a little dicey. Her only family is a half-sister named Betsy Rausch, renting here in Sunrise. And she's one of our four suspects. I don't know if Ms. Holden has a do-not-resuscitate order. None was found at her home."

Chief Barajas had never been accused of being slow. "Holy crap! If Rausch is the attacker, and if she gets to decide on pulling the plug, we'd be letting her finish the job. That's one hell of an ethical dilemma. You have to eliminate or confirm her as the likely murderer, assailant, whatever— and soon. I don't know how long Ms. Holden has to live. Come on, Villegas. Live up to that reputation for creatively rewriting the book when it suits you and get us some real evidence."

"Well," Villegas said, "seems to me the dilemma would apply to the hospital as well. I'm sure their lawyers will be looking for a living will. I'll pull my team together here and see if we can possibly eliminate Rausch as a suspect. I'll get back to you. Oh, and one other thing, Chief. If we're going to continue to get 'real evidence,' we're going to need some overtime. My team has really been stretched, including a midnight trip to Phoenix and back by Rasmussen and Washington."

Chief Barajas's answer was a grimace and a wave of dismissal.

Well, he didn't say no.

As he closed the door behind him, Villegas could just hear the chief's sonorous voice: "Is he up to this?" Villegas couldn't hear Dubrow's much softer response.

"None of our suspects has an ironclad alibi," Villegas said. He was seated in front of Captain Dubrow's desk in one of the suffocating chairs he despised, briefing her on the suspects in more detail. "And all of them had time enough, by car or golf cart, to get to the scene and back." Dubrow was in full uniform today, gold badge and gold stripes on the sleeves set off by the dark navy jacket. Her highlighted brown hair was pulled back into a bun and small gold studs in her ears caught the light. Despite her erect carriage and authoritative air, she still looked as if she'd borrowed a male colleague's uniform, with the men's tie carefully knotted under the white shirt collar—but it was standard dress for her position. Villegas fleetingly pondered whether the required men's tie symbolized power or implied its opposite, but Dubrow's cocked eyebrow prompted him to continue his report—immediately.

"Peter Jackson, our victim's, uh, significant other...."

Dubrow gave a sharp nod, suggesting she would not need reminders about the identity of the suspects. "The one who denies sending the text invitation to Ms. Holden," she confirmed.

"He's the one with the tightest window of opportunity, no apparent motive, and the best alibi. The message could easily have been spoofed," Villegas said. "Google gives you

DIY instructions. Someone could even do it from a burner phone or some public computer."

"Could he have spoofed himself, to throw us off?" The question reminded Villegas that Dubrow had been an astute detective herself.

"Possibly, but according to his poker buddies, his trip to get beer was brief—twenty to twenty-five minutes. By our timing, that's hardly long enough to get to the tower, commit the assault, and return with cold beer and in pristine clothing. And, as I said, no motive that we've found yet. According to the man who called nine-one-one and stayed by her until the fire crew arrived, our victim tried to say something. Could have been 'Peter,' but might have been 'please.'"

"And if she did say Jackson's name, what does that tell us?"

"Not much, although Terry thinks it's incriminating."

Dubrow nodded. "Okay, tell me about the guy who wants the victim's property in California. Rod Staley, right?"

Now she's showing off her famous memory. "Guess you've been reading our reports," Villegas said.

Dubrow smirked. "Bedtime reading. Puts me to sleep every time."

Cheap shot, Villegas thought, *given the rumor that her real sleep remedy is a slug—or two or three—of single malt Scotch.*

"Staley's alibi is Swiss cheese," Villegas persevered. "He attended a Diamondbacks game, but could have dodged in and out again with plenty of time to drive down here from Phoenix and attack Ms. Holden."

"How about the guy Terry told me about? Antonelli, right?"

Villegas suppressed a wince at the reference to Rasmussen's end run. "Yeah. Turns out Antonelli has at least two known assaults: a bar fight here in Tucson and the one up at Yavapai. And Ms. Holden felt threatened by him in a meeting about her construction project. Until we found out about Betsy Rausch, I would have said he has the strongest motive. His retirement money just went into the toilet. He gambled on a fraudulent startup. They need to sell their house and Renee Holden's proposed extension reduces their property value a lot."

"Alibi?"

"Just his wife. Says they were both home all evening. But I think she'd say anything he told her to."

"Which brings us to Betsy Rausch. What's her alibi?"

"Watching television." Villegas decided not to recount in detail his team discussion about the show.

"Any of you Love Island *fans?" he had asked his three colleagues. Weatherby looked up with a small, hesitant nod.*

"Denise. You happen to watch the show the evening of the assault?"

"Ah, yes, guilty as charged." Weatherby glanced at Rasmussen, who was openly smirking at her admission. "What!" Weatherby said indignantly. "Hey, that's the only romance in my life these days!"

Partridge chuckled. "Well, Ms. Rausch says she was also watching the show. Of course, even old farts...," she glanced at Villegas, "ah, senior citizens can work a TVR. So she could have recorded it, watched later, then deleted the recording."

"Or read about it on the internet that night or next morning," Weatherby said. "Those shows get covered in a lot of detail," she added, with another annoyed glance at Rasmussen.

Villegas summarized the team's discussion for the captain: "Rausch's alibi is weak but impossible to prove or disprove. Unless, of course, someone saw her outside the house during the critical time. Sarah Partridge is going to talk to her neighbors. And," he added, "we haven't found blood on any of our suspects' cars or golf carts, and whoever did this had to have been covered with it."

"So," Dubrow said slowly, "either you have the wrong vehicles or the wrong suspects."

"Or both," Villegas admitted glumly. He started to rise from his seat, but the captain waved him to sit back down. She sat in silence a few moments. *Here it comes,* Villegas thought, recalling the chief's question to her. *I'm going to be taken off the case.* Villegas's stomach roiled nervously. Her first few words did little to dispel the fear.

"The chief is not convinced," she said, "that just because you were first on the scene, you are the right lead for this case." She held up a hand to silence him as he started to protest. "I told him we were lucky to have you. Bringing in the civilians to help identify suspects seems to be paying off. You get along with everyone—*most* everyone," she amended. He knew she was thinking of Rasmussen.

Seeing that comment as dismissal, Villegas stood and turned for the door. But Linda Dubrow's final words stopped him.

"But Jose, the chief's giving you one week to put this to bed."

What? He wheeled about to face her. "Or?"

She looked down at her desk and shuffled some papers. Finally she looked up and said, "Or he'll get someone more experienced to take over the lead."

MIKE

"Do you like Indian food?" Mike asked Molly, hoping for an affirmative. Preparing dinners for the family had always been one of Mike's pleasures. He had enjoyed planning the menus, with an emphasis on ethnic dishes. But after Andrea's death he found little pleasure in cooking creatively just for himself. Now he again looked forward to preparing meals for Molly once or twice a week. Tonight, he was hoping to return to one of his favorite ethnic meals.

"Indian as in indigenous peoples or South Asian?"

"I guess someday I may learn how to make a meal out of prickly pear pads and mesquite pod flour, but for the time being I'm talking about curries and flat breads. Nothing too spicy, I promise."

Over a dinner of chicken tikka masala over basmati rice, mango lassi, and dal makhani, augmented with garlic naan from Trader Joe's, he told Molly about an idea for catching Renee's attacker.

"Last week I came home to find my Mont Blanc pen on the floor. I figured it must have rolled off. A couple of days later when I got back from pickleball there was more of my desk stuff all over the place. And then today when I came back from shopping, I found the TV remote on the floor, popped open, batteries everywhere. I accused the cats, but both Arlo and Woody just stared at me with those big yellow innocent eyes. So I was thinking about how I could catch the guilty one in the act, and that led me to think of some kind of nanny cam to mount over my desk. And *that* led me to wonder if the police could set up a trap for Renee's assailant. They have several specific suspects. If they were somehow allowed to come visit Renee...."

"Hmm, you mean like in the movies, where the attacker would be anxious to finish Renee off before she could wake up and tell anyone what happened?"

"Well, yes, exactly. Renee would be the bait," Mike said. "Of course, as Detective Villegas said, it's unlikely she would have any memories around the attack, but the assailant wouldn't necessarily know that."

"Yeah," Molly nodded slowly, "very creative plan, but I don't like the idea of Renee as the goat tethered for the lion."

"It's not a plan! Just, just an idea, or a germ of an idea. Besides, the cops would probably not even listen to us, but I'm going to call Villegas on the off chance he'll see us. He did tell us to contact him if we had anything more to contribute. Maybe he can find a way to make it work. And as for identifying suspects for Villegas, it wouldn't have to be someone in our community," Mike reasoned. "Renee did have a life before she came here. And as we've said, she's not one to avoid confrontation. Probably what made her a successful lawyer."

"But face it," Molly persisted, "whoever did it had to know about Peter, know his phone number, know Renee's phone number, know that Renee exercised on the stairs at the tower, so that she'd immediately know what tower the text meant. Isn't it likely to be someone in Sunrise?"

"Probably, I guess. But of course, a motivated outsider could get those phone numbers easily enough. All they'd need is a Sunrise directory. In fact, anyone smart enough to spoof Peter's phone could surely use the internet to find phone numbers. And couldn't an outsider watch Renee from a distance for a few days and see her running up and down the stairs every day at the same time?"

"But," Molly asked, "how would an outsider know about Peter and Renee's relationship?" She shrugged, then answered her own question. "Talk to folks here? It's not exactly a secret, and most people are friendly and like to, well, gossip. Or maybe he—or she—saw Renee with Peter. Or," she said thoughtfully, "maybe Renee herself told whoever it was. Rod Staley knew about Peter, probably from when he and Renee went to California right after her father's death. When Staley called me a few days ago, he asked for Peter's phone number."

"Huh," Mike said, antennae up. "What else did he ask you?"

"Not much. Hey, stop looking at me like that. It seemed like an innocent inquiry, and remember, I did tell Detective Villegas about the call. Staley just wanted to know how Renee was doing. Like everyone else, he'd tried to get more information from the hospital, and they weren't giving it out. He wanted to talk to Peter to see if he knew more. I said it was unlikely. Anyway, it was really awkward. When I told Staley that Betsy was Renee's half-sister, he seemed at least as shocked about that as about Renee's...fall. And then he wanted Betsy's number."

"I wonder if Villegas has followed up with him—probably has."

"So maybe Staley's a suspect. I kind of hope he is. Villegas questioned Peter a long time, so he's obviously high on their list. But they must know by now that the text didn't really come from his phone. I'd like to see them look at some other people."

"Be careful what you wish for," Mike said with a laugh. "Could get *us* on the list. Did Peter say why they're still on his case even after looking at his phone?"

"Well, remember," Molly said, "Peter told us that he left his poker game for a few minutes when he went home to get some beer. And when he tried to use the fact that the beer was cold as part of his alibi, Villegas said that Peter could have had the beer in his car in a cooler and that he had plenty of time to get to the tower and back to the game."

"How would Peter have known that Jerry wouldn't have enough beer?"

"Didn't Peter tell us that he was supposed to bring it, but he forgot?"

"Yeah, but it still doesn't make sense to keep hounding him. I think the cops have glommed onto Peter as the prime suspect and just aren't looking beyond him. Did the time he was gone match the time of the assault?"

"I don't know," Molly said. "And I don't think we can go around asking the guys who were at the game. Peter wasn't sure either, just that it was shortly after they started playing when it was clear there wouldn't be enough beer to last the evening. I want to help Peter. So I do like the idea of pointing the police in a different direction. But I don't know about suggesting this notion of a trap. Seems kind of far-fetched. And we're not giving them additional information. I don't want to spoil the rapport we've built. What if they think we're trying to tell them how to conduct their investigation rather than helping?"

46

VILLEGAS

July 18: Day Ten

Villegas eyed the espresso machine. *If you have one more cup of that concentrated caffeine, you know you'll regret it,* he warned himself. But they were another day closer to the chief's one-week deadline. The knot that had taken up residence in his stomach tightened more with the thought. Fear? Anger? Maybe both. The pressure to solve the case within an arbitrary time period was unreasonable. He decided to fight his exhaustion by calling home instead of drinking more coffee. Just hearing his husband's voice would help. But as he reached for the phone, Denise Weatherby approached.

"Bunch of new info," she said, plopping down on the straight-backed chair next to Villegas's desk and opening her tablet. She clicked to her most recent notes. "Elizabeth Rausch's background, the alibi for Sanford—Ms. Holden's ex—and preliminary report from the lab about the brick. What would you like first?"

"Which is most likely to keep me awake?" Villegas asked wearily.

"None of them. Maybe Sanford. But the brick's quick. Nothing much to discuss. So I'll start there."

Villegas was tempted to ask why Weatherby had bothered to ask his preference, since she was ignoring it. *But*, he chided himself, *I'm being cranky. Denise has the nose of a bloodhound for researching backgrounds, and I need to be appreciative.*

"As expected, the brick fragments tell us a bunch of nothing. The only thing the lab can say so far is that the fragments don't match the bricks used in the tower stairs." She glanced up at Villegas. "But we already figured that."

"Still, good to have the confirmation," Villegas said. "And," he added thoughtfully, "it also suggests our assailant is possibly somewhat naïve." At Weatherby's inquiring look, he explained. "Assuming that he or she thought we might believe the wounds came from the stairs. Why else use a brick for the weapon?"

"Dumb," Weatherby agreed.

"Unless our assailant didn't realize the power of the blows would leave fragments. A skull is a lot harder than people realize."

Weatherby shook her head. "Dumb," she said again.

"No mastermind, for sure," Villegas agreed. "But then, we aren't dealing with a practiced murderer—at least if one of our current suspects is the attacker."

"Well, as it turns out, Daniel Sanford isn't likely to be added to our list," Weatherby said, referring to her notes. "After he and Renee Holden divorced in 2013 he moved as far away from Silicon Valley as he could. Likely a deliberate choice. Works as a cabinetmaker, remarried—to a much younger woman—has a toddler and a baby on the way. His alibi for the time is solid. He was in Maine with his in-laws for two weeks in a cabin on a lake, lucky devil. It's on an island, accessible only by boat."

Weatherby shook her head. "Man, to be that rich.... Anyway, he's got a bunch of witnesses who can vouch for his being there the entire time. And despite his move clear across country, he doesn't seem particularly bitter toward Ms. Holden. In fact, he's either an Oscar winner like Tom Hanks or he was genuinely shocked and concerned about her. I let him think it was an accident until we'd talked maybe twenty minutes, and then I asked him about who might have it in for her. He doesn't know anyone here, so he went immediately to that trial she won and all the African Americans angry about the way she got the shooter off. But he couldn't give me any names. Said to ask her old partners in the law firm."

"We may have to pursue that angle," Villegas said, rubbing his forehead at the very thought. "But right now, we have suspects a lot closer to home."

"Which," Weatherby said, "brings us to Rausch. Elizabeth Rausch has no arrests, not even a moving violation. A couple of parking tickets—one in Woburn, Massachusetts, where she lives, one in Lexington, Mass, where she works. I couldn't find out much about her at all. Google's never heard of her. She's just a boring sixty-two-year-old woman from New England. Tom Rausch—the father who raised her —ran a small hardware store but went bankrupt a few years ago. Her mother died last January and judging from her obituary, was a housewife. We don't really know for sure what Rausch's financial situation is, but she works in a garden center—or did before coming out here in March."

Weatherby looked up from her notes. "So," she said, "unless Rausch is a wizard in the stock market, or inherited from somewhere other than her folks, she could probably use some dough."

47

VILLEGAS

As Molly and Mike sat down in one of the interview rooms, Villegas looked from one to the other inquiringly. "Okay, you asked to see me...."

Molly gestured an "after you" to Mike. "I had an idea about identifying Renee's attacker," Mike said. "Unless you already know who it is?"

Villegas merely shook his head.

"This may sound melodramatic," Mike said hesitantly. "But we were wondering if it would be possible to set up a kind of trap. We are assuming that whoever was responsible for the attack actually wanted Renee to die. If so," he hurried on, as Villegas had assumed his usual impassive expression, "that attacker might want to finish the job, so to speak. Maybe you could have someone, um, like a policewoman, all bandaged up, pose as Renee and the hospital would allow visitors. Of course, the policewoman would have to be armed and ready to protect herself. And there would be a camera focused on the bed, like one of those nanny cams, with police officers in the next room watching.

When the assailant came over to, uh, finish off Renee, the officers would come to her rescue. To the policewoman's rescue, that is."

Villegas struggled to maintain his straight face. His mouth twitched and a small dimple appeared on one side.

"Guess there are a few flaws in the idea," Mike said.

"A few," Villegas said, an unaccustomed smile breaking out. "First of all, we would never allow a policewoman to take that kind of risk. What if the attacker brought a gun, or even a knife? The decoy could be dead before we could get to her. Second, the hospital would probably not let us set up two rooms like that. They need to keep rooms free in case of some major accident. Third, how would we notify all possible suspects that they were invited for a second try at Renee? You know the hospital won't answer questions about a patient's condition."

"Yeah, I see your point," Mike said, looking a bit dejected. "Guess it was a lame notion." Villegas started to thank them for coming in, but Molly switched to another topic.

"I hate to ask a dumb question, but can you narrow down the suspects by height? I mean, can't you tell by the blows, or maybe by blood spatter, how tall the assailant is? There's a huge difference in height between Rod Staley or Steve Antonelli and Betsy Rausch—if you're considering her a suspect," she added awkwardly.

"Wish it were that easy," Villegas said. "We can tell a lot about the attack from Ms. Holden's injuries and from blood spatter—but not about the height of the attacker. The first blow sent her to her knees. The blood spatter came from the second blow, and anyone standing above her could have delivered it."

Villegas stood. "Thank you for coming in. I appreciate your...creativity," he said tactfully. "But *mirabile*...uh, miracles happen, and there's always a chance that Ms. Holden's doctors will succeed in bringing her around, and then she might be able to tell us something that will help us identify her assailant."

48

MOLLY

"Huh," Molly said to Mike. "This is a bit weird." She was checking her voice mail as Mike drove them both back from their meeting with Villegas.

"Betsy has been kind of angry with me ever since I insisted that I go with her into Renee's house, but she just left a message asking me for a favor. Remember I told you that I gave Betsy's number to Rod Staley? Apparently, he called her, saying he wanted to come down from Phoenix and talk with her in person about a 'business proposition.' She thinks it must be about Renee's land. Anyway, she's asking if I'd be willing to come to her house tomorrow while he's here. I don't know whether she wants me as backup in case he's a threat or she wants me for my knowledge of real estate."

"Well, let's call her back. If she's worried about his temper, maybe I'd better come too."

But when Molly reached Betsy, it was clear that she was interested in Molly's real estate smarts.

"I'm just sure the 'business proposition' has to be about

Renee's land. What else could he possibly want to talk to me about? I tried to put him off, but he was really pushy. I have no idea what that land is like or why he's so eager to buy it. I don't even know what questions to ask him. If it is valuable, well, I'd like to know that. Just in case."

Then, after an awkward pause when Molly said nothing, "I mean, of course, just in case Renee recovers and I can give her the information. Anyway, are you free tomorrow at one o'clock? That's when he'd like to talk with me."

"Let me just see...," Molly said, checking her calendar. "Yes, that works. If Mike's free, would it be okay if he comes too? Just in case Staley gets physical? He's a big guy."

There was another pause before Betsy said, "Do you know something about this guy that I don't? Never occurred to me he'd get violent. But then he seemed pretty threatening when I saw him at Renee's house. So okay, I guess. You and Mike seem like twins joined at the hip these days."

Molly laughed. *More like conjoined hearts.* The thought made her unreasonably happy. "See you tomorrow at one."

JULY 19: Day Eleven

"Is that him?" Mike asked, looking out Betsy's window as an SUV with tinted glass pulled into the driveway promptly at one o'clock the next afternoon.

"Must be," Molly said, glancing at her watch. "I can't see through his window yet. At least he's on time. But it's not the same car he had when he argued with Renee. Remember, Betsy? He was in a cute little convertible."

"Yeah," Betsy said, watching as Rod stepped down from the driver's seat. "Maybe it was his daughter's car. Although why anyone in Arizona would drive a convertible is beyond me. Seems as if you'd be asking for sun poisoning. Great car for Massachusetts, though," she added a bit longingly.

"Hey, Betsy," Mike asked suddenly. "Did the police search your car the way they did Peter's?"

"Yeah. Pretty insulting. They didn't search yours, I'll bet. They made some feeble excuse about it's being routine, looking for DNA or something, in case Renee had ever ridden in it. I almost made them get a search warrant, but I figured that would look suspicious."

Mike stood in apparent deep thought as Betsy went to open the door.

"Come on in," she said to Rod. "You said you had a business proposition to discuss?"

Noticing the other two people in the room, Rod halted right inside the door. "What's this, a convention?"

As usual, Molly tried to defuse the situation. "Hi again, Mr. Staley." When he looked blank, she offered a hand. "Molly Levin. We met at the Hole-in-One and I'm the one who gave you Betsy's telephone number."

"Oh, right. Sorry. Guess I forgot what you looked like." He turned to Mike, who emerged from his reverie long enough to introduce himself.

Rod still looked puzzled at the unexpected presence of Molly and Mike, but he seemed determined to put the discussion on a social footing. "Nice house," he said, looking around at the studied Southwest décor. Stucco fireplace painted terra cotta, extruding a round belly onto the hearth in imitation of a wood-burning clay chiminea. Native American pots on the mantel. Framed prints and photographs of desert scenes on the walls. Colorful Mexican clay tiles around the baseboards and more neutral-colored tiles on the floors.

"It's a rental," Betsy said curtly. She waved him toward a leather couch with bronze studs outlining the arms.

To Molly's mystification, Mike signaled to her that he was going outside, and he held his phone up as if in explanation.

Betsy perched on the edge of a tall, uncomfortable-looking leather chair and looked at Rod expectantly.

"You said on the phone that Renee's condition is very serious," he said, glancing a bit nervously at Molly and at Mike's back as he went out the door.

She nodded.

"How serious? Is she expected to survive?"

"Why do you want to know that?"

"Well, if she...should she...um, not survive, then I take it you are her only living relative."

Betsy just looked at him steadily. He blundered on.

"In that case, you would inherit her estate, right?"

"Maybe."

"Well, you know that land Renee and I were, uh, discussing when I met you a couple weeks ago?"

"All I know is that Renee does not want to sell it to you."

"It's totally irrational. She's holding a grudge against me because of something my mother did over twenty years ago. I offered Doug, Renee's father, a really good price for his land a while back and he agreed to sell it to me. But then he died very unexpectedly."

"How inconvenient," Betsy said.

"I see you've been influenced by Renee's attitude toward me. I was hoping you and I might...that if you got to know me...you might be more, um, amenable...."

"Lots of 'ifs' there," Betsy observed. "*If* Renee dies, *if* I inherit, *if* I want to get to know you, *if* I want to sell some land I've not even seen...."

"Well, at least assure me that you won't sell it without giving me right of first refusal."

Molly stood up from the corner of the room where she had been sitting on the hearth. "Mr. Staley, can you give Betsy the exact location of the land and the acreage involved?"

He looked at her warily, clearly disconcerted by her intrusion. "Why?"

"To look at comparables in the area. How would she know if the price you offered was competitive? I'm in real estate," she reminded him. "Renee would know the value of the land, but if it turns out that...." She paused uncertainly. "If you're going to be asking Betsy to make a decision, she'd need a lot more information."

Despite having asked Molly to bring up such points, Betsy's face displayed a bit of discomfort with the turn the conversation was taking. "But I find this whole conversation ghoulish, Mr. Staley. Renee is alive. As long as she is, the decision about the land you want to buy is hers. In the meantime, please get me the information Molly mentioned." She stood, as if to bring the conversation to an end.

"Sure, I can get that. In fact, I already have some figures on recent property sales in the area. I could email them to you. You'll see what I'm offering is more than fair. Then...." He stood awkwardly, not moving toward the door as she so clearly wanted him to. "Can you at least let me know if she comes out of the coma you said she's in?"

"Why do you need to know that?"

"You just said, it's her decision unless she dies. If she recovers, maybe she'll change her mind and sell to me. If she dies, then the decision would probably be yours. And you don't have any sentimental attachment to the land.

You could be objective about selling. It's a really good price."

Betsy eyed him shrewdly. "Renee said it's been in the family for a hundred years or something. Why is that land so important to you right now? What's your big rush? If it were in Texas, I'd think you'd found oil on it."

She smiled at the startled look that flashed across his face.

"There's not much undeveloped land left in California," he said. But he didn't sound convinced of his own explanation. "And, uh, the trees, uh, there's a good market for timber and, well, I'll keep in touch. Thanks for seeing me."

Molly and Betsy watched through the front window as Rod walked toward the SUV. Mike stopped him before he opened the car door, and they had what appeared to be a rather tense exchange. Mike handed Rod his phone, apparently to speak to someone. After a brief conversation, Rod shoved the phone back at Mike, who grabbed it just in time to keep it from falling. Rod shook his head angrily, got into his car, and drove off.

"Well, Molly, what do you think?" Betsy asked.

"I think he really wants to buy that land. But I agree with you that it's—what did you say?—'ghoulish' to be so insistent while Renee's still in a coma."

"Yeah, he knows something about that land that makes it especially valuable, and I don't think it's trees. He's way too eager. When I had the estate sale after my mom died, an antiques dealer was awfully anxious to buy an old dresser. I could just tell she was trying to get it on the cheap and I wound up getting a good price for it. I'm getting the same greedy vibe from this guy."

When Mike walked back in the house, they both spoke

at once: Betsy asking, "What was that about?" and Molly, "What did you say to Rod?"

"I called the police station," he explained. "Detective Villegas did tell us to let him know if we had any ideas that might help. I spoke to Detective Rasmussen—he's part of the case team. In fact, he's the one who first interviewed Staley. Anyway...." Mike glanced at Betsy, and Molly saw he was unwilling to say much in her presence. He ended his explanation rather abruptly. "They want to talk to him down at the station."

After Molly and Mike got into his golf cart to return to her house, she asked, "Okay, Master Sleuth, there was more to your conversation than that, right?"

"I got to thinking about what you and Betsy noticed— that Staley was driving a different car today than when he had that argument with Renee."

"So what?"

"Well, it might not have any significance. As Betsy said, the convertible may have been a borrowed car and then he needed a rental. Or vice versa, I guess. But the point is: Which car did the police search for blood residue? Rasmussen, the detective that I just spoke with, seemed very interested; he asked if we could confirm that the two cars were different. I got the distinct feeling that Rasmussen had looked for blood in the SUV, not the convertible, though of course he wouldn't tell me anything. I think Villegas might have been more forthcoming with me if he'd been available. Anyway, Staley's on his way to the station now."

"What did you tell Staley?"

"About what?"

"To get him to go to the station? He must have been angry at you for getting the police on the line. Did you mention our noticing the different car?"

"No, I'm leaving that up to the police. I just told him that we were asked to let the police know when he was down here so that they could follow up with a few more questions."

Molly cocked an eyebrow at him dubiously.

"Okay," he admitted. "I was stretching the truth a bit—but Detective Villegas did ask us to let him know if we came up with anything interesting."

"Are you sure he went to the station?"

"What do you mean? I gave him the address."

"Well, he might not go there. Maybe he'll just drive back to Phoenix. They can't make him come, can they?"

"He wasn't pleased, that's for sure. But he told Rasmussen he'd give them a half hour. I don't think it would be smart of him to ignore their request."

49

VILLEGAS

"Thank you for extending your time down here," Villegas said, shaking Rod's hand and preceding him down the corridor to the interview room.

"Yeah," Rod said. "Do you grab anyone who comes from out of town for questioning?"

Villegas smiled politely. "No, certainly not." He stood aside, then followed Rod into the room. "We are talking with as many people who know Ms. Holden as possible. And you have made several trips here to see her or Ms. Rausch."

"Didn't know that was a crime," Rod said. His lips curled up slightly in a smile, but his eyes remained wary. Villegas was reminded of a dog uncertain of its attitude—tail wagging while its neck ruff stood up aggressively.

"Please, have a seat." Villegas positioned himself across the narrow table from Rod, with Rasmussen at his side. "You've met Detective Rasmussen."

The two shook hands and Rasmussen said, "Thanks for sending the photo of your ticket stub."

"I would have brought the stub with me if I'd known you were going to haul me down to the station."

"No need," Rasmussen said. "The photo's fine."

"Mr. Staley, would you mind if we record our conversation with you?" Villegas asked.

Rod hesitated. "That seems a bit...formal. I thought you just wanted some background on Renee since, as I told the detective here, I've known her since she was knee-high to a grasshopper."

"Yes, that is the purpose of meeting," Villegas said easily. "But Detective Rasmussen's handwriting is awful and mine's worse. So we'd rather not rely on our notes and memories."

"And actually it's for your protection," Rasmussen added. "We are legally bound to record any interviews conducted here in the station."

"Uh, okay I guess."

After the formalities of establishing Rod's name and address and recording the time and who was in the room, Villegas pushed himself back from the table and spread his legs out, crossing them at the ankles.

The pose seemed to reassure Rod, who visibly relaxed.

Rasmussen took the lead. He smiled at Rod and asked in carefully neutral tones, "Just to clarify a point that puzzles me, can you help me understand the discrep...difference between your son-in-law's recollection of when he told you he could not go to the ball game with you, and your memory of when that conversation took place?"

Rod began to tense up again, not at all reassured by Rasmussen's casual approach. "No big deal," he said. "I didn't remember his telling me he couldn't go until I was ready to go out the door that evening. Otherwise, maybe I could have sold his ticket. So maybe he did tell me earlier and I forgot. So what?"

"It's just one of those little details we try to get straight. But he definitely didn't go with you to the game, right?"

At Rod's nod, he continued. "Did you happen to see anyone you knew at the game?"

Rod frowned. "Do you know how big that stadium is? Thousands of people."

"Yeah," he said easily, "I've been to Chase. Good hot dogs. Did you get some that night? Or maybe some nachos at that Mexican stand? Beer?"

"Yeah, I had a beer. But what are you after? I showed you the ticket stub; you know I was there. What more do you want? You expect some guy hawking beer to remember selling me one? Gimme a break!"

"Had to ask," Rasmussen said, with a shrug and a glance at Villegas, as if Villegas was insisting on the question. Switching gears, he asked, "How about if you tell us why you've visited both Ms. Holden and Ms. Rausch—aside from the slightly cooler weather down here than in Phoenix."

Rod launched into a long explanation about the California property, his friendship with Doug Holden, and his offer to buy the Holden land.

Villegas and Rasmussen heard him out, although the family history he recounted seemed irrelevant to their purpose.

When at last he wound down, Villegas sat up. "Very interesting," he said. "But what makes that land so valuable to you?"

Rod sat forward and rested his elbows on the table. "It's wonderful forest land," he said earnestly. "Gorgeous firs and pine and black oak, even some yew."

"So you would sell the timber? Is that real profitable these days?"

"Sure."

"We've heard that you're offering a very high price for the land."

Rod looked startled. "How do you know that?"

"We've also heard that the market for timber is depressed, especially for fir," Villegas observed, ignoring his question.

"What, the police in the forestry business now?" Rod asked indignantly.

Villegas just shrugged. "Just wondering why that land is so valuable."

"I can't see why that's relevant. Why do you care about the land?"

"We don't; we just need to know why you do. Apparently, you've been very persistent about buying it. And Ms. Holden has been very clear that she doesn't want to sell it to you. You've argued with her about it."

"Wait a minute. I see what you're doing. You know I had nothing to do with Renee's accident. I wasn't anywhere near here that night. The detective here came all the way to my daughter's home to check it out. Yeah, Renee's been real stubborn about selling, so we've had some words, but nothing serious. I...I don't like the way you're talking to me. I came here voluntarily, remember. And now I'm going to leave—unless you're arresting me." He stood to go.

"No, of course not. But I do have one last question for you. Please."

"If it's the last one," Rod said grudgingly, sitting back down in the chair.

"Why did you switch your rental car the morning of the day Detective Rasmussen came up to see you?"

"Huh?" Rod looked wildly back and forth between the two of them. "How did you.... What difference does it...."

"Just answer the question, please," Villegas said politely.

"The first car I rented had mechanical problems."

"So if we checked with the car rental company, they would have a record of the necessary repairs."

Rod's gaze fell to the floor under the table, as if he would like to crawl there. He ran his finger along the rim of the table before answering. "Uh, well, actually it wasn't so much a mechanical problem. I just didn't like driving a convertible. It turned out to be hotter than a regular sedan—I thought it would be cooler." Gaining confidence, he added, "I only put the top down once anyway. The extra rental fee was a waste of money."

Villegas shook his head, visibly reminding Rod that lying to the police wasn't wise. "Okay, Mr. Staley." He stood. "Thank you for coming in." He offered his hand and Rod took it automatically, still stinging from being caught in a lie.

After he left, Rasmussen mused, "So we don't really know if there was blood in the car he used the night of the assault. Should we try to track down the convertible he was driving that day?"

"Not sure his lying is enough to get a warrant," Villegas said. "But it does raise him a notch as a suspect."

"By the way," Rasmussen asked, "how did you know that about the price of fir lumber?"

Villegas grinned. "I didn't. But clearly, neither did he."

50

VILLEGAS

July 20, 2019: Day Twelve

"Renee Holden is unlikely to ever regain consciousness," Villegas announced as he began the meeting of the case team Saturday morning. "I just confirmed with the hospital that her condition is unchanged. So at some point, perhaps in the near future, we'll be dealing with a homicide. This is a really big deal for a town that hasn't had a homicide in at least the four years I've been here. Chief Barajas is getting pressure from the mayor, and he's expressed his displeasure to Captain Dubrow with what he sees as lack of progress, so both the chief and Dubrow are leaning on me." He considered whether to tell them about the chief's threat to remove him from the case if it was not solved in the next four days, but rejected the notion. *Rasmussen would love that! He might even be a candidate to take over. And that possibility would give him a strong incentive to slow down the investigation.*

Villegas reviewed with the others the ethical dilemma of possibly leaving one of their suspects in charge of deciding when Renee Holden would die. "If Rausch is given any say in the life-or-death decision about her half-sister before the case is solved, we and the hospital could have a legal and PR disaster on our hands. Can you see the headlines? 'Murder suspect allowed by police to finish the job.'

"We need to find out what influence, if any, Ms. Rausch has in her half-sister's care. Chief Barajas told me that our lawyer says she would first have to be appointed guardian by the court, and there would be no relatives left to sue her if they didn't like the court order. The hospital's lawyers are probably chewing on that one as well."

At the nods of agreement, Villegas went on: "Now, back to the evidence." He turned to Weatherby. "What's the word on the brick fragments we sent to the lab, Denise?"

The detective looked down at the notes she had just taken over the phone. "They'll send the full report over to Brandon Liao in the Forensics Lab this afternoon, but in short: They can likely identify the manufacturer of the brick used in the attack, given a bit more time. It turns out that each company uses its own blend of clays, and while they fire the brick within a certain temperature range, there can be a bit of variance in that."

"And knowing the manufacturer would help us how?"

Weatherby shook her head and rubbed the back of her neck, a familiar gesture that Villegas recognized as frustration. "Not much," she admitted. "It's likely the manufacturer is domestic or Mexican, since long-distance shipping is expensive for something so heavy. But there are dozens of places in Arizona that supply bricks. We could probably find out which suppliers buy from that particular manufacturer, and we could likely track down any reasonably large orders, but that still wouldn't tell us who actually picked up that brick for that purpose. And all of these places will give individual customers a sample or two to use while they are planning their patio or walkway or whatever. Maybe the actual brick used in the attack would give us some better info."

"No disagreement there," Villegas said. "But," turning to Detective Rasmussen, "you said earlier you didn't see any obvious places around Sunrise Acres to ditch one."

"None that jumped out at me while I was timing the routes between the attack site and the suspects' houses. I did paw around under two of the bridges, but the washes are full of shrubs and grasses. I was trying to think like the attacker: Say I'm covered in blood spatter; it's dark and I'm in my golf cart or car, driving home. Or maybe walking, since we didn't find anything in the suspects' cars and golf carts. So, obviously, I want to get rid of the weapon. It's covered in blood and probably tissue and hair, and it's pretty heavy. I could toss it anywhere, but I want to be sure I throw it somewhere it won't be obvious once the sun comes up. Or I could wait until morning and bury it. But that's a bit risky also. People go out early for their walks, as soon as it's light, and the landscaping crews are also out early. I'd look pretty suspicious heading out into the desert with a bag, a shovel —and probably a crowbar or a caliche bar, because if I wanted to bury it more than a few inches, I'd have to break through the caliche layer. That's not easy; it can be as hard as cement in places. Not to be sexist, but frankly I can't see our female suspect being able to dig down far. And if Staley's our man, I doubt we'll get many volunteers to search both sides of the interstate between here and Phoenix."

Villegas stood up from his chair and stretched. "Then let's just suppose for the moment that our suspect is one of the three locals. He or she has thrown the brick or buried it, but not deep. How do we find it?"

"There's one more thing," Rasmussen said. "We're well

into monsoon season, and we haven't had a storm since the assault. I checked the latest forecast. Today's good and so is tomorrow. But there's a sixty percent chance of thunderstorms starting late Monday afternoon and continuing through the next morning. So, I think we need to find the brick ASAP, today or tomorrow if possible. Maybe do a grid search behind Jackson's and Antonelli's houses. Rausch's rental is surrounded by other houses."

"Does it even make sense to look behind Jackson's house?" Weatherby asked. "We've established no motive for him and a really small window of opportunity."

"It's probably very low probability," Villegas admitted. "But we haven't been able to totally exclude him. We don't know what's in Ms. Holden's will. He's smart and, according to his poker buddies, a good bluffer—which means he's really good at getting people to misread him, maybe us as well."

"If we do a search behind the houses, can we get some extra manpower before the thunderstorms hit? Maybe we could borrow some of Tucson's or the sheriff's guys?" Rasmussen asked.

"I wonder how smart Jessie is," Villegas mused.

"Huh? Jessie who?"

"Ms. Holden's dog. No," he quickly added, shaking his head, "dumb idea. She's totally untrained. But it does make me wonder if we could borrow a dog from Tucson PD's K-9 unit. It would have to be a cadaver dog. There's got to be blood and tissue on that brick. If we could get one of their units to help us, we could cover a heck of a lot more territory sooner. We'll have to stick to common areas and county land since we have no search warrant for anyone's private property, but if we don't find it there, we can try for warrants to search yards."

"And by then, any evidence would likely have been washed away. Want me to call about the dog?" Rasmussen asked

"No, I'll ask Captain Dubrow to make the call. I'll brief her, she'll appreciate the time pressures, and she knows the people downtown. We may have to jump the queue—those dogs and their handlers can be in high demand. Hope to hell we can get one on short notice. It's too late to organize anything today, and if we get that storm on schedule Monday afternoon, that gives us only tomorrow and half of Monday. Let's hold off on searching Sunrise Acres home-owner property and focus on nearby desert. And hope that Dubrow can work her magic with her pals downtown."

Just as the team was filing out, Maria came into the squad room. "Detective," she said, "there's a Peter Jackson on the phone. He asked to speak with you urgently. May I put him through?" Villegas asked her to go after Rasmussen and Weatherby and to put the call through as soon as they were back in the room.

"Mr. Jackson?"

Peter sounded nervous. "This is kind of awkward," he said. "But I have Bert O'Shea on the line with me. I met him when I was in California with Renee."

"Yes," Villegas said, "we've spoken with him. He's Ms. Holden's neighbor, right?"

"Yeah, and he kind of looks out for her land. He has an idea about why Rod Staley is so determined to get Renee's land. And I thought you'd better hear it directly from him. Better than from me," he added, with a touch of resentment in his voice. "It won't take long; I'll merge the calls, okay?"

"I'm going to put you on speaker," Villegas said. "Detectives Rasmussen and Weatherby are in the room." Weatherby had her phone out and held it up to show Villegas that she would record the conversation. Villegas nodded. "And we are recording this conversation," he added.

"Uh, okay, I guess. Let me ask Bert before I merge the call with you. I told him he'd be talking just with you, not a roomful of cops. And I didn't know you'd record him."

"Please assure him it's standard procedure," Villegas said.

"Yeah, for sure," Peter said sarcastically. "When have I heard that before."

But in less than a minute, a growly but pleasant voice came on the line. "Hello?"

"Mr. O'Shea," Villegas said. "I understand you have some information about Rod Staley to give us. As Mr. Jackson told you, I am going to record our conversation. Standard practice."

Bert gave a short laugh. "Well, first of all, call me Bert. And that ain't 'xactly what Peter said, but it's okay by me. I got a lotta cop friends out here. Now it ain't what you'd call information, 'xactly. More like a hunch."

Rasmussen rolled his eyes, looked pointedly at his watch, and stood up. Villegas held up a finger and mouthed, "Five minutes." Rasmussen remained standing.

"Go ahead, Mr. O'Shea, ah, Bert."

"See, I've been thinkin'. 'Bout why Rod'd be so all-fired in a hurry to buy Renee's land. 'Specially the swamp. It's turrbul land. Good fer nothin'. Poison oak and mosquitos big enough to carry off little kids. But ya know where we live, right?"

"Northern California," Villegas said.

"Placer County," Bert said. "Gold country. See, that swamp is like a catch basin for the crick runnin' down off the mountain. Doug—that's Renee's dad—allus said he should drain the swamp, 'cuz there was likely gold collected there. And could be. When Renee was little, I useta take her pannin' where the crick comes out. And we'd find color, ya know. Nuthin' big—just flakes."

Rasmussen sat down.

"But, see, last Jan'ry, we had one hell...uh, heckuva storm and the crick was jist roarin'. And it was jist after that, I seen Rod headin' out with his shotgun toward the swamp. I figgered he was goin' to try and see if there was enough water there'd be ducks. But I niver heard no shots. And then he started buggin' Doug to sell the land."

"So," Villegas asked, "you think he found—"

"Somethin' bigger'n usual. Probly some good-sized nuggets. And then, Rod bein' the ijit he is, he'd be sure there's a fortune in there. He's been tryin' to get rich all his life. Full of stupid schemes."

"Would he have found enough to make it worthwhile for him to...um, turn to violence to get the land?"

"I dunno. But now Doug's dead and Peter tells me Renee is real critical," Bert said sadly."Mebbe I'm jist a bad judge a people. Ya know someone almos' your whole life, ya just can't think they'd...." His voice trailed off.

"Bert? This is Denise Weatherby. A question, please, sir. Say Mr. Staley found a nugget. How would he know it was gold?"

"Well, he'd be purty sure, 'cuz most of the families 'round here have kept one or two that got passed down to them over the years; we know what gold looks like. But he'd take it to one a them assayers to make sure. There's a couple right near here, probly more over to Reno."

Rasmussen was interested now. Without introducing himself, he asked, "Did Ms. Holden inherit mineral rights to the land when her father died?"

Bert sounded surprised at the question. "Sure! That

land's been in her famly for years and they din't never give 'em up."

Villegas looked at the other two detectives, raising his eyebrows in a silent inquiry as to whether they had more questions. When they both shook their heads, he said to Bert, "If we have any follow-up questions, may we call you again?"

"Sure, if you'll lemme know how Renee's doin'," he said. "Peter 'n' me. We're both real worried. We're the only famly she's got now."

Villegas ended the call by thanking both of the men and with only a vague response to Bert's request about Renee's condition. In all likelihood, the next news he would be allowed to convey would not be what they hoped for.

"What do you think?" Villegas asked the other two detectives.

"Not sure it helps us," Rasmussen said. "We already knew Staley wanted to buy her land. And could be Jackson just wants to deflect attention from himself."

"But," Villegas pointed out, "it does strengthen Staley's motive for wanting to buy her land before anyone else discovers what he found."

"Especially Ms. Holden," Weatherby said.

"Exactly."

51

VILLEGAS

July 21: Day 13

Finally—a chance at some progress on the case, Villegas thought. Captain Dubrow had managed to impress upon her counterpart in Tucson the seriousness of the crime and that their best chance of locating the weapon was the K-9 unit. In another pleasant—and unexpected—development, Chief Barajas had assigned twelve additional officers to help in a search for the brick.

The trained cadaver dog, Skookum, and her handler, Doris Reimhold, arrived at nine o'clock in the morning, along with the additional twelve police officers, ready to go. Both Peter Jackson's and Steve Antonelli's houses backed up to public land, crisscrossed with hiking trails. Betsy Rausch's rental house had only a tiny backyard and backed up to a neighbor's, so they had no common area to search there.

With the abundance of recruits, Villegas decided to split into two teams. He assigned eight to go with Rasmussen to set up a search grid in the desert behind Peter Jackson's house. Villegas would lead the second team, comprised of the remaining four officers, Weatherby, Skookum, and her handler. They would search behind the Antonellis'.

Gathering his team, Villegas looked them over, assessing how prepared they were for what would be an arduous task. "It's going up to 105 later today," he said, "so be sure you have plenty of water. I don't need to tell you that every cholla, every cactus, is armed and dangerous." His humorous reference to all the spines and prickles they would encounter while fighting their way through the undergrowth elicited a few knowing smiles. "And if anyone missed breakfast," he waved some protein bars, "come grab a couple of these."

The officers formed a line about twelve feet apart, perpendicular to the row of houses, starting a quarter mile from the suspect's house and working their way toward it and beyond for another quarter mile.

At eleven forty, the Antonelli team members paused. They had gone the requisite quarter mile past the house. Their long-sleeved shirts and gloves helped protect against cactus spines but added to their discomfort; the mumbled curses had increasingly grown in length, volume, and creativity. Skookum's handler had brought extra water, but every member of the search team, human and canine, was wilting.

Rasmussen's team was similarly stressed, and he telephoned to report that they had found nothing.

Villegas called his team of searchers together. "Thank you all for your efforts—truly heroic, given the heat. We knew it was a very long shot, but it's time to call off the search. Let's head back."

"Yeah, should have handed this off to firefighters," one officer said, mimicking wringing sweat out of his wet bandana. "They're used to being broiled alive. Where are we?"

Villegas checked his GPS. "We're about fifty yards directly in back of Renee Holden's house." He pointed out a likely path up the embankment. The most direct route toward their vehicles ran between the Antonellis' and Renee Holden's houses. Without a trail, they had to bushwhack their way. They took it slow, in follow-the-leader single file behind Villegas until they reached the houses.

As Doris Reimhold and Skookum were about to pass Renee's back patio, the dog sat down abruptly. The dog handler looked puzzled. She pulled gently at Skookum's leash. "C'mon, girl."

One of the passing officers said, "Maybe she's exhausted. I know I am."

Reimhold took her own water bottle from her pack and offered it to Skookum. The dog opened her mouth and the handler squirted water in.

"Eeew," another officer said as he passed with a colleague. "Look at that. Do you know where that dog's tongue has been?"

His partner was apparently not too tired to get in a dig. "No worse than where yours has been."

"Bite me," was the cheerful response.

Doris Reimhold ignored the banter. "Skookum smells something in the yard over there."

"Could it be a dead squirrel or some other animal?" Villegas asked.

Skookum's handler was a bit insulted. "No way. Skookum would never make a mistake like that."

Weatherby, who was leading the group toward the road, had turned back when Villegas and Reimhold stopped. "If it was something big, we'd smell it ourselves," she said.

"Skookum has 300 million olfactory receptors in her nose—that's fifty times as many as you. And the part of her brain used for analyzing smells is forty times greater than a human's. She can smell a tiny bit of rotting flesh from fifty feet. This dog's nose," Reimhold added, stroking Skookum's head, "is still the most powerful piece of equipment anywhere for finding human remains."

Weatherby held up her hands in surrender. "Got it," she said with a smile. Not waiting for Villegas's command, she was already dialing. "Judge Worth, for a search warrant, right?"

Villegas nodded. "I'm sorry to ask you to wait," he said to Skookum's handler, "but we should be able to get a warrant to go inside the yard within twenty minutes or so—we can move on a verbal one from the judge and have her email a hard copy to the station. Let's move into some shade over there." He indicated the shadow of the Antonelli house.

Weatherby's phone rang within twenty-five minutes with the verbal warrant.

Inside Renee Holden's back patio, two pallets of bricks had been unloaded against the bars of the metal fence. Skookum went immediately to the first pallet and sat by one corner. The pallet had been completely encased in plastic, but the end Snookum sat by was open and folded back. A number of bricks had been removed and were scattered around the ground in pairs, each pair standing next to a different piece of hardscape: two different-style pavers, a slab of slate, and two different-colored pieces of flagstone.

Skookum ignored the bricks on the ground. She sat, her gaze intent on the rest of the stacked bricks in the pallet. Her handler started to reach inside. "Wait," Villegas said quickly. "Please don't touch anything."

"I think Skookum is indicating one of the bricks inside."

Villegas looked carefully at the stacks. The plastic was open to about two feet and folded back a foot or so. "We need to get a crime scene team here before we find the brick we're looking for. But I can't see anything on any of them. Can you and Skookum give us just another half hour?"

Reimhold looked at her watch wearily. "I guess so. What do you need us for?"

"I can't tell which brick she's pointing us to. I need the crime scene team to take photos and dust for fingerprints before we take the stack apart. And given what you've told us about Skookum's nose, I think she's much more likely than any of us to know which of these bricks has been used as a weapon. They all look the same to me. Someone has apparently cleaned it off."

When the crime scene crew showed up, to Villegas's surprise it included forensics lab chief Brandon Liao. "Much more interesting than burglary scenes," Liao explained his presence to Villegas as he pulled on latex gloves. The crew dusted the entire outside of the pallet and carefully disassembled the stack of bricks that could be reached through the hole in the plastic, laying them on the ground.

"The plastic is covered with fingerprints," Liao told Villegas, "but a few of them are on the underside, right where someone who has cut through the plastic with a sharp object, probably a box cutter, would grasp the plastic to pull it open and fold it back. And these few fingerprints are superimposed on older ones that were likely placed by workmen wrapping up the pallet. I'm having your suspects' prints sent to my tablet. Should know something in a few minutes."

Weatherby surveyed the array of a dozen bricks on the ground. "All look the same to me." But as soon as Reimhold was given permission to loose Skookum, the dog went immediately to one of the bricks and sat down, fixing her gaze on her handler.

Villegas needed no explanation. He picked up the brick in gloved hands and slipped it into an evidence bag. Liao could look for fingerprints later.

Liao brought his tablet over to Villegas. "Look at these prints of your suspects," he said. "We'll have to confirm this back in the lab, of course, where I can enlarge them, but I'll bet you a bottle of that Señor Rio tequila you like so much that the fingerprints from the plastic around the pallet match these."

52

VILLEGAS

"Have a seat," Villegas said, motioning Betsy to a metal chair on the other side of the table. The interview room was spare and intimidating. Villegas was seated across from Betsy, and Rasmussen stood against the beige wall near the door. Villegas stated the time and the names of the people in the room for the recording before beginning in a pleasant tone of voice.

"Ms. Rausch, could you tell us again why you decided to rent in Sunrise Acres this summer? It isn't exactly high season."

The question appeared to be unexpected. Betsy glanced at Rasmussen and sat forward in the chair before stammering, "Well, I...I don't see why that's relevant to your inquiry into Renee's...into what happened to Renee."

Villegas just continued to look at her in silence.

"She's my half-sister," she said, with a hint of indignation. "You know that, right?" Villegas nodded. "But she didn't know that until just recently, right?" He sounded a bit accusatory.

Betsy stared at him. "How the.... My God, Molly Levin has a big mouth!"

"So was Renee Holden the reason you came to Sunrise Acres? Renting in the hottest months of the year? You've been here, what, over three months? Surely you had time to talk with her before last week."

"Not that it's any of your business," Betsy said angrily, "but we were just getting to know each other. I was helping her with her landscaping. We'd have coffee together. I thought...I thought she liked me." There was a slight catch in her voice, hastily covered with a cough. "I was waiting for the right time...."

"But why did you come all the way out here?" Villegas repeated. "In person. You could have contacted her by phone or email—wouldn't that have made more sense than going to all the expense and trouble of coming to Arizona? Especially in the summer when visitors generally stay away?"

"Aren't you listening? I told you. I wanted to get to know Renee. How am I supposed to do that with a phone call? I wasn't sure how we might get along. So I wanted to be able to leave without saying anything if I could see we weren't compatible, or wouldn't...couldn't be friends. We've led such different lives."

Villegas changed his approach. "So you knew she's quite wealthy."

"That's insulting!" Betsy half stood, but Villegas waved her back down into the chair. She sat down sulkily. "I just told you, I didn't know that when I found out we were sisters, back in Massachusetts," she said, her voice rising. "I didn't know that until I got here."

"Really!" Villegas said as if mildly surprised. "Didn't you do some research on her before you came? Even a simple

Google search would have told you that she must have been more than comfortable financially, retired criminal defense lawyer and all."

"You're making this sound like...like some kind of cold-blooded, sneaky, premeditated plan. No, I didn't do a lot of 'research' on her." Betsy spit the word out disdainfully, like a bite of rancid meat. "I found out I had a sister I never knew I had. A little bit of family. An aunt for my son, my only child."

"A *rich* aunt," Villegas emphasized.

"So what? You're making me out to be some sort of money-grabber!" Betsy stood. "You're just badgering me. Is this some sort of bad-cop," she glanced over at the impassive Rasmussen, "no-cop routine? You have no real reason to suspect me of anything. I don't have to sit here and listen to this. Am I under arrest or something?"

"No, you're not under arrest. Let's just say that for the time being I would consider it...a responsible act for you to remain sitting here," he said. "You see, we have found your fingerprints in a very, uh, interesting place."

Betsy sat back down with an audible thump. "My fingerprints? Where?"

"We found the weapon used in the attack on Ms. Holden —a brick."

"Well, you couldn't have found my fingerprints on that!" Betsy exclaimed.

"Why not?" Villegas noted her certainty. *Because she was the attacker and had worn gloves? Or maybe because she knew porous materials like bricks were unlikely to provide fingerprints? Or both?*

"Obviously, because I didn't attack Renee," Betsy said sarcastically. "So where do you *say* you found my fingerprints?" She sat back in the chair, folding her arms as if she were daring him to admit he was baiting her with a lie.

"That particular brick came from a pallet in Ms. Holden's backyard. And your fingerprints were on the plastic covering the pallet. You took a number of bricks out of the pallet—and," Villegas said with deliberate brutality, "one of them was used to smash in the back of Renee Holden's head."

Betsy seemed unfazed. "Oh," she said, with an airy wave of her hand. "I can explain that. I was helping Renee design her back patio. She had ordered those bricks for a new wall, but we wanted to see how their color would go with the samples we had of pavers, flagstone, and slate. So we opened the plastic and took a few out. Hey, I already told you I was helping Renee with the landscaping. I've been back there several times; my fingerprints are probably all over the place."

That was quick, Villegas thought. *She was expecting to be questioned about those fingerprints.*

"Or," Villegas said, "perhaps you opened the plastic to get that one particular brick we found. Given Ms. Holden's condition, we have no way of verifying your story."

"It's not a *story*. It's the truth. And I can prove it. I ordered plants and two trees for her. I could show you a copy of the order." She sat back, a slight satisfied smile on her lips.

Again, well prepared. "That substantiates your...that shows that you were planning some landscaping for Ms. Holden. But it doesn't prove that you didn't take a brick out of the pallet to use in an attack."

"It doesn't prove I did, either. If all you've got is my fingerprints on the plastic covering the bricks and I can easily explain how they got there, you shouldn't be throwing accusations around." She stood up and strode to the door, still with that faint smile on her lips. Rasmussen barely had time to step over and open it for her.

"It's a good explanation," Rasmussen said after Betsy had left. "We can check, of course, and make sure Ms. Holden's address is on the order for delivery, but Rausch's story does make sense."

"Agreed," Villegas said. "But we have no idea when that plastic was opened—or that the bricks were taken out for the purpose she stated. Did you notice how well prepared she was to be questioned about the fingerprints? She didn't hesitate a moment before producing an explanation. And while the explanation is certainly credible, we might consider another possible scenario.

"Suppose we have a very clever assailant who opens the pallet to get at the brick to use in an assault, hoping it's a good weapon because of the bricks in the tower stairway. She's afraid that even wiping down the plastic could still leave an unnoticed fingerprint or a tiny bit of DNA somewhere. So she makes sure she has a good innocent explanation for why we might find either. She washes off the brick used in the attack and slips it back into the pallet. To the naked eye it looks just like all the others in the pallet. We would never have found it without Skookum. But Liao has been able to confirm that there's human blood soaked into it. He's testing now to be sure it's Holden's—but it likely is."

"If I'd been the attacker," Rasmussen said, "I'd have wiped down the plastic and counted on the rain to wash any remaining traces away. And I would have thrown that brick into some wash during the monsoon, when there was going to be a running stream of water. Why would she put the brick back in the pallet?"

"Actually," Villegas said, "that wasn't so dumb. Hiding it

in plain sight. If it hadn't been for Skookum's nose, we never would have found it. All of our suspects had opportunity to put it there—Antonelli and Jackson—even Staley, for that matter. But Rausch is the only one who left fingerprints on the pallet covering."

53

MOLLY

July 22: Day Fourteen

When daytime temperatures inevitably hit three digits, Molly walked Jessie just at dawn. The sky was light, the morning air soft and cool. The exotic harmonies of the birds' dawn choruses provided a soothing prelude to her day. She knew they were making avian claims on territory, not singing for fun, but the music still always filled her with a primal joy. She and Jessie's usual morning route took them a couple of miles through the neighborhood, and by the time they returned home, Jessie had identified traces of recent visitors on almost every boulder and lamppost, and had made several contributions herself.

This Monday morning, Jessie woke Molly just as the first bird announced its claim. Finding two humans in the bed, she padded from one side to the other, but settled on Molly's to carry out her usual ritual. Leash in mouth, she sat bedside with ferocious concentration. She didn't bark, didn't whine. Just sat and stared. Renee had trained her well. Closer to the edge of the bed than usual, Molly was unfortunate enough to have awakened with her face turned outward. Jessie was close enough to waft less-than-fragrant doggy breaths her way. And when Molly opened a wary eye, she was confronted with two large brown eyes, only inches from her own.

"All right, all right," Molly groaned softly. "It's not even light yet, Jessie." Hearing her name, Jessie wagged her tail ecstatically. Walking carefully around a still dark bedroom, Molly pulled on jeans and a T-shirt. Mike stirred.

"What time is it?" he asked groggily.

"A bit before five," Molly whispered. "Please go back to sleep. I'll be back in a half hour." She started to stick her feet into sandals but then decided that caution dictated tennis shoes rather than bare toes. In the height of summer, rattlesnakes could be out at any hour.

It was trash pickup day, and she'd need to wheel the second of her large containers out to the curb when she returned from walking Jessie. She always put out the recycle bin at night, but after one experience with the boar-like javalinas tipping over the trash barrel during the night, strewing yogurt containers, meat packaging, and corncobs all over the street, she waited for morning to put out the garbage bin.

She turned on the small lights under the kitchen cabinets, unwilling this early to face the harsh glare of the overheads, pushed the controls on the electric teakettle, and loaded her tea caddy with a tablespoon of her favorite tea. Mike, in shorts and a T-shirt, came into the kitchen and put coffee beans in the small grinder Molly had bought as an enticement to have breakfast together once or twice a week. Jessie was now doing a little jig, the doggy equivalent of a human's crossing legs, in evident urgent need to go outside.

Molly sighed. "Sorry you didn't get back to sleep. Guess

I'll have my tea when we return. I need to put out the trash anyway."

"I put mine out last night."

"Good luck. Hope you weren't cursed with a visit from the local javalina troupe."

"I'll get the trash bin," Mike volunteered, and headed for the garage. He glanced out the window, stopped, and watched for a few seconds. "Hey Molly, come look." Molly joined him as he pointed to a figure that had emerged from the Antonellis' house, barely lit by the one lamppost in front of Renee's house next door.

"That's just Julie. So what?" said Molly.

"I don't know, doesn't she look kind of sneaky, looking up and down the street?"

"You're right." Molly turned off the lights in the kitchen. For some reason she didn't quite understand, she didn't want Julie to know she was being observed.

"Julie, Julie, what are you doing?" Molly murmured, intrigued now. Julie had a small bundle under her arm, and Molly expected to see her tuck it into her own garbage bin at the curb. Instead, she walked two houses down, past the Bowers', and put the bundle into the Jeffersons' trash. Then, again with that oddly intense look up and down the street, Julie walked quickly back to her own house and shut the door behind her.

"Huh!" Molly said. "Why would she walk all the way down there?"

Mike shrugged, but Molly's curiosity was now at full boil. "While you put my bin out, I'll walk Jessie." She attached the leash, crossed the street with Jessie, and casually walked past the Bowers' house, allowed Jessie to baptize a few rocks, then, equally casually, pulled her to a stop by the Jeffersons' trash bins and, mimicking Julie, looked up and down the street. It was still barely light and most of the houses were completely dark. Puzzled, Jessie tugged at the leash. "Poop here!" Molly whispered urgently. Jessie didn't recognize the command, but she interpreted the tone of voice to mean she should do something, so she sat.

Her heart pounding, Molly silently lifted the lid of the four-foot-high bin just enough to see a small trash bundle in a white plastic bag on top, obviously the one Julie had just deposited. The rest of the Jeffersons' trash was mostly shrub cuttings, she was relieved to see. She was not eager to paw through garbage. *Why would Julie put trash in someone else's barrel? Is hers full?* After checking around to see if anyone else was out, she slipped the bundle out, holding it tightly to her side, and walked back toward the Antonellis' driveway, where their trash barrel stood on the sidewalk.

She glanced around nervously again. *I will look awfully suspicious if someone sees me.* She hesitated. The desire to flee was almost overwhelming. *It will take only a few seconds,* she urged herself. In one quick motion, she grabbed the lid of the barrel and lifted it just enough to peek inside. It was only half full. The lid slipped from her fingers and fell with a soft thud that sounded like a clap of thunder to her. She half expected one of the neighbors to come out and ask what she was doing, but there were still no lights on in any of the houses, and the newspapers lay as yet unclaimed in the driveways.

As she walked quickly back to her house, she took a deep breath, only as she reached the yard realizing she had been holding it. Jessie trailed behind obediently, obviously confused. "Jessie, sit. I'll be right back, girl," Molly said as she looped the leash over her gate and hastily dropped the mysterious trash bag inside the front door. She would explore the contents after Jessie completed an abbreviated walk.

When Molly opened the front door on her return, she saw that Mike was about to pour his first cup of coffee of the day from his French press into his favorite mug, an old birthday gift from his son Andy. Mike had explained that he had brought it to use in Molly's house because of its capacious size, not because of the "Big Six-Oh" it sported. He took his first sip with an audible "ah."

"Wow," he said, pointing to the plastic bag Molly had picked up on her way in. "Either Jessie has a real plumbing problem or you're raiding a neighbor's trash."

"This is what Julie was putting into the Jeffersons' trash bin," Molly said. "Feels like cloth." She peered into the bag, unwilling to stick her hand in or dump out the contents before she was sure there was no garbage inside. She opened the mouth of the bag wide and turned it so that Mike could see inside. "Clothing," she said. "Dark-colored clothing." She pulled out the top piece. It was a man's T-shirt, black, extra large.

"Hm, interesting. Looks like Julie's ditching Steve's clothes," Mike said. "What else is in there?"

Suddenly aware that the kitchen could be visible from the street, Molly moved to the back of the room. She shook out the remaining item: a pair of dressy petite size 10 women's pants. They, like the T-shirt, looked to be in excellent condition. Neither appeared to have any spots or tears. Under Mike's increasingly bewildered eyes, she raised them to her nose.

"Smell," she commanded, holding the clothes out to him.

Mike obediently bent his head to them and took a sniff. "I don't smell anything."

"Exactly!" she said triumphantly. "These have been laundered. Why wash clothes if you're going to put them in the trash? And why on earth would she throw these away to begin with? Even if they no longer fit, there are dozens of organizations begging for 'gently used' clothing, and many of them pick up curbside. And if she's throwing them away, why not put them in her own trash?"

"I'm sure there's a reasonable explanation, but I sure as hell can't come up with one. She did look as if she was trying to hide them."

"Mike," she said slowly. "What if...what if there was blood on these clothes? I know Detective Villegas considers Steve a suspect, and the police said there would have been blood everywhere on whoever hit Renee. And this sure looks like Steve's T-shirt."

Mike gave her his full attention. "That's a heck of a leap. Just because you saw her throwing away some old clothes."

"But these aren't old, Mike. They are in really good shape. Think about it. Someone intending to remain invisible at night would wear dark clothing like this."

"Well, I can't see Steve wearing those pants!" Mike said with a laugh.

"That's part of why it's so odd. Why are these two pieces together? One is Steve's and the other obviously belonged to Julie. Even if, say, Julie wanted to wear Steve's T-shirt for some reason, no woman with any fashion sense at all would wear a black top with navy pants. Especially since the T-shirt is really casual and the pants are definitely dressy. And look at this!" she said, examining the label on the pants. "Wow! YSL!"

Mike started to laugh but checked himself at the warning look Molly shot him. "Ah, okay," he said. "I'm totally, totally with you on the horribly mismatched colors...." Another glare from Molly. Then, hurriedly, "I assume YSL means something?"

"Means Yves St. Laurent—means five hundred dollars or more somethings," Molly said. "No one would throw away such an expensive pair of pants unless...."

"Okay. Why don't we look and see if there's blood on them."

They took the clothes into the bedroom and held the T-shirt directly under the strongest light. No stains at all that either of them could see. Same with the pants. "Of course the clothes are dark," Mike said, "so it would probably be difficult to see any stains."

Molly was not ready to give up. "What if there *was* blood? They've been washed."

"Can you get blood out that easily?" Mike asked.

"Sure, if the blood is fresh and you use cool water," Molly said confidently.

"How do you know this stuff?"

Molly just looked at him. "Guys!" Molly grinned, then addressed Siri on her phone and showed Mike the result. All traces of blood on clothing would be removed if the blood were fresh and the washing thorough. One article even specifically mentioned the inability of police to retrieve useful evidence from bloody clothes that had been well washed.

"But maybe it depends on the material and how much blood," Molly said. "Maybe a police lab could still find traces if there had been a lot." She shuddered at the realization that she was possibly talking about Renee's blood. It was such a horrible thought and mental picture. She sat down heavily on the edge of the bed.

Mike fingered the weave on the pants. "The police have never considered Julie a suspect. But didn't you tell me she used to work in IT? So she'd know how to spoof Peter's phone. And she has the same motive Steve does."

"Oh, let's run down to the station and suggest her to them," Molly said, shaking her head in disbelief. "Meek little Julie?"

"Minnie Mousy little Julie?" Mike joined in.

"Whoa, that's sexist, or...something-ist. Julie's little, but she's in good shape. She rides her bike to all her club meetings and classes."

"Except," Mike said, hands up in appeasement, "when you offer her a ride, like to your sessions getting the *Sunrise Notes* ready to print. By the way, that's always struck me as amusing, the way people go to great lengths to go to exercise classes but avoid opportunities to exercise in daily routines. Park the car right by the gym...."

"It makes perfect sense. You should come work out with Billy and you'll understand why we might avoid exercise on off-days. Besides, the *Sunrise Notes* committee meets way at the other end of Sunrise. And I'm happy to give her a ride— it's not as if she lived miles away."

He raised a defensive hand. "Peace! I take it all back. 'Julie is the very model of a modern pint-sized se-ni-or,'" he sang, doing an *HMS Pinafore* patter.

"That's pretty good, Mike, but you just keep digging that hole deeper, don't you," she said with a chuckle.

"Let's stay with this for a bit," he said, more seriously. "Detective Villegas obviously thinks a woman could be the assailant, or he would already have eliminated Betsy as a suspect. He didn't seem inclined to do that."

"So you're saying we should have given him Julie's name as well as Steve's?"

"No, Steve's the one who has publicly argued with Renee and he's the one Renee accused of poisoning Jessie. And he certainly could swing a weapon at someone's head better. I'm just saying they had the same motive to harm Renee—to get her to stop that extension she's building."

"I hadn't thought of that," Molly said quietly. "I would just hate being suspicious of Julie. She seems so...pathetic, so unlikely to be a homicidal maniac."

"Now who's being sexist? You were okay with suspecting Steve."

"Touché," she said with a laugh. "I'll treat them both as equal opportunity suspects. Maybe I should take these clothes to Detective Villegas? Tell him what I saw Julie do?"

"I don't think I would. We're batting no more than .500 at the moment with Detective Villegas. The tip about Staley's switching cars gave us some credibility, but our—my —little suggestion about a trap was pretty dumb. If there were bloodstains, that would be different. But as far as we can tell, there aren't. Maybe she just didn't want Steve to know she was throwing out some good clothes."

"Huh. Yeah, that's a possibility I hadn't thought of."

AFTER MIKE LEFT for his bike club outing, his words echoed in Molly's ears. "If there were bloodstains, that would be different." *Where else would there be bloodstains, if Julie were the attacker? I think I know. And I think I know how to find out for sure.*

Fortunately for Molly's plan, it was Julie who answered the phone. "Hi, Julie, I'm not able to go with you and Aki to work on *Sunrise Notes* today. I'm not that much help, anyway. You're the only one who can figure out that software. But Aki is going to come by and pick you up." At Julie's protest that Aki needn't bother, Molly said, "Actually, she'd really like to, and she's planning on it. She'll be by at seven forty-five. See you next time." She hung up before Julie could argue further.

Now for part two of the plan. Everything depended on whether Steve went out or not. Molly watched through her front window as Aki pulled her red Prius into the Antonellis' driveway. Julie came out and the two drove away. Molly waited several minutes until it was unlikely they would be coming back for some forgotten item. Then she crossed the street and rang the bell.

When Steve came to the door, Molly put on her friendliest smile. "Hey, Steve, how are you?"

"What do you want?" he asked quickly, with a businesslike "don't-waste-my-time" intonation.

He's still mad because I didn't help them fight the RIC. Or maybe he hasn't had his coffee yet.

"I have to run to the center to get some cash, and my car's getting fixed. Could I borrow Julie's bike for about twenty minutes?"

Steve hesitated. *What if he refuses, or worse, offers to drive me?* Molly worried. *Unlikely. Not Steve.* He apparently decided to be gracious. Or at least his version of gracious. "Okay. I'll open the garage door for you to get it. But don't be long. Julie will need it when she gets home from working on that newsletter. Hey, how come you didn't go this morning?"

"I'm supposed to get a call from the car dealer," Molly said breezily. "Sometime after eight thirty."

She went to the front of the house and when Steve opened the garage door, she wheeled Julie's bike out onto the short driveway. From what the police said about the attack, whoever did it would have been covered in blood. *Where would that blood show up besides on clothing?* She waited until the garage door came down behind her. For the second time that morning, Molly's heart began to race and her breath came ragged. *What if someone comes by?* She took a few deep breaths to steady her nerves and then stooped to scrutinize the seat, the handlebars, and the pedals. *I could say I was deciding whether or not to adjust the seat for longer legs. Is that rust on the left pedal or...?*

She took out her phone and with a nervous glance at the house, bent to snap a close-up. *The police said the attack weapon was a brick. If they'd found it at the tower, we'd know. So if Julie was the attacker, she might have carried the brick away with her. How?* Behind the seat, Julie had suspended over the back fender a two-sided leather saddlebag pannier that she used to carry water and other small items.

Molly looked down the street both ways. A car appeared a few blocks away, but to her relief, turned off. She returned to her examination, more nervous with each passing moment, trying to focus on her observation—not what it might mean. She saw nothing on the outside of the leather. *Hurry! Steve could come out any second! I can't do this! Let the police take over,* she thought. *But they can't—not without more evidence, and what if I'm wrong? Julie would never forgive me and neither would anyone else in Sunrise.* She took a deep breath. Cautiously, covering her fingers with a Kleenex, she flipped open one side of the pannier. It was deep, narrow, and dark. She could see nothing inside until she turned on her phone flashlight.

She gasped. On the sides of the pannier, deep inside, were rust-colored smears. A lot of them. Red sand-like debris gathered in the folds at the bottom. Making sure her flash was on, Molly reached the phone deep into the pannier and took photo bursts all the way around and then at the bottom. Then she pulled the pannier as wide as she could to allow sunlight in. Carefully standing so that she did not cast a shadow, she videoed the insides. Her fingers were shaking so badly that she was afraid she might have hit the wrong button activating the video, but she didn't dare take time to check the recording. She reached over to open the other pannier, but it seemed clean. She stood with her back to the street, blocking the view of anyone who might walk by. *Steve could open the garage door any time or come out through the front door.*

She started at the grating sound of the garage door beginning to open and felt a wave of panic so strong that she felt light-headed. *How do I explain not leaving before now?* She had just time enough to step back from the bike and put the phone to her ear. She spoke into it, "Okay, see you soon." Her voice came out in a high-pitched squeak. She cleared her throat, put the phone in her pocket, and turned to Steve, who was walking to the side of his car. He was obviously surprised to see her standing there by the bike.

"Oh, Steve—glad you came out." She was surprised at how normal she now sounded. "I was just talking with Mike, and he says he'll take me to the ATM, says it's too hot to bike, so I'm not going to need it after all. Shall I put the bike back for you?" She turned away quickly, knowing that her flaming face could reveal she was lying.

"Yeah, okay." Steve climbed into his car and waited for her to return the bike to the side of the garage before backing out. She waved at him as he drove off and gave a great sigh of relief. Then she crossed the street and called Mike.

He could scarcely believe both the risk she had taken and her discovery. "Are you sure you got the shots? Check your Photos."

Nervously, she opened her Photos folder and saw a series of photo bursts and a one-minute video. The images were even crisper than she had hoped. The rust-colored stains showed up prominently.

"Yes. Really clear. Of course, they may not be blood."

"Let's get them to Villegas; it's up to him to decide what to do next. I could pick you up in five. And Molly? I'd suggest you bring along those clothes you found this morning. Just in case."

54

STEVE

When Steve returned home from the hardware store with a replacement fluorescent bulb for the laundry room, he found Julie in the living room, feet up on the couch hassock. She looked up from the newspaper and noted the long bulb in his hand. "Good. Now can you put it in today for sure? Otherwise, I'm going to have to do the laundry by flashlight!"

"Could do it now if you'll help me get the ladder in from the garage without banging the walls."

Her face told him she regretted suggesting the chore. "I'm beat," she admitted. "Molly didn't help out with composing the *Sunrise Notes,* so it took Aki and me a lot longer than usual."

"Yeah, I know Molly didn't go. She came by here after you left."

"Why?"

"She asked to borrow your bike," he said, walking down the hall toward the laundry.

"What?" Julie sprang up from the couch and hastily followed him. "And you let her?"

He turned, surprised at the accusing note in her voice.

"Well, I said she could; she's having some problem with her car, but then Mike called her to take her to the ATM and she ended up not needing it."

"So she never rode it?" Julie's voice was shrill with anxiety.

"I don't know if she ever got on it; she was out in the driveway, and I was in the house. What the hell? What's the big deal? You've loaned that bike to people before. In fact, you're always loaning stuff out, like my electric sander last week." He was resentful, remembering that he didn't have that sander back yet.

"But she took it out of the garage? For how long?"

"Just a couple of minutes, and then when she got that call from Mike, put it back in. I don't get why you're getting so worked up over this."

Before he finished speaking, Julie was racing toward the garage. She turned on the light and looked relieved when she inspected the bike. But then she opened the garage door, wheeled the bike into the strong sunlight, bent down, and looked carefully at the pedals.

Steve had followed her out, bemused by her actions. He stood watching her scrutinize the bike. It looked fine to him. Did she think Molly had somehow damaged it? "Julie?" She paid no attention.

She took the pannier off the bike and turned it so the two compartments were facing toward the sun. She sighed with relief. But then she turned on her phone flashlight and peered inside one compartment, then the other. "Oh my God," she murmured.

"Did she open these?" Julie demanded in a tone Steve had never heard in their forty-three years of marriage.

"How would I know? I told you I was inside. But why would she? What the hell, Julie?"

Using the outside keypad, she mystified Steve by closing the garage door, then began rapidly wheeling the bike around the side of the house to the back patio. He followed, still asking for an explanation, now sharing in her anxiety. She ignored him, throwing the pannier on the pink-and-red-flow-ered cloth seat of a patio chair. Then she seized the garden hose and sprayed the whole bike, especially the pedals.

"Julie? Babe? You're acting crazy. What's going on? Talk to me."

Steve might as well not have been there, as Julie picked up the pannier and stood with it in her hand, staring at it. She picked up the hose again but then stopped, rubbing the leather top nervously.

"Julie?" he said again, now definitely worried about her.

Finally, she turned to him, still holding the pannier. "I can't wash this; I've got to get rid of it, Steve. Fast, and not here." She looked out at the wash as if considering throwing it there. "Not anywhere in Sunrise. Come on," she said, heading back through the house toward the garage. "Get the car keys, quick. We'll take it miles away."

"Why? Julie," he said, arms akimbo and his voice hardening. "I'm not budging from this spot until you tell me what's going on."

She looked at him in despair. "Now, Steve, *right* now. Jesus! Get the car keys. There's too much—I'll explain on the way."

Steve had never seen his docile wife like this, never. He looked as bewildered as if she had transformed into a wraith. "Where are we going?"

"I don't know yet. Goddamn it, Steve, just this once, trust

me! Get the keys!" Her voice had risen to a frustrated angry wail.

Finally yielding to her hysteria, Steve hurried inside the house and then to the car while Julie climbed into the passenger seat, clutching the pannier.

But as the garage door rose, they could see the flashing lights of a police cruiser parked sideways in their short driveway, close enough to block any hope of exiting.

"Those mother—" Steve threw open his door and charged out. "What the hell do you think you are doing? Get out of my way. I've answered all your questions. This is harassment!"

Julie stayed inside the car, the pannier still on her lap. She started quietly sobbing, tears streaming down her face and splashing onto the bags, where they left wet marks on the leather.

Detective Villegas held up his hands like a traffic cop at Steve. "Please take it easy, sir. We have a warrant to search the premises."

"What? Why?" Steve could not help a quick nervous glance back toward Julie. "Where is this warrant? Let me see it!" He was shouting by now, gesturing wildly. Rasmussen removed a set of handcuffs from his belt, in preparation.

"At the moment, it's being sent over to my office. But we already have verbal, recorded permission from Judge Barrett to proceed. Now get out of the way, Mr. Antonelli, and let us do our job." When Steve made no move, Villegas added sternly, "*Now*, Mr. Antonelli!"

Steve eyed the handcuffs and realized his jeopardy. He pulled his phone out of his pocket. "Wait, wait," he said. "I'm calling our lawyer. What's this shit about a verbal warrant? You can't do this...."

A siren announced the arrival of Detective Weatherby in

another patrol car. Jumping out, she ran to Villegas and handed him a paper. He skimmed it quickly and handed it to Steve.

Making a quick connection between Julie's frantic pleas and the pannier she clutched, Steve yelled to her, "Stay in the car!" He read the warrant quickly. "Doesn't say you can search my car."

"The warrant covers the house and the grounds as well as the garage and everything in it," Villegas said. Then he turned quickly to Weatherby. "Don't let her take anything out of the car. And, Mr. Antonelli, the warrant also specifically includes your wife's bicycle and the saddlebags on it."

By now, Weatherby had quickly donned a pair of blue latex gloves. She reached into the front seat, took the pannier off Julie's lap, and held it up over the top of the car roof for Villegas to see. Julie continued to sob, her head in her hands. "Oh God, oh God."

Detective Rasmussen emerged from a tall wooden gate at the side of the house, where pebbled stepping-stones led to the back. "The bike's on the back patio. And it's been hosed down. But on flagstone," he added. The significance was not lost on Villegas.

"Get Brandon Liao over here," he said to Weatherby. "Tell him to bring the tools he needs to take up the stone and bring it in for testing—just in case there's residue."

Steve whirled to Rasmussen. "Testing for what?" he yelled. "You can't dig up my patio, for God's sake! Residue of what? Tell me what's going on!"

"Ask your wife," Villegas said. "Read her her rights," he said to Rasmussen, who walked to the passenger side of the car and opened the door.

55

VILLEGAS

July 23: Day Fifteen

"I want to see my husband," Julie told Detective Villegas.

After Julie's arrest, she had been transported to the Cactus Heights police station and placed in a holding cell, where she had spent the night.

"Mrs. Antonelli, I'm afraid that's not possible at this time. You're going to be held here briefly, then transported to the Pima County, uh, facility. After you've been there for seventy-two hours, excluding Sundays, you will be able to see your husband. From here on you're going to be in the Pima County justice system. Tomorrow you'll go before a judge, and he or she is again going to advise you of your rights before you see another judge for a preliminary hearing. And if you continue to plead guilty, there won't be a trial. Do you understand all this?"

"Yes, I just want this over with. Can I call him now?"

"You may speak with your husband by phone while you are here, but I'll be able to hear your conversation and everything will be recorded. Since you have waived your right to an attorney, anything you say to your husband can be used against you. Do you understand that?"

"Yes. Can I call Steve now?"

Villegas escorted her outside the cell to a telephone placed on a small table in an interview room and turned on the recording equipment.

Steve picked up immediately. Before allowing Julie into the conversation, Villegas warned that he was listening in and recording it all.

Steve started talking immediately, not waiting for Villegas to exit the room. "Julie, why did you refuse to see Jim Yeager? He's one of the best criminal defense lawyers in town. I've already paid him a retainer."

Villegas observed the changes in Julie Antonelli's appearance since her arrest. Her face was haggard. Her hair was matted on one side, probably from lying on it when her pillow was wet with her tears. It hung in dirty ribbons around her face. She seemed to have aged twelve years in as many hours. Her eyes were swollen from crying and her whole body seemed shrunk into herself. But her voice was firm.

"See if you can get the retainer back. Please, Steve. There's no use spending what little money we have left on a lawyer. I am guilty and I will plead guilty."

"Julie, stop. Stop! They're recording this. You can't say stuff like that—they'll use it against you. I don't think you really know what you're saying."

"Oh, Steve, I know exactly what I'm pleading guilty to. The charge is aggravated assault, although I heard them talking about maybe making it attempted murder. Nothing for a lawyer to do. No sense throwing money at one when all I have to do is stand before the judge and say, 'I did it.'"

"Oh, Julie, please, think—"

She interrupted him. "Steve, I've done nothing but think about it for the past two weeks. I have made up my mind. You must hold on to what money we have. My future is paid for," she said, smiling faintly. "It appears I'm going to be a guest of the state—possibly for the rest of my life. I'll be fed and—"

"But, I thought Peter.... Didn't the police arrest Renee's boyfriend?"

"I set him up. It was so easy. When you dropped me off a couple of weeks ago at the mall while you went to the drugstore I bought a disposable, untraceable phone—what they call a 'burner.' I used that to spoof Peter's phone. Steve, just a minute. Let me finish. You know I'm still pretty good with technology, and believe me, it's easy to do. I could see that Peter's car wasn't in Renee's driveway, so I figured she was alone and it was a good night to do it. I sent Renee a text to meet at the top of the bell tower at eight o'clock. It looked like it was from Peter, and she obviously bought it."

"Spoofed.... Julie, I just can't believe this. How could you.... Renee's a bitch, but—

"Steve, we're on the verge of bankruptcy, and that woman was going to push us over the edge! I did what I had to do." Her voice was quiet but controlled and full of certainty.

"This is all my fault," Steve said quietly. "If I hadn't lost our money, that damned phony startup.... Oh Julie," he moaned. "Oh Christ...."

"Steve, stop! It's not your fault. I guess I made a really stupid decision. I thought I could save us and get away with it. Maybe I could have if I hadn't hit her a second time. You see," she said, her tone as reasonable as if she were explaining the plot of a fairy tale to a five-year-old, "my plan was just to push her down the stairs—just injure her enough to put her out of commission for a while, delay things. But then I remembered how athletic she is, and I wasn't sure I could push her hard enough, so I took the brick with me. It was actually Renee's brick, from her big project." She paused. "How's that for poetic justice!" she said in a slightly surprised tone, as if it had just occurred to her.

Villegas briefly considered interrupting to remind her that this confession would be used against her, but she was clearly of sound mind and understood what she was doing. *I'd better not interfere. The assault was deliberate, after all.*

Julie continued. "It was amazingly easy. I wore dark clothes and waited at the top of the bell tower and hunched over the railing at the far side so she couldn't get a good look at me. She called out for Peter and of course I didn't answer, so I waited for her to head back down. I followed her down the first flight of stairs, and when she started down the second flight, I hit her on the back of her head. She never knew I was there. I thought I could just kind of stun her with it and then give her a shove. And because the stairs are brick, if they figured out she was hit by a brick, it would look like she hit her head as she fell. But when I first hit her and she didn't fall down the stairs, she just kind of sank to her knees on the edge of the landing...I thought about what she has done to us, and how cruel she was, and somehow it just seemed too much to bear and I got so angry."

She paused a moment, then spoke louder. "Actions have consequences—maybe she never learned that. It was *her* fault. She did it to herself. I kept thinking, 'This is your fault, yours! Your fault!' I probably even said that out loud. I've never been that angry in all my life. I hit her again—really hard. And," Julie's eyes filled with tears, "this time she did fall down the stairs. It was awful. There was blood everywhere. It was dark, but it felt like I was covered in her blood. Even my face...." Her voice broke on the last words.

"I didn't even know you went out that night," Steve said dully. "If I'd seen you go...."

"You were on the computer. I knew you'd be on it for a couple of hours. And you're always completely absorbed when you work on finances. So I figured you'd never notice my absence for forty-five minutes or so."

"You rode your bike there?" He was incredulous.

"How else was I going to get there? Ask you to drive me? I parked it at the end of that big oleander hedge by the Activity Center. I was a little lucky because a dog almost sniffed me out, but the woman who was walking it spotted Renee lying there and started screaming. So no one saw me leave."

"Why didn't you tell me what you were going to do? Julie, why? We could have talked about it. I could have stopped you."

"Exactly. You would have stopped me," she said matter-of-factly. "I had made up my mind. I wanted to save our...our lives, our future. It was something I could do. You had already tried everything you could think of, and so had I. Besides, the police suspected *you*. The only time they talked to *me* was about where you were that night. I'm sorry you got questioned, but I knew they couldn't have any evidence against you."

"But how...."

"I came in through the garage and put all my clothes and my tennis shoes in the washer. Then I ran in and took a shower. I was counting on your still being glued to your computer, because if you had come into the garage earlier while I was loading the machine, or come in to use the bathroom while I was getting in the shower, you would have seen what a mess I was and realized what I'd done. When the police came to the door that night, I thought for sure they'd figured it out already."

Never occurred to me, Villegas thought ruefully. *Probably not even if she'd been the one to answer the door freshly showered instead of her husband.*

"I'd barely gotten into bed when you came in and asked me who had access to Renee's house. The dryer was still running, and I could hear the shoes banging around inside. I was afraid you would notice and ask me why I was doing laundry at that time of night. And if you had, I might have broken down and told you. I was about out of my mind, I was so nervous. But even if I had told you, that wouldn't have changed anything; I'd already done it. " She started crying silently. There was a box of tissues on the table, but she made no move to use them as the tears ran unheeded down her face.

"The brick—what did you do with the brick? And your clothes? You said they were covered in blood."

"The brick was still in my saddlebag. I went out back the next morning when it was just barely light and washed it off with the hose by my roses. I figured anyone who saw me would think I was watering the flowers. Then I let it dry there out of sight, and that evening I walked over to Renee's and stuck it back in the stack she had there. I really don't know how the police found it. I could swear no one saw me in her backyard. But it didn't matter much, because I knew they couldn't get my fingerprints or other evidence from the brick since I wore gloves.

"My big mistake was not getting rid of the saddlebag." She closed her eyes and shook her head. "Stupid. It was stupid. I was just thinking of getting rid of the brick, and never thought to check for blood left behind in the pannier.

The clothes were another stupid mistake. After I washed them I should have hidden them in plain sight, the way I did the brick. But I knew the clothes had been covered with blood, and I was afraid maybe there was some special way the police could find traces—especially in the pants, because they're woven. So I bagged them and hid them in the garage, and then threw them out. Somebody, maybe Molly, must have seen me put them in the Jeffersons' trash barrel. And I guess that made her suspicious. I thought I was being so clever, putting them out on trash pickup day. And then she tricked you into letting her look in the pannier. If Molly weren't so damn nosy, no one would have suspected me," she added angrily.

I'm afraid she's right, Villegas thought.

"The Jeffersons' trash," Steve repeated. "I just don't…. How…." Then he gave a sudden sob and yelled into the phone angrily, "You should have told me earlier! I could have helped. At least I could have helped you hide that damn pannier."

Julie remained calm. "And then both of us go to prison? If you even knew about it—and they may try to say you did—you'd be as guilty as me." She paused. "Actually, *you* may need that lawyer's help. You were ready to drive away with me and the pannier when the police arrived. Protect your-self, please, Steve."

Just then, Rasmussen entered the observation room and placed a note in front of Villegas. The handwritten message was brief. Villegas closed his eyes and murmured a few words of prayer. Then he walked into the room where Julie was sitting, her head down, the phone still at her ear as she listened to Steve's agonized pleading. She looked up as he entered and told Steve, "The detective is here. I've got to go. I love you." She hung up and faced Villegas.

"Mrs. Antonelli," he said, "I'm afraid I have bad news. Ms. Holden died a few minutes ago."

Julie paled and sagged heavily against the wall. She had immediately understood the significance of this development, even before he stated it.

"The charge is now first-degree murder."

56

MOLLY

Later in July Peter and Molly had arranged a memorial service for Renee and a reception afterward at one of the larger community halls. Advance rumors of lavish eats and drinks ensured a large turnout. Sunrise residents could out-rival grad students in their dedication to free food. However, a few attendees were skipping the reception and leaving at the end of the service.

Molly stood at the door, thanking people for coming as they exited. She was astonished to see a tall man with an impressive mustache join the group filing out. Just before he got to the door, she retrieved his name. "Mr. Staley! Good of you to come."

"Bert told me about this, uh, this..." he said awkwardly, gesturing to the hall with the hat he'd taken off. "Hope it was okay to come. I was in Phoenix with my daughter, so...."

"Of course," Molly said. Honesty compelled her to add, "I'm just a bit surprised to see you here. You weren't exactly, uh, I didn't think...."

He shuffled his feet, looking embarrassed. "I know," he said. "Renee and I had our disagreements. But I was her father's friend for over 30 years. And I've felt terribly guilty that I wasn't home when he called that day to get help felling that damn tree. Never really told Renee I was sorry. Not that I could've done anything about the heart attack, but he might have survived that. If I'd been there, at least I might have gotten him to help."

"Heart attack?" Molly said. "Renee never said anything about that; she said the tree falling on him killed him." *And that you pushed the tree,* she thought.

"Yeah, the tree probably killed him all right. But he'd had a lot of heart trouble, and when I found him, he had his hand under him, curled up to his chest, like he'd grabbed it when he fell. I think he fell down first and then got hit by the tree. Since they didn't do an autopsy, I guess we can't be sure, but why else didn't he get out of the way? Even if he didn't hear it, he must have seen it start to fall his way." He shook his head. "And there wasn't a service for him, you know. I just felt I kinda needed to come to this one. For Doug's sake." He bobbed his head in her direction and strode out the door. *What would Renee think of* that? Molly wondered.

She went back to where Peter, Mike and Betsy were directing the hungry hordes into a more orderly stampede toward edibles. When the tables were bare of food, the hall emptied quickly, leaving Renee's friends to clean up.

As Mike and Molly were clearing the tables of debris, Mike nudged Molly and pointed unobtrusively to Maude, who was in animated conversation with Peter. "Think she's offering him a casserole dinner?"

Unaware of Mike's appellation for the women who had brought him unwanted food after Andrea's death, Molly was puzzled. "What? Maude doesn't cook. Why would she offer him a casserole?"

Mike grinned. "Just a thought," he said innocently.

They stacked the paper plates and dumped them into the large black trash bin at the end of the serving table. Betsy emerged from the kitchen that ran behind the far wall of the auditorium, carrying some large white porcelain platters that had been used to serve the finger food. "Where do I put these?" she asked Molly.

"They belong to the kitchen. We usually wash them and put them in the lower cupboard."

"Thanks. I figured you would know."

Molly followed her into the kitchen to show her which cupboard to use. "So, how are you doing? Must be kind of weird for you, finding a half-sister and then losing her almost immediately."

"More than just weird, losing a mother, an unknown father, and a half-sister in the same six months. I was stupid. Maybe if I had told Renee right at the start, when I first got here, things would have come out very differently."

"How so? Julie still would have killed her."

"Yeah, I guess I couldn't have stopped that. But at least Renee might not have been angry with me for not telling her. We might have had a few weeks of being...family. And I might have made it into her will."

"Who found her will? It wasn't hidden somewhere in the house, was it? I thought we did a pretty good job of looking for it."

"No, the police tracked down her lawyer in California and he had it, along with all the other documents we were looking for, the living will and so forth."

Molly didn't push but continued to stand by the double

sinks in the kitchen. After a few seconds, Molly looked at Betsy, head cocked. "And?"

Betsy relented and explained. "Turns out, she left almost everything to a conservation organization. All her land in California will be left as forest in perpetuity."

"Rod Staley will be bummed," Molly observed. *I wonder if he knew, when he came today.*

Betsy laughed. "Yeah, now he'll never get his hands on Renee's land. And she left the house there to another neighbor, some Irish guy."

"Bert O'Shea?"

"Yeah, the name sounds right. And the house here in Arizona wasn't mentioned—guess she didn't get around to changing the will after she bought it. I'm going to see if I'm entitled to that, but the state will try to shut me out. My lawyer thinks we have a good chance, given that I'm Renee's closest living relative."

Mike poked his head around the corner into the kitchen. "Hey, come look who's here." He beckoned to Molly to join him in the auditorium.

Jose Villegawas wending his way toward them. He had attended the service but left before Mollly even got to the door. "I thought I'd catch you still here. The Cactus Heights police force owes you thanks for your help. Julie Antonelli was not at the top of our list of suspects. And I have a little something for each of you."

"What? Are these what I think they are?"

"You tell me, super sleuths."

"Um," said Molly. "These say 'Texas Rangers' on them."

"Yeah, sorry about that. Those were the only tin stars available at Walmart."

"Well, thank you, Detective. It's the thought that counts.

But I trust you'll never need us to pin these on in the future," Molly said. "I can't imagine ever having a similar situation."

"Nor can I," he agreed. "*Lauda finem*."

Molly looked to Mike for translation, but he shrugged. "Beats me," he said. "I almost flunked Latin in high school."

"Loosely translated," Villegas said, "Thank God it's over." He shook their hands and left the hall.

The community of Sunrise Acres appeared to agree. With the equanimity born of long life and experience, the residents returned to their usual activities with no additional precautions. Except that the Renovations and Improvements Committee noted they were receiving fewer applications for construction of house extensions than usual.

ACKNOWLEDGMENTS

Writing for the first time a book outside our own expertise, we necessarily leaned on the deep smarts of others. We are grateful to: Judge Ted Borek, who took us through the legal niceties of search warrants; Dr. Barton Epstein, an expert on blood spatter; Scott Restivo and Kevin West on EMT procedures; Donald Teiser on "spoofing"; Dr. Mark Wenner, on saving a poisoned dog's life; retired police chief David Johnson and several officers who asked to remain anonymous, on police procedures. Whatever we got wrong, we'll blame on senior moments—ours, not theirs.

We are also indebted to brave volunteer readers, whose comments on earlier drafts identified inconsistencies and guided our progress by asking for "more" or "less" of various narrative elements: Dawn Larmer, Jim Haber, Ali Wilkinson, Michelle Barton, Jane Lutz, Marina Margetts, Jef McAllister, Jennifer Thomas-Larmer and Patricia Heine. They cheered us on—tactfully!

Finally, our thanks to our editor and publisher, Cornelia Feye, who collaborated with us at each step of the way and taught us a lot. Next book that we write, we'll have a head start on "show, don't tell!"

ABOUT THE AUTHOR

Andre Charles is the pseudonym for two retired professors, one from Harvard Business School and the other from Tufts University. They've co-authored three books previously, including the award-winning management book on group creativity, *When Sparks Fly,* and are currently writing the second Molly and Mike mystery.

Active hikers and pickleball players, they strenuously resist being referred to as "spry." They live in Sun City, Oro Valley, Arizona, with two cats of dubious ancestry.

www.andrecharles.com